NOT
JUST ANY MAN

A Novel of Old New Mexico

LORETTA MILES TOLLEFSON

ISBN: 978-0-9983498-5-5

While many of the events in this novel are based on historical record, it is a work of fiction, not biography or history. The thoughts, words, and motivations of the 'real' people in this book are as much a product of the author's imagination as are those of the fictional ones.

Palo Flechado Press
Santa Fe, NM

A Note about Spanish Terms

This novel is set in northern New Mexico and reflects as much as possible the local dialect at that time. Even today, Northern New Mexico Spanish is a unique combination of late 1500s Spanish, indigenous words from the First Peoples of the region and of Mexico, and terms that filtered in with the French and American trappers and traders. I've tried to represent the resulting mixture as faithfully as possible. My primary source of information was Rubén Cobos' excellent work, *A Dictionary of New Mexico and Southern Colorado Spanish* (University of New Mexico Press, 2003). Any errors in spelling, usage, or definition are solely my responsibility.

For Lowell

CHAPTER 1

When Gerald tops the low rise and sees the mule-drawn wagons strung out along a rutted track across the prairie, it takes him a moment to adjust. After five days walking westward, he is still absorbing the healing beauty of the wind bending the grass, the bulk of buffalo in the distance. The sweep of the land has been a balm to his eyes. So the eight mule-drawn wagons jolting along the rutted trail below are a bit of a shock.

A loose collection of mules and horses meander to one side. Gerald stops, considering. Approaching the train is the sensible thing to do. It's pure luck that he hasn't encountered any Indians so far. But he isn't quite ready to give up the silent grassland, regardless of the risk to his light brown skin.

Then a long-haired man with a wind-reddened face canters a chestnut-colored horse out from the wagon train. A firearm is braced in the crook of his right arm. Gerald moves toward him, down the slope.

The man on the chestnut reins in at a safe distance, rifle still in a position to be easily lifted and fired. Gerald stops walking and lifts his hands away from his sides, palms out.

"Ya'll stranded?" the man calls.

Gerald takes off his hat, runs his hand through his curly black hair, and shakes his head. "Headed west."

The man turns his head and spits. "Lose yer ride?"

"I figure my feet are more dependable."

The man snorts. "And slower."

"They also give me a lower profile, out of Indian sight."

The other man nods begrudgingly, then jerks his head toward the caravan. "Wagon master says come on in, he'll trade ya for a mount 'n some food."

"Where are you headed?" Gerald asks.

"Santa Fe, where else?"

"I'm hoping to reach Don Fernando de Taos."

"Same thing, pretty much. North o' Santa Fe a couple o' days." The man jerks his head toward the wagon train again. "Young's got a mercantile there."

"Young?"

"The train master. Ewing Young. He's been merchanting, bringin' in goods from Missouri, selling 'em, then goin' back fer more." The chestnut stirs restlessly. "Come on in an' he'll tell ya himself."

If he refuses, they'll suspect him of trouble and who knows where that will lead? Gerald nods and follows the horseman toward the wagons.

As he gets closer, a tall powerfully built man wearing fringed buckskins and a broad-brimmed felt hat walks out from the lead wagon. In his early thirties, the man's air of command is enhanced by intelligent brown eyes under a high forehead, a hawkish nose, and a mouth that looks as if it rarely smiles.

"Well now, it's not often we find someone walkin' the trail," he says in a Tennessee drawl. He looks steadily into Gerald's face.

"A horse seemed like an unnecessary expense and more than likely to make me a target," Gerald says.

"It's a slow way to travel, though," the other man observes.

Gerald glances toward the wagon trundling past at the pace of a slow-walking mule. The way it lurches over the rutted track says it's

2

heavy with goods. "If I had what you're carrying, it would be," he says.

The man sticks out his hand. "I'm Ewing Young, owner of this outfit." He jerks a thumb toward the rider who'd met Gerald on the hill. "This here's Charlie Westin, my scout."

Gerald nods at the scout and reaches to shake Ewing Young's hand. "I'm Gerald Locke Jr., hoping to one day own an outfit." He grins, gray eyes crinkling in his square brown face. "Though not a wagon outfit."

Young chuckles. "Well, out here just about anything's possible." The last of the wagons trundles past and he gestures at it. "Come along to camp and we'll talk about how you can get started on that."

Gerald falls into step with the older man, cursing himself for a fool. He doesn't need to tell his intentions to everyone he meets. It comes from not speaking to another living being in the last five days, he thinks ruefully. Solitude makes a man too quick to speech. How often has his father repeated, "Words can be a burden"? He'd do well to heed that idea. Especially until he knows the character of the men he's fallen in with.

So when the small train stops that night, Gerald says nothing of joining his father or of his desire for land. That he's from Missouri and going west to try his fortune are all that Young needs to know.

It seems to be all he wants to know. The men with him are silent, clearly playing subordinate roles, and the wagon master does the talking, mostly about himself and the part his merchandise is playing in opening up the Santa Fe trade.

"It's slow goin' though," he says. "Now, trappin's a way to make yourself some real money. But it's a risky business. You've got to throw in with the right men and steer clear of the Mexican officials as much as you can." He grimaces and shakes his head. "The Mexican

3

government's as changeable as the weather when it comes to what's allowed and what's not." He takes a sip from his tin cup of coffee. "The best way to do it, is to find a seasoned man to work with. Someone who can show you the ropes and knows whose hands to grease."

Gerald raises an eyebrow. "New Mexico sounds like it's not much different from Missouri."

Young chuckles and looks into the fire. "Oh, it's different all right. For one thing, the women are more forgiving. And the houses the people live in are like nothin' you've ever seen. But government's government no matter where you go, so the main thing is to steer clear of it as much as possible. That's why I like Taos. It's a good stretch from the official center of things. And it's within strikin' distance of good fur country. Trappers bring in the furs and I trade for 'em. Do a little trapping myself, for that matter." He swings his head, eyes on Gerald's face. "But Charlie says you're headin' there, not Santa Fe. Where'd you learn about Taos, anyhow?"

Gerald shrugs. "I don't rightly know," he lies. "Someone passing through, I suppose."

And that's all it takes. Young gives him a sharp look, then nods as if he approves. "We could use another man on the remuda," he says.

Gerald feels something like hope stir in his chest. Could it be this easy?

But then he turns his head and catches the flat contemptuous gaze of a big man with long, matted dirty-blond hair, who's leaning against a nearby wagon bed. He knows. In spite of Gerald's light skin that could pass for a tanned white man, and the red highlights in his wavy black hair, he knows.

Rebellion stirs. Gerald's eyes tighten and he looks deliberately at Ewing Young. "Remuda?" he asks.

4

Young gestures toward the herd of mules and horses grazing beside the wide, dusty track that breaks across the prairie. "What in New Mexico they call the extra mounts we've brought along as spares. I could do with another herder. Not much in wages, but bread and board and a mount."

Gerald's lips twitch as he remembers the Missouri farmer who refused his back wages and predicted he'd be back within a month. He looks into Ewing Young's eyes. "I can do that," he says.

As he unrolls his bedding that night, Gerald shakes his head. His father's letter said a man isn't judged by his color out here. Is it possible that it's not even noticed? Then he tamps down the tingle of hope. Some men do notice and judge. The dirty-haired blond man with the narrow blue eyes certainly seems to suspect something. Can somehow tell that, along with the Irish and Cherokee blood in Gerald's veins, there's blackness in there, too.

Gerald scowls. Somehow, that piece of his heritage outweighs everything else. But not, apparently, for everyone, he reminds himself. And Young is the boss, not the man with the sneer. He'll just have to wait and see. To work for a man who accepts him as just any other man would be a new experience in itself.

The work is simple enough: keep the loose horses and mules alongside the wagon train, spell a teamster when it's needed, brush down whatever mount he's ridden that day. The days are long and, when sundown comes, no one's in much of a mood for talk.

There's also guard duty. Each man takes a shift every three nights, watching to make sure the animals don't stray, or that interested coyotes or wolves don't get too close. No one speaks of the possibility of human interest in the resting animals, but there's always that danger, as well.

But it's another week before there's any sign of other humans on the prairie. Young's merchandise train bumps steadily along the dusty Santa Fe Trail, the grass beside it growing ever more golden-brown as the autumn heat bakes the ground, the loose herd wandering a little farther off trail each day as they search for tender shoots in the occasional water seep. Gerald follows their wanderings on his plodding horse, both of them half-asleep in the warm fall sun.

Enoch Jones, the man who'd scowled when Gerald and Young were negotiating Gerald's pay, is also with the remuda, but he's made a point of steering clear of Gerald, so Gerald's lost his edge of concern about the big man. He's stretching himself sleepily, trying to stay awake, when there's a sudden hail from the head wagon.

Gerald looks up to see Ewing Young half-standing on the wagon seat. He's leaning out from the wagon and rotating his arms over his head, signaling the herders to move the remuda closer to the train. Charlie's on his horse beside the wagon, his head turned to focus on a low ridge to the south.

As the spare animals move closer to the train, Young swings onto a horse and rides out to meet the herders, the scout behind him.

"Charlie tells me we're goin' to have company shortly," Young says. "We'll make a halt up on that rise ahead." He gestures toward the loose animals. "When we do, I want all these hobbled or staked close by so they can't be run off."

"Comanche?" someone asks.

Young shakes his head. "Pawnee. They should be friendly. They don't look painted up and he didn't see any war shields." He turns to gaze at the ridge to the south. A line of men on ponies is strung out along its top, facing the train. They could be trees, they're so still. Young turns back to his men. "Go cautious, though. No gun waving. No heroics."

Enoch Jones growls "Coward," and there's a low mutter from the men at the back of the group.

His mount moves restlessly, but Young just turns to his scout. "Charlie, why don't you go see what they want. Raise both hands comin' back if they're lookin' to trade."

The scout's face tightens, but he nods and turns the chestnut's head. They all watch silently as he trots toward the waiting Indians. When he reaches sign-language distance, half a dozen yards below the ridge, there's a long tense moment. Charlie moves his hands, then one of the Pawnee moves his. Finally, Charlie turns and begins to trot back, both hands up and waving.

The tension goes out of the group. The herders scatter to gather the remuda and follow the wagons up the trail. When the train stops, the teamsters leave their mules in their traces but the herders vault from their mounts to hobble or stake out the spares. When Gerald's finished his work, he heads for the train, where the teamsters are pulling boxes of goods from the wagon beds.

Young moves along the little train, confirming what should be displayed and what left covered. "No liquor," he says as he passes the third wagon. "Move those jugs farther back and cover up that barrel. We don't need them to know we've got all that on board."

"Too good for 'em anyway," a teamster chuckles. "Let 'em go t' Taos for some lightning."

Young grins. "Make sure it's well covered," he says.

Gerald watches in fascination as the Pawnee canter toward the train. Their ponies are full of energy and seem to respond to the slightest touch. The men have no hair on their faces at all, whiskers or eyebrows. Gerald tries not to stare. The sides of their heads are also shaved, leaving a mop of hair and feathers on top. This has been stiffened with something that glints red in the sun, and arranged so it

7

curves up and out over the men's foreheads like the prow of a ship. Ridges of hair run from this puff toward the back of the warriors' heads, then hang down their backs in a kind of braided tail. Silver and brass earrings dangle from the Pawnees' ears.

The Indians vault off their horses and stalk alongside the wagons, looking imperiously at the goods Young's men have pulled from the boxes. The cloth shirts the warriors are wearing with their buckskin leggings say the Pawnee have traded before. The shirts are weighted down with necklaces of shells and beads.

But it won't do to stare. After all, Gerald's seen Indians before, in the Missouri settlements. They aren't a brand new phenomenon. But they seem different out here, somehow. More at home.

Certainly more confident. A tall young man strides up to Gerald and reaches toward the tooled leather scabbard at Gerald's waist and the carved wooden handle of the knife protruding from it. Gerald starts to flinch away, then catches himself and forces himself still. He raises his eyebrows and stares inquiringly into the man's face. The Pawnee points his index fingers into the air, then begins crossing his hands and swinging them up and back, in a kind of arch.

"He's wantin' to trade for yer knife," Charlie says from behind him.

As Gerald turns toward Charlie, the Indian reaches out and pulls Gerald's knife from its sheath. Gerald's hand clamps instinctively on the man's wrist. "Leave it alone!" he snaps.

"Easy now," Charlie cautions. "Ya hafta agree it's a right purty thing."

Gerald turns to the Pawnee and holds out his hand. The man lays the knife in Gerald's palm. The ten inch double-edged steel blade gleams in the prairie sun. The knife guard is well balanced and solid, the finely carved maple handle cool to the touch. Gerald's fingers curve around it protectively.

"My father made this for me," Gerald says. He looks at Charlie. "I won't trade it."

Charlie nods and turns to the Pawnee. His hands gesture rapidly and the man looks again at the knife, then into Gerald's face. He nods, looks at Charlie, moves his own hands in a few fluid gestures, then turns and is gone.

"This talking with the hands is hard to get used to," Gerald says. "What did you say?"

"That it was made by yer father fer you only, an' its medicine would be bad fer anyone who takes it away from ya."

Gerald grins. "He swallowed that?"

"He said it's good for a man to own such a thing from his ancestors and yer a wise man to protect it."

"Thanks Charlie. I appreciate it." Gerald looks down at the knife again, then slips it back into its sheath. He grins. "Guess I'd better try to learn some sign language."

It's another eight days before they see more Indians. They're Kiowa this time, and they also want to trade. Ewing Young agrees and again orders his men to cover the liquor in the third wagon and place a guard on it. "That bourbon isn't intended for the likes of them," he says, turning away. He looks at Charlie. "In fact, let's put all the trade goods up front by the lead wagon."

But the Kiowa don't seem at all interested in the third wagon. The older men cluster around the trade goods while the younger men wander freely along the rest of the wagons, stopping now and then to chat in sign language with a teamster or herder, or standing to gaze at the hobbled horses and mules nearby.

Gerald hasn't been assigned guard duty, but he happens to be passing the fourth wagon when the shoving starts. Enoch Jones staggers to one side and his spine scrapes against the wagon wheel. He comes up in a crouch, long bone-handled knife at the ready. Steel flashes in the hand of the long-haired teenage Kiowa who pushed him, and the men standing guard on the liquor wagon, Charlie included, form a silent circle around the combatants.

Gerald glances toward the third wagon. A younger Indian, no more than a boy, is climbing over the tailgate, his yellow-painted leather moccasins braced on the rim of the big wheels as he leans to push the wagon's canvas cover to one side.

"Hah!" Gerald shouts. Startled, the youngster looks toward him. Gerald laughs. "Good try!" He waves his hands as he walks toward the wagon, shooing the boy away. The boy looks toward the combatants, shrugs, pushes his long black hair away from his face, and hops down. The wagon guards turn to look. They grin sheepishly, then move back into position.

The teenager who'd pushed Jones glances toward them, then tosses his knife into the dirt and lifts his empty palms toward Jones. He grins mischievously, his silver earrings flashing in the sunlight. Jones scowls in confusion.

"We've been had," one of the guards tells him. "Bloody devils were tryin' to distract us to get at the liquor."

"Bastards!" Jones growls. He lunges toward the Kiowa boy, but the Indian dances backwards, swoops down to retrieve his knife, then flashes Jones another smile and turns on his heel to trot toward the men clustered around the lead wagon.

"It's just a couple of kids," Gerald says.

Jones glares at him and opens his mouth, but then Charlie says, "They'll be trying the mules an' horses next," and Jones sticks his knife back into his belt and heads off toward the remuda.

That night, Ewing Young settles beside Gerald as they drink the last round of coffee by the fire. "Good work there today," Young says. "Kept a battle from starting."

"Would it have gone that far?" Gerald asks in surprise.

"You never can tell. How'd you know what they were up to?"

"I guess I've learned to watch out for the unexpected."

Young grins. "Even Charlie got caught by that one. And here I thought you were a green hand."

"When it comes to the wilderness, I am," Gerald says. "But when it comes to people, I've got more experience than I would prefer."

Young studies him, a question in his eyes, but Gerald turns his face to the fire. Once again, he's said more than he should have. But it doesn't seem to matter to Young, who nods thoughtfully, then rises to name the men who'll take the first watch.

CHAPTER 2

The train trundles uneventfully southwest after that. They're on the Cimarron Cut Off, so the only real issue is lack of water, a lack that gives Gerald a new appreciation for the wide and steady flow of the Missouri River. And the taste of fresh water, which they don't experience until they reach the springs near a rocky outcropping unimaginatively called Point of Rocks.

From here, the Sangre de Cristo mountains break blue across the western horizon. Men and animals are travel weary and dusty, but Young doesn't give them more than a day to rest and clean up. He begins almost immediately to divide the horses and mules into two groups: those who'll tolerate a pack and those who won't.

The second morning finds the one who will being fitted with loads of merchandise to be carried over the mountains to Don Fernando de Taos. The other, smaller group will tow the remaining merchandise in the now half-empty wagons to Santa Fe, where the Mexican government officials will levy a tariff on the goods. Apparently there's no such tariff levied in Taos and this division of goods is common practice. Certainly, the teamsters seem to consider it routine.

"I guess you'll be wantin' to head straight to Taos," Young says to Gerald as they watch the packs being loaded. "Since you've got business there."

"I do, if you don't need me with the wagons," Gerald answers.

Young nods. "I'll meet you and the others there and pay you all off," he says. "You can find me at my store or at Peabody's."

Gerald nods. "That'll be fine," he says. "Where—"

A scuffle breaks out just then between two horses and a teamster, and Young heads toward them, leaving Gerald with his question unasked. He shrugs. He'll learn soon enough how to find his way around Taos, locate Young's mercantile, or this Peabody's place of business.

He moves out with the pack train the next morning. They head due west, the animals strung together with ropes in long groups of ten, a man at the head of each group and one halfway back. Charlie is master now and he tells Gerald to settle in beside the middle of the second string, the one led by Enoch Jones.

The scout steers the mule train toward a gap in the hills. As they move west, the grass thickens. The late summer rains have greened the landscape nicely. Yellow sunflowers brighten the ground wherever there's a bit of an indentation to hold the moisture. Gerald looks at them approvingly.

The next day, the grassy slopes begin to tilt upward and the sunflowers shrink in size and number. Juniper bushes scatter the landscape and fill the warm afternoon with a sharp urine smell. Farther up, there's a type of tree Gerald's never seen before: a kind of resinous pine, its trunk gnarled as if it's been wind blasted for at least a hundred years.

The route moves uphill, along the side of a rocky slope, and the path narrows. Gerald focuses on his work. There's not room for both man and mule, and he drops into the trees below the path to give the animals room to maneuver. Dirt and small rocks break under his feet and dribble down the slope to the gully below. He has to work to stay in line with his string.

Then the trail ahead becomes little more than a rocky outcropping. Gerald's string of mules comes to a halt as the animals ahead of them edge cautiously across the ledge. The mules bunch together on the narrow path and snuffle at each other as if commiserating on their lot. Gerald scrambles up the bank to them, then farther up the slope to get out of their way but be within reach if they need him.

At the sound of rocks skittering down the bank, Enoch Jones turns and glares. "No time t' be explorin'," he growls.

"There's not room on the path for both man and beast," Gerald points out. The dirt moves under his feet and he clutches at a juniper branch for support. "I'll be down as soon as we start moving again."

Jones scowls and yanks on his lead mule's chin strap, forcing the animal's muzzle toward him. The mule pulls its head back, baring its teeth, and Jones whips the free end of the lead rope across its nose. The animal snorts angrily and jerks away, but this puts its hooves off the trail, scrambling in the dirt and rocks. The pack on its back tilts precariously.

Jones is pulled forward by the mule's weight. Just as his feet hit the edge of the trail, the mule lurches backward down the slope, wrenching the rope from Jones' hands. He drops to the ground and his right foot twists awkwardly under his left leg. "Whoa, damn you!" he yells.

But it's too late. As the lead mule slides down the bank, the animals linked to it are pulled inexorably toward the edge of the trail. They brace themselves, their eyes rolling.

Gerald slips gingerly down the bank, trying to move as smoothly as possible to keep from knocking gravel onto the trail and frightening the animals even more.

"Whoa, now," he says soothingly. "Whoa now."

The mule nearest him turns its head, its eyes wild with fright. Gerald stretches to touch the mule's neck, then moves cautiously to its head. He grabs the animal's halter and peers over its shoulder and down the hillside. "Whoa now," he says again.

Fortunately, the lead mule has found its footing. It stands, huffing irritably, on a small flat space below, its pack still intact but tilted to one side. The four mules strung behind it are stranded in an uneven row between it and the trail above. They scuffle rocky dirt anxiously as they try to find secure footing. They look more puzzled than frightened.

Gerald pats the mule he's standing next to soothingly and moves past it, grateful that it and the four still behind it stalled when they did.

He looks at Jones, who's still on the ground, his hands on his twisted ankle. "No harm done," Gerald says.

Just then, Charlie appears on the trail ahead. "Ya'll all right back there?" he calls. As he gets closer, Jones pushes himself upright, his right foot carefully lifted from the ground, his face twisted in fury.

"You give me green help, this is what happens," Jones jabs a thumb toward Gerald. "He was too busy wandering uphill to keep 'em in line." He puts his foot on the ground and winces. "An' now I can't walk."

Charlie gives Jones a long look, then turns to Gerald. "On slopes like this, it's best if ya stay below 'em, when ya ken," he says. "Or directly behind. They get nervous when there's somethin' on the hillside above. Think yer a catamount or somethin'."

Gerald nods. There's no point in pointing out that Jones triggered this particular nervousness.

The scout moves to the edge of the path and peers down. "Looks like nothin's lost." He turns to consider Jones' foot, then Gerald.

15

"Think ya ken lead 'em up? Jones is gonna need to favor that foot a mite."

Gerald nods and maneuvers around the other men to find a way down the hillside to the lead mule. As he passes, Jones mutters, "Damn green hand!" and Charlie answers evenly, "A man ken't do what he ain't been told, now ken he?"

Once all of the string is back on the path, Gerald and Charlie straighten the lead mule's pack and tighten it down again, then Charlie returns to his own string and Gerald keeps the mule steady until it's their turn to make their way across the outcropping.

Jones limps behind, alternately cursing damn mules and green hands. He soon falls behind the entire mule train, so Gerald doesn't have to listen to him for long. But Jones is still fuming when he limps into camp that night, well after everyone else.

"Coulda been killed," he growls, tossing aside the stick he's been using as a crutch. He sinks onto a large piece of sandstone and begins loosening his bootlaces. "There's Apaches out there, ya know."

"There was nothin' for ya t' ride," Charlie says mildly from across the fire. "And we weren't that far ahead."

Jones grunts and reaches down to pull off his boot, but the angle is wrong and he wrenches the swollen ankle out of position. "Hell!" he yelps.

"Want some help with that?" Gerald asks, moving toward him.

"Stay away from me!" Jones snarls.

"You know, Jones, if you'd been a little easier on that mule, she wouldn't of jumped," says the man who'd been leading the set of mules directly behind Jones and Gerald's string. He glances at Jones, then Charlie, then the fire. "Looked to me like she was pretty calm 'til you slapped her muzzle with that rope."

16

Charlie looks first at Jones, then Gerald. Jones glares at the man on the other side of the flames, who ignores him, but Gerald returns Charlie's gaze steadily.

"You don't know nothin'," Jones growls. He glares at Charlie. "I got stuck with a idiot mule and a damn green hand. What'd ya expect?" The scout doesn't respond and Jones turns his scowl on Gerald. "You green hands come out here and think ya know everything there is t' know, an' ya don't know shit!" He moves his foot impatiently, then flinches and reaches for his swollen ankle.

"If ya wrap that up good and tight, it'll help bring that swellin' down," Charlie says. "We ken redistribute goods in the morning and set up somethin' fer ya to ride on fer tomorrow, at least."

Jones nods sullenly. "In the meantime, someone could bring me some food," he grumbles and Charlie nods to the other stringer, who rises quietly to make the arrangements.

Early the next day, with Jones riding at the head of the mule train, Charlie and his men drop into the south end of a valley thick with ripe grass. A small sparkling stream winds its way through the valley floor, heading north through more grassland. Mountains glimmer at the valley's head, a good ten miles away. The bank of the little creek below has broken off in places, exposing a soil so black and fertile that Gerald's fingers itch to run through it. Now this is land a man could raise a crop on.

He looks up at the almost-black fir-covered mountains in front of them, then northwest to taller, stonier peaks, the largest a massive, curved wall of rock. They've been climbing the last two days. The growing season here would be short, and the winters strong.

But still— Gerald looks down at the thick grass on the valley floor. Cattle would do well here. If a man built them adequate shelter, they could feed all through the cold season on hay harvested from these rich bottom lands.

But he has no money for land and the outlay needed to raise cattle or anything else. And this is Indian country. It's an impossible dream. Even so, as the mule train moves into the trees on the other side of the valley, toward what Charlie says is Apache Pass, Gerald finds himself glancing back toward the bright trickle of water running steadily north.

CHAPTER 3

As they move closer to Taos, Gerald begins to ponder just how best to go about locating his father. The pack mules move steadily through the ponderosa forest, then turn and follow a small green valley to the canyon of the Rio Fernando, a river that seems like a mere creek by Missouri standards. By late morning the next day, the men and mules move out of the juniper at the mouth of the canyon and gaze at the sweep of the Taos Valley. It's so broad it hardly seems like a valley, the mountains on the western edge a dim blue in the distance.

"That there's the Taos Gorge," Charlie says, ahead of him.

Gerald nods. It's a gash in the earth that cuts the valley in two along its length.

"Doesn't look like much from here," the Scout says. "You oughta see it from the south. It's somethin' else agin."

Gerald nods politely, his gaze moving to the objects nearer at hand, the town of Don Fernando de Taos. Though to call Taos a town seems rather pretentious. Flat-roofed mud houses cluster along narrow dirt streets that straggle out from a central square, or plaza. The town's a hamlet, really, although the walls around the square look substantial enough. As the train draws closer, Gerald sees that the plaza walls are actually the back side of long low adobe buildings, all facing inward in a protective stance. The early afternoon sunlight reflects bits of mica in their walls. There are perhaps eight or nine

19

buildings in all. Surely it won't be difficult to find his father in a community this small.

The problem is how to go about asking for him. To need the services of a blacksmith is common enough, even if one doesn't own a mount. The blade of a knife might be loose, a belt buckle might need to be mended. But looking specifically for a black-skinned smith whose last name is Locke is bound to raise questions. Why would a white man be looking for a black man with the same last name?

And there's no guarantee that his father is actually in Taos itself. Gerald's already discovered from the campfire talk that when someone says "Taos" they can mean one of a number of different locations: the village of Don Fernando de Taos, the Taos Indian pueblo north of the village, or the widespread Taos valley and one of the many hamlets it contains. So, while knowing his father is in Taos keeps him from having to search the entire Rocky Mountain region, it doesn't narrow down his location as much as Gerald would like.

Well, he's closer to his father here than he was in Missouri. That's something. The question is whether to drop this attempt to pass as a white man and acknowledge their relationship. He isn't sure how his father, ever the practical one and yet a man who treasures his son, will feel about that. Hopefully, they'll have an opportunity to discuss the situation in private.

But while Gerald is still trying to decide how to go about his search, Charlie announces that he has business to take care of and needs help to accomplish it.

The men from the mule train are still together and camped on the northern edge of Don Fernando de Taos on land controlled by Ewing Young. No one wants to move on until Young shows up to pay them. Besides, he's still providing the rations. But none of the men have been doing much to earn their keep, so when Charlie appears at the campfire two nights after they arrive, he isn't in an asking mood.

"I need some of ya to head south to Ranchos with me tomorrow, first light," he says abruptly. "We got a passel of animals that need their shoes looked after an' the only smith Young trusts is in Ranchos."

"Nothin' in Ranchos I wanna see," Enoch Jones says. "'Sides, it's too far, with this ankle."

"It's three miles," Charlie says dryly. "Yer ankle was well enough this mornin', chasin' the girls on the plaza like ya were."

"Gonna cost you," Jones says.

"None of ya's been exactly pullin' yer weight the last few days."

Jones gestures toward Gerald, on the other side of the fire. "Green hand can go. It's his fault I'm tied up."

Charlie looks at Gerald, who nods agreement, then swings back to Jones. "I ken't promise you extra," he says. "That's up t' Young. But I'm sure he'd look kindly on a little help."

Jones grunts and nods unwillingly. "When?"

"First light." Charlie turns away and nods at two other men who are sitting at the far edge of the fire. "You, too." They nod back, and he turns and disappears into the night.

"Gotta go visit his señora," Jones says derisively. He pulls out his bone-handled knife, reaches for a flat stone, spits on it, and begins to draw the blade across the stone, honing the steel.

Gerald glances up and speaks in spite of himself. "He's married to a Spanish girl?"

Jones snorts derisively. "Keepin' her. Gotta turn Catholic t' marry one of these gals." He examines the knife's blade, slips it back into the beaded sheath at his waist, then pulls out a flask and takes a swig.

"But you don't have t' get religion anyways. These putas are all easy enough to come by."

Gerald stares into the dying flames. Jones seems to make a habit of quick judgments. Not that the characters of the girls here really matter. Gerald's more interested in land than women, though he doesn't have the funds for either of them. His thoughts turn to the mountain valley with its black soil and long grasses, its tiny sparkling streams, running even in the fall. From what he's seen of this land so far, that much water in the landscape, the thickness of those grasses, is unusual.

The men are up at first light, preparing to move out, the animals balky with sleep. They see no reason to move any further than Ewing Young's grassy meadow.

The fall nights and early mornings here are cooler than Gerald is used to. He shivers a little as he waits for the others. The two mules he's responsible for crowd him a little, as if they too are chilled. The mule with the missing shoe pushes its nose against Gerald's shoulder and the jenny with the two loose nails shakes her hoof impatiently.

Gerald gives her a reassuring pat and looks over her shoulder. Enoch Jones seems to be adjusting a halter strap on his far mule. Gerald's animals block his view somewhat, but he can see that Jones' mules seem agitated.

Then the nearer one pulls back sharply, ears flat against his head. Gerald catches a glimpse of a sharp object in Jones' hand as his fingers slap up and against the far mule's lip. The mule's right hoof comes forward and catches Jones in the left leg, knocking him off balance, and Jones lets out a howl of protest.

Gerald's own mules stir anxiously and he speaks softly to them as Charlie materializes from the gray dawn.

"What's goin' on?" Charlie demands.

Jones gets to his feet. The object that had been in his hand is nowhere in sight. "Damn mule kicked me," he says.

Charlie looks at Jones' leg, then the mule, which stands, panting slightly, its ears still back. "If yer leg ain't broke, keep usin' it," Charlie says. He turns away. "We need to get goin'." He moves toward Gerald. "You ready, Locke?"

"Yes, sir."

"Glad someone's got some sense," he mutters, just loud enough for Gerald to hear, as he passes him on the way back to his own animals. "Here we go!" he says over his shoulder as he snaps his lead rope. "Let's get 'er done!"

The mules are slowed by missing shoes and loose nails, and it takes a full hour to reach Ranchos, but Gerald doesn't mind the leisurely pace. As the sun rises behind the eastern mountains, the landscape begins to glow with light. The adobe walls of the houses are soft in the light. Then their flecks of mica begin to spark as the sun strengthens and fingers its way across the flat plain to the west and the mountains bulking beyond.

Gerald is craning his neck to see more when the view is abruptly blocked by a row of rangy narrow leaf cottonwoods strung out along a small stream and the men and mules reach the blacksmith's shop. It's not much of a shop. Just a ramshackle structure at one end of a barren compound of small adobe buildings. Thick posts support a loosely-spaced layer of thin, unpeeled poles. Sunlight filters through the gaps and dapples the dirt floor. A waist-high chimneyless adobe hearth stands in the center of the space, a small leather bellows on the ground beside it.

The coals on the hearth are cold and no one stirs in the compound. Gerald and the others hold the mules while Charlie knocks on the door of the nearest hut. He speaks to the man who opens it, then comes back to the mules. "It'll be a minute," he says. He gestures to the men behind Gerald. "Those ken wait a bit. He's gonna hafta get a fire goin' before he ken shape the shoes. Jest take 'em to the corral in the back." He turns to Gerald. "We'll get the loose nails done first."

Gerald nods and leads his animals around the building, then returns to the smithy with the jenny with the loose nails. The blacksmith has come out of his hut now and is building a fire on the smithy hearth as he and Charlie talk.

"We got us a pretty good set o' men this time," Charlie's saying as Gerald approaches the shed. "No Mexicans this time, though. All white men."

As Gerald steps into the shed, the smith's head swings toward him and his hand, reaching for another handful of coal, freezes. Then he recovers himself and continues feeding the fire.

Gerald's a little slower. Joy surges through him and his face breaks into a broad smile. Then he realizes what he's done and flattens his face. But Enoch Jones, standing in the corner has seen both reactions, and his pale blue eyes narrow with suspicion.

"No mulattos this time?" the smith says to Charlie with a small grin. "You didn't want another Jim Beckworth in your crowd?"

Charlie grins. "Ah, old Jim's well enough. Ya jest ken't expect to believe anything he says."

The smith chuckles and turns to insert his bellows into a small hole halfway down the side of the hearth and give it a light pump. He glances over his shoulder. "No green hands this time?"

In the corner, Jones snorts derisively. Charlie grins and jerks his head toward Gerald. "Well, we're still trying to figure out what Locke here is. He says he don't know anything but he keeps provin' himself wrong." He grins at Gerald and nods toward the smith. "This here's Jerry Smith." Gerald and the smith nod politely at each other, Jones

24

watching them with narrowed eyes. "And you know Enoch Jones, I think," Charlie continues. "He's been around a while."

The smith nods to Jones. "I think I did some work for you last spring," he says politely. "Reset the blade of that big knife of yours."

Jones shrugs. "Could be."

Smith looks at Gerald. "You plannin' on stayin' for a while?"

"I hope to," Gerald says. "If I can find a way to make a living."

"He's got the brains to be a trapper," Charlie says.

Smith chuckles and shakes his head. He picks up a small bucket and pours more coals onto the fire, then pushes down on the bellows handle again. "Beggin' your pardon, but I'm not sure how many brains that takes," he says dryly.

Charlie laughs as the black man gathers up his hammer, files, and shoe nails and heads for the mule tethered outside. "Let's see what we've got here," the smith says.

CHAPTER 4

Ewing Young appears at the Taos campsite three days later and pays off his men. It's heading toward late October now, the cottonwoods gold along the stream banks, the temperatures cold at night but still warm during the daylight hours. Most of the teamsters leave the next morning. They hope to sign on with a Santa Fe train that will head east to Missouri before winter sets in. A small group remains behind in the pasture. Most of them plan to either winter in Taos or join a beaver trapping group and overwinter in the mountains.

Gerald isn't sure how he wants to proceed. He'd like to see his father again and have a real conversation with him, but he can't figure out how to do this without rousing suspicion. Jones is still in the Don Fernando de Taos area, though Gerald isn't sure where. The matted-haired man sloped off with a lewd reference to Mexican señoritas as soon as he'd collected his pay. His going certainly makes Ewing Young's meadow more comfortable and, since Young has told the men to stay as long as they need to, Gerald sees no reason to leave just yet, despite the chill nights.

Young comes by late one evening and sits talking with the remaining men, his big frame bending toward the fire as he warms his hands. When the last of Gerald's companions has slipped off to their bedrolls, Young turns to him. "You lookin' to trap?" he asks.

"I don't know," Gerald says. "I'd hoped to find work clerking, but I haven't really started searching yet."

"Still gettin' your bearings?"

26

Gerald smiles slightly. "I suppose you could call it that."

Young rises from the dead log he's been sitting on. "I'm puttin' together a band and headin' out late next month. If you want to learn, you're welcome to tag along. It might be a good way to earn the money for that farm of yours." He grins. "If that's what you're still thinkin' of doing. New Mexico has a way of turning a man's mind in new directions."

Gerald looks at him noncommittally and Young studies him. "I'm assuming you've got the wherewithal for the gear," he says. "Traps are runnin' ten dollars apiece and you'd need at least six, plus food and sundries. You'd be free trappin', which means everything you bring in would be yours, but everything you put into it will be at risk, as well."

"The investment resources aren't a problem," Gerald says, looking up at the big man. "And I appreciate the offer." He shrugs and smiles. "I just may take you up on it."

"I can sweeten the offer by assurin' you that Enoch Jones won't be comin' with me," Young says. "He made noises, but I've had just about all of him I can take for one year." He stretches his hands over the flames. "Well, you know where t' find me. We've got another week or so before headin' out. I'm either at the store, my house, or Peabody's place." He turns away from the fire. "I'll see you around."

Gerald nods to the empty night and turns thoughtfully back to the flames. He picks up a stick and pokes at the fire, separating the pieces of burning wood so the flames will die out faster. He knows where Young's mercantile is, and his house is on the other end of the pasture. But in the little time Gerald's spent wandering the village, he's seen no sign that identifies Peabody's store.

He chuckles. But then, signs aren't a major part of Don Fernando de Taos' streetscapes. It's an interesting place: half American, half

27

Mexican, with a good dose of Taos Pueblo added in. The buildings are all brown one-story adobe mud that glint with flecks of mica in certain lights. In fact, in certain lights, the hamlet's downright pretty.

And the people are pretty much live and let live, from what he can see. Best of all, he blends among them in a way he never has before, his skin simply another shade of the prevalent brown. In fact, he feels so comfortable here, he hates to leave.

But his money won't last forever. He has only a few more weeks in which to decide what to do with himself. He hasn't seen any need in the shops for another clerk. And Ewing Young is right. He doesn't have the resources to set himself up as a farmer. Although if he did, he knows where he'd want to do so. If that's possible so high in the mountains. On land surely already owned by someone. He pushes the thought of the long and fertile mountain valley out of his mind and douses the fire. Trapping seems like the best option so far.

~ ~ ~ ~

Gerald heads to the Taos plaza the next day for supplies, thinking again about how to approach his father in Ranchos. He'd truly like to get some advice about the idea of free trapping, not to mention passing as white.

He's still accustomed to walking with a prairie-eating stride and he passes several groups of blanket-swathed Taos Indians who are also heading toward the plaza. He nods politely each time, but notices that their eyes tend to veer away from him. Even as they nod back at him, they don't look directly into his face.

He frowns irritably, then remembers the slaves in Missouri. They did the same thing, carefully avoiding eye contact. Is it the sign of an oppressed people? Or simply politeness, not wanting to challenge or be challenged? It must be difficult to continue here in this land, with first the Spanish and now the Americans crowding in, encroaching on what was once only theirs.

Gerald reaches the plaza and slows to saunter past the cloths laid out on the ground and the produce and other goods carefully arranged on them. He finds he isn't as interested in any of it as he probably ought to be, and veers off the plaza onto a street lined with adobe walls and the houses behind them.

All this vast land, yet the houses are so close together. There's safety in that, of course. Although there are also plenty of shadowed corners for activity that might be suspicious in the full light of day. For example, this man facing the corner made by those two walls, his arms up and blocking the young woman who's crowded into the niche, her back to the light brown adobe.

Gerald frowns. The man's back is to him, but the matted white-blond hair under the dirty hat looks familiar. Jones? Then the man speaks, low and threatening, and there's no doubt. Gerald stops in his tracks.

The girl speaks, in surprisingly good English, her voice sharp and clear. "I apologize if you have misunderstood me, Mr. Jones," she says firmly. "I have no interest in keeping company with you."

Jones reaches for her arm. "You think yer somethin'," he growls. "But yer just another Mexican slut."

"How dare you!" She twists, trying to get away, but Jones reaches for her shoulder and forces her back, against the adobe.

Then Gerald is behind him, fingers clamping Jones' upper arm. "Let her go!"

Jones, startled, turns his head. "You!" His grip on the girl loosens involuntarily. She slips out of his grasp and darts down the dirt street. She looks back as she reaches the corner, dark eyes wide, and nods her thanks to Gerald, then is gone before he's had time to do more than glimpse a light brown face and black hair neatly pulled up in an old-fashioned American hairstyle, soft tendrils framing her cheeks.

Gerald turns back to Jones and tightens his grip. "She clearly doesn't want your attentions."

Jones jerks his arm away and Gerald lets him go. "It's none o' yer business," Jones growls. "'Sides, she's just a Mexican. Just like yer just a nigger."

Gerald's eyes narrow. "She's still a woman," he says. "To be treated with respect."

"Respect ain't what they want." Jones grins lasciviously. "They want tamin'."

"It certainly didn't sound that way to me."

Jones shoves past Gerald into the narrow street. "You just stay out of my way."

Gerald watches him go, then looks again toward the corner where the girl disappeared. She's taller than the other women he's seen in Taos. Her clothes are different, too. More American style, with an old-fashioned high waist and straight skirt that reminds him of the dresses his mother used to wear. Her skirts are longer than those of the other Mexican girls. He'd caught only a glimpse of ankle, instead of the half calf so common here. And her hair was tucked up. Off her neck, not down her back. A long, narrow back. A truly beautiful tawny-brown neck.

Impulsively, he moves down the street after her. But rounding the corner only reveals more adobe walls and a little boy playing in the dirt. The girl spoke perfect English too, although with a slight Spanish lilt. A very pleasant lilt. Who is she?

Perhaps his father will know. It's yet another question to ask him, apart from whether it's wise for Gerald to continue to try to pass as white and what he would advise Gerald to do for a living, now that he's here.

But when Gerald arrives at the Ranchos de Taos smithy early the next day, he finds that both the smithy and the casita beside it are empty. A middle-aged Mexican woman is pulling water from a well in the center of the compound. She looks at him inquiringly. He gestures toward the smithy and raises his eyebrows in a questioning look.

She smiles in amusement, shakes her head, and carries her water bucket through a doorway at the end of the compound.

A minute later, an American man comes out. He scratches at his scraggly blond beard and scowls at Gerald. "You wantin' the smith?" he asks. "He took off. Said he was goin' trappin'. Paid me my month's due an' hightailed it." He peers into Gerald's face. "You wouldn't happen to know anything about blacksmithin', would you?"

Gerald shakes his head. "Did he say where he was going?"

The man waves a hand toward the mountains to the north. "Rockies, I guess. I dunno. He's left me in a helluva bind." His face brightens a little. "You needin' traps? I've still got a half dozen he made before he took off."

Gerald shakes his head again, then pauses. Maybe trapping would be the best way. "I'm not sure," he says. "But if I do, I'll come back for them."

"Don't know if they'll be here by then." The man scratches at his beard again. "They're likely to go fast, once word gets out that Smith's gone. He's the best damn blacksmith we've seen in these parts for a while now."

Gerald grins. "Then you should get a good price," he says, turning away. "I apologize for waking you so early."

"You come on back now, if you need anything," the man says.

31

Gerald lifts a hand in farewell. "I'll do that."

He heads back to Don Fernando de Taos. His father has answered at least one of his questions. He's left the area, leaving Gerald free to continue to pass as white. Gerald isn't sure how he feels about this. Although most people don't seem to care about his ancestry, clearly those who do care, care deeply. At least, Enoch Jones seems to.

And is it the right thing to do? Is it fair to others to not tell them up front? His jaw tightens. Why should it matter what color his skin is? He's just a man, like any other man. The same hopes and desires, the same needs.

He stops in the middle of the path back to Taos and gazes up at the golden cottonwoods, the intense blue of the sky above them. It's not like he set out to pass. In fact, he hasn't actually told anyone he's white. He's just let them assume it. For that matter, he hasn't denied his race to Jones. Although he hasn't confirmed it, either.

But living on an equal footing with other men these past weeks has felt good. Gerald chuckles. 'Good' is such an inadequate word to describe the expansion he's felt, the way he seems taller, somehow. He's always known that he's equal to any other man. Certainly, his parents made that clear enough to him.

Gerald grins, thinking of his Irish mother's blazing blue eyes as she snapped, "You just be who you are inside and that'll be good enough for anybody who has any sense, whether your mother's a mere bondservant or your father a free negro." He lifts two fingers to his forehead in a mock salute. Yes ma'am. Then he sobers. But to be treated as equal is another thing entirely. It makes a man's shoulders a little straighter, somehow.

He continues walking, his hands in his pockets. Maybe he'll just continue on as he is and see what comes of it. Why cause trouble when it isn't asking to be caused? Why not enjoy the experience and see where it takes him?

CHAPTER 5

But there's still the matter of how he'll spend his winter, whether he'll plunge into the world of fur trapping or try to find some other way to earn his keep. He's thinking about Ewing Young's offer as he wanders Taos plaza two days later, with one eye out for the tall girl in American clothing. He idly contemplates a blanket covered with fat pumpkins, then glances up and sees Ewing Young striding diagonally across the plaza. A tall thin buckskin-clad man with long red hair in disheveled braids stalks beside him. The man gestures wildly and his nasal high-pitched voice echoes off the adobe buildings.

When Young sees Gerald, a relieved look crosses his long face. He slows as he reaches Gerald, although his companion is still talking.

"And he's workin' on a new-fangled trap that might hold some promise, if—" the man is saying.

Young puts his hand on the red-haired man's arm. "Here's someone you'll be interested in knowing," he says. "Gerald Locke Jr., meet Old Bill Williams. He came in yesterday with that bunch that's surveying the Santa Fe Trail."

There'd been talk around the campfire the night before about the Santa Fe Trail Survey team the U.S. Congress has sent out under Major Sibley, but Gerald had assumed they'd all be in uniform. He looks at the buckskin-clad man in surprise.

Williams snorts. "Expecting a little more dudin' up?"

"I thought the survey was an army project," Gerald says.

34

Williams shrugs. "They had to have an expert in the country to guide 'em."

"You'll find that Old Bill here isn't shy about his talents," Young says drily. "Fortunately, he usually manages to keep to subjects he's got some knowledge of."

Williams snorts. "Know more'n you about trapping!" he says. "And Injuns!"

"So you say." Young's eyes crinkle with amusement. He turns to Gerald. "Williams here has lived a lot of years in Indian country and thinks he knows all about it. Fact is, he's so damn confident that he goes out trapping on his own in places where the rest of us hunt in groups in case of Indian attacks."

Williams grunts. "I don't plan on gettin' sent to the other side any time soon, not 'til I feel like takin' a few with me."

Young grins and shakes his head. Then he glances toward the mercantile behind Gerald. "I need to go in and talk to Baillio." He nods to Old Bill, then Gerald. "I expect we'll be meetin' again."

Gerald and Williams watch Young duck through the store's heavy wooden door frame, then stand in the dusty plaza and consider the vendors and the goods spread in front of them. Williams glances up at the turquoise sky, but Gerald's eyes stray across the plaza, still watching for the tall girl with the American hairstyle.

"So," Williams says abruptly. "You new to nuevomexico?"

"I came in with Young's most recent trade caravan." Gerald brings his eyes back to the older man's face. He's probably about forty. Older than most of the Americans Gerald's met here so far.

"You lookin' to trap?"

"I haven't decided yet." Gerald looks around the plaza. Still no sign of the girl. He looks at the red-haired man. "I'm still trying to sort out my options."

"Well, that sounds like a mighty tall order." Old Bill jabs a thumb in the direction of the nearest taberna. "Like Ewing says, I know about trappin' and a few other things besides. If you're lookin' for advice about the lay of the land, I can share some pearls of wisdom for the price of a tangle foot."

"Tangle foot?"

"A drink. Taos Lightnin'. Whisky."

Gerald chuckles. "It's a deal."

They're a long while in the bar and Gerald buys more than one drink, but he does learn a good deal: which of the Americans has the most experience trapping, who buys the resulting furs and at what prices, which groups are forming for the coming season. What Williams says accords with and expands on what Gerald's already picked up from the campfire talk, so he's inclined to believe this scrawny man with the long red braids.

Williams holds his liquor well, too. Three whiskeys in short succession have no impact on his speech or the brightness of his brown eyes. The only change Gerald can detect is that the mountain man's sentences become longer and more complex, his diction more precise.

"And now that I've told you the sum and total of all my most profound knowledge about the art and technique of beaver trapping, let us proceed to more essential information," Williams says. "Where is it you hail from, young man?"

"Missouri," Gerald says. "I—"

"Ah, Missouri," Old Bill says. He leans back. "I also consider myself to be of Missouri, though my natal state is North Carolina, of all the benighted places to be born. But when I was seven years old, my paterfamilias hightailed it for greener pastures and I've always been grateful for his sense of adventure. We landed far enough away from St. Louie to keep the stench of its sinful ways from my mother's nostrils but close enough to take advantage of the fur market when we needed cash money." He takes another sip of whiskey. "I was just a young whippersnapper when my daddy showed me how to set my first trap line and it sure did give me a taste of what it is to be independent. Then when I was sixteen I took me a notion to go live with the Osages and Christianize them." He shrugs and grins. "That was most righteously green of me. In the end, they taught me more than I ever taught them, that's for damn certain."

Abruptly, the mountain man pushes away from the table. "Well, that was a mighty fine respite, that was, and we've had ourselves a healthy palaver, but I think maybe we could do with a feed and I know where to get it. Have you had the pleasure of meeting Jeremiah Peabody yet?"

Gerald shakes his head.

"Come along with me and I'll introduce you. He's always got a feed going. The man's got a good cook and has the righteous sense to keep her busy."

Gerald nods. He'll finally learn where Peabody's is. A restaurant of some kind, apparently. But by the time they're halfway across the village, the loquacious trapper has set him straight on that, too.

According to Williams, Peabody is a New England man who came into the country around '09 and set himself up as a teacher and scribe so the Spaniards would let him stay in the country legally. He holds open house for the trappers when they're in town, as long as they aren't liquored up when they arrive.

Gerald smiles slightly at this, thinking of the amount of whisky Williams consumed at the taberna, but holds his tongue. The man doesn't appear to be drunk. Perhaps that will suffice.

And it does. The house is built in a U-shape. A gated adobe wall blocks the open end, but the wooden gate stands invitingly open. As Gerald follows Williams into the plant-filled courtyard beyond, a tall thin man with a black chin beard comes out of a short wooden door set into the adobe wall to their left. A Mexican man chops wood in the far corner.

"Well, Mr. Williams!" the man with the beard says. "It's a pleasure to see you again, sir!" He gives Gerald a questioning glance.

"Jeremiah Peabody, you old scholar, you!" Williams says. "How are you?" He jerks a thumb at Gerald. "This here's a young man I think you might wanta know, name of Gerald Locke the younger. He's got a good head on his shoulders, according to Ewing. More importantly, he's got the good sense to listen to my pearls of wisdom."

Jeremiah Peabody chuckles and gives Gerald an amused glance. "That would imply that he has excellent manners and the patience of Job."

"He might even have the patience to listen to you!" Old Bill laughs.

"And if I know you, William, you have neglected to eat since you rose this morning, although you have probably imbibed at least a drink or two." Peabody turns back toward the house, waving them after him. "Come in, come in!"

Williams and Gerald follow him past a well, two small garden beds, and the man chopping wood. They duck through the door and move past a kitchen area, then down a short hall.

Jeremiah Peabody waves them into a fire-lit room crowded with tall bookcases and men sitting on carved wooden benches and cushion-topped chests. A narrow-shouldered blonde man and a slim dark-haired girl face each other in the center of the room.

The girl's back is to the door. As Gerald enters, she says "Oh! Thank you, monsieur!" and the young man glances at the door and sees Jeremiah Peabody. His face flushes guiltily. There's a general chuckle from the other men in the room as the girl turns, smiling, toward the door, a cloth covered package in her hands.

"Well, Mr. Bill Williams!" she says. "Hello!" Then her eyes touch Gerald's face and her black eyes widen. Her smile deepens. "Hello," she says.

Jeremiah Peabody looks puzzled. "Have you met Mr. Locke already, my dear?"

She shakes her head, eyes glinting with amusement. "Not formally, no."

Peabody turns to Gerald. "My daughter, Suzanna." Then, to Suzanna. "Mr. Gerald Locke Jr., newly arrived." He glances at Gerald. "With Ewing Young's train, I believe?"

Gerald nods, but his eyes are on the girl. "It's my pleasure," Gerald says.

She bobs a curtsey, her hands still full, eyes on his.

"And what is it you have there, my dear?" her father asks.

Suzanna lifts a corner of the cloth. "Look what Monsieur Beaubien brought me!"

Jeremiah Peabody frowns at the thin young man with the sharp nose who stands facing him, looking doubtful.

Peabody's black eyes narrow and his gaze sweeps the room. "I know girls here marry at an early age," he says, his tone clipped. "But my daughter is too young for gifts from eligible men."

Beaubien shakes his head, spreading his hands. "They are merely the potatoes of Ireland," he says in a polished French accent. "And most inedible, I assure you. I meant nothing by them."

Jeremiah turns to Suzanna, his eyebrows raised. "Potatoes?"

Suzanna nods, eyes shining. "Mr. Young's cook was going to throw them out, but Monsieur Beaubien thought I might be able to get them to grow here." She unties one corner of the cloth. "Look, they already have eyes starting to form." She lifts her chin at her father, her eyes just slightly defiant. "It's a fair trade. I'll give him some of my first crop."

"Though she's promised not to cook them herself," Beaubien says mischievously. "I'll let someone else have that honor."

Jeremiah shakes his head and permits himself a small smile. "Very well. We'll consider it a commercial transaction and leave it at that."

Suzanna smiles triumphantly and carries her treasure out of the room. Old Bill crosses to the fireplace and turns, warming his long buckskin-clad legs. "Like you got a choice, Jeremiah," he chuckles. "Who's gonna tell that girl she can't do what she's already decided on doin'?"

"Must take after her daddy or somethin'," a big broad-faced young man observes from the adobe seat that forms the sill of the multi-paned window overlooking the street. The panes are made of milk-white sheets of mica and the resulting muted light gives the room a sleepy, church-like glow that's balanced by the color of the cushions on the chests and the light of the fire.

Jeremiah grins ruefully and crosses to the tea table in the right hand corner. "Did you all get enough to eat?" he asks. "I'm sure you will be wanting something, William." He lifts a small china plate. "What's the news from Sibley's survey expedition?" Then he turns. "I apologize, Mr. Locke. Have you met Carlos Beaubien and Ceran St. Vrain? And of course you know Ewing Young here in the corner, guarding the table for us."

Young lifts a hand in acknowledgement, and Gerald nods to him and then the other men. They nod politely, then go on with their talk.

Gerald drops into a chair near the door and tries not to watch it for the girl's return. The way her eyes widened in apparent delight at the sight of him, the way she looked directly into his face. She's unlike any girl he's ever encountered.

When she returns, she has a book in her hand. The conversation stops when she enters and the men all watch her cross the room to Ceran St. Vrain in the window seat. She hands him the small brown volume. He takes it, looks at the spine, and shakes his head. Suzanna laughs as he hands it back to her. "You can face Apaches and Mouache Utes, but Samuel Johnson is too much for you?" she teases.

"You can face Samuel Johnson, but a skillet and oven are too much for you?" he answers.

Williams barks with laughter as Charles Beaubien chortles, "He caught you out that time!" But the girl only chuckles, crosses to a bookcase, and inserts the book in a row of similarly-bound volumes.

"We all have our strengths and weaknesses," Jeremiah Peabody says, smiling. "While she serves the food we eat, her training is in literature and horticulture, not cookery."

Suzanna tilts her head, gives him a small smile, and crosses to the table. "Shall I ask Encarnación for more tea and rolls?" she asks. She swings around, looking at the men in the room. "I suspect Mr. Williams and Mr. Locke have not partaken as much as they might like to." She smiles mischievously at Old Bill. "You, of course, are always hungry for more of Encarnación's rolls." She turns to Gerald. "And you? Are you still hungry?"

Then she looks at his hands, empty in his lap. "Why, you haven't eaten at all, have you?" She picks up a small plate, places two rolls, a piece of soft white cheese, and a napkin on it, and crosses the room to him. "That tea water is cold. I'll bring more in a minute, along with some fresh bread."

41

As Gerald takes the plate, he looks up into her eyes. Again, the straightforward quality of her gaze strikes him. There is nothing flirtatious in this girl. Yet he can barely move his lips to acknowledge her attention. "Thank you," is all he can manage to say.

~ ~ ~ ~

Gerald sits beside the campfire that night long after the others have gone to their bedrolls, and gazes thoughtfully into the flames. Other than Enoch Jones, everyone he's met in the West has made no reference to the color of his skin. It's almost as if they can't see that he's a shade darker than the most sun-burnt of any of the Americans or Frenchmen here. He chews thoughtfully on his lower lip. That might not be true. A few of the French trappers, exposed for decades to the elements, are darker than he is. And, of course, the natives. Although some of them have both Spanish and Indian parents, so they're also of mixed race.

For example, the girl Suzanna appears to be the daughter of Peabody and an Indian woman. Or perhaps half-Indian? There's something about her, a creaminess to her coloring, that sets her apart. His mind strays, thinking about her height, the way she bears herself so confidently in her strangely old-fashioned American clothes. The way her eyes look straight into his—

Then he shakes himself and goes back to the original question. The question of his own parentage, whether he should be more upfront about his race. Even though he's already settled the issue for the time being, he finds it rising again. Perhaps because of the girl? He pushes the thought away and considers. No one seems at all interested in his background. Although Jeremiah Peabody might be, if Suzanna takes a liking to him.

42

Gerald catches himself. The girl clearly has many admirers. It isn't just her father's table that brings the trappers and merchants to his parlor, men of standing and resources like Ewing Young. Even if Gerald's parentage isn't an issue, what chance does a poor man have against men of substance like Young or someone with the experience and way with words of Old Bill? He'd need a good deal more money than he currently has to even begin thinking of speaking to a young woman like that. A girl who reads Johnson but can't cook. It would require a house with room for books. And a cook.

Gerald shakes his head. It will doubtless be a long while before he's in a position to offer such a thing. She'll have found someone else by then. Someone who can give her all she's worthy of, long before he can even think of approaching her. Besides, he'd have to tell her about his father, about his race.

He stands, stretches, and heads to his bedroll. He knows it's foolish to think of her, but the last image across his mind as he drifts into sleep is Suzanna Peabody's face, her eyes widening with surprise and something akin to delight. It hasn't even occurred to him that he knows virtually nothing about her.

CHAPTER 6

"So how is it that you knew Gerald Locke Jr. yesterday, even though you had not been formally introduced?" Jeremiah Peabody asks Suzanna the next morning as he cuts into his egg-and-corn-tortilla breakfast.

Suzanna reaches for another tortilla. "You know, Encarnación's tortillas are so delicious, I'm sure our visitors wouldn't mind having them for tea instead of wheat rolls."

"The cost of wheat flour may be high, but it means a great deal to these men to have a semblance of home in the shape of wheat bread, tea, and a pretty woman to serve them," her father says. "And, as you say, Encarnación's corn tortillas are well made, so it's no sacrifice to eat them at our other meals. That young woman is quite a cook. I thank the day she appeared at our doorstop." He looks up at her with a slight frown. "Unless you have grown weary of tortillas, my dear. In which case—"

"Oh no," Suzanna says. "I could eat Chonita's tortillas at every meal and never weary of them." She pops the last bit into her mouth and lifts her cup of milk. "That and this good cow's milk that Ramón so thoughtfully brings us."

"Well, we do pay him for it, although Ramón has also been a great friend to us. Although I have reason to believe that we are no longer the primary attraction for him." He smiles. "He seems to think Encarnación's acquaintance is worth cultivating." Then his eyes narrow. "However, if you think you are going to deflect me from my purpose, you are very sadly mistaken. How is it you know this Gerald Locke?"

Suzanna chuckles as she places the milk back on the table. "I couldn't help but try," she says. She looks at her plate. "I— I didn't want to worry you."

His head lifts sharply. "Should I have not invited him in? Shall I forbid his return?"

"Oh no!" She looks up in alarm. "He's a good man who saved me from a very uncomfortable encounter. I was glad to meet him properly."

"An uncomfortable encounter?" Jeremiah's hands fall away from his plate and flatten on the edge of the table. "I think you had best start at the beginning."

His knuckles have whitened by the time Suzanna finishes her story and his compressed lips are one thin angry line. "That Enoch Jones is a man who cannot rise above his station and so resents anyone who looks as if they might do so," he says angrily. "Or anyone who has already surpassed him." He takes a deep breath, picks up his knife and fork, and gives Suzanna a sharp look before reapplying himself to his food. "And Gerald Locke Jr. has clearly done so."

She smiles at him radiantly. "I'm so glad you like him, papá."

He raises an eyebrow. "So, it's 'papá' now, is it?" He smiles and shakes his head. Then his face sobers. "But please be more careful as you traverse the town, my dear. There may not always be a Mr. Locke nearby to save you from men like Enoch Jones."

Suzanna sobers. "I know it. I've thought about my route that day, and decided on a new path for getting safely to and from the plaza." Her chin lifts. "But I have no intention of allowing the likes of Enoch Jones to keep me from enjoying my life."

45

Her father chuckles, tosses his napkin onto the table, and pushes back his chair. "I have no doubt that is the case," he says. "Not even I am likely to stop you from achieving your wishes. Are you prepared for your Latin lesson this morning?"

"Of course," Suzanna says. "But before we begin, I need to check on the courtyard plants. I put straw on the greens last night, to protect them from the frost, and they need to be uncovered."

"Has the frost reached the courtyard?"

"I thought that it might, so I was worried about the lettuce. I want to keep it going as long as I can. There's enough for at least another salad or two."

"And did you find a way to protect your seed potatoes until spring?"

Suzanna's eyes brighten. "I placed them under the straw, as well. This afternoon I'll find a dry space for them in the root cellar. It may be difficult to keep those tiny eyes from growing too long before it's time to plant them."

Jeremiah smiles at her. "I'm sure you'll find a way."

But her plants aren't enough to keep Suzanna Peabody from thinking about Gerald Locke at odd times over the next few days. The way he looked into her face, didn't let his gaze drift lower. The shy but somehow confident smile. The broad forehead above his gray eyes. The tone of his voice as he spoke to her father: low-timbered, respectful, self assured. There's something about the way the man carries himself, a kind of firm gentleness.

She wonders what he'll decide to do during the coming trapping season. There are groups going up to the Platte River country. At least that's what their leaders are telling the government officials. They're claiming that they'll head north to trap outside Mexico's boundaries. But word is they intend to sneak back across the border, then move south, all the way to the Gila's rich beaver country. Somehow, she doesn't think Mr. Locke would misrepresent his intentions in that way. He just doesn't seem the kind of man who would intentionally deceive others.

He seemed interested in her potato project, Suzanna reflects as she picks pieces of straw from between the leaves of loose-leaf lettuce. He had leaned toward her a little, his gray eyes on her face as she explained how she planned to overwinter the pieces Carlos Beaubien gave her. She smiles a little to herself as she reenters the house, thinking again of that broad forehead, that kind-looking mouth. She doesn't pause to think that she knows virtually nothing about him.

CHAPTER 7

The day after the visit to the Peabody's, Gerald shares yet another whisky with Old Bill in yet another Taos taberna. In the middle of a story about his life among the Osage Indians, Williams interrupts himself. "So how is it you happened to already know our Miz Peabody?" he asks abruptly.

Gerald shrugs. "A man was paying her what seemed to be unwanted attention and I intervened." He lifts his drink. "Anyone else would've done the same thing."

Old Bill lifts a scraggly red eyebrow. "Would the gentleman who was providing this unwanted attention happen to be named Enoch Jones?"

Gerald sets his drink on the table. "Do you know him?"

Williams' back straightens and his eyes narrow. "I know him all right. I'll wring his fat neck for him, the mothersuckin' balls for brains bastard!"

Gerald frowns. "Has he been after her before this?"

"He's made eyes," Old Bill says grimly. "You sure it was him?"

"Oh yes. We were in the same train coming out."

"He'll be waitin' for you t' turn your back, you know."

"He already disliked me." Gerald shrugs. "This will just give him another reason."

Williams raises an inquiring eyebrow and Gerald briefly describes the incident with the Kiowa boy, then—more fully—Jones' treatment of the mules.

48

"He's a godforsaken bastard, that one," Old Bill says. "I've known a few craven-hearted men in my time, but he's one of the worst." His eyes snap. "To think he'd have the gall to put his hands on our Suzanna."

"It was the way he spoke to her," Gerald says. "As if she was dirt under his feet."

"Well, he's got this mothersuckin' idea that a white skin makes him better than the rest of the human race," Williams says. "And Miz Peabody being part Navajo but so well bred and nice mannered must just stick in his craw."

"She's part Navajo?"

"Now there's a story for you." Old Bill leans forward and lowers his voice. "No one talks about it much, because Jeremiah doesn't like to be reminded how he was boondoggled." He tilts his red head. "At least, that's how he figgers it." He shrugs. "Any other man would of known what the girl was up to, but he was still green and those New Englanders, they expect everybody else to have their same standards."

Gerald frowns, confused.

Williams stretches back, fingering his whisky. "See, what happened was, Peabody showed up out here from the East along about 1809. He was still pretty much just a whippersnapper, runnin' away from some trouble with a gal and another man." Williams shrugs. "The usual. Anyway, he got out here safe enough and managed to sweet talk the ricos into letting him stay, but then this puta started after him. She was the daughter of a French trapper and a Navajo gal the trapper had bought from the Comanches."

Williams grins ruefully. "The girl was a righteously pretty little thing and she pretty much got what she wanted. Jeremiah fell in love, or so he thought, and when she told him she was enciento, he hooked up with her. Didn't marry her, though. He wouldn't turn Catholic, even for a girl. But he swore he'd take care of her and the child. And he did, even when she started running around with other men."

Old Bill shakes his head. "Should of turned her out. I would of. But by that time, the little girl was born and they say she was a righteous beauty even then. Her daddy fell in love for real then, that's for certain sure."

Williams pauses, looking incongruously bemused. "Babies'll do that t' a man if you're not careful. Tie you down faster'n any woman can." He shakes a finger at Gerald. "My advice is, don't stay around long enough to find out if there's gonna be a kid, and if you do find out, then cut out before the coon actually arrives. If you stay, you're lost, sure as oil and water don't mix."

Gerald grins. "I'll remember that."

Williams raises both hands, leans forward, and slaps the rough wooden table with both palms. "So what're you gonna do with yourself this winter? You decide yet?"

Gerald shakes his head.

"Why don't you throw in with me?" the trapper asks. "I've got nothing to do here except play court to Sibley on his road commission work and I ain't much good at payin' court." He snorts. "Sibley'd tell you that." He leans back, hands still flat on the table. "I'll show you the ropes and we'll split the results. Just you and me, private like. I'm not about to share my hunting grounds with just anyone."

"Your hunting grounds?"

Old Bill winks. "I know some places up in the hills that they all think are trapped out. But it's good hunting if you know where to look and there ain't too many out looking."

Gerald studies the opinionated mountain man. There's something about Williams that's quite appealing. Or maybe it's just that Old

50

Bill's loquaciousness means Gerald doesn't have to talk much when they're together. There's certainly little need to explain himself or where he comes from.

Gerald nods thoughtfully, then more firmly, looking into the trapper's face. "I'd be honored to throw in with you," he says. "When do you expect to start?"

"Well, there ain't no time like the present!" Williams scrapes back his chair. "Let's get a move on."

Gerald follows him out the taberna door, squelching his desire to make a farewell visit to the Peabody home, aware that he has no right to make such a call, hoping against hope that he might chance across Suzanna before he and Old Bill leave town. Or that Williams will decide he needs one last meal of the Peabody cook's wheat flour rolls.

But when the old trapper decides to do something, he throws himself into it completely. He and Gerald are busy from dawn to dusk: stocking up on flour, coffee, and salt; purchasing Gerald's gear, including elk hide moccasins and buckskin trousers and shirt; and locating and bargaining for two sturdy mules for their gear. Gerald keeps an eye out for Suzanna Peabody, but doesn't catch so much as a glimpse of her in the next three days.

They slip out of Taos in the middle of the night. Williams has mentioned casually to several of the other trappers that he's heading up the Rio del Norte, and he and Gerald move out in that direction under a star-studded sky.

The next morning, the wheat fields of Taos Valley give way to rolling hills covered with forty-foot juniper and occasional long-needled thick-barked ponderosa pine. But Old Bill is paralleling the Rio del Norte, not heading toward it. He moves due north, then slightly east, to hit what he calls Red River Creek well east of its confluence with the del Norte. They camp beside the creek that night,

51

in the shadow of the mountains it flows from. According to Williams, the stream is called "Colorado" in Spanish, in honor of the reddish sediment that stains it during spring runoff.

The next morning they follow the Red's narrow canyon east into the Sangre de Cristos. Williams leads the way, the gap between the men too far for any real conversation and Old Bill anxious not to be spotted. Gerald's not sure if Williams is more concerned about Indians or other trappers.

He takes the opportunity to study the massive granite and sandstone boulders that jut from the canyon walls, dwarfing the men and mules, and the ponderosas that cling precariously in the gaps between them. There's a brooding beauty in the darkness of the pines. Sunlight breaks around the rocks onto the clear-running river below, then cuts off abruptly as the canyon rim narrows overhead.

Where the canyon is wider, broad grassy areas stretch beside the stream. Even Gerald can spot the old beaver sign in these meadows. Graying tree stumps stick up from the grasses and show themselves among the alder and willows along the river bank. Their tops, gnawed long ago into dull points by beaver incisors, are chipped like poorly sharpened pencils.

The men find no truly marshy areas or ponds with active beaver lodges until well into the second day. Williams is ahead and Gerald's beginning to wonder when he'll decide to noon, when the older man raises his reedy voice. "Well now, that's a beaver dam if ever I saw one!"

A windblown snag straddles the river from bank to bank. Ten- and twelve-foot lengths of two-inch thick branches are jammed hard against the snag at every possible angle. River mud has been smudged between them, whether by beaver or water flow, it's hard to say.

The dam is massive, perhaps eight feet tall and fifteen long. Grasses dot its top and sides. They're well rooted in the sediment and enhance the dam's strength. Water slips around its near end, trickling downstream just enough to keep the pond behind it in check. There are no discernible banks to the pond itself. The impounded water seeps through a swath of cattails, then into a tangle of coyote willow. Beyond the willows, long grasses rise from mucky soil, creating a bog that blocks the canyon floor for a good quarter mile upriver.

Williams pushes his hat back on his head and scratches his scraggly red beard as he studies the dam and the pond. Then he turns to Gerald.

"This is where moccasins are better'n boots," he says. "We're about to get damp." Old Bill's mule nickers at him and he looks at her impatiently. "Ah hell, let's noon first." He pulls off his hat. "Then we'll start slogging."

They loose the mules to graze among the water-rich grasses, and munch buffalo jerky while they study the bog. "We could trap it from here," Williams says. "If we're careful, the beaver won't know which direction we come from." He snorts. "There's sure enough water around here to wash our stink out." He glances up at the sheer canyon walls. "But we'd only have one way out if any Utes or Apaches show up." He clucks his tongue as he shakes his head. "We're gonna have to get past this. Come at it from upstream."

"And if Apaches or Utes show up when we're above this?" Gerald asks. "Won't this mess block us from moving out of here quickly?"

Williams grins mischievously. "Then we'll have to head upstream instead." He glances at Gerald's feet. "Better put your moccasins on. Those leather boots will take a month of Sundays to dry out good and proper."

53

Gerald grimaces. He suspects the elk hide moccasins aren't going to be much protection against the icy water.

And he's right. When he steps into the stream, the shock to his feet is truly breathtaking.

Ahead of him, leading a reluctant mule through the water-logged grass, Old Bill looks back over his shoulder and grins. "They'll numb up soon enough," he says. "Then you won't feel a thing."

Gerald grins wryly and clucks at his mule, who seems more interested in eating than wading. Smart animal, he thinks grimly.

They move upstream and well beyond the pond before Williams finds a camping site to his liking. The next morning, he gathers gear enough for a day's trapping, hands Gerald a long piece of deadwood sharpened on one end, hoists a pack onto his back, and leads the way back to the beaver dam.

They maneuver downstream perhaps a mile, though it seems longer. Gerald's feet are blocks of ice before the trapper abruptly halts. "Here it is!" Williams hisses. "Looks different, this direction."

Gerald wades through the water to stand beside Williams in the eddying stream. A wall of willow lines the river's banks, marking the edge of the beaver pond. On their left, there's a narrow muddy incline between the willows. Neatly-clipped willow sticks lie beside it. A small bush has been sheared off to within a foot of the ground, the tip of each stub angled and sharp.

"Beaver feeding?" Gerald asks.

Williams hisses, "Quiet!" Then he nods and jerks a thumb toward the strip of mud. "That there's their slide," he whispers. "We'll be settin' the trap out from that, a good three feet or so." He points at a small section of water that's noticeably darker than the rest, a sign that the pond bottom drops sharply in that location. "Right about there."

Gerald considers the dark spot and wonders just how deep the pool actually is. But he only nods.

Old Bill wades forward cautiously. He stops, extends his foot, and taps it along the bottom of the pond, then grunts approvingly. He turns and beckons to Gerald. "Come and see."

Gerald edges closer, staying between Williams and the bank.

Williams moves his foot from side to side. The water swirls, turning brown with silt. "I'm using my foot to move some of this here mud into a little hill," he explains. "When I'm done, the top of it'll be about a foot below the surface."

Gerald nods his understanding, if not his ability to see what the trapper is actually doing.

"I've got to make it wide enough to hold the trap and all," Williams explains, gesturing with his hands, forgetting to whisper. He yanks the bag on his back around to rest against his scrawny belly, then pulls out a trap and begins unwrapping the steel chain that's wound around it. "You know how to set this beast?"

"Well, I do on solid ground," Gerald says.

Williams grins. "It ain't so theoretical now, is it?" He lifts the trap chain to one side, out of the way, then flips the trap itself onto its side and braces it against his thigh. He wraps his hands around the metal clamps at each end and squeezes steadily, forcing them together. As the springs compress, the trap jaws are forced open and into position.

Old Bill gives Gerald a little nod and jerks his chin at the trap. "Just flip that trigger piece into that there dog."

Gerald gingerly uses his free hand to snap the dangling piece of narrow, angled metal into the notch on the opposite side of the trap. This will keep the trap's jaws open until an unwary animal ventures too close and bumps the trigger and the metal jaws clamp shut around the animal's leg or other body part.

55

Williams lifts the trap carefully, gives a satisfied nod, and grins at Gerald. "That's the way to do it."

Gerald grins back at him. "That approach requires some real strength."

Williams nods complacently. "It's all in the hands." He deftly slides the trap under the water and onto the pile of dredged-up mud, then lifts the chain and moves farther into the pond. When he finds the anchorage spot he's looking for, he motions Gerald to bring him the trap stake.

Gerald wades across and hands Williams the piece of sharpened deadwood, and the trapper slips its blunt end into the final loop of the chain. Then he pulls a leather cord from a pocket, wraps it around the stick twice, then threads it through a loop of the chain, and knots it into place just below the top of the stake. Once the chain is attached, he grabs the stick with both hands and shoves the pointed end firmly downward, driving it into the pond floor. He nods in satisfaction and turns to follow the chain back to the trap site. Gerald wades after him.

"Cold yet?" Old Bill asks over his shoulder.

"Startin' to feel it," Gerald says, his lips so stiff he can hardly form the words.

Williams chuckles. "You got sand, I'll say that for you." He gestures toward the stake. "All that's the preliminaries. This next step's the crucial piece." He wades to the willow bushes along the bank, pulls out his knife, and slices off a long switch. He scrapes the bark from one end, then reaches into a pocket. "I'm gonna need you to take care of this," he says. He holds out the corked piece of antelope horn that serves as his bait container.

Gerald has smelled castoreum before, but the choking scent of it is always a shock to his senses. He grimaces as he removes the cork and tilts the contents toward the trapper. Williams grins at him, sticks his

56

gloved forefinger into the goop, and smears it onto the scraped end of the willow switch.

As Gerald recaps the bit of horn, Williams chuckles. "Look at your face!" He shakes his head. "Better get use to it, sonny. That stuff's what fortunes are made of."

"It stinks like a lot of necessary things," Gerald says dryly.

Old Bill laughs and moves to the edge of the pond. He forces the thicker end of the willow stick into the bank at an angle, so that the baited end hangs out over the water and dangles perhaps six inches above the surface and the set trap underneath.

"That should do it," Williams says. He turns and begins wading upstream. "We need to make tracks up a ways before we can climb out. We don't want that beaver smellin' us. These critters can be mighty intelligent when they take a notion to be."

There's a good sized male beaver in the trap when they return the next morning. Gerald carries it back to camp, where Williams proceeds to demonstrate how to skin and butcher the carcass, then how to stretch the skin onto a hoop he constructs from willow branches and thin strips of rawhide. When he hangs the hooped pelt from a ponderosa branch, the sun shines through the skin and gives it a reddish hue.

"You ever eat beaver flesh?" the trapper asks.

Gerald shakes his head.

"Well, you're in for a treat," Old Bill says. "Beaver tastes like beef and even has a little fat in it, unlike venison or antelope. They're so dry you've got to add fat to the pot to make them righteously edible." He squats next to the fire and reaches for the coffee pot. "With all that grease, beaver flesh doesn't last long, but it's good the first day, at any rate. And it's a nice change from deer or elk or those other hoofed creatures."

"I understand beaver tail is quite tasty."

Williams grunts disparagingly. "If you're craving fat, it'll pass for it," he says. "It's too bland for my tongue. Though that cook of Jeremiah Peabody's knows what to do with it. Someone brought her some last fall and by the time she was done with it, Peabody said it was like ambrosia." He shakes his head. "That Chonita is a looker, too. It's beyond my understanding why she's not married yet. Waiting for the best proposition, I suppose. A female like her can take her time, be righteously choosy."

Williams pauses, still holding the coffee pot, staring up into the golden narrow leaf cottonwoods between them and the river. "I knew another one like that once. An Osage gal." He shakes his head and puts the pot back on the stone next to the fire. "Pretty, too." He looks at Gerald. "Have you met her?"

"Jeremiah Peabody's cook?" Gerald shakes his head.

Williams grins mischievously. "Well, you met his daughter, so nobody else matters much now, I reckon."

Gerald looks away. Suzanna Peabody's name isn't something to be bandied about around a campfire.

"Ah, come on now," the trapper says. "It's not a thing to be ashamed of, that spark between you. And you can't deny it was there. I saw it."

Gerald glances at him, then rises. "I'm to bed," he says.

Old Bill chuckles knowingly and reaches for the coffee pot again. Gerald's face tightens. Is the man taking liberties because of the color of his skin, or is he just taking liberties? How dare he talk about Suzanna Peabody in that way! He has no right!

Gerald pulls himself together and spreads out his blankets. He has no rights either. No permission to think of the girl with such a combination of sweetness and longing. And no reason to think he'll

58

ever have such permission. She may smile that way at every new man she meets. She certainly must meet plenty of them in her father's parlor. He seems to keep open house.

Despite these obvious facts, Suzanna Peabody's dark eyes still sparkle in Gerald's memory as he lays down, covers himself, and tries to force his mind elsewhere, away from the look on her face in that first unguarded moment in her father's small Taos parlor.

CHAPTER 8

Over the next two weeks, Williams and Gerald trap their way steadily up the Red River. As they move higher, the temperatures drop a little more each night. The cottonwoods and the heart-shaped foliage of the white-barked aspens turn ever more golden.

Then snow falls for the first time. Williams stands by the morning campfire and studies the sides of the canyon. Its sharp rocks are outlined in white. The trapper swings his head toward the stream and the fingers of ice that edge its banks. Then he nods eastward, up the canyon.

"I reckon it's about time for us to head on to greener pastures," he says. "We're not going to spy much more beaver up this creek. From here on, it's too narrow and steep for them to have much chance at damming it solid. And anything dammable that runs into it is gonna be froze over anyway. We're high up enough now that the snow's likely to be nothing but serious from now until March. I reckon we'd better head on across Bobcat before it really sets in."

"Bobcat?"

Old Bill jerks his head to the southeast. "There's a pass thataway. It'll drop us down into the prettiest little valley you ever saw." He grins. "Well, not so little. But it's a sight." He swings toward his mule. "We'd best get to moving though, if we want to get over it before nightfall."

The trail to Bobcat Pass is a steady climb up a rocky path dominated by snow-dusted ponderosas and other pine that cling improbably to almost perpendicular slopes. Gerald feels the upward incline in his ears. First a dull pressure, than a sharp pain until he sets himself to yawning and swallowing air. How high are they climbing, anyway?

High enough to be above the river, which slices through a steep sided and heavily treed ravine below. The actual pass itself is more grass than trees. The snow is thick, but drifted enough that the dried herbage is still evident. The men pause to let the mules blow and browse for a few minutes. They pull jerky for themselves from their packs, then begin the descent, into the trees again, on a slant almost as steep as the one they've just scaled. Elk lift their heads from pocket meadows too small even for beaver as the trappers and their animals move down the mountainside.

They drop into a narrow defile and follow it east and south below slopes dotted with twisted brown scrub oak and green-black pine. The snow hasn't reached this side of the mountains yet and a small stream, not yet frozen, trickles merrily through narrow meadows thick with willow and drying grass. Just ahead, a flock of perhaps twenty wild turkeys moves silently away from the other side of the stream and weaves uphill through the trees. None of the birds turn their heads toward the men and mules, but they're clearly moving away from the foreign presence.

Gerald takes a deep breath, breathing in the cold pine-scented air. Though the tree-covered slopes are almost close enough touch, the sky to the east feels more open, somehow. He suddenly realizes how closed in he's felt in the last few weeks in the Red River's canyon.

They reach the valley early the next morning, just as the sun is rising behind the massive snow-dusted rock abutment that Williams

61

calls Baldy Mountain. As they move south beside the creek in the valley's center, Williams gestures to the west. Gerald turns his head. The snow-clad peaks opposite Baldy glow pink, reflecting the sunrise.

Gerald shakes his head, bemused. The sun rises in all directions in this valley. In fact, the way the sunlight glints from the dew on the brown grasses makes it feel as if the light rises from the ground itself. The grass is long and healthy. It sweeps from the bushes scattered along Baldy's slopes down into the valley floor and then west over the foothills to the edge of the pine-covered and pink-topped mountains. It's thickest along the creek bank. Gerald's farmer heart twinges with desire.

Old Bill and his mule drop back to walk beside Gerald. "This little bit of a stream's called the Moreno River," he says.

The younger man grins. The strip of water is so narrow he could jump across it, but they call it a river.

"Here in nuevomexico, if it flows all year, then it's a river. It don't rightly matter how much water actually runs in it," Williams adds.

"Doesn't Moreno mean black?" Gerald asks. The water isn't black, but the soil the stream cuts through certainly is. Dark and loamy. Inside his buckskin gloves, his fingers twitch, wanting to know how such a soil might respond to the touch. It looks as healthy as the grasses that weave their roots into its heart. He glances toward Baldy again and blinks. What he'd taken for bushes on the lower slopes have resolved into a scattered herd of feeding elk. Involuntarily, he wonders what Suzanna Peabody would say to such a sight.

But Williams is talking again, his voice high and querulous, a sure sign that he's about to launch into a story. "First time I saw this valley, there was a foot of snow on the ground and a group of Utes camping just yonder, under that stony outcrop."

He points to the right, where a mass of stone juts from the side of a flat-topped grassy hill. "I'd just pushed over Bobcat Pass in snow so deep the mules could barely plow through it. I'd been walkin' three days. I figured if I stopped, I'd just righteously freeze to death."

Old Bill shakes his head. "I tell you, I was mighty pleased to see that little camp of Utes down there and even gladder when I realized its chief was a friend of mine. They welcomed me well enough, but he wouldn't tell me a righteous lick about what they were doin' up here in that kind of weather. They should of been down Cimarron Canyon feeding their families and waitin' out the winter like sensible men. Instead, they were laying here, waiting on something they probably weren't supposed to be tanglin' with. Mexicano soldiers, most likely. I got myself thawed out a little, then I hightailed it outta there with just my rifle, one beaver trap, and the clothes on my back."

Williams shrugs. "Old Three Hands got two good mules for feeding me a couple of days, but I got out of tanglin' in a fight that was none of my business. So I reckon it washed clean, although I sure did miss the use of those mules. I just hope they didn't get turned into stew meat when those damn fools stopped waitin' for a fight and headed for home."

He pauses. Gerald knows he's expected to prod the story forward. "You never got your mules back?" he asks.

"Nope, I never did. And the next time I saw Three Hands, he didn't recall having seen me at all that whole winter." Old Bill grins. "It turns out they'd had a bit of a scrap with the Mexican soldiers. He didn't have much to say about that, neither. Those government troops seem to have got the better of them . Old Three Hands sure didn't want to put his jaw to talking about anything that happened that season." Williams chuckles. "The Utes ain't ones for dwellin' on their defeats."

"Like most men."

Williams snorts in agreement and points ahead, to a cluster of ponderosas in the curve of the stream. "We'll stop there to noon. That'll give the mules a chance to feed up. This grass may be brown, but it's still tasty." He nods southward. "If you're thinkin' this is pretty, wait'll you see the south part."

"There's more?"

"You could say that." Old Bill chuckles. "You might just be able to say that."

The mules are reluctant to leave the long grasses, but once the men have eaten, Williams seems eager to push on. They follow the stream through a mile-long passageway that winds between the hills. The ground is thick with grass and spotted with thick-trunked ponderosas. Then the trees end and the land opens before them. Williams halts, grins at Gerald, and waves a proud hand at the view. "Now that's something, ain't it?" he says.

They're standing at the top of a broad slope that angles gently down to a grassy basin that's perhaps a mile wide and extends south toward haze-covered blue peaks. The valley is bisected by a series of low grass-covered ridges that block his view of the valley floor, but Gerald suspects the grass continues right to the edge of those southern mountains. If it's anything like the growth at his feet, this is a rich valley indeed.

Elk are scattered across the hillside to his right. At its base, a stream narrower than the Moreno slips from the west and joins the Moreno, then snakes slowly southeast. Gerald's gaze lifts and moves along the mountains that line the valley, east and west. He squints, puzzled. There's something familiar about this place.

Williams gestures toward a low point in the peaks to the left, south of Baldy and a flat-topped ridge that bulks beyond it. "Those streams are headin' there, where the Cimarron starts," he says. "There's a crag above the marsh there that the Injuns favor for gatherin' eagle feathers. There were three big scraggly nests perched up in there the last time I come through. There's likely more further up the slopes."

He waves his hand at the grassland. "That there's prime eagle hunting grounds for keeping their young fed up, what with the smaller birds and le petite chien."

Gerald lifts an eyebrow. "Prairie dogs? The more the eagles eat, the better. They'd wipe out the grasses with their mounds. And that's prime hay meadow, from the looks of it."

Williams chuckles. "Prime elk browse, at any rate. Even the occasional buffalo." He clucks at his pack mule. "This valley gets a mite windy and cold this time of year. We need to get a move on and get under the lee of one of those ridges before nightfall. I'm lookin' to scout east along the Cimarron tomorrow and see if there's any beaver come in since I was here two seasons back."

Gerald follows the trapper down the broad slope, but his mind isn't on beaver. The broad grassland and small streams move his thoughts inevitably to cattle and farming. The length and thickness of the grass here tell him there's water available pretty much year-round.

And there are no people. No farmers, at any rate. The Indians apparently come through to hunt and even camp. Do they stay long? How would they feel about a man who wanted to actually put roots down here, build a house? Put in a garden? Grow a family along with it?

Suzanna Peabody's straightforward black eyes rise before him and Gerald shakes his head. That's presuming too much. But wouldn't it be something if she should decide— He forces his mind back to the more plausible daydream of ranch, house, hay, and cattle.

"Does anybody actually live up here year-round?" he asks that night as he and Williams crouch next to a fire at the base of Eagle's Nest rock. The canyon wall soars above them, black in the darkness. They're right up against it, out of the way of the cattail-strewn marsh that absorbs the waters of the Moreno River. Gerald can hear it trickling from the marsh into the intermittent stream that runs through the canyon they'll enter tomorrow. Cimarron Creek, Williams calls it. "Cimarron" because it's as wild and unpredictable as the mountain sheep also called "cimarron." "Creek" because it doesn't flow year-round.

"This here valley's too cold for perching in durin' the winter months," Williams says. "It's a righteously beautiful place in the summer, once summer finally makes it this high up. It takes a mite longer than most places to warm up and the cold comes in earlier, too." He shrugs. "It ain't good for beaver though. Not enough trees and willow to make it worth their while."

"I was thinking about how it would be to farm," Gerald says casually. "But from what you say, it sounds like the growing season's a bit short."

Williams snorts. "The growin' season's short and the winter season's long," he says. "I surely wouldn't try it. But then I ain't a farming man." He points to the rock abutment overhead. "I'd rather be on top of that rock, seein' what I can see, lookin' for new trails to blaze. Not cramped up in a cabin with nothin' to do." He shrugs. "But if a man was goin' to venture livin' up here, he could always run cattle. There's grass enough. Though you'd have to fight the elk for the range and the wolves and the cougars for the calves."

"And watch out for prairie dogs," Gerald says wryly.

66

Williams nods. "And then you'd have to get those cows down to market." He pushes back his hat. "I hear tell some of the Taos folk run their goats and sheep up here in the summer. Between them, the Injuns, the elk, and the weather, it'd be a contest who'd wear you out soonest."

Gerald nods, gazing into the dark toward the marsh, his mind drifting toward the richness of the soil in the valley beyond.

"And you'd have a tough time findin' a woman who'd be willin' to live this far from nowhere." Williams grins mischievously at Gerald. "Even Suzanna Peabody."

Gerald's head jerks toward Old Bill in spite of himself.

Williams stretches his legs toward the fire. "You ain't the only one who's dreamed that particular notion, you know. We've all had that idea, one time or the other."

Gerald feels a tight fist of disgust in his belly and fights to keep it from showing on his face.

Williams shakes his head at the fire, a rueful smile on his lips. "Not that any of us'd touch her. She's that fine a lady." He nods at Gerald companionably. "But she does make you think of what it'd be like to settle with a girl like herself, don't she now? Educated like that. Smart as a whip. Not takin' sass off a soul, not even her daddy. But not mean like. It's just she can talk him so sweet he don't even know he's been twisted around her little finger." He chuckles. "'Course, that might be a reason for some of us to think twice about a gal of her caliber."

Gerald permits himself a small smile. To think of another man thinking of Suzanna Peabody in that way makes his stomach clench, but he does like that Old Bill admires her qualities, knows what she's worth.

Not that he himself really knows the girl, Gerald reminds himself. But what Williams says of her fits what Gerald instinctively feels.

The true heart of her. The strength. As to her taking no sass off anybody, he knows that isn't quite true. He's seen her frightened, though not cowed. And he's very glad that he happened around the corner of that narrow street where Enoch Jones had her cornered against that adobe wall.

Not that his intervention lays any obligation upon her, he reminds himself later, as he spreads his bedroll on the rocky ground beneath the cliff. Or means she's special to him in any way. He would do the same for any woman in such a predicament.

Yet, as he dozes off, Gerald's mind drifts to the image of black eyes looking straight into his, slim brown hands offering him a plate of food.

CHAPTER 9

Williams and Gerald move down the Cimarron over the course of the next week, trapping as they go, a day or two in each location, setting traps, pulling in beaver, skinning carcasses, and stretching plews. They eat what they trap until the aroma of fatty flesh drifting from the fire begins to turn Gerald's stomach.

Occasionally, they see wild turkey. The sleek birds slip through the forest without any apparent awareness of the humans, but keep well out of reach. Old Bill claims he doesn't want to shoot them for fear of bringing larger, two-footed varmints into range, but Gerald suspects the red-haired man has an affinity with the birds that precludes killing them unless absolutely necessary.

Gerald himself finds the turkeys unaccountably beautiful. There's a wild wariness to them unlike anything he's ever encountered in barnyard fowl. Although he has to admit that an alternative to beaver flesh would be nice. When the men and their mules break into the small snow-drifted valley Williams calls Ute Park, it's more than the scenic value that lifts Gerald's heart. A herd of perhaps thirty elk browses at the base of a small rocky cliff to his left.

Williams halts, studying the herd. Although the elk seem unaware of the trappers, they also seem restless. Suddenly, a large cow bolts toward the river on the other side of the valley. As the other elk follow, three wolves—two small grays and a big black—circle into sight, tagging the stragglers.

69

The elk barrel across the snow and grass, surge into the icy stream, then scramble up the far bank into the trees. A young bull, its left hind leg dragging, balks at the river's edge, perhaps wishing for a more shallow ford. The wolves move in swiftly. As they cut the elk away from the stream, a raven caws overhead.

Williams chuckles, drops his mule's lead rope, and lifts his rifle. As its muzzle roars, an identical blast erupts from the base of the stone outcropping, and the bull stumbles and goes down. The wolves dart in, then pull slightly back. The big black looks over his shoulder, toward the cliff.

Williams' head swivels, following the wolf's gaze. "Well, I'll be hornswoggled," he says.

An Indian man, his hair in the long braids and tall pompadour characteristic of Ute men, moves from the cliff. He waves an arm at the wolves and they slink, tails between their legs, toward the leafless willow brush that crowds the riverbank a half-dozen yards downstream. Then they turn and crouch in the grass, eyes flicking between the approaching man and the elk.

"Waagh!" Old Bill groans. "That Ute's gonna claim that bull, and now him and those wolves have that whole herd most righteously spooked. We don't have a chance in hell of gettin' another one, and all we've got for supper is that quarter beaver that's on the edge of sour, and that little bit of tail."

"It may have been your shot that brought that bull down," Gerald points out.

"Don't matter," Williams says. His eyes rake the valley. "He appears to be alone," he adds thoughtfully. Then he shrugs. "Well, it's worth a try anyhow. We're two against one."

He grabs his mule's lead rope and moves forward, Gerald and his mule slightly behind.

70

The Indian looks up as they move toward him. Then he raises his knife and slices deep into the elk's belly. He yanks out a long handful of glistening entrails and turns to toss it toward the wolves. The black darts in, mouths the food, and drags it off, his companions following obsequiously.

"That's us," Williams says over his shoulder. "Those grays."

Gerald grins and nods, his eyes on the Ute, who's pulled off his buckskin shirt and gone back to work on the elk carcass, pointedly ignoring the two trappers. Gerald and Williams are within ten feet before he looks up again.

Old Bill signs "Hello" and the other man nods noncommittally as his knife continues to slice into the elk.

"That there was a good shot," Williams says, then repeats himself with a few fluent hand signs.

A smile flashes across the Indian's face. "You shot wide," he says in English.

Williams chuckles. He looks down at the carcass and gestures toward its front quarters. "Mind if I just turn him a mite?"

The Indian, who's now crouched at the elk's tail, incising careful circles around its hooves, nods and pauses in his work. Williams moves forward, grasps the bull's neck in both hands, and lifts, twisting the body first one way, then the other.

"There's a bullet in each shoulder," he says.

The Indian grins. "I arrived first. Made first cut."

"You did at that," Williams agrees. "But that's a whole lot of elk for one man to feed on."

The man's eyes flash and the knife in his hand lifts slightly. Gerald shifts his rifle, but the Ute's eyes remain on Old Bill's face. He gestures toward the rocky outcropping and the mouth of the narrow valley that stretches further north. "My family waits."

"I don't suppose we could trade you a bit of beaver for a haunch?" Gerald asks.

Williams nods at Gerald. "Beaver fat would be just the thing to flavor that elk," he says. He turns to the Ute. "You know how dry and tough elk can be. Especially this time of year, when the little grass they've had is all dried out and worthless."

The Indian's gaze moves across the valley's patches of still-thick brown grass, then to Williams' face.

"Though, I have to tell you we've got a righteous hunger for beaver," the trapper says. "My partner here likes it so well he just truly can't get enough of it. So you could say he's makin' a sacrifice, offering you some. We can spare you some tail, too, for that matter." He looks at Gerald. "If that's all right with you."

Gerald nods and Williams looks at the Ute. "We just thought we'd do you a favor, is all. Give you somethin' to sweeten the pot and put some taste in that rangy old winter elk."

"Show it me."

Gerald fumbles with the leather thongs that secure the wrapped portion of beaver to his mule's packsaddle and lifts the meat down. "It was fresh yesterday morning," he says.

The Indian leans forward slightly, his nostrils flaring. Then he pulls back, nods, and gestures toward the elk carcass. "I trade front left shank," he says. He grins at Williams. "Your piece."

Gerald grins. The front pieces are smaller than the hindquarters.

Old Bill nods. "That'll do right well." He sticks out a hand. "My name's Old Bill Williams and this here's Gerald Locke."

The Ute frowns at Gerald. "I know older man this name."

Gerald smiles. "My father and I are both named Gerald Locke," he says. "I am called Gerald Locke Junior." The man looks puzzled. "Gerald the younger," Gerald explains.

The Ute nods, studying Gerald's face. "I can see it is so." He lifts a bloodied hand toward his chest. "I am Stands Alone." His gesture takes in the valley, then the peaks upstream. "This my place."

Gerald nods. How far does the Ute's place extend? But he merely says, "We've been trapping beaver on the river here. Is that all right with you?"

Williams swings his head, glaring, but neither Gerald nor Stands Alone respond. They stand, looking into each other's faces, then the Ute says, "For beaver to flavor the pot," and Gerald grins and nods.

Williams shakes his head in disgust. He jerks his thumb downstream. "We're trappin' that direction." His tone makes it clear that he's not asking permission.

Stands Alone nods. "No beaver there beyond a half-day journey," he says. "The water is swift." He jerks his head southwest, toward the other side of the river. "That way, toward the black valley, there may be beaver."

Williams frowns. "Not in the Moreno Valley," he says. "We was just there and there ain't any there. Never has been, far's I know."

Stands Alone gestures toward the peaks that rise above the opposite bank. "That way is a smaller valley with many seeps. I have seen beaver." He shrugs. "Too far for too little meat." He spreads his hands and a ghost of a smile glimmers in his eyes. "I give them to you."

Old Bill throws back his head and barks a laugh. "We can have all we want, huh? As long as we leave the elk here for you?"

Stands Alone smiles noncommittally.

Gerald chuckles and gazes toward the pine-covered slopes. "I suppose the quickest way there is back the way we came."

Stands Alone nods. "There is a way when grass is green," he says. "But when snow comes, following water is best." He bends and goes back to his work, deftly cuts a section of meat from the elk's shoulder, then proffers it to Old Bill.

Williams shrugs, wraps the meat in a piece of buckskin, and attaches the bundle to his mule's packsaddle. Stands Alone returns to his labors and doesn't look up as the trappers turn and move up the valley.

As the canyon narrows around them, Gerald glances back. The Ute man has been joined by two female figures and a horse-drawn travois. The women bend over the elk while he washes his hands in the river.

~ ~ ~ ~

Intermittent snow slides in over the canyon brim as the trappers move west. The flakes become steadily smaller and more intense, and the cold increases proportionately. Gerald and Williams camp again at the foot of the eagle nesting cliff. When they wake, the snow has stopped and the valley beyond is blindingly white. As Gerald squints, trying to see the peaks on the other side, Old Bill grabs charcoal from the coolest edge of the fire and begins smudging it onto his face below his eyes.

"You best be doin' this, too," he tells Gerald. "It keeps the glare from gettin' your eyes. Your skin's darker'n mine but even the Injuns do it this time of year."

Gerald swings his head, waiting for Williams to speculate on the difference in their skin tone, but Old Bill has turned away and is smearing charcoal on his mule's cheeks, as well. The animal pulls back, resisting, and Gerald chuckles and reaches for his own piece of burnt wood.

They move out, into a sweep of icy, concentrated sunlight. The glare bounces from the snow and forces the men's eyes into mere

74

slits. Gerald's head feels like it's being split in two, first by the dry sharpness of the cold, then by the piercing light. Even with the charcoal smudged on his cheeks, he has to work to see Williams, a mere ten feet ahead.

Old Bill hugs the valley's eastern edge, skirting the base of the snow-covered hills as they move south. On the west, the mountaintops are buried behind a mass of gray clouds that seem to only intensify the blaze of the sun above them.

Then a breeze springs up. It lifts the top layer of snow and spins an icy spray around the men and mules. "Might as well be snowin' again!" Williams yells. His voice drops, still muttering, then rises. "That Ute can have it!"

Gerald's lips are too stiff with cold for him to even smile in response, but when they stop to noon in the lee of a snow-covered ridge and he's recovered a little, he grins at Williams. "You think Stands Alone spends much time up here in winter?"

"Not in a teepee!" Old Bill says. "These winds'd blow his lodge poles to smithereens." He grunts disparagingly and uses a finger to work a piece of jerky from behind a molar. He pulls the half-chewed meat out, looks at it, puts it back in his mouth, and tilts his canteen. Nothing comes out. "Frozen solid." He looks at Gerald. "You got any?"

Gerald reaches for his own water container and jiggles it. "It sounds like something's still liquid," he says. He hands Williams the canteen.

"See, that's the difference between an Injun and a white man," Williams says. "You just hand it to me, knowing I'm wantin' a drink. An Injun'll bargain with you, daylight to dark, to see what he can get out of you. Make you beg for what he's planning to give you."

Gerald tilts his head. A white man, huh? Well, that answers that question. But he can't, in all fairness, let the mischaracterization slide. "I wish my experience bore that out," he says. "I've known white men who wouldn't so much as let you step on their land without making conditions."

Williams shrugs. "I reckon there's bad apples in every lot," he concedes. He turns and looks up the valley. "But that Ute saying this valley is his? Well, that just ain't so. For one thing, the Apaches come through here regular-like. They might have a difference of opinion about who all it belongs to." He nods toward the cloud-covered peaks on the other side of the valley. "And, sure as shootin', the Taos Injuns on the other side of those mountains would have a righteous something to say about his claim. It's their hunting grounds, too."

He shakes his head as he returns Gerald's canteen. "But see, most Injuns don't see the land the same way we whites do, with clear boundaries marked out and a man's right to work it. To them, the country's just something to hunt on and gather from, not to plant and work and turn it into more than it was at the start. Except for the Pueblos, it takes a righteous amount of palaver to get them so's they're willing to divide it up between them and actually plow it. Not like us."

Gerald looks at the other man, thinking of his preference for blazing trail over living in a cabin. Yet here he is, asserting the value of making the land more than a place to hunt and gather. Gerald's own propensities are toward plowing and planting, so he tends to agree with Old Bill, but the Utes and Apaches have been hunting and gathering on this land for generations. Which gives them some rights. It's a different way of looking at it, is all. They just don't feel the need to sink their fingers in the soil, the way he does. A need which is very strong.

Old Bill rises and Gerald grimaces at the quandary, wraps his mule's lead rope around his gloved hand, and prepares to follow Williams back into the wind-driven snow.

The cold intensifies as the setting sun silhouettes the western clouds. When Gerald lifts his hand to his face, his glove bumps numb cheeks as stiff as boards. He turns stiffly, scanning for another sheltering abutment. Then, out of the corner of his eye, he sees Williams move abruptly left. Numbly, Gerald follows.

A trickle of half-frozen water flows from the tree line, forming a slushy black line in the snow. The men and mules move along the rivulet and into the trees. The wind drops sharply in the lee of the hill and Gerald releases breath he hasn't realized he's been holding.

The next morning they discover that Stands Alone spoke truly. Beaver ponds dot the small valley that parallels the larger one. And they're not completely frozen over. It takes a good two weeks to trap them out.

When the men return to the larger valley, the snow has abated and the grass is visible again. Gerald pauses beside the small, still slushy stream, and gazes at the western peaks, especially the massive middle one. He looks south, then north, and nods. Yes, he has seen this before. From this angle, it's recognizable as the valley he crossed with Ewing Young's mule train. The one with the long grasses, the winding streams, the soil so black his fingers itched to to touch it, to tuck seed into its fertile protection.

As he follows Williams' mule down the valley, he studies the pine trees on its slopes. They're black against a now-turquoise sky. And to think that same sky was thick with grey snow-bearing clouds just a week ago! What a changeable place it is! He has a sudden urge to laugh out loud.

CHAPTER 10

There are no beaver in the valley itself, so the men and mules move steadily through the ponderosas and occasional cluster of white-barked aspen that close in at the southern end. The land tilts up, then down again, and the trappers are once more in beaver country. Their pace slows as they trap steadily south over the next few weeks, through a rich grassland that contains a cluster of small lakes, then down Coyote Creek to the edge of another, smaller, snow-bright valley. In its center, adobe houses huddle together at the edge of a narrow iced-over river.

"Saint Gertrude's," Williams says. "It ain't worth much. They don't even have a taberna." He turns and looks at the pack mules, now loaded with a substantial amount of furs. "No place to sell these furry bank notes, either. Or to resupply. Which is too bad, because that coffee supply is righteously low."

Gerald nods. He feels an unexpected stab of disappointment. It would be good to see other faces, acknowledge the presence of other beings. He doesn't consider himself a particularly social person, but he finds himself suddenly wishing for an adobe casa to sit in, a hot drink from the hands of a pleasant girl.

Suzanna Peabody's face, dark eyes looking directly into his, comes to mind and he flinches away from it. He has no right to such thoughts. He flicks his mule's lead rope and follows Old Bill as he circles the village and its snow-covered fields.

They head west, following the river Williams calls the Mora upstream into yet more mountains. They work their way north and west, halting wherever a beaver lodge bulks from the snow-covered ice or where clusters of willow have been clipped back by sharp teeth. Then, after a day or two setting traps in bone-chilling water, they move on, heading further into the hills as the snow deepens and the icy cold sharpens further.

As the year turns, Gerald, who had initially welcomed the adventure of it all, the opportunity to learn a new skill, begins to feel the drudgery of trapping. His experience has narrowed to cold water, half-frozen dead beaver, cold air, and cold bedding.

And Old Bill's continuous string of advice and opinion. But at least Williams has dropped the teasing about Suzanna Peabody. There is that to be grateful for. As Gerald and the mule trudge up yet another gully behind Williams' pack mule, he tries to talk himself into some kind of positive mood, but at this point all he really wants is to return to Taos and the warmth of the Peabody parlor.

On the slope above, a mountain lion coughs menacingly and Gerald snaps back to his surroundings. Daydreaming is a good way to discover that the wilderness isn't as boring as it might seem. He clucks at his mule and quickens his step so he's close enough to Williams' mule to hear the low monotone of Williams' running commentary.

~ ~ ~ ~

They camp that night in yet another narrow mountain defile smothered in two feet of early February snow. Heavy gray clouds block the sky and promise more snow in the night. The lower branches of the aspen thickets on the slopes above have been gnawed raw by hungry deer and elk. Strangely, the snow-laden alder and rose bushes beside the iced-over stream don't appear to have been browsed. The only explanation is the presence of wolves or mountain lion stalking the few clearings near the stream. The browsers feel safer among the trees.

Williams and Gerald pull the packs from their mules, lash them into the protection of a nearby pine, then cut thin aspen branches for the animals and create a feed pile. The mules come eagerly to investigate.

"Anyone passing through's gonna know we were here," Old Bill says ruefully. "Not that it's likely anyone'll be passin' through." He shakes his head. "Only americanos like us are crazy enough to be out in this kind of weather. The Injuns have enough sense to stay in their lodges this time of year. And the mexicanos ain't no fools, neither." He looks up at the thick dark-gray clouds in the narrow bit of visible sky. "It don't matter much what we leave behind us, anyhow. With that snow coming in, by noon tomorrow this feeding pile will be just another white mound of windfall."

Gerald nods without really listening, moves to add more wood to the fire, then hunkers down beside it and pulls his wool blanket tighter around his shoulders. He's too cold to care whether anyone knows they're here. They've been wandering the mountains for weeks now and have seen little sign of other humans. The only person they've spoken to is Stands Alone, the Ute who thinks the black valley belongs to him. This whole expedition is beginning to seem rather pointless.

Gerald grimaces. He knows he's being uncharitable, but they haven't collected any beaver in a week, and the cold and snow is becoming monotonous. But he isn't the one leading this expedition, so he doesn't have much say in what they do. Maybe Williams knows something he doesn't and there's a reason they're still wandering these frozen streams.

Old Bill joins him by the fire and huddles into his own blanket. "I sure do wish I had me some coffee," he says. "Or some Taos lightning. Yes siree, some liquor would feel righteously fine right about now." He shakes his head and his long red braids, frosted with tiny white flakes, glint in the firelight. "Snow melt water'll warm you a mite, but something with a kick in it would go a lot farther. As long as there wasn't enough of it to create a temptation to foolishness." He chuckles. "I ever tell you about the time me and Old Pete got to drinking up on the Platte and that band of Crow found us?"

Gerald lifts his eyes from the flames. He hasn't heard the story, but he doesn't want to. "Yes," he says.

Williams studies the younger man. His lips twitch, then he glances at the packs strung up in the pine. "I'd say we've accumulated a respectable amount of pelts for one season's worth of work," he says. "And it's clear to me that the beaver up here are peterin' out. We ain't seen action for going on a week now, and the streams are gettin' narrower and their ice is growin' thicker. I'd say it's about time to cash in our chips."

Gerald glances up from the flames.

"Yes sir, I'm thinking it's about time we headed back to the land of the living." Old Bill glances up at the snow-encrusted slopes on either side of the campsite. "I've got a notion that if we head due west and a little north from here, we'll get ourselves into Taos in pretty short order." He shakes his head. "I'm getting powerful thirsty for a little inside warmth and some whisky."

Gerald rouses himself. "Do we have enough furs to make it worthwhile?"

"I calculate we've got enough to get you set up real good for the next go-round, with a little something extra to buy a certain girl a trinket or two." Williams grins at him.

"I'm looking for more than the next go 'round and a trinket or two," Gerald says. "I want enough for land and a home." He glances at the other man, then returns his gaze to the flames. "As much as I appreciate the skills I've learned from you, I'm not sure trapping is something I want to do for the rest of my life."

Williams nods. "Some like it, some don't," he says. "But you've got to start somewhere." He shrugs. "And to learn when to pack it home. There's no point in hangin' on when the beaver ain't biting. By my way of thinking it's time we hightailed it on back to Taos."

Gerald nods, trying to look disappointed, and rubs his chin. "So it's time to pack it in?"

"For the time bein'." Williams lifts a stick from the fire and pushes the ash at its edges closer to the flames, banking their warmth. "We'll still be getting in before the rest of them, so you'll have a good chance of getting to know Miz Suzanna a little better before the competition arrives." He wraps himself more securely in the blanket, lays himself down next to the log he's been sitting on, and winks at Gerald before he covers his face and goes to sleep.

Gerald grins in spite of himself, then shakes his head, and stares into the fire. Williams seems to think he has a chance with Suzanna Peabody. If only it were true and not the dream he knows it to be. A dream as likely to turn into reality as the smoke from the fire is likely to coalesce once again into sweet smelling pine.

But there's no time for dreaming the next morning. Gerald wakes to a sharp intake of breath from Williams' blankets and sits up abruptly. It's still dark, the heft of it just starting to lighten as dawn filters through the clouds. But it isn't the light that causes the hair on

Gerald's neck to prickle. There's something different in the air. A smell? A movement? Something dangerous.

"Act natural," Old Bill hisses. "But be quick. Something's circlin' us. More than one." He's out of his blankets now, rolling them efficiently into a tight tube. "Nah, don't turn your head. Act natural, dammit!" Just beyond the clearing, a mule stomps anxiously and Williams responds with an encouraging cluck.

Gerald reaches for his boots. "What is it?"

"Apache, I reckon." Williams lifts his pack and moves toward the mules.

Gerald scrambles to gather his gear, trying to move swiftly but nonchalantly in the darkness, as if he and Williams pack at this speed every morning. He glances at the snow-laden trees on the slopes above. He can see nothing, yet there's a definite menace in the air. As if the shadows have shadows. He carries his pack to the mule, then returns for the food bundle. As he reaches up to unfasten it from the pine, dead wood slaps rock behind him.

Gerald whirls, knife half out of his belt, but it's only Williams, kicking the fire apart to ensure that the coals from last night's fire won't re-ignite. It doesn't seem likely, given the cold and the snow. But this is a precaution every mountain man takes, no matter the weather conditions. You just never know.

And taking care of the fire is part of the ritual of acting naturally, Gerald reflects ruefully as he slips the food pack from the pine and carries it to the mules.

Old Bill follows him. "Ready?" he asks as he reaches for his mule's halter rope.

Gerald lifts his rifle from its scabbard. "All set."

"That thing primed?"

"Ready to go."

83

In the time he's known Old Bill, the man has never used such short sentences, Gerald reflects as they move out, following the stream. Or been so alert: spine straight, head up, eyes scanning the way ahead as he maneuvers through the trees. The slope on the other side of the stream is steep here, almost straight up, and when a dark shape emerges between the pines above them, Williams' mule rears back and screams in terror.

Williams drops the lead rope and fires, the shot echoing from the canyon walls. Then there's a rustle behind Gerald and he whirls, dropping his mule's rope and lifting his gun in one swift motion. As the muzzle roars, another sound rises, a wild scream that pierces Gerald's ears and sends the mules crashing upstream through the brush. The scream comes again, closer this time, and everything in the forest seems to freeze in response.

Williams is half crouched, his gun ready, making a full, cautious circle.

The early sunlight has pushed through the clouds. It fingers the tops of the pines, confusing the shadows below. Gerald blinks, and stares up the slope.

Though he knows he's seen at least two shapes, apparently human, and believes Williams' gun, at least, found its target, there's no sign of anyone among the trees on either side.

Old Bill straightens and scowls. "Hell and damnation!" he says. "Those Injuns were aiming to scare off the mules, not hit us! The damn scoundrels are after our plews!" He turns to peer upstream. "All we can hope is that those animals are smart enough to keep running and get away from them, whole and all."

He stalks away, to the edge of the frozen creek, and begins forcing his way through the brush, following the mules' trail. "Apaches," he says in disgust. "I should of known it was too good to last," he grumbles. "I might of known they were hanging around, waitin' on us to finish up and put together a righteously fat pack or two before they bothered to sweep in and steal everything we had." He snorts. "Well, we'll just see about that."

He stomps on for a full mile, pushing violently through the underbrush, making no effort at silence. Gerald follows close behind, a sharp eye on the slopes overhead.

Then Old Bill stops abruptly at the edge of a break in the bushes and scratches his matted red head.

"Well, what do you want to know about that?" he says softly. His voice rises, all of its anger gone. "Now that's just something you've got to see with your own eyes to righteously believe it done happened."

Behind him, Gerald frowns. He can see nothing but William's buckskin-clad back and fuzzy red braids. There are twigs in the braids, where they've been snagged by the brush. Then there's a huffing sound and the click of shod hoof on rock.

Williams moves slowly forward. "Here now, you jennie, you," he says soothingly. "That's a good and a right righteous mule. How you doing, now, huh? Did you get a little roughed up there, or did you manage to outrun those damn Apaches and that screaming old catamount, too? That screeching got you in a grand righteous panic, now didn't it?"

He moves slowly toward the mule, still talking, his hand out. The mule backs away, eyes rolling. "There now, it all ain't so bad is it?" Old Bill asks. "And you've done proved yourself a right clever mule, too. You took off through that brush and left us all to the mountain lion, now didn't you? And that hellacious old catamount scared those Apache so bad they didn't follow you after all." He shakes his head. "There's somethin' to be said for Apaches believin' those lions are

85

devils." His hand touches the mule's haler rope and he gently reels her in. "Now let's just take a look at that there pack and see what kind of shape it's got in."

He edges around her. "Not bad, not bad at all." He nods at Gerald. "It looks like my bedroll's gone, but the plews are all right." He pats the mule's neck encouragingly. "Now all we've got to do is find your partner in crime. You were smart enough to both break the same way and I can tell you I truly appreciate that."

He turns to Gerald. "We'll head on upstream and see if yours—"

Then the mule's head lifts toward the stream. The willows rustle and the men brace themselves. Their spent rifles lift, then drop as Gerald's mule appears.

Her pack hangs to one side, and Gerald's rifle scabbard dangles precariously under her belly, but everything is still attached and the mule herself is unscratched. She moves into the tiny clearing and nuzzles at Gerald impatiently, as if asking him to straighten her load.

The men chuckle and get to work, checking the loads and tightening straps. They've lost a skillet and Williams' bedroll, and Gerald's rifle scabbard is badly scratched, but the beaver pelts have come through without damage.

"Now this here's quite a sight," Old Bill gloats. "I'd never have thought I'd be so damnably glad to have such a righteously skittish pack animal as this one. Or hear a catamount scream just when that one did. Yes siree, it makes you want to believe in a gracious almighty that takes personal care of you, don't it?"

Gerald, tightening the straps around the food pack, grins to himself. They are definitely out of danger. Williams has fully regained his loquacity.

~ ~ ~ ~

They stop at the top of the ridge above the hillside road that will take them north to Taos and simply stand there, absorbing the view. On their right, the mountain slopes are black against a monotonously white sky, as if all color has been wiped from the world. But to their left, a broad swath of golden brown grassland sweeps west and north from the base of the hill. The sky is a clear blue behind the rapidly thinning haze of clouds. Brown cattle, white sheep, and black and white goats dot the fields. There's no snow in sight.

Gerald's eyes linger on the animals, then move farther west. He blinks and looks again. He's seen it before, but not from this angle, and the difference is truly breathtaking. A mile-wide gash bisects the flat Taos plain, north to south. It drops abruptly from the green pastures and plunges straight down, between reddish-brown rock walls. There's a narrow glint of water far below. Gerald shakes his head at the wonder of it.

"Rio del Norte's gorge looks diff'rent from this direction, don't it?" Williams asks. "It's a righteously grand sight, even if it ain't got no beaver in it." He shakes his head. "There ain't nothing but a few river otter in that there river canyon. There used to be, but not now. This section's no use for hunting at all, now." He turns and flicks his mule's lead. "But we ain't got time for sight seeing anyhow. The way that sun's moving, we're gonna have to make some steady tracks if we want to get to Taos before dark."

They move down the rocky slope to the road, Old Bill and his mule taking the lead. Then the red-headed trapper stops abruptly. "God damn him to hell and perdition!" he mutters. He raises his hand in a half-hearted greeting.

87

Gerald cranes his neck. A man with a stiff back and a military-looking hat rides a large black stallion up the hill toward them. Two men on shorter horses hang deferentially behind.

The man in the hat reins to a stop in front of Bill. His shoulder-length auburn hair glints in the afternoon sun and the tip of his long hatchet-sharp nose is red from the cold. "Mr. Williams," he says formally. "You've returned earlier than I expected." There's an edge of disapproval in his voice, as if the trapper has failed to live up to some unspoken agreement.

"It appears that I did at that, Señor Sibley," Williams says. He grins and gestures toward the pack mules. "We got so many plews we done run out of animals to carry 'em!" He chuckles. "But don't go tellin' the customs official I said so."

Sibley nods absently. His eyes sweep over Gerald and turn back to Williams. "I am to Santa Fe to meet with the Governor," he says. "I will then proceed to Chihuahua to consult with the officials there regarding the road survey." His stallion sidesteps, away from Williams' mule, and Sibley reins him in impatiently. "I presume you are to Taos."

"It would appear so," Old Bill says drily.

Sibley nods. "I will see you when I return." It's more of a command than a polite goodbye and Sibley doesn't wait for an answer. He spurs his mount forward and his companions follow silently, not making eye contact with Williams or Gerald.

Williams watches them with narrowed eyes. Then he spits into the dirt, turns abruptly, and heads downhill toward Taos. Gerald can hear him muttering angrily to himself, but he doesn't move close enough to hear the actual words. It isn't necessary. There's clearly no love lost between Old Bill and the head of the Santa Fe Trail Survey expedition.

CHAPTER 11

Gerald steps out of the trader's store and pauses in the late February sunlight, waiting while Old Bill seals his own fur-trading transaction with a drink or two. He looks up at the sky appreciatively. It's deep blue and holds only a handful of small, fluffy white clouds. The sun catches the flecks of mica on the Plaza's adobe walls. The glitter reflects his mood. There's $332 dollars and fifteen cents in his money belt, more than he's ever possessed.

His hand moves unconsciously toward the belt and a passing young woman with long black hair, short skirts, and a low cut blouse looks flirtatiously into his face. Gerald smiles slightly and shakes his head. Is it that apparent? But then, any trapper just back from the mountains and standing outside a trader's store is likely to have money to spend.

Old Bill bends his lanky frame through the low wooden door frame and straightens beside Gerald. "Ah, it's a wonderful thing, ain't it?" he asks. "Those furry banknotes." His breath smells of whiskey. Another young woman passes, this one flicking her skirts around her knees, and Williams' eyes follow her appreciatively. "I think I'll get me a drink and a señorita," he says. He glances at Gerald as he claps his hat on his head. "I don't suppose you'd care to join me."

"Perhaps for the drink," Gerald says. "But not for the señorita."

"Ah, what a wondrously righteous thing is young love," Williams says. "You keepin' yourself pure for Miz Peabody, are you?"

Gerald scowls and Old Bill raises a hand. "That's that there Taos Lightning loosening my tongue a might, that's all that is," he says apologetically. "I'll take myself off now, before I say something we both find regretful."

He grins at Gerald mischievously and Gerald smiles back in spite of himself. He watches the long-legged trapper lurch across the plaza to the nearest taberna and considers Williams' remark. It isn't so much that Gerald is keeping himself pure for Suzanna Peabody. After all, he has no claim on her affections. And the fact of his black heritage weighs on him, makes him reluctant to put himself forward. He can't bring himself to even think how her face might change in the instant she knows the truth about him.

But he's never met another girl even remotely like her. And why would he chase after other girls when there's someone like her in the world? He can't imagine being attracted to anyone else. Not that there's much hope for him. He doesn't even know her father well enough to approach their house on his own. He certainly doesn't have the impudence to take her a gift. Her father's eyes darkened at the idea of potatoes. Gerald can't imagine what he would say to jewelry.

He turns away from the plaza and spends the next three days restlessly wandering the village or meandering down to the still-empty blacksmith shop in Ranchos to confirm that his father hasn't returned. There's nothing for him here. He's wasting his time. He should locate someone else to trap with in the fall.

Or go to Santa Fe and try for a place on a mule train returning to Missouri. He has enough now for a small farm of his own there, if he's careful. If prices haven't risen with the onslaught of farmers and slaves from the southern states that had begun well before he left.

But he feels only a sinking sensation in his stomach when he thinks of Missouri and he knows he won't return. After the freedom of movement he's experienced here, the acceptance, he can't imagine returning to an American slave state.

What he will do is less certain. All he knows is that he continues to find himself wandering Taos' plaza and few streets, especially the small lane where he first glimpsed Suzanna Peabody.

He sees little of Old Bill, who seems to be trying to spend all of his season's earnings in the plaza tabernas. Other trappers have also drifted back into town and several, including Enoch Jones, are making themselves at home in the saloons.

Gerald himself visits the plaza at least once a day, walking in from his campsite beside Ewing Young's pasture north of town. He tells himself he needs provisions and that it's best to buy them fresh daily, but this task somehow takes up most of each day, and while he's about it, his eyes tend to stray toward any girl taller and slimmer than usual.

On the fourth day, he's just purchased a small clutch of eggs and a few still-warm tortillas when voices erupt in front of a saloon on the opposite side of the square.

"You devil! You pig! Get your filthy hands off of me! How dare you accost me!" The young woman's shawl has slipped off her dark head and the full force of her glare is focused on Enoch Jones, whose hands are reaching for her shoulders.

She slaps at him and her palm connects with his cheek. He grabs her upper arm and she yanks away and faces him, hands on solid hips, large black eyes blazing. "You sorry excuse for a human being! You four footed beast! Eres más mala que Judas! You are more evil than Judas!"

Jones laughs and lunges at her again. He grabs her shoulders, one in each dirty hand. "Just one little kiss!"

The girl twists, trying to get away, but his face darkens and he jerks her toward him. As she turns her face from his slobbering mouth, Gerald moves forward, eggs and tortillas still in his hands.

Then a long red-headed form erupts from the taberna door and Old Bill has Enoch Jones by the scuff of the neck. "Let her go," the trapper growls.

Jones' hands falls away from the Spanish girl's arms. "I was jus' askin' fer a kiss," he says.

"I am not one of your putas!" the girl blazes. "How dare you!" She backs away, still glaring, then nods at Williams. "I thank you, Mr. Williams," she says. She looks him up and down as she straightens her shawl. "Though I would prefer to have met you without so much liquor on your breath."

Williams releases Jones from his grip and draws himself up to his full lanky height. "I apologize for inconveniencing you, Señorita Encarnación," he says with drunken dignity. He turns back to the taberna door.

Jones snickers. "Yeah, Carny," he says. "Make him apologize. Make 'im grovel fer yer favors."

She looks at him contemptuously. "Filthy pig!"

Jones scowls. "You think yer so high 'n mighty in Peabody's kitchen, but yer just a Mexican slut like the rest of 'em." He waves his arm, encompassing the plaza and the silent brown-faced men and women watching. "Yer all a bunch o' greasy Mexicans too lazy t' do anything but take the money o' anyone man enough to winter in th' mountains an' take what's rightfully ours."

"Yours?" Jeremiah Peabody strides into the plaza, his mouth a thin angry line above the neat black chin beard. He pauses at Encarnación's side and looks down at her. "Are you quite all right?"

She nods and raises her shawl to cover her now-disheveled black head. Peabody turns to Enoch Jones, his eyes steely. "I will thank you to leave the members of my household in peace."

Jones scowls but doesn't respond. Williams reappears in the taberna doorway and Peabody looks him up and down. "And when you have recovered from your drunk, I will be pleased to see you once again under my roof." He turns away. "And now, gentlemen, I will leave you to your recreations."

Then Peabody catches sight of Gerald, halfway across the square and still holding his eggs and tortillas. Peabody's face softens. He says something to Encarnación, pats her on the arm, then crosses the plaza toward Gerald. "Mr. Locke, you appear to be a man who knows how to provision himself," he says. He smiles. "If you would care to visit us, I'm sure Encarnación will be happy to provide you with even fresher tortías. And my daughter would be happy to make your further acquaintance." He touches his finger to his hat and moves away as Gerald nods dumbly.

Movement returns to the plaza as the vendors, marketers, and Encarnación begin once again to go about their business. She smiles slightly as she passes Gerald, and drops him a small curtsy. "Señor," she says pleasantly.

Gerald, still processing Jeremiah Peabody's words, can only nod. 'My daughter would be happy to make your further acquaintance.' Gerald tamps down the surge of delight and the smile on his face. The man is merely being polite. There's no more to the invitation than that.

He stalls for two days, unwilling to believe Peabody is serious. But then they meet again, again on the plaza. This time, the New Englander is accompanied by Suzanna herself, her hands tucked into his elbow, her eyes tight with irritation. The eyes relax a little when they meet Gerald's. She glances at her father and releases his arm.

"Mr. Locke," Jeremiah says. "How fortunate to meet you here." He glances down at Suzanna, who gives him a small nod, then returns his gaze to Gerald. "I hope you will join us this afternoon for tea. I believe we will be quite alone, so we can have a nice chat."

Quite alone? The phrase sends a shiver of alarm through Gerald's spine, but the look Suzanna gives him is so friendly, he finds himself smiling an acceptance to her father's invitation.

"About three then?" Peabody asks. A smile flashes across his thin face. "Or have you acclimated so well to Mexican time that we must be more general than that? Mid-afternoon?"

Gerald laughs. "No, I haven't adjusted that thoroughly," he says. "Three o'clock, then."

He arrives at the Peabody's door a few minutes before three and loiters outside the gate, not wanting to enter before his time. Besides, his boots are muddy. As he scrapes them against the edge of a nearby rock, the young woman Enoch Jones accosted in the plaza appears in the gateway. She puts her hands on her sturdy hips.

"The boots, they are dirty?" she asks.

He nods and gestures at the street. "The roads have become muddy with the spring rains."

"Sí, but the rains have also watered Señorita Peabody's plants," she says. She smiles at him. "I am called Encarnación Mora. I believe you are Señor Gerald Locke."

"Yes ma'am." He pulls his hat from his head. "I am Gerald Locke Jr." He bows a little, not sure if he should offer his hand, and she chuckles.

"I am not a señorita, sir," she says. "I am only the cook."

"And a quite accomplished one," says an amused voice from behind her. "She makes up for my shortcomings." Suzanna appears at the shorter and plumper woman's elbow. "Welcome again to our home, Mr. Locke." She dips him a small curtsy.

"Please, call me Gerald." He moves forward, his hand out, and she takes it with a smile.

She looks into his eyes and something moves within him. It's as if his heart has adjusted itself to a different rhythm. "And I am Suzanna," she says.

"Yes," he says. "Suzanna." Then feels like a fool.

But she only smiles, turns, and leads the way across the courtyard, between the two small garden beds, and into the house.

Her father is in the parlor, reading beside the fire, and truly alone. Suzanna enters ahead of Gerald, then immediately turns and disappears back into the hallway. Anxiety rises in Gerald's chest. But then the older man puts down his book, smiles, rises, gestures Gerald into the chair on the other side of the fire, and sits down again. "I've been re-reading Susanna Rowson's novel *Charlotte,*" he says.

He waves at the cloth-bound book on the table beside his chair as Suzanna comes in with a tray piled with sandwiches. Her father stands again, takes the tray, and sets it on a table in the corner. "Do you know the book?" he asks Gerald.

Suzanna shakes her head at him and smiles at Gerald. "He reads more novels than I do," she says. "I prefer Shakespeare or botanical texts." She perches herself on the brightly cushioned and painted wooden chest opposite him as Encarnación carries in a tray with a teapot and three cups.

Gerald grins. "I prefer Shakespeare, myself." He turns to Jeremiah Peabody. "Although I have not read Miss Rowson, so perhaps 'prefer' is too strong a term."

95

Peabody chuckles. "You are a diplomat! But Suzanna is teasing me. She knows I enjoy Shakespeare as much as she does."

"Though I think you prefer your Latin authors above all else," she says. She moves to the table and begins preparing the tea.

"My daughter can read Latin as well as I can," Jeremiah Peabody tells Gerald, pride touching his voice.

Gerald looks at Suzanna. "I envy you," he says. "My education never extended that far."

Suzanna hands him a cup of tea. "Oh, I forgot," she says. "Do you take milk or sugar?" She wrinkles her forehead in a self-deprecatory smile. "Somehow I just assumed you take your tea black."

"Actually, I do," he says. Their eyes lock for just a moment, then she moves hastily away to prepare her father's cup.

Gerald turns to Jeremiah Peabody. "I'm afraid I learned to read at my mother's knee," he says apologetically. "I had no opportunity for a formal education."

"You have the speech and carriage of an educated man."

"Speaking correctly was important to both my parents." He looks into his teacup and smiles. "My mother was something of a stickler for proper manners." He looks up. "As was my father, but he wasn't quite so insistent." He chuckles and shakes her head. "My mother was passionate about everything she did."

"They are both deceased?" Jeremiah Peabody looks into Gerald's face as if he wants to read his very soul.

Gerald lifts his chin slightly, holds his voice steady. He will not lie to any man. And he will not be ashamed, no matter the outcome. "My mother died when I is still a child," he says calmly. "My father— My father is here in the Mountain West. I don't know where or with whom."

"You came here to find him?"

Gerald nods, a slight trace of sorrow in his eyes.

"Well, give it time," Suzanna says. "Sooner or later all the mountain men and traders pass through Don Fernando de Taos. It's a kind of magnet, drawing them. Even Major Sibley was here this winter, when by all rights he ought to have been in Santa Fe speaking with the Governor."

"He had business to attend to here and he believes our air to be more salubrious than that at Santa Fe," her father says drily. He turns to Gerald. "I came here myself to escape the confines of the States and have not had reason to return." He smiles at Suzanna. "Or perhaps I should say I found a reason to stay."

She smiles back at him affectionately, then turns to Gerald. "A sandwich?" she asks. "I think Encarnación's bread is the only norte americano bread in nuevomexico."

"Yes, please," he says. He turns to her father. "I have been trying to pick up a little Spanish. When you first arrived here, did you find the language a difficult barrier?"

The talk moves on then, to language, to Shakespeare, to Suzanna's plants and her plans for her spring garden beds. Gerald finds himself relaxing in spite of the slight formality of the New England man's diction and bearing. He clearly cares deeply for his daughter and she clearly respects and loves him, although she feels no obligation to bow before his opinions.

Finally, the conversation turns to Gerald's recent trapping expedition with Old Bill.

"And Mr. Williams has again debased himself with drink." Suzanna shakes her head. "It's such a shame that he carries on in that way. He's such a— A nice man when he's sober."

"For a moment I thought you were going to call him a gentleman," her father teases.

"Well, he can behave in a gentlemanly way when he wishes to," she says tartly. "Though all of that seems to disappear when he's been imbibing."

"Even when he's been drinking he doesn't quite forget himself," Gerald says. "Your Encarnación can attest to that."

They look at him, startled.

"She didn't tell you?" Gerald frowns, uncertain. "The interchange with Enoch Jones?"

"Father entered the plaza just as that ended," Suzanna says. She chuckles. "Chonita said a good deal about her interaction with Jones, but most of it was not repeatable. At least, not by me." She hesitates, then gives Gerald a slight frown. "She said nothing about Mr. Williams."

Briefly, Gerald tells them what happened before Jeremiah arrived in the plaza.

"The entire incident demonstrates the goodness of William's heart," Jeremiah says.

"And the filthiness of liquor, and the pain and sorrow it causes!" Suzanna says. She turns and begins rattling the tea things on the table beside her, her black eyes snapping. "That Enoch Jones is a disgusting man made even more disgusting by drink! Sometimes I think trapping is the very essence of evil. The men endure incredible deprivation to accumulate furs in order to satisfy the vanity of folks back in the States and in Europe, people who have no inkling how their luxuries are obtained."

She glares at her father. "Then when the trappers come out of the wilderness and exchange their plews for gold, they're like springs wound too tightly for too long and they go on a binge fueled by Taos Lightning. Aguardiente indeed! Water of fire? Water of poison! They fling away a season's hard earnings in a matter of days and are left with nothing to show for the misery they've endured!"

She flounces a little in her chair, as if the irritation she feels is too much to hold in, and turns to Gerald. "It's just nonsensical!"

Jeremiah grins at Gerald. "I suppose you have no idea what her opinion is about such matters," he says drily.

Eyes still bright with anger, Suzanna stands and paces to the window. She peers out. "I wish I could actually see through these selenite panes," she grumbles. "The light may come in, but I can't see out."

She turns back to the men. "And the impact the trappers' nonsense has on the women in this town is just unconscionable," she says. "They wait all winter for men who don't actually return when they return. They're too busy carousing. Most of them have completely forgotten the promises they made, even to women who have born them children. Instead, they squander their money on women of the street, some of whom have sunk to that condition as a result of mistreatment by other men who've wandered into the mountains and never returned."

She scowls at her father again. "I swear, this town would be better off without hunting and trapping, without the furry banknotes that Old Bill Williams is always lauding. The income it brings is more of a curse than a blessing."

Gerald studies her as she stands there, her tall gently-curved figure in its old-fashioned narrow gown silhouetted against the dim light from the mica-paned window. "There are some men who are able to endure the discomfort of the wilderness, obtain their financial reward, and yet not succumb to the temptation to squander their wealth when they return," he says mildly.

Suzanna looks down at her hands and crosses the room back to her seat by the table. Gerald turns to her father. "Not that I would call what I obtained on this expedition true wealth," he says ruefully. "But it's certainly more than I've been able to accumulate in the past."

Jeremiah Peabody takes his pipe from the small table beside his chair and begins filling it with tobacco. "Will you return to the wilderness?"

Gerald nods. "I think so. I'd like to gather enough of a nest egg to set myself up with a farm."

"A farm?" Suzanna's voice is calmer now. She leans toward him. "What would you raise?"

"I know a little about wheat," Gerald tells her. "And cattle always seem to bring a good profit, if you can over-winter them safely. My daddy is a blacksmith, so I know enough to do most repairs myself."

When Gerald turns his head, Jeremiah Peabody is studying his face, his eyes slightly narrowed. "Your father's a blacksmith?"

Gerald nods. Has he said too much? His chin lifts a little. He won't deny who he is, even if it means losing this girl. Not that he has this girl. "Yes," he says. Best to just leave it at that.

Peabody nods and leans into his pipe, lighting it.

"You would only grow wheat?" Suzanna asks. "What about corn and potatoes and peas?"

"Those also, perhaps," Gerald says. "That reminds me, have you planted the potatoes Charles Beaubien brought you?"

"It's too early to plant them just yet," she says. "And I'll need more space than what's available in the courtyard." She glances at her father. "I'm trying to find a small plot outside the village that I can rent."

Gerald feels his muscles relax as they plunge into a discussion of site requirements and potato spacing, as well as the best types of fertilizer and what might be available here. Jeremiah Peabody returns to his book, and the rest of the room recedes until there's nothing but the subject at hand and the spark in Suzanna's intelligent black eyes.

Finally, the light beyond the window's small panes dims so much that even Gerald becomes aware that he's outstayed his time, and he tears himself away. He moves briskly through the dusk toward his campsite, his spine energized by conversation and hope. What a girl. What eyes, what smooth hair, what enthusiasms. He smiles. The intensity of her opinions is something else again. He spins on his heel and faces the village, its adobe walls glowing in the light from the setting spring sun.

What he would give for the right to return to that adobe house and its courtyard, to continue talking to the girl with the fiery eyes and strong opinions. To sit in the parlor with her father and watch her hands move over the tea things. To tell her that there are men in this world who want nothing more than a woman to return to. A woman like her.

Gerald shakes his head, straightens his shoulders, turns, and heads himself firmly toward the edge of Ewing Young's pasture.

CHAPTER 12

"I'm glad you invited him and that he came," Suzanna says at dinner that evening, interrupting her father's silent train of thought.

He looks up from his plate. "Who, my dear?"

"Mr. Locke, papá."

"He's quite a nice, gentlemanly young man," he agrees. "Although I fear you may have frightened him off with your diatribe about trapping and the resultant drunkenness."

"He didn't seem frightened," she says. "Besides, if he's going to visit us, he'll have to get used to my opinions." She dips her spoon into the bowl of mutton stew, then pauses to look up at him with narrowed eyes. "And what do you mean by 'frighten him off'? Why should it matter to me whether he visits or not? After all, he's not coming to court me. You've made it clear enough that I'm not of an age for such things."

She takes a bite of stew, chews, swallows, then adds firmly, "Not that I'm particularly interested in him or any other young man."

Her father's lips twitch. "It would be wise to not become interested in a trapper," he observes mildly. "Theirs is an unsettled life and prone to discord. Unlike that of, for example, New England." He bends his head over his food, his eyes clouded.

Suzanna puts down her spoon and studies him. She's never been certain just why her father left New England. Something about a girl, pistols, and the wounded heir of a powerful family. Jeremiah had just read Lt. Zebulon Pike's newly-published book about the far-away land of New Mexico, so that's where he headed. Suzanna knows more about his journey west than the events leading up to it.

Her father rarely speaks of New England, although it's reflected in the intonation of every word, the turn of his narrow head, his firm and piercing eye. To him, his true life began somewhere on the trek from New England to the Rocky Mountains, found its purpose when he held Suzanna in his arms for the first time.

She doesn't know much about his early life in the Rockies, either. Once in a long while, a man who knew her father in the two years between his New England life and Suzanna's birth shows up in Taos. Their reminiscences have given her a glimpse of a man quite different from the dignified scholar she knows. A warrior, a man who dealt with the natives in a way that won their grudging respect, a skilled fur trapper and hunter.

She looks at him thoughtfully. "Did you dislike trapping so very much?" she asks.

He shrugs. "Any man can hunt and trap if he must," he says. "But it is not well for a man to get caught in that life if his heart is elsewhere."

"And that appears to be the case with Mr. Locke."

Her father nods. "It does so appear." He shakes his head. "He seems to be a man with a dream. Whether or not he can achieve that dream will depend on many things, some of which he cannot control." He reaches for a tortilla and begins tearing it into small pieces and dropping it into his stew. "I would not desire any daughter of mine to be dependent on the dream of a man without the means or the will to accomplish what he sets out to do."

Suzanna's lips tighten. She's already said she's not interested in Gerald Locke, Junior. Why does her father persist in this train of thought? Besides, Mr. Locke appears to be perfectly capable of making any dream he may dream a reality.

The thought creates a small bubble of something like hope in her chest, but Suzanna only shakes her head at her father and smiles. "Since you only have one daughter that I know of, and that daughter is known for her independence of mind, I doubt there's any real danger," she says lightly. She reaches for a tortilla. "At any rate, your concerns are of a purely hypothetical nature. I'm not interested in becoming dependent on Gerald Locke or anyone else."

Jeremiah Peabody smiles at his stew, then asks, "Is your garden in the courtyard ready for the soil to be turned? I believe Ramón is bringing us more firewood tomorrow morning. Shall I ask him to start digging?"

"I'll ask him," Suzanna says. She grins mischievously. "It's still cool enough outside that Chonita can invite him into the kitchen to warm his hands. She seems to enjoy feeding him."

CHAPTER 13

Gerald stops in the middle of the path and stares at the small fenced-off area beside the brimming irrigation ditch, what in nuevomexico is called an 'acequia'. The plot is perhaps an eighth of an acre and filled with vibrant green sprigs of pigweed, a sign both that the soil has been turned in the past year and that it's fertile. The weeds will be easy to pull once the plot is flooded with water from the ditch.

He puts a hand on the rough rail fence. A shallow indentation extends from the acequia along one side of the plot. Only a small ridge of dirt blocks the ditch water from moving down the furrow and into the weeds. Gerald crouches, reaches through the fence, and picks up a small clump of dirt. He lifts it to his face. It smells good. As if it's been fertilized. Potatoes would do well here.

"Señor?" a boy's voice asks.

Gerald looks up. A thin dark-skinned teenage boy with large brown eyes and a mass of straight black hair stands behind him, clearly trying to understand why this americano is holding a clod of dirt to his nose.

Gerald doesn't know the Spanish for 'garden' or 'rent,' so all he can do is gesture at the garden plot and ask "A cómo?"

The boy frowns, puzzled, then lifts a hand. "Un momento," he says. He circles around Gerald and the plot of pigweed to the acequia. He moves nimbly across it on a narrow plank of thick wood and disappears into a tangle of young narrow leaf cottonwoods.

Gerald waits, not sure if the boy understood. The sun is warm on his shoulders and he breathes in the green smell of the plants in the plot. It's good to just stand here, soaking it in.

Just as he's beginning to think the boy won't return, two figures emerge from the cottonwoods: the boy and a solidly-constructed woman in a knee length black dress. Gerald holds his breath as first the boy, then the woman, use the plank to cross the ditch.

The woman's dress is spotted with damp, her long sleeves pushed up, and her hands pale and wrinkled, as if she's been interrupted in the middle of her washing. Her eyes are narrow and her lips tight. She puts her hands on her hips. "You want buy land?" she asks brusquely.

Well, at least she speaks English, even though she looks ready to do battle. Gerald shakes his head. "I apologize," he says. "My Spanish is not good."

Her expression softens a little and she nods.

"I want to know if the plot is for rent," he explains. "Not to me, but to someone who may wish to use it for her garden."

The woman looks at him impassively. "How much?"

"I—." He stops, unsure. After all, he has no idea what price would be appropriate, if this is something that Miss Peabody truly wishes to do, or if her father has the resources to rent the plot. "I would need to consult with the young lady," he says.

"Ah, una señorita." She smiles a little and tilts her head to one side. "It depends on la señorita and what it is she wishes to plant."

"I will need to consult with her," he says again. What a fool he is. What has he gotten himself into?

The woman shrugs and turns away, then back. "I am Maria Antonia Garcia," she says. "It is my land." She gestures across the ditch. "If your young lady wishes to speak to me, she can find me there."

Gerald hesitates, then nods. The woman turns and heads back across the plank. The boy smiles shyly at Gerald, then follows.

Gerald puts his hands in his pockets and watches them disappear into the trees. Then he turns back to study the garden plot. Would it be presumptuous to use this as an excuse to call on Miss Peabody and her father again? He grins. It's better than nothing. And she did say that she wants to find a plot for her potatoes.

~ ~ ~ ~

Suzanna Peabody strides so eagerly beside him that Gerald has to lengthen his stride to keep up with her. "I know Antonia Garcia," she says. "She and Encarnación are related somehow. Antonia does laundry for us sometimes, when Chonita has more baking than usual, or when the load is more than she and I can do on our own." She glances at him with a small smile. "I may not cook, but I do know how to clean."

He smiles down at her. "I suspect, though, that you would rather be gardening."

She laughs. "You suspect rightly!" She looks eagerly up the path. "Is that the plot? Oh, that's where they were holding the pigs last spring!" She purses her lips, eyes dark with thought. "The fence was too low for them, so they weren't there very long. Certainly, it's been enough time that the manure will have cooled sufficiently." She looks up at him, eyes dancing. "Potatoes could do well here!"

He nods. "I think they might."

They stop at the fence and gaze into the plot. "There's access to water from the ditch," he points out.

She peers across the pigweed at the acequia. Gerald looks at her in amusement, then finds his gaze dropping. Her breasts strain slightly against the cotton of her dress. He pulls his eyes back to her face as she turns to him. "If I'm allowed to access the water, it will do nicely," she says.

A figure moves in the trees on the other side of the ditch and the teenage boy materializes on the opposite bank. Suzanna waves her hand. "Hola Juan Gregorio!" she calls. She gestures at the acequia. "May we cross?"

The boy smiles and makes a beckoning gesture. Suzanna moves around the garden plot and trots briskly over the wooden plank. She stops on the other side and grins at Gerald. "It looks more narrow than it actually is," she says.

He raises an eyebrow and follows her gingerly. As he steps onto the opposite bank, his foot slips and he throws his arms out for balance. Suzanna grabs his hand, pulls him to safety, then releases him the instant he's upright again.

"Thank you!" Gerald exclaims, but she's already turned away. She and Gregorio plunge into the cottonwoods without looking behind them to make sure Gerald is following.

He lags behind glumly, but by the time he can see the Garcia's low adobe house through the trees, Suzanna has turned twice to glance behind her, and Gerald's confidence returns. He's beside her as they enter the yard. Wooden washtubs stand in a neat row along one side of the building and men's drawers hang from clothes lines that have been strung from the adobe's vigas to cottonwoods on the other side of the yard.

Señora Garcia invites them inside and they sit on blanket-covered adobe benches that jut from the walls while she and Suzanna negotiate terms. The Spanish is too rapid for Gerald to follow, though he has the impression that the conversation has moved on from the garden plot when the señora glances at her son, then Gerald, and frowns irritably. She almost seems to puff up with annoyance. But then Suzanna says something soothing and the woman settles.

Finally, the conversation ends. Suzanna and Gerald say their farewells and slip back through the trees. "Isn't there another route to this house?" he asks.

"There is." Suzanna waves an arm. "It's in that direction, but it's very long and involves trespassing across the land of a man who Antonia is angry with. There was some kind of boundary dispute a number of years ago and she believes she was cheated of her rights. Antonia isn't one to forgive and forget easily."

They reach the irrigation ditch. Gerald waves Suzanna ahead of him and she slips easily across the plank. He follows more slowly and makes sure his footing is secure before he steps onto the opposite bank. Suzanna stands back, giving him plenty of room as she pretends to examine her new garden plot.

They head back toward the village. "It's a good bit of a walk to Taos from here," Gerald says. "I wasn't sure if that would be an issue for you."

"Oh, I love to walk," Suzanna says. "I constrain my ramblings when the American hunters are in residence, because my father worries, but when you all aren't here, I often walk to Ranchos and back."

"You walk for health reasons?"

She looks at him in surprise. "No, I walk because I like to walk." She smiles mischievously. "I find an errand that requires that I go to Ranchos, and then I go." She shrugs. "But the garden plot isn't nearly as far as Ranchos. I'll explain to Father why it's important to me, and he won't protest." She chuckles. "Not too much, at any rate."

"Are we American hunters so dangerous?"

She smiles. "Not all of you." She looks up at him. "Certainly, I wouldn't be worried about meeting you on the streets." She makes an annoyed flapping movement with her hand. "But you saw how Enoch Jones is. And there are others like him." There's a long pause, as she studies the trees beside the path. Then she glances at him shyly. "I never thanked you for intervening that day."

"I was happy to do so," Gerald says a little stiffly.

"Jones is—" Suzanna sighs. "How can I say it? I don't believe he is an evil man, but he seems persuaded that all women are his property, especially if they are women with brown skin. And that, as his property, we are required to do whatever he wishes."

Gerald feels a surge of revulsion. "His wishes are pure filth!" he says, more sharply than he intends.

She smiles at him. "That's what I like about you." She slows her pace slightly and takes his arm. "That and the fact that you know how to walk quickly."

"While I'm here, will you allow me to accompany you?" he asks impulsively. "Then you can walk as far as you like."

"I would like that," she agrees, her eyes on the path. Then she looks at him again. "Though I expect you won't be here much longer. You'll be going out on another hunt soon, will you not?"

He nods glumly, wishing he could walk this path with her for the rest of his days.

"Did you see the look Antonia sent your way?" she asks abruptly.

"She seemed quite annoyed with both me and her son," Gerald says.

Suzanna chuckles. "She is," she agrees. "I told her you're a trapper. Her son has expressed interest in going with the men this fall and she's unwilling to allow it, but he's insisting quite strongly. He says he can make more money being a camp keeper than he can staying at home."

The girl shakes her dark head. "He's quite strong, although he doesn't look it. I'm sure you noticed the wash tubs and clothes lines. She may not like trappers, but she does washing for them. Gregorio helps her with the heavy lifting. But he wants very badly to go trapping instead."

She lifts her hand in a helpless gesture. "Antonia worries that he will be in danger in some way or that he will be treated unjustly. But in the end he will undoubtedly have his way." She grins ruefully. "As my father says, we only children can be quite willful." She lifts an eyebrow at Gerald. "Didn't you say you also are an only child? Did your parents find you willful?"

He laughs. "My mother used to say I was the sweetest obstinate child she ever knew."

"I'm not sure my father would include 'sweet' in his description of me," Suzanna says ruefully. "I suspect he'd use the term 'verbal' instead. He claims that I can talk him into almost anything." She grins. "I prefer to think of myself as logical." Then she sobers. "I wasn't sure what to say to Antonia about Gregorio going out with the hunters. Do you think it would be safe? After all, he is her only child."

Gerald shrugs. "Is anything completely safe? If he goes with responsible men, he will be as safe as staying here. Even here, there are dangers."

Suzanna nods. "Yes. A group of Comanches raided some ranchos in the cañon east of here just a week or so ago."

He looks at her in alarm. "And you still walk alone?"

She laughs. "They weren't here in the valley. They were out on the fringes." She grins. "Actually their presence is something of a boon to the American trappers. Governor Narbona stationed soldiers at Taos to monitor the trappers' activities, but the troops have been too busy chasing Indians to pay much attention to the Americans." She shakes her head and shrugs. "Even if the Comanches get closer to town, I know enough sign language to communicate with them. And they have dealings with my father. I don't believe they would harm me."

Gerald chews on his upper lip. He has no rights, but still— "I hope that while I'm here you will allow me to accompany you when you should feel the need for a walk," he says, his eyes on the path in front of his feet. "I would blame myself greatly if something were to happen to you as you go to or from that garden plot."

She pulls her hand away from his arm. "I am quite capable of looking after myself," she says stiffly.

"I am sure you are," Gerald says. What has he done? He has no rights. And now she's angry. "But I cannot forget Enoch Jones and his attitude," he says lamely.

They walk several more minutes before Suzanna takes his arm again. "It's just that I dislike being constrained," she says. "Even the Taos, as small as it is, seems to constrict me sometimes. I long for movement and space."

"And plants?" he asks, his spirits lifting.

"And plants!" she laughs. She waves a hand at the wild rose bushes between the path and the acequia. "Have you noticed how plump last year's rosehips are this spring? I must bring a container next time and collect some. Encarnación makes an excellent rose hip jelly which my father particularly enjoys."

Gerald smiles at her, marveling again at the way her eyes are level with his. But as they enter the town and turn down the lane to the Peabody gate, his spirits drop. He wishes the distance between the house and the garden plot is longer, that there's somewhere else she

112

wants to go, some other destination to which she needs an escort. But he can think of no good excuse to prolong their walk.

His pain lessens when Suzanna turns at the open gate and looks into his eyes. "Would you mind very much if I ask you to accompany me to the garden plot tomorrow?" she asks. "Gregorio has agreed to irrigate it and pull the epazote for me, but before he does, I'd like to harvest the smaller leaves so Encarnación and I can dry them for her cooking pot this winter."

"The pigweed?" Gerald asks in surprise.

"Oh yes. It's an essential addition to the beans that we eat so often here. Besides enhancing the flavor, epazote increases the bean's digestibility." She grins mischievously. "My father says it civilizes the beans. Or at least the bean eaters."

~ ~ ~ ~

Gerald spends the next several weeks accompanying Suzanna back and forth to the new garden plot and helping her plant the seed potatoes. He notes with a relief he doesn't dare express that she carries a cutting knife with her at all times. She uses it for her gardening, but its sturdy eight inch blade would do substantial damage if she had to use it against a human foe. She calls it her cuchillito and says Encarnación gave it to her as a gift.

Gerald's eyes narrow at that. So the Peabody cook also feels Suzanna needs protection. But he has no right to further caution Suzanna. Perhaps someday he will have that privilege— Even then, it's unlikely. She isn't a girl who likes to be cautioned.

Somehow this train of thought converts into a mental tally of the funds in Gerald's possession. His only option for increasing them is to trap. Although he hates the thought of leaving Taos, he pays close attention when the fur brigades begin to form up in August. At least three parties are heading south and west to the Gila River and its tributaries. But that's all owned by Mexico and a man needs a Mexican passport to trap there. At least, nuevomexico's Governor is insisting that passports are required, even though no one seems to have actually seen the directive that says so.

But, according to Old Bill, passports aren't an insoluble problem. "You just got to sign on with someone that has one," he explains one afternoon in the Peabody parlor. "One guía is good for however many men you tell his Excellency the guvner you're taking, and after that nobody's counting." He leans toward Gerald, whisky on his breath, and Gerald exchanges an uneasy glance with Suzanna.

"Me and St. Vrain, we're sayin' we've got around twenty men," Old Bill says. "But that don't include camp keepers and such." He winks and leans back. "We ain't truly decided just yet where we're headed, neither." He grins. "The paper we got says we're going south to Sonora." Suzanna looks at him disapprovingly and he swings his red head toward her father. "What do you think, Jeremiah? Think we'll find beaver in the deserts of Sonora?"

Jeremiah Peabody glances up from the two-week-old newspaper he's been thumbing through. "I'm sure I couldn't say," he says. "Although I understood from St. Vrain that the guía you obtained was for trading, not trapping."

"Ah, it'll cover it all!" Williams chuckles and slaps his knee. "And it'll take in the Gila River quite nicely. Even the mountains to the north of it."

He looks at the three faces gazing back at him. "Well, I can see you all have more interesting things to cogitate on than mere beaver," he says mischievously. "So I'll just mosey on back to the taberna."

They all say muted goodbyes and Suzanna rises to see him out.

"Are you anticipating a return to hunting with Mr. Williams?" Jeremiah Peabody asks when he and Gerald are alone.

Gerald shakes his head. "He hasn't suggested it," he says. "And I doubt I would take him up on such an offer if he did." He gestures toward the door. "He's very knowledgeable about the ways of the wilderness, but—"

"I suspect that you may have learned all he can teach you," Peabody says drily.

Suzanna comes back into the room. "I wish he wouldn't drink so," she says. She moves restlessly to the dimly-lit window. "Why must men throw themselves away on whisky?"

"Not all men do so, my dear," her father says mildly.

"They have nothing else to give their lives meaning," Gerald says.

She glances around and his eyes meet hers. Her cheeks flush scarlet and she turns back to the window. "I suppose you'll be leaving with one of the fur brigades soon?" she asks. She moves back across the room, and seats herself beside the tea table. "With Mr. Williams, I presume?"

"Ewing Young has suggested that I join the group he and William Wolfskill are organizing for the southern mountains and the Gila River," Gerald says. "I believe he has the appropriate permissions." He turns to her father. "Young will be leading it and some of the men going with him will be free trappers, but he's offered me a contract. I'd earn a wage instead of taking the risk of bringing back enough furs to make it worth my while."

"Leaving the risk of a good take to Young is a fine strategy," Jeremiah Peabody says. "You may not make as much as you would if you were free and your catch was good, but you don't risk losing all of it, either. And Young and Wolfskill are two men with a fine reputation for good sense." He accepts a fresh cup of tea from

Suzanna, then adds, "I'm glad you aren't thinking about going out with the party that Michel Robidoux is putting together for the Gila. He doesn't seem seasoned enough to be heading up such a venture."

Gerald nods absently and glances at Suzanna. "I hope to add a decent amount to what I've already earned," he says. "Though I'm reluctant to take with me the funds I already have. I understand some men put theirs in trust with a merchant here or in Santa Fe."

"Either way is a risk," Peabody says.

"I wondered if you would be so good as to keep my small earnings for me." Gerald hesitates. "Though, if you don't wish to carry the burden—."

"I would be delighted to take on that responsibility for you," Jeremiah Peabody says with a smile. He glances toward Suzanna. "You honor me with the request to entrust your resources to my care. And I'm sure you'll come back from this venture with more to add to it. A group led by Young has every chance of doing well."

But Gerald barely hears this last sentence. He has turned toward Suzanna and is too busy looking into her smiling eyes.

CHAPTER 14

But Jeremiah Peabody's last sentence has registered on some level. By mid-October, after a month in the pine-covered southern mountains, Gerald has begun to seriously wonder what 'doing well' really means when it comes to trapping beaver.

A few days before the trappers left Taos, Ewing Young took ill and remained behind, so William Wolfskill is in charge. Wolfskill is a dark-haired, solidly built man with a broad forehead and determined eyes and mouth, and he sets a hard pace.

He has to, with twenty men along. As they move through the Gila wilderness, anywhere from eighty to one hundred traps are in action at any one time, and the beaver seem to evaporate from the landscape. Wolfskill's band is rarely in the same place more than a night. Each morning they lift traps, skin the night's catch, then push on to the next location, stopping in the early evening to fan out and set yet another round in the streams that thread the headwaters of the Gila River.

The pace is rough and there's little time to enjoy a quiet smoke or conversation. When there is talk, it doesn't focus on trapping. These men aren't about to share what they know. Free trappers don't talk about where and how they set their traps, and they don't share tips for getting better results, either.

Instead, big-bodied Milton Sublette and short, round Thomas Smith brag about sharp trades they've made and Indian battles they've fought. Their impetuosity always comes out triumphant, of course. Trapping partners Alexander Branch and Solomon Stone swap travel stories with Richard Campbell, as well as tales of encounters with animals of various types and size, some of them more exaggerated than others. The trappers don't always win these conflicts, but even when they're worsted, the resulting scar is worth showing off, and there's usually another story about the size of the wound and how quickly it healed.

Not everyone is loquacious: Smith's partner Maurice LeDuc and the big Pennsylvania Dutchman George Yount say as little as possible. They simply listen and smoke.

The half-dozen Mexican camp keepers have little leisure time. While the trappers chat, the Mexicans go about the business of cooking, keeping the campsite organized, and preparing the beaver plews the trappers have collected.

Most of the workers seem content with their routine, but twenty-year-old Ignacio Sandoval apparently expected to actually learn how to trap on this trip. Wolfskill ignores the younger man's dark looks, but Gerald is curious.

He can also see that, when the traps are full each morning, the Mexicans have more work than they can easily handle. Gerald begins skinning his catch himself and trying to re-teach himself the art of stretching the beaver pelts tight on their willow hoop frames. He's surprised at how much he's forgotten.

He's hung his second attempt for the day from the lower branch of a pine tree and is standing back to admire the way the late-morning light glows red through the stretched skin, when Ignacio Sandoval approaches him.

"El señor, he say I stretch pelt for you," the boy says.

Gerald turns. "Hmm? Thank you, but that's not necessary. I only have two more to do." He gestures toward the tree and smiles ruefully. "I'm still remembering how to go about it, so these are a bit rough, but I'm sure I'll improve with some practice."

Ignacio moves toward the pine. A grin flashes across his face as he examines the furs, which sag badly to one side. He starts to shake his head, then stops himself. "Si, señor," he says politely.

Gerald chuckles. "They're that bad, are they?" He moves toward the pine. "Perhaps you can help me tighten them up a bit."

The boy gives him a swift, anxious look, but Gerald's face shows only a desire for help.

Ignacio smiles. "Four hands son necessario a veces," he says as he lifts the hoop from the tree.

Gerald chuckles. "Sometimes four hands truly are necessary to make it work," he agrees. "Especially when two of them are mine and don't know what they're doing."

The boy gives him a swift grin, then bends his head over the knots that hold the beaver pelt in place.

~ ~ ~ ~

By the time the trappers follow the Gila west out of the pine-covered mountains and into the juniper and piñon that scatter the foothills, Gerald has mastered the art of stretching beaver pelts. This is partly because there are fewer streams here and therefore fewer pelts and more time to string them.

Wolfskill doesn't seem concerned about the reduced number of beaver. There'll be more when the trappers reach the Colorado. What worries him is the increased sense of an Apache presence.

It starts while they're still in the mountains. Although no one in the party actually sights an Indian, items disappear from camp: a sugar loaf from the mess, a beaver pelt hung on an outlying tree, a knife left

119

on a rock, meat from a plate unattended while its owner takes care of private business.

If a horse or two had been stolen, it wouldn't be so nerve-racking. They'd at least know for sure that Indians are around. But the disappearance of these smaller items makes their owners question their own perception. Did they actually leave the knife on the rock? Perhaps it slipped into a crevice or was picked up by one of the other men.

Yet the knife doesn't reappear and the very pines themselves seem to wait for someone to turn his back. It's a relief to get into more open country, where the landscape gives less cover to whoever is trailing them. But small items continue to evaporate in the December sun. Even when there's no cover to speak of.

"I'll warrant it's that same band Sylvester Pattie was yammering on about when I saw him and his son James last summer, before Sylvester headed to the Santa Rita copper mines," Thomas Smith says. "He and his boy were up in these parts last season and a group of Apaches harassed them all winter. Stole Sylvester's Kentucky ridin' horse and generally made their lives hell."

"But here we are," Maurice LeDuc observes philosophically. "Because here is the beaver."

"We just need to stay out in the open as much as we can," William Wolfskill says. "And keep a sharp lookout."

~ ~ ~ ~

But a camp needs cover of some kind, if only to keep personal business personal. And the trappers are forced to stay along the river, among its cottonwood and willow, if they want to collect pelts. As the men move down the Gila toward the mouth of the Salt, small things

NOT JUST ANY MAN

continue to disappear and the tension continues to rise. It's almost a relief when a small band of Apaches finally materializes.

The trappers are in the process of breaking camp. Thomas Smith, roping a half-pack of pelts onto his mule's off-side, is the first to glance up and see the line of six warriors standing motionless beneath the rugged cottonwoods on the opposite side of the clearing.

"Holy shit!" Smith exclaims. Around him, men turn swiftly, following his gaze. Their hands move swiftly to rifle, knife, or hatchet—whatever is closest to hand—and William Wolfskill barks, "Settle and steady now!"

The Apaches are solidly built and menacing in their silent impassiveness. The very length of their black hair exudes a dangerous strength. Only one wears a shirt and something resembling trousers. There's a broad palmetto-leaf hat on his head and red sleeves and leggings on his limbs, clearly the marks of a chief. The others wear strands of shell on their bare chests. Their legs are covered with thigh-high moccasins that reach almost to their breech clouts.

The Chief's hands are empty, but two of his men carry battered rifles. Two others hold empty bows at their side. A younger man stands slightly behind, a notched reed arrow in the curved wooden bow he holds casually at his waist.

The man in the palmetto hat moves forward. His eyes sweep the trappers and land on William Wolfskill, who moves toward him. Wolfskill raises his eyebrows questioningly and lifts his hands. He closes his fists, points both index fingers toward the sky, then sweeps his hands swiftly down and across each other and up again, making the sign for trade.

The Apache chuckles and shakes his head, then stretches a hand toward Wolfskill, palm up, and gestures toward himself in a scooping motion.

Wolfskill scowls. "Give you?" he asks. "Why should I give anything to you?"

Thomas Smith moves forward with a hatchet in his hand. He snaps a few words in Apache. The Indian gives him a contemptuous look, then turns and speaks to Wolfskill.

"He says we ain't goin' any farther if we don't give him gifts," Smith says, his eyes on the Chief's face.

The man glances at Smith, then speaks to Wolfskill again, rather impatiently. There's a low chuckle from the men behind him.

"He says he's the Chief of all o' this land and we gotta pay to be here," Smith translates.

"And you can just tell him to go to hell," Wolfskill says pleasantly, his eyes scanning the men behind the Chief calmly. "They've been pilfering and we don't have anything left to give, even if we wanted to. They don't even hunt beaver, far as I know. We've got just as much right here as anyone else."

Smith grins malevolently and nods at the Indians behind the Chief, then says something in Apache. The warriors' postures shift slightly, then an arrow flies over Smith's head and hits his mule's left flank with a dull thud.

As the animal screams in terror, Smith's hatchet flies across the clearing. In the same instant, rifles roar from both sides and more Apaches appear from the trees.

"To me!" Wolfskill bellows and Gerald finds himself beside the man, Ignacio Sandoval behind him, loading a rifle. Gerald takes a deep breath, aims carefully, and fires into the gunpowder haze that rises from the trees.

As he begins to reload, a hand touches his shoulder blade. Gerald turns his head and Ignacio offers him a newly-loaded rifle. Gerald nods, trades weapons, and turns back to the fight. Another mule screams.

A few yards to Gerald's right, Milton Sublette howls with anger and charges across the clearing toward the trees. Then his legs crumple beneath him and he sits down abruptly and clutches his right thigh. An arrow protrudes from his buckskin leggings.

Gerald pulls his eyes away from Sublette and fires into the cottonwoods, then trades weapons with Ignacio again, the acrid gunpowder bitter on his tongue. The flurry of arrows from the cottonwoods has slowed. Gerald pauses, considering whether it's worthwhile to fire again.

William Wolfskill raises a hand. "They're gone, boys!" he says.

Gerald lowers his rifle and takes a deep breath. He and the others keep an eye on the trees as William Wolfskill moves around the campsite, assessing the damage, then heads toward the hobbled animals in the clearing beyond.

"Shit!" Milton Sublette says as he tries to sit up.

Thomas Smith goes to Sublette's possibles sack and rummages through it. When he pulls out a whisky bottle, Sublette smiles grimly.

"Well, at least I've got a reason to get soused," he says.

"Save some for sousin' that wound," Smith says. He pulls a clean shirt from Sublette's pack and begins tearing it into strips. "Hey Locke, you game for helpin' me with this?"

Gerald nods and moves forward. Then he pauses and reaches for his canteen. "Give me a minute to wash."

"Naw, use the whisky," Smith says, holding it out.

Gerald washes a swig of water through his mouth, swallows the bitterness that still clings there, then takes the whisky bottle from Smith and splashes liquor on his hands as Smith slices into Sublette's buckskin trousers. He peels the leather back to reveal the Apache arrow and the bloody gash it's made in Sublette's leg. He carefully cuts off a strip of the buckskin, folds it into a narrow band, and hands it to Sublette, who grimaces and slips it between his teeth.

"Ready?" Smith asks.

Sublette nods, his eyes slitted with pain.

The arrow's shaft is made of some kind of thick reed. Smith grabs it with both hands, one fist above the other, and snaps the shaft off six inches above the wound.

Smith raises an eyebrow at Sublette and the big man nods grimly.

Smith gently moves the shaft back and forth, working it away from the edge of the wound. "It's a good thing Apache arrow heads ain't barbed," he says. "I ken pull it straight out." He looks at Sublette, who nods again. A little impatiently, Gerald thinks. Sweat drops stand out on Sublette's broad forehead.

"You're gonna hafta hold his hands," Smith tells Gerald. "Or he'll grab at me in spite of himself."

Sublette's eyes are clenched shut. Gerald takes his right hand and reaches across for his left. "Go!" the wounded man grunts around the leather in his mouth.

"Got him?" Smith asks Gerald.

Gerald nods and Smith turns to the arrow. He moves the shaft gingerly, as if testing it, then tightens his grip and gives a little grunt as the blood-smeared head lifts free of Sublette's leg.

Sublette gasps, shudders, and lies still, his chest heaving. As Smith begins binding the wound, Gerald releases Sublette's hands. The wounded man takes a deep, shuddering breath. "Coulda done that quicker," he grumbles. He turns his head. "Where's the whisky?"

As Gerald hands Sublette the whisky bottle, William Wolfskill walks up, his hands on his hips. "Well, we got at least a couple of the bastards," he says. "But we lost three of the mules and yours is wounded, Smith. It looks pretty bad."

"The hell she is!" Smith exclaims belligerently. He scrambles to his feet, the piece of arrow still in his hand. "Those damn red skinned mother suckers! That's the best mule in the whole damn outfit!" He scowls at Wolfskill. "I ain't puttin' her down, William."

"I didn't say she had to be put down, now did I?" Wolfskill asks reasonably. He looks around at the silent trappers, then turns back to Smith. "The more important issue at hand is how much we have remaining in the way of supplies. And it's not much. We're going to have to pull out."

"Retreat?" Smith spits. "After they attacked us and wounded my mule and put a arrow in Milt's leg? You wanta retreat?"

Wolfskill lifts a hand. "We need to regroup," he says. "I say we go back to where we can get word to Taos for reinforcements and more supplies, then we come back and teach these bastards a lesson they won't forget."

There's a murmur of agreement from the other trappers, but Smith only says, "We're takin' that mule with us."

Wolfskill gives him a skeptical look. "You'll need to practice your doctoring skills on her," he says. "But if she can keep up, we'll take her with us."

Smith crosses to the mule, who's standing at the edge of the clearing, blood seeping steadily from the arrow in her left flank. He runs a hand over her rump and she jerks away from him, her ears back. "Hurts, don't it?" he asks. "Thata girl. We'll fix you up so you'll be in high beaver."

"She's going to have to keep up," Wolfskill says again. "And we can't be waiting around for her, either." He studies the other trappers, then turns to Sublette. "Milt, do you think you can ride?"

Sublette moves his leg slightly and winces. "Give me a day and I'll be ready to go," he says.

Wolfskill nods. "Day after tomorrow then." He turns to Smith, who's pulling a jar of ointment from his possibles sack. "Day after tomorrow early," he says, raising his voice slightly, but Smith doesn't respond.

The doctored mule is limping and irritable, but she's in the train that turns back up the Gila River within an hour of sunrise two days later. Unlike the other animals, she carries no packsaddle and there's an oily smear on her left flank. But she's moving. Smith is in good spirits.

While Milton Sublette's leg heals more slowly than he would have liked, it is healing. By the fourth day, he's able to walk for short distances. But the mule isn't so fortunate. She's weaker than when they began the trek and her wound is giving off a rotting-meat smell. The other animals, and then the men, give her a wide berth.

"That's going to start attracting mountain lion," Wolfskill tells Thomas Smith that night. "She's not going to make it, Tom."

Smith scowls at Wolfskill's back as the group's leader walks away. He strokes the animal's neck, trying to coax her to eat, but she only rolls her pain-ridden eyes and gingerly lifts her hind leg, as if this will ease the discomfort.

"Godforsaken mothersuckin' Apache!" Smith growls.

Gerald watches sympathetically but knows there's nothing he can do to help. When Smith leads the limping animal out of camp the next morning, no one accompanies them and they all pretend not to hear the gunshot that reverberates across the mountainside half an hour later.

Everyone avoids Smith's eyes when he returns. "Damn Apaches!" he mutters as he drops the mule's halter and rope onto a log near the fire. "Coyote bastards! She was the best damn mule I ever had!"

Sublette, perched on a big piece of sandstone at the end of the log, shifts his leg into a more comfortable position. "Damn Apaches, is right," he says. "We'll come back and take that mule outta their skin, Tom. That and some payment for this leg."

Smith drops down to sit beside him and leans forward to lift a stick from the ground. He pulls out his knife and begins whittling ferociously. "I'll cut off more'n their scalps," he vows. "That there was my best mule. Best one I ever had."

Gerald looks at the two men thoughtfully. Is this what trapping in Apache territory does to a man? Winds them up so tightly that they value a mule's life over that of another man's? At least two Apaches died in that fight. But then, not everyone thinks an Indian's life is equivalent to a white man's. Or a Mexican's. Gerald watches Ignacio Sandoval move to the fire with an armful of wood. Would Smith have been so upset if Sandoval or one of the other camp keepers had died?

Gerald stirs uneasily. If an Apache or Mexican life isn't worth much to these men, how would they value a black man who's also part Indian? Especially one who's passing as white? His stomach clenches. It seemed so simple at the time. On the prairie. On the road between Ranchos and Taos. And surely some of them have guessed. But no one has confronted him and they certainly seem to treat him as an equal.

His tension eases a little and his back straightens. He'll just have to play it out and see where it takes him. But the fact remains that he's not like these other men. He's not just any man.

Smith is still muttering about losing his mule when the trappers break out of the mountains a week later and see the Rio del Norte winding like a silver ribbon through the dry land below, the bosque's gnarled gray cottonwoods running beside it. The hamlet of Socorro, surrounded by fields and sheepfolds, lies between them and the water.

"Well, it ain't much, but it's bound to have food," Milton Sublette says as they gaze down at the dusty clutch of adobe casitas.

Suddenly, Ignacio Sandoval is at William Wolfskill's elbow, looking at him pleadingly, his voice low and urgent. Wolfskill gives the young man a quizzical look, then throws back his head and laughs aloud. He turns to the others. "I guess we're gonna have to take the long way to the river," he announces. "Sandoval here says his Daddy lives down there and he don't know Ignacio's with us. He'll likely cause quite a ruckus if we show up with the boy in tow."

"Thought you was from Taos!" Thomas Smith says to Ignacio.

"He believes me there," the younger man says reluctantly. "He sent me to study."

"You're supposed to be goin' to school?" Sublette asks incredulously. "You're a Mexican! What the hell do you need schoolin' for?"

Ignacio gives him a sheepish grin and shrugs.

"I know his daddy and he's got a sharp streak to him," Wolfskill says. "We'll just ease on around this little mud town and head on up to Los Chavez. Señor Chavez is likely to be more welcoming and he has a bunch of pretty daughters, besides."

"Well, for a pretty girl I guess I can go a little farther on this bum leg," Sublette says. There's a general chuckle of agreement and the trappers move out, heading north across the dead grasses of the llano, keeping the gnarled gray cottonwoods that line the Rio del Norte well in sight.

CHAPTER 15

The ground is dry and the going easy, and two days bring the trappers to the Chavez rancho, which is sprawled along the river. As Wolfskill's party moves toward it across the llano, they pass shepherds grazing mixed flocks of goats and sheep. There's no apparent move to get word to the Los Chavez padrón and former nuevomexico governor Franscisco Javier Chavez that the trappers are coming, but by mid-day a man on horseback has appeared to welcome them and lead them politely to a campsite under the massive cottonwoods beside the river.

Once the animals are unpacked, the men disperse to make themselves presentable to the Don and his daughters. The river is too shallow for proper bathing, but its waters are warmer and wider than the mountain streams in the highlands. Gerald finds a depression near the bank where he can shed his layers of clothing and weigh them down with some rocks, then lower himself into the water and let the river wash away at least some of the stink.

As he's climbing back into his clothes, Ignacio appears, waving at him. "Come," he says. "El señor prepares for us a feast."

Don Chavez's women have roasted two lambs and cooked several kilos of tortillas, as well as a tender cheese, or queso. Though there is no opportunity for interaction with the Chavez daughters, the food is a welcome change from camp fare. The trappers are in a mellow mood when they head back to the campsite. But their faces darken when William Wolfskill announces that they're heading up to Taos the next day.

"We don't all need to go," he adds. "In fact, it'll be quicker if most of you stay here." He grins. "Especially those of you with Taos sweethearts. There just won't be time for all that. We need to get there, consult with Ewing, and then hightail it back here and decide how to proceed."

"Decide?" Thomas Smith growls. "What's t' decide? We're gonna go back in there and teach those mothersuckin' Apaches a lesson they ain't gonna forget! Damn Indians!"

"We'll need more men to do that," Wolfskill points out. "And more supplies. Since Ewing has the biggest share in this outfit, it's going to depend on what he wants to do and how much more money he wants to lay out."

Smith scowls. "It's my mule that got killed. I've got a right to a voice in this."

"I know it," Wolfskill says. "And that'll be part of the considerations. But my partner and I need to confer. And if the decision goes the way I think it might, we'll need more men." He shakes his head. "There's not likely to be many left in Taos this time of year. We'll be scraping the barrel." He looks around the circle. "Now, I need a few to go with me. Enough that we can fend off anyone layin' in wait and get through t' Taos in good time." His eyes rest on Gerald, then pass over him. "Sublette, you'll be wantin' to stay and rest up that wound."

Milt Sublette stretches his leg slightly and grimaces. "I'd just slow you down," he agrees.

Wolfskill's eyes move on. "I'm thinking Stone and Branch and Dutch George." He grins. "As far as I know, none of you have sweethearts to distract you." He nods to Ignacio. "And Sandoval to do the cooking." He chuckles. "You can check in with your teacher, so he can send news to your pa that you're workin' hard."

Ignacio grins sheepishly and Gerald feels a pang of something almost like jealousy. Had Ignacio been studying with Jeremiah Peabody before he joined Wolfskill's trapping group? Would he see Peabody's daughter? It's more likely that he was working under Taos' new Catholic priest, Padre Martinez. But there's still a chance that the boy's path will cross the Peabodys' while he's in Taos, and Gerald feels a twinge of envy. It would be good to see Suzanna again.

But he has no rights to such thoughts. He considers the fact that William Wolfskill didn't name him as a man with no Taos sweetheart to distract him. He has to admit that Suzanna Peabody would be a distraction, but Gerald isn't sure whether he's pleased or annoyed by Wolfskill's silence. Are others besides Old Bill aware of the pull the Peabody casa has for him? He feels a glimmer of amusement, then discomfort, and remains in the background the next morning, lest someone should decide to ask him what message he wants delivered to the Peabody parlor.

While the Taos party is gone, Gerald devotes himself to grazing his mule along the river in locations that won't interfere with the Chavez stock and getting his gear back into shape. He also studies the way the Chavez acequia system channels water to the hacienda's fields, and the primitive but effective wooden gates the laborers use to send it where it's most needed.

The soil is sandy here, but rich wherever the river has flooded, and he's told that it produces bountiful crops of chili and corn. The fields are barren now. Brown leaves rattle in the cottonwoods along the river. But Gerald can see that it's a good land, and fertile wherever the irrigation system's channels have been extended.

His mind strays to the girl in Taos who's growing potatoes beside a similar water course, but he forces himself back to the ditch at hand. He has no right to think of her long-limbed stride, her black eyes gazing into his face. He has no right.

CHAPTER 16

"I met William Wolfskill in the plaza this afternoon, on my way back from Padre Martinez's house," Jeremiah Peabody says as he helps himself to more mutton stew.

Suzanna's head jerks up involuntarily. "They're back?" Then she stops herself. There's absolutely no reason to sound so delighted.

Her father smiles at the tortilla he's tearing in two. "Just Wolfskill and a few of his men. Not Mr. Locke, I'm sorry to say." He glances at his daughter, who's examining her bowl of stew, and forces the amusement from his voice. "I would have enjoyed hearing his reaction to a prolonged expedition with a large group of men. I expect the experience will be quite different from what he experienced with Old Bill."

"I expect so." Suzanna's voice is carefully neutral. She will not ask whether Gerald Locke has sent a message. She has no right to expect such a thing. And he's too much of a gentlemen to presume to do so. She forces herself to eat another spoonful of stew. "Chonita has done an excellent job of flavoring this stew." She grins at her father. "Did you notice that it includes Irish potatoes?"

"I did!" he says. "Are these from your harvest?"

She nods, forcing her thoughts away from the memory of Gerald Locke helping her plant the seed for the potatoes, walking beside her along the acequia ditches toward home. To her home, that is. Not his. She looks up at her father. "They've stored nicely," she says. "And the straw Ramón brought me to cover them was extremely clean, so Encarnación found no bad spots when she prepared them."

Her father nods, knowing a change of subject when he hears one. "They're quite tasty," he says.

Suzanna watches him. She wants badly to ask if he's invited William Wolfskill to tea, but this once quite ordinary question now feels somehow dangerous. "And did Padre Martinez have any news of interest from Santa Fe?" she asks.

CHAPTER 17

Gerald tells himself that his restlessness is triggered by the Chavez fields and acequia system. The wide pastures and black soil make him wish for land of his own to cultivate. His yearnings have nothing to do with an American/French/Navajo girl who grows Irish potatoes beside a Spanish acequia. He feels a surge of relief when word comes that the men are on their way back from Taos.

But he's surprised to see that William Wolfskill is not with them. Ewing Young has apparently recovered enough from his illness to head up the dozen and a half men who ride into camp a good two weeks after Wolfskill had headed north.

Yount and Stone are with him. Ignacio Sandoval trails behind with another young mexicano. Gerald's heart jumps when the rider lifts his head. It's Gregorio Garcia. He'll have news of the Peabody household.

Then Gerald's surge of anticipation is replaced by something else. Enoch Jones rides with the men clustered around Ewing Young.

But there's no time to do more than greet Gregorio and avoid Jones' half-drunk scowl before Young gets down to business.

"Wolfskill's mindin' the store," he says brusquely in response to Thomas Smith's question. He releases his mount to a camp keeper and reaches for the coffee pot, on a rock by the fire. "He told me what happened, but I want t' hear it again from you all."

135

Smith hunkers down on the other side of the fire and launches into a detailed narrative that begins with the first pilfering and ends only when his mule has suffered a lingering death. His ire rises as the story progresses. "Damn Apaches!" he finishes with a growl.

Young is silent for a long while, staring into the flames, then looks around at the other men. "So that's what happened, is it?" he asks.

Gerald suppresses a smile. Young's eyes rest on his face and Gerald looks away. Who is he to contradict Thomas Smith: merchant, veteran trapper, and seasoned Indian fighter?

"Close enough," Solomon Stone answers as his big hands snap small cottonwood branches into kindling for the fire.

"Jest like he says," Maurice Leduc asserts rather belligerently.

Young's eyes swivel back to Gerald's and Gerald gives him a small shrug and a nod.

"I'm not too sure it's worth the time and trouble to go back in," Young says. He looks at Milton Sublette, who's perched on a chunk of cottonwood log with his legs straight out in front of him. "We've already had one man wounded. How's the leg, Milt?"

"It's doin', Captain," Sublette says. "Long as I can keep the witch woman away from it."

"La curandera try to help, he no want," the oldest of the camp keepers explains as he hands Young a bowl of mutton stew.

Young shakes his head and stirs the stew with his spoon. "Those woman healers generally know what they're about," he tells Sublette. "You ought to have taken her up on that."

"She wanted to put some stuff on it that she'd been chawin' on!" Sublette moves his leg impatiently, then grimaces. "I'll cut it off before I pack it with stuff some old Mexican woman's been chawin' on for who knows how long!"

Young chuckles. "Well, as long as you can walk or ride, it's no business of mine." He spoons a bite of stew into his mouth as he scans the faces of the men around the fire. He swallows, takes another bite, then says, "I'm thinkin' we should call it a loss and get out while the gettin's good."

Thomas Smith jumps to his feet. "You ain't lost nearly what I have! And I'm goin' back!"

"We all run risks every day of our lives," the Captain says mildly. "I'm just not sure there's enough beaver there to make it worth our while. Maybe we should try headin' in a different direction entirely."

"If we don't go back, I'm out!" Smith snaps. "I'll head in there on my own! Those bastards need t' pay for what they done!"

"And I'll go with him," LeDuc says from the shadows.

"And we'll take anyone else who wants t' come," Smith adds.

"You'll be breakin' our agreement," Young says. "I footed the bill for some of your gear. You'll be owin' me."

"And you'll be owin' me for a mule!" Smith blusters. "We made an agreement to hunt the Gila and the Salt and beyond. As far as I can see, if you don't go back, you're the one breakin' that contract, not me! Those Apaches need a lesson, or no white man'll ever be safe to trap that way again! They're gettin' way too cocky for my taste!"

Ewing Young gives Smith a long look. "I'll think on it," he says.

Smith stomps away from the fire, still muttering, but he gets what he wants. The next morning, Young announces that they'll head back into the Gila that very afternoon. "We're gonna have to make good time if we want to get any furs worth mentioning," he observes. Surprisingly, Smith reacts only with a curt nod.

The mid-day meal includes a last treat of wheat flour tortillas from the Chavez hacienda and a visit from the courtly old man himself. "Vaya con diós," he tells the assembled trappers. "May He bless all

137

your ventures." There's a hush as he turns to leave. Even Enoch Jones is suppressed by the man's white-haired self-possession.

Then Smith gets to his feet, breaking the spell, and they break camp. The band of thirty trappers moves west across the llano in clusters of threes and fours, the camp keepers trailing behind with the pack mules, Gregorio and Ignacio among them.

Gerald has still not found an opportunity to speak more than two words to either of them. But to lag behind would attract attention and he can feel Enoch Jones' eyes on him, as the big dirty-blond man stalks silently beside George Yount and Milton Sublette, the only trapper on horseback. Gerald stays where he is, alongside Smith and LeDuc.

It's an hour past full dark and they're still on the llano when Young calls a halt for the day. In the interest of time, the evening meal is served cold. Gregorio lays a piece of buckskin on the sand and rock ground and crouches over it to slice mutton off the haunch Señor Chavez has sent with them. He layers the pieces between cold tortillas and hands them to the men as they meander over to him in the moonlight.

When Gerald presents himself for his portion, Gregorio looks up with a smile. "Hola, Señor Locke," he says. "Señor Peabody and his daughter send greetings." His eyes twinkle. "Mi mamá también."

Gerald smiles. "She allowed you to come, after all."

The boy's smile widens. "Señorita Peabody, she persuaded her."

Gerald chuckles and is about to reply when a rough voice demands. "What's takin' so long? The resta us gotta eat too!"

Gerald turns. Enoch Jones scowls back at him.

"You wanta talk, do it later!" Jones growls. Then he leers into Gerald's face, his breath foul on Gerald's skin. "It's plenty dark. The boy'll be waitin' for you, if you ask him nice like."

Gerald looks at the man in disgust and brushes past him without speaking.

"Gotta get it anyway you can, don't ya, ya black—"

"Your food, señor," Gregorio interrupts, thrusting the tortilla-wrapped meat into the man's hands.

Jones jerks back and the meat and tortilla fall to the ground. His closed fist strikes out, hitting the boy in the arm. Gregorio jerks away and half-falls onto the buckskin, knocking the remaining meat into the dirt.

"You greasy mex bastard!" Jones howls. "Look what ya done!" He grabs Gregorio by the arm and yanks him to his feet. "That's good food yer throwin' around!"

As Jones pulls back to slug the boy again, Young appears. He grabs Jones' arm. "That's enough! Let the boy go." He nods at Gregorio. "Use your canteen water to wash off that meat and see that everyone's fed." He turns brusquely away. "Sandoval, help him clean it up. We don't have all night."

As Ignacio moves toward Gregorio, Young swings around, his eyes taking in Gerald and the other men. "We're moving out at first light, so the sooner we eat and bed down, the better. And don't guzzle your water. There won't be any more until late tomorrow."

As he says this, Ignacio and Gregorio pull out their canteens and begin pouring water over the dirt-covered mutton. The haunch is still a good-sized portion, in spite of feeding half the men, and the grit is well embedded. By the time they're done, neither will have enough water to get them through the next day.

When everyone's eaten, Ignacio and Gregorio begin repacking the food in the dark and the trappers roll themselves into their blankets. Even with no fire to center them, they stay close to one another, an instinctive reaction against the darkness and the empty grassland.

Gerald is a little behind the others in his preparations. He lays out his blankets, then moves to the two camp keepers. He holds out his canteen. "Let me top off your water," he says.

Ignacio extends his canteen and Gerald begins to carefully pour water into its small opening, but Gregorio turns to look at the sleeping men and shakes his head anxiously. "Gracias, señor," he mutters. "But no. They will not like it."

Ignacio glances at his friend and then at Gerald, then gestures for Gerald to stop pouring. "Gracias, señor," he mutters. "It is enough."

Gerald nods and holds the canteen out to Gregorio. The boy looks again at the sleeping men, then reluctantly hands over his own container. Gerald dribbles the precious liquid carefully, not wanting to drip any down the side. It's hard to see in the dark. When the container feels perhaps a third full, Gerald hands it back. "I'm sorry I brought Jones down on you like that," he says quietly.

The boy shakes his head. "He's been that way since we left Taos." His mouth twists. "It is difficult to avoid him."

Gerald nods grimly. No wonder Gregorio's mother didn't want him to join the trappers. There's a frail look to him that incites negative attention from men like Jones. He looks at Ignacio.

"Nothing is ever what it seems," Ignacio says bitterly. Gerald raises an eyebrow, inviting an explanation, but Ignacio turns away and Gregorio follows him.

Gerald shakes his head and heads for his own bedding, careful not to trip over any of the sleeping men. It isn't his problem, yet he feels somehow responsible for both these Spanish boys. Though they aren't truly boys. They're young men. He was barely their age when his father left him behind in Missouri, essentially alone.

Yet still he feels responsible, especially for Gregorio. If nothing else, he's a link to Suzanna Peabody. Who seems very far away at the moment.

CHAPTER 18

The next day they move into the pine-filled mountains of the Gila and Gerald's spirits lift. He grins at himself. He's a mountain man in the sense that the mountains feel more like home to him than anywhere else. He wonders if Suzanna Peabody feels the same way. She has, after all, grown up in Taos, the mountains behind her, the broad flat fields of the Taos Valley spreading westward toward yet more mountain peaks. Which does she prefer? Someplace where she can garden, that's certain. He chuckles and glances down. Not that this soil would be right for that. It's entirely too steep and rocky for potatoes.

The men push hard through the territory they've already trapped. There's no sense in trying for beaver again here, and Young seems determined to make up for lost time. The trappers move steadily through the mountains, bedding down late, rising before the sun is truly over the canyon rims, living on short rations. Their only fresh meat is what happens to cross their path. The pace is so intense that it's something of a shock when the line of trappers halts abruptly the afternoon of the fourth day.

Then a string of four trappers and three mules comes into view. They're working their way up a dry arroyo that intersects with Young's trajectory. He holds up a hand and his men all stop to watch the other group scramble toward them, though Enoch Jones huffs impatiently at the delay.

"Chalifoux!" Young says when the newcomers get within speaking distance. "I thought you were trapping south with James Baird!"

"Baird, he is dead," the tallest of the two long-haired Frenchmen says. "La maladie, it got him."

"I'm sorry to hear that."

"We came on anyway," Chalifoux says. He gestures behind him. "Me, my brother, Grijalva, and him."

The men behind Chalifoux nod at Young politely. The youngest, the one with the dark skin and tightly-curled black hair, seems to tense as Young's gaze lands on him, but Young only nods absently and turns back to Chalifoux. "We've got thirty in our troop," he says. "I figure that's about all the Gila can handle at any one time. You headin' that way?"

"It is as God wills," Chalifoux answers. "Perhaps to the north, toward the salt bluffs of the Navajo." He shrugs. "It is possible we go to the Mariposa villages, but it is also possible that Monsieur St. Vrain and Monsieur Williams are there now and nothing will remain for us. Have you heard of this?"

Ewing Young chuckles and shakes his head. "I heard they were headed that general direction, but you never know with Old Bill. He could be on the Yellowstone for all I know."

Chalifoux grunts. "That is the God's truth," he agrees. He looks down the line of Young's men. "It is a full group you have." He scratches his bandanna-covered forehead and nods toward the third man in his small train. "Grijalva here, he shot a buck." He jerks his head toward the pack animal being led by the dark-skinned young man. "A good size one. You want we share the meat tonight?"

143

"Sure, why not?" Ewing Young grins and nods toward the end of his own train. "Fall in behind and we'll help you to cut that deer down to a more packable size."

The Frenchman's party stands and waits as Young's men file past. Gerald eyes the dead buck as he passes the men on the side of the trail. His stomach rumbles. A good meal of venison will make for a pleasant evening.

But the evening turns unpleasant when the visitors produce whisky to accompany the meal and Enoch Jones takes more than his share. When he drinks, Jones is apt to be more surly than usual, and the presence of the young black man seems to aggravate him.

He's leaning sullenly against a large rock that juts from the ground a few yards beyond the fire, nursing yet another drink, when the younger man approaches, a small book in his hand. The stranger nods to Gerald, who's mending harness on the other side of the fire, then crouches down, opens the book, and angles its pages so the light will fall on them.

Jones scowls and leans forward. "What're ya doin' there?" he demands. He sets his tin cup on top of the big rock, steps forward, and nudges at the black man with his foot. "Hey! I asked a question! What're ya doin'?"

The man looks up. "I'm reading," he says. He turns the book so Jones can see the spine. "It's a play by Mr. William Shakespeare called Othello."

Jones scowls at him. "What's yer name, anyway?"

"I'm called Blackstone." The man considers Jones for a long moment, then asks. "And what is your name?"

Jones stalks away into the night. Blackstone's eyes follow him thoughtfully, then return to his book.

But Jones is back a few minutes later, followed by Chalifoux. Jones jabs a thumb toward Blackstone. "You see what he's doin'?" he demands.

Chalifoux grunts. "It appears to me that he is reading." He turns away, but Jones blocks his path.

"That's illegal!" Jones says. "You can't let him do that!"

"He is a free man, Mr. Jones," Chalifoux answers. "He can do as he likes."

Jones' face turns red. "He's a nigger! He ain't allowed t' read!"

Chalifoux raises an eyebrow. "This is a new law? One I know nothing of?" He turns to Blackstone. "What is this law?"

The younger man looks up, moves a small ribbon to mark his place, and closes the book. "I believe there is a law in South Carolina which makes it illegal for slaves to learn to read or write." He shifts the book into his left hand, lifting it as if its very bulk is pleasant to him. "However, as you say, I'm a free man. So the law wouldn't apply to me even if we were still in the United States."

"Which it is certain we are not," Chalifoux says. He bends, picks up a stray pine cone, and tosses it into the fire.

Blackstone glances at Jones, then away. "And there's certainly no such law here," he says.

"Damn uppity nigger!" Jones growls. He surges past Chalifoux, leans down, and grabs Blackstone's arm. "You talkin' back t' me?"

Blackstone rises in one easy motion, elbowing Jones aside. "I was speaking to Mr. Chalifoux," he says evenly.

Jones reaches for the Shakespeare, but Blackstone lifts it out of his reach. Then Jones' foot strikes sideways, into Blackstone's shin, and the younger man stumbles and loses his grip on the book, which lands, page end down, on the stones beside the fire.

145

"You bastard!" Blackstone turns and shoves Jones with both hands. Jones sprawls backward and onto the ground beside the big rock.

Blackstone swings back to the fire and the Shakespeare, but Gerald has already risen, leaned across, and lifted it away from the licking flames.

As Gerald hands Blackstone the book, Jones heaves himself from the ground. He's halfway to the fire again, his fists doubled and ready for battle, when Ewing Young steps from the darkness.

"What's goin' on?" Young asks.

Jones stops short. "Nigger bastard sucker punched me!" he growls. He jerks his head at Blackstone and Gerald. "They're two of a kind," he says. "I'd string 'em both up if rope wasn't worth more'n they are." He glares at Blackstone. "You ain't seen the last o' me." Then he turns and stalks into the night.

"Is he always so pleasant, that one?" Chalifoux asks Young.

Young spreads his hands, palms up. "There's one in every bunch." He turns to Blackstone. "We aren't all of his opinion."

Blackstone nods as he brushes soot from the book's pages. "I can see that," he says. He looks up. "No harm done, thanks to some quick action on this gentleman's part."

Young grins. "Yes, I hear Gerald's become especially partial to books since he arrived in nuevomexico. Books and the people who read them."

Gerald smiles unwillingly and turns away. Has his time with the Peabody's been that noticeable? First Wolfskill and now Young. But then, Taos is a small village. It's natural enough for everyone to know everyone else's business. But he isn't sure he likes that they do.

And Young didn't remark on any other similarities between him and Blackstone. Only the books. Was Young just being polite, skirting the issue of his race?

Gerald shakes his head. Is he really passing?

"It appears that I am," he mutters. He's not sure if he's glad or anxious about that. The lack of total honesty goes against the grain. But then, he's never claimed to be white. He just hasn't brought the subject up. And he's ignored Jones' remarks. Of course, that's the only thing any decent man, either white or black, would do. The man's a bastard. The best way to deal with someone like that is to have as little as possible to do with him. But Gerald wonders how feasible that would be in the long run in a town the size of Taos.

Don Fernando de Taos is still on Gerald's mind the next day as he and the rest of Young's party continue on through the Gila wilderness. If he's going to stay in nuevomexico, find some land he can make his own, continue to pass as white, it might be best to do so away from Taos. Santa Fe might be a better option. It would be easier to blend in there.

Gerald grimaces. Perhaps. But with Sibley's survey of the Santa Fe Trail, more people will be coming in from the States, including men with Enoch Jones' prejudices. Besides, Santa Fe is several days journey from Taos. Suzanna will be reluctant to separate herself that far from her father.

Gerald chuckles and shakes his head at himself. He's aggravated by comments from Wolfskill and Young about Suzanna Peabody, yet here he is, making assumptions himself. Or at least daydreaming. He has no right to such thoughts. Yet the images linger—slim brown hands reaching for the teacups, that willowy form striding beside him toward her plot of potatoes, her face turned toward him, steady black eyes level with his.

When he comes out of his reverie, he finds Ignacio Sandoval beside him, head down, watching the path. "Where's your mule?" Gerald asks in surprise.

Ignacio gestures toward the back of the line. "We strung them together," he says. "Gregorio and I." He shrugs. "It is more interesting to walk together than to see only the back end of a mule."

Gerald chuckles and glances ahead, where the back end of Thomas Smith's new animal blocks his own view forward. "I see what you mean," he says.

"And I wished to speak to you privately," Ignacio says. He glances ahead uneasily. "When there is little chance of being overheard."

"Yes?"

But Ignacio is silent, his head turning to examine the pine and cedar through which they're climbing. Gerald studies the younger man's face, then turns to cluck at his mule. The animal twitches his ears, huffs impatiently, and looks away.

They walk perhaps thirty minutes before Ignacio speaks again. "There was a letter from mi papá waiting for me in Taos."

Gerald grins. "That was excellent timing," he says. "Did you answer it in a way that will allay your father's suspicions?"

Ignacio nods, his eyes anxious. "I do not like to lie to my parents," he says. "But it is sometimes necessary."

Gerald nods sympathetically.

"In the letter, he gave me news." Ignacio breaks off to move ahead and allow Gerald and the mule to negotiate a particularly rocky, and therefore treacherous, piece of trail. When he rejoins them, he seems reluctant to go on. "Perhaps it is nothing," he says. "My father worries a great deal about almost everything." He makes a small hopeless gesture. "My mother believes it is nothing."

Gerald chuckles. "In my experience, it's the mothers who worry."

Ignacio laughs. "It is not so in mi familia. I think sometimes my mother has decided mi papá worries enough for both of them." His voice changes, the anxiety gone. "One day when they were newly married, he told her with great excitement that the well had gone dry. Even she was concerned at the possibility that this was true. He was beside himself with worry. But when mamá went out to investigate, she discovered that the bucket, it had developed a hole!" He laughs. "Papá was muy, how do you say—"

"Embarrassed?" Gerald asks with a grin.

"Si, embarrassed. He was embarrassed." He laughs again. "Poor papá. Now when he begins to worry, mamá asks if he has checked for a hole in the bucket." He chuckles, his eyes sparkling.

Gerald smiles and clucks at the mule again and they walk on. Whatever has been bothering the younger man seems to have been removed by the story, and after the mid-day break he rejoins Gregorio and the pack mules they're responsible for.

The trappers push through the mountains for ten long days, following the Gila as it drops west out of the pines and into dryer country, toward the mouth of the Salt. They begin to see Apache sign again—moccasin tracks, old fires—but this time nothing disappears from camp. Ewing Young establishes two-hour watches. With thirty men, this means no one watches every night, so there are no complaints, except from Enoch Jones, who demands an extra ration of whisky for his trouble. Young isn't forthcoming.

Jones mutters for a solid week, becoming more and more surly, but Ewing Young ignores him. He has his hands full with Thomas Smith and Milton Sublette, who are hell bent on making the Apaches pay for what they did to Smith's mule and Sublette's leg.

Young vetoes the idea of trying to locate the Indians' camp and taking the battle to them. For one thing, it's unlikely that even the most experienced American tracker can find the Apache encampment, unless the Indians want him to. For another thing, hunting Apache will take time away from the trappers' primary task. Now that he's reached untrapped waters, Young wants to focus on beaver, not revenge.

But Smith isn't taking 'no' for an answer. In fact, he's even enlisted Enoch Jones in his schemes.

"I'm for just cuttin' out on our own and doing a little huntin'," Gerald hears Smith telling Jones one morning as he rubs oil onto the stock of his rifle.

Gregorio is kneeling on the ground nearby, mixing tortillas for the morning meal. Jones spits toward Gregorio's big wooden bowl, but the boy shifts slightly, blocking the bowl. The spittle lands on the ground next to the barrel of flour, which stands beside him. Gregorio looks away from the two men. He glances at Gerald, on the other side of the fire, then toward the pine and rocks beyond.

His hands freeze in the batter. "Apache!" he exclaims.

The trappers all turn at once. A loose line of long-haired warriors stands among the rocks and pines at the far side of the clearing. The man in the center sports a large palmetto hat and scarlet leggings and long sleeve shirt. It's the Chief who confronted Wolfskill. Three warriors are positioned on his left, two on his right. As before, another warrior stands slightly back, an arrow fletched in his lightly-held bow.

There's a long silence, then Ewing Young makes a welcoming motion.

The man in the hat moves forward. He stops beside the fire and looks slowly around the clearing, as if he's appraising the value of every item in sight, including the rifle in Thomas Smith's hands.

Then his gaze falls on Gregorio. He points at the barrel of flour. "Meal!" he commands.

Ewing Young frowns, then nods. The Chief picks a wool blanket up from a nearby rock and flicks it open, an edge in each hand.

"That's mine!" Enoch Jones protests.

Smith shakes his head at him. "I'll give you mine," he says. Then he steps backward into the trees, and begins circling toward Gregorio and the flour.

The Chief positions himself in front of the barrel and lets Jones' blanket sag slightly between his hands, forming a kind of container.

Ewing Young waves Gregorio aside, leans over the barrel, and begins scooping out double handfuls of flour. As he drops them into the blanket, a dusty haze rises into the morning air.

The Apache turns his head and gives his men a satisfied smile. He doesn't see Thomas Smith step from the trees behind Gregorio, rifle cocked and ready.

Young pours another double handful of flour into the blanket and holds up his white-dusted palms to show that he's finished.

The Apache leader growls something unintelligible in response.

Young scowls and raises two fingers. "Two more," he says.

The Chief nods and lifts the blanket slightly, ready for more.

As Young reaches into the barrel again, Thomas Smith steps past Gregorio, shoves the rifle muzzle up under the blanket, and pulls the trigger. The bullet explodes through the cloth and blood-spattered flour splashes the Chief's torso.

As the Apache crumples to the ground, his men dash into the clearing. Gunfire erupts. Arrows fly. A trapper drops, then an Apache, then another.

Ewing Young, his upper body coated in white flour, shakes his deafened head. Then an arrow flashes through the air and bites into

151

the ground at his feet. He lunges for his rifle and aims into the trees. But the Indians are already gone, vanished into the rocks and the pines.

The Chief lies where he fell, his red sleeves dusted with flour, his chest an incongruous paste of flour and blood.

Thomas Smith stands over him, his own face and hair coated in white. "That'll teach 'em!" he says triumphantly. He grins at Enoch Jones, who's crouched beside a dead Apache, the man's beaded knife sheath in his hands. "That's worth a hole in a blanket, ain't it?"

Enoch Jones grins back at him, his eyes glittering. "Three dead, four t' go!" he agrees. "They can't be far yet."

"Three dead's enough," Ewing Young says grimly as he beats flour from his clothes. "That was a stupid stunt, Smith. You think that's all of them? If that band doesn't come after us by nightfall, it'll only be because they can't decide who their new leader is." His eyes glare from the flour still spattered across his face. "Next time you decide to shoot an Indian, don't do it in my face, or I may just mistake you for one."

"Well, I wasn't gonna stand by and just let you give 'em our flour!" Smith snaps. "Then they'd just be wantin' more. You ain't got the courage of a lizard!"

Young gives him a withering look and turns to Gregorio. "You all right, son?"

The boy has positioned himself behind the barrel of flour. He nods reluctantly and Jones looks up, then barks with laughter. He points at Gregorio's thin cotton pants, which cling damply to his thighs. "He wet himself! Did more than that!" he chortles. "I can smell ya from here! You never seen a man die before, Miz Mollie?" He laughs again and yanks his bone-handled knife from the sheath at his waist. "Here's something else for you to think on!"

He bends, grabs the dead Apache's hair, pulls it out straight, then moves the steel blade swiftly down and across, cutting away the man's scalp. He straightens and waves the bloody mass at Gregorio. "Here's what happens t' weaklings!"

The boy turns and stumbles out of the clearing. Jones laughs again. "Needs a good fuckin' to make him a man," he says. He looks down at the Apache's body and nudges it with his moccasined toe. He swings his head and sees Ignacio Sandoval. "You! Mexican!" he barks. "Get rid o' this thing!"

Ignacio looks at Young questioningly and Young nods. Gerald pushes his own nausea aside and steps forward. "I'll help you with that," he says.

"Two of a kind," Enoch Jones sneers as Ignacio and Gerald lift the body, one on each end. "Gonna have a little fiesta after yer done, are ya?"

Milton Sublette limps into the clearing, leading a tall sorrel mare with a notch in its left ear. "Look what I found," he says. "It must of got loose from the Injuns."

"That ain't no Injun horse," Thomas Smith says. "Look at that head and those shoulders. That's an American horse that's been bred to run." He narrows his eyes. "Seems to me like I've laid eyes on that sorrel before."

Ewing Young steps to the mare, palm up, and she nickers softly. Young runs a hand over her withers. "This looks to me like Sylvester Pattie's horse," he says. He turns to Smith. "Didn't you say he and his son were up this way last winter?"

"Yeah, they complained all last summer about how Sylvester's horse was stolen by the Apaches around here last season," Smith says. "The damn Injuns gave those Patties fits all the time they were here."

153

"It's always the same group causin' the trouble." Sublette says. "It don't surprise me that this outfit had Pattie's horse." He shifts slightly, easing his leg. "Say, isn't Jim Pattie comin' back this way with Michel Robidoux's group? I wonder if he knows his daddy's mount is still kickin'."

CHAPTER 19

Ewing Young tells the camp keepers to link the Pattie horse to one of the pack mules when they head out the next morning, and orders the two-hour night watch rotation to continue. He's convinced they haven't seen the last of the Apaches.

Three nights later and two days march from the attack site, Gerald is assigned first watch. It's a bitter night, desert-cold and no moon. At ten o'clock, when no one comes out to the herd to relieve him, Gerald heads back to camp.

Blanket-wrapped men lie in mounds around the fire. Only Enoch Jones is awake, warming himself with a tin cup of stewed coffee, a pistol stuck in his waistband. Gerald steps to his bedroll and drops his rifle beside it, then moves into the light, opposite Jones on the other side of the flames. Jones continues to stare into his cup, studiously ignoring him.

Gerald holds his hands over the fire and waits. A coyote yips in the distance. Finally, Gerald says, "Aren't you up for the next watch?"

"In a minute," Jones growls.

"Young wants them monitored closely," Gerald observes mildly.

Jones scowls, his eyes narrow. "You tellin' me what t' do?"

Gerald's stomach tightens as he resists the urge to respond in kind. But then a distant voice calls "Hallo the camp" from the darkness, and Jones' head swings away. He half rises, hand to his pistol.

155

Gerald squints into the night. His hand moves to the pistol at his own waist as he silently curses himself for leaving the rifle by his bedding.

"Come on in," Gerald calls cautiously. A blanket lifts on the ground behind him, and then Thomas Smith is standing next to him, rifle barrel pointing toward the voice.

One shadowy form appears, then two, their hands well away from their sides, rifle barrels pointing to the ground. Americans, by the look of them. Certainly not Apache.

As they step into the firelight, a voice from a blanket on the far side of the fire says, "Well, I'll be!"

"Jim Pattie," Smith says. He lowers his rifle barrel. "And LeCompte too, by God."

The younger man's dirt-streaked face breaks into a grin as he takes off his battered hat and runs a hand through his curly blond hair. "I sure am glad to see you all," he says.

"Sacrebleu!" the man beside him says. "C'est une miracle!"

"We've got Michel Robidoux back there," Pattie says, jerking his head in the direction he's come from. He scowls. "We're the only ones left, thanks to him."

Ewing Young materializes from the dark, gun at the ready. "Only ones left of what?"

"Of Robidoux's thirteen." Pattie's eyes sweep the men around the fire, all of them roused now. "We got hit by Papagos." Pattie's voice rises. "I told him, those dirty Indians weren't to be trusted, but he wouldn't listen!"

"Better go get him," Young says. "Then we can talk."

Pattie scowls and turns. He says something in broken French and his companion nods and turns away.

"There's Apache around," Young says. "You'd best go with him."

Pattie's scowl deepens. "I've been on the move since yesterday morning."

"A little longer won't hurt you."

"I'll go with you," Smith says. He flourishes his rifle. "Just let those Injuns get near me and I'll be bringin' back a scalp or two."

Pattie nods unhappily and turns back into the darkness, LeCompte and Smith close behind. They return an hour later with several mules, two horses, and Michel Robidoux, his face and shirt stained black with blood and dirt, his jaw swollen to twice its natural size.

All of Young's trappers are awake by now. They crouch around the built-up fire and listen attentively as Pattie tells the grim story. This is rightfully Robidoux's role, as the party's head, but the Frenchman's jaw is too swollen to allow him to do more than mutter a few phrases in confirmation or denial of Pattie's version of events, and LeCompte has too little English to do more than nod his thanks for the freshly brewed coffee and study the fire-lit faces surrounding him.

As Pattie tells it, Robidoux's trappers were on the Salt River a mile or so above its junction with the Black, when Robidoux foolishly let a group of Papago warriors talk him into visiting their village, then piling his men's weapons in a single stack between their huts. Even worse, to show how much he trusted them, Robidoux allowed the Papago men to sleep alongside the trappers in their camp just beyond the huts.

Pattie hadn't liked the looks of things from the start, and he and LeCompte slept away from the others, rifles to hand, horses saddled, mules packed and ready to light out at a moment's notice. When the attack came, they hung around just long enough to confirm that they could be of no use to their fellows, then lit out. Robidoux glares at the assertion that they even considered coming to his rescue, but his jaw

157

is so battered that he can do nothing but growl wordlessly and shake his head.

According to Pattie, he and LeCompte headed up the Salt as fast as they could. The next morning, watching the back trail for Papagos, they spied Robidoux instead. They retrieved him, gave him food and water, then laid up the rest of the day while he recovered.

Robidoux scowls at this assertion and shakes his head. "Weren't tha ba," he mutters.

Pattie ignores him, his eyes on Ewing Young. He runs his hand through his hair. "When I seen your fire, me and LeCompte slipped close enough to make out you weren't a bunch of Injuns," he says.

Gerald raises an eyebrow at this. The two men had been at least 200 feet out when they'd hailed the camp and the night is pitch black and moonless. They couldn't have seen anything but the fire's glow. Only desperate men would head for a fire of unclear origin.

"We've got your daddy's horse," Milton Sublette says abruptly. "The one the Apaches stole last season."

Pattie turns toward him eagerly. "You don't say! What happened?"

But Ewing Young isn't about to be sidetracked. He's looking at Robidoux. "Are you three truly all that's left of your bunch?" he asks.

Robidoux nods. He holds up his hands, fingers splayed out, then grimaces and shakes his head.

"The Papagos got ten men?"

There's a sharp intake of breath from Young's trappers. Robidoux nods, eyes grim.

Young turns to Pattie. "Where's this village?"

Pattie gestures vaguely south and west. "Down river maybe five miles."

Robidoux grunts and shakes his battered head. When Young looks at him, he raises both hands and lifts seven fingers. He tries to speak, but pain spasms across his face.

"Seven miles?"

Robidoux nods just enough to answer the question but not enough to start the pain up again.

"Right on the Salt?"

Robidoux shakes his head slightly, then puts his hand to his jaw, his eyes squinting against the pain.

Young looks at Pattie. "How far is the village from the river?"

Pattie shrugs. "A mile. Maybe a mile and a half."

Robidoux nods slightly, his hand still holding his swollen jaw.

Ewing Young's head turns, taking in his circle of men. "No trapping tomorrow," he says. "We're huntin' justice instead." He pauses. "But not everyone. The camp keepers can stay here, except for Gregorio." He nods at him. "Bring what we'll need for a couple of days. And the shovels." He rises to his feet. "We leave at first light."

They don't go far the next day, just a few miles, to a protected bluff near the river bottom where they wait under the gnarled cottonwoods while Thomas Smith and Leduc head downstream to reconnoiter. The two men return looking satisfied, and report that a four-foot deep arroyo curves along one edge of the Papago camp, between it and the river. Young nods at the lines they draw in the rocky sand. "That'll do," he says.

The trappers head out an hour before dawn, moving cautiously through the tree-lined river bottom and into the narrow sand-and-gravel wash Smith and LeDuc have spotted. They crouch below its banks and wait silently in the cold darkness. Smith and Leduc are positioned in the center of the line of trappers, at the deepest part of the curve. Young is to one side of them, Gerald to the other. Michel Robidoux crouches just beyond Gerald.

Quiet settles. There's only a mouse scurrying, a man's weight shifting on the gravel, Robidoux's labored breathing. A slight breeze rattles a dead cottonwood leaf overhead.

Finally, the sky begins to gray toward dawn. Small birds rustle in the trees. Young gestures to Smith and Leduc. They grin at him happily and scramble up the side of the gully, their moccasined feet pushing the gravel behind them and into the wash. As they crest the top, they both let out a blood-curdling yell. They raise their rifles over their heads and run toward the cluster of Papago huts, howling like maniacs as they go.

Young raises his head above the gully's edge just far enough to watch them, his face immobile. Suddenly, without turning his head, he settles his rifle in the dirt in front of him, lifts his hands, palm up, and moves them slightly upward. The trappers rise in a single fluid motion, the edge of the wash at chest height now, and ready their weapons.

The morning light is still uncertain and it's difficult to see at any great distance, but it's clear that Smith and LeDuc are now moving back toward the gully, still yelling. Forms materialize behind them as almost-naked Papago warriors respond to the apparent attack. Smith and LeDuc take their time, stopping every few yards to take a pot shot at the warriors, who gain shape and increase in number, their round white shields glowing in the early morning sun.

As the gap between warriors and trappers narrows, Gerald keeps one eye on Ewing Young. the Captain's arms are still stretched out, his hands sideways now, signaling Gerald and the others to hold their fire. Gerald hears Robidoux huff impatiently.

160

The Papagos are within a few yards of Smith and Leduc now. The two trappers reach the edge of the wash, turn to fire once more, then drop over the edge of the gully as Young shouts "Fire!" and reaches for his rifle.

Gerald feels his gun blast before he's aware that he's squeezed the trigger. Then he and the others are firing, reloading, and firing again, putting up a solid wall of bullets. The Papagos waver, realizing they've been tricked, and begin to retreat.

As the warriors fall back, the trappers scramble up the bank, maintaining a steady rain of fire as they curse the rock and sand that slides out from under their feet and slows their ascent. Then they're over the lip of the arroyo and moving after the Indians.

As the Papagos retreat, women and children pour out of the village and scatter into the fields beyond. The trappers follow. When they reach the huts, James Pattie and a few others give up the chase and begin investigating the buildings for stragglers. Gerald slows too, not wanting to participate in more killing than he has to, though it seems unlikely that there's anyone left in the village.

He stands in a broad path between two rows of wooden huts and studies the encampment. The only substantial part of the buildings are the posts at each corner, which are set deep into the ground. The hut walls are simply dead tree branches attached to the posts with leather straps. Rough porches much like the freestanding Ranchos de Taos blacksmith shop stand in front of the huts. Like the shop, the gaps between the poles on the roofs allow light and air to filter through while still providing shade. The bare wood glints like dull silver in the morning light.

Gerald turns and glances beyond the village. Milton Sublette, slightly behind the others, limps between two fields, gun at the ready. The winter-brown fields are neatly laid out. Thin lines of what appear to be irrigation ditches run between them. Gerald's eyes narrow, automatically trying to identify the plants from their remains. What would grow out here in this desert?

But then his attention is pulled back to a hut just ahead and to his right. He hears a man growl a curse, then a scuffling sound. Enoch Jones appears in the door opening. He's dragging a Papago girl by the arm. She's perhaps twelve years old, her breasts just beginning to show her womanhood. Her eyes are wide with fright. She wears only a clumsy grass skirt around her waist.

Jones drops her to the ground under the hut's porch and leers down at her as he fumbles at his crotch. Gerald takes a step forward, but then Gregorio Garcia appears from the other side of the building, a rifle in his hands.

"Déjela de paz!" the boy yells. The rifle barrel wobbles, then straightens and fixes directly on Jones' chest. "Let her go!" he repeats.

Jones' pants fall open, revealing his pale cock, which stands straight up. He looks down at it with a kind of glee and waggles his hips at Gregorio. "I'm gonna show ya how it's done," he says. He leans down and yanks the girl around, reaching for her buttocks. "See, ya—"

"I said, let her go." The boy takes a step closer. The rifle barrel dips, aiming at Jones' crotch. "I will blow that thing off." It's a statement of fact more than a threat.

Jones looks into the boy's face and his smile disappears. His eyes narrow. Then he looks down at the girl. "Tell ya what," he says. "You can have her for yerself." He reaches down and slaps her on the thigh. "She'll be jest right fer a first time."

He tucks himself back into his pants and refastens his buttons. "She's all yers, Miz Mollie." He turns on his heel and walks away, up the path toward the fields. He looks back. "You do know what t' do with her, don't ya?" He laughs harshly. "That's a favor ya owe me now, Mollie boy!" Then he disappears around the corner of another hut, doubtless in search of another victim.

Gerald and Gregorio look at each other, then the girl. She lies motionless on the ground beneath the porch, her terrified eyes fixed on the boy with the gun. Tear marks streak her face. Gregorio lowers his rifle barrel and gestures at her to go. She stares at him blankly.

"Adelante!" he yells, waving his free hand. "Go!"

She blinks and turns her head. She sees Gerald and her eyebrows contract. He nods and waves his hand toward the fields with a shooing motion.

Suddenly, she seems to understand. She pulls herself cautiously into a sitting position, looks at Gregorio, then Gerald, then leaps to her feet and scuttles away from the porch, toward the field.

Gregorio moves toward Gerald. "I did that," he says, his voice shaking. "I would have killed him. I felt it."

Gerald put his hand on the boy's arm. "It's over now."

Gregorio snorts, his eyes anxious. "That Jones, he will be angry and full of the vengeance." He shakes his head. "It is not over, señor."

CHAPTER 20

But there are other things besides Jones to think about. After the fight, Michel Robidoux leads Ewing Young to the other side of the village, where he and his men had bedded down beside the Papago warriors. The trappers' animals, guns, and ammunition have disappeared, but their bodies are still there. Even the most experienced men gag at the sight. Naked corpses are strewn across the campsite. Arms and bashed-in heads have been severed from torsos. Torn holes gape in stinking bellies and chests, although it's not certain whether knives or beaks did the work. Ravens and vultures wheel overhead.

The trappers turn immediately to the task of burial. Once the top crust of sand and rock is clawed away and the damp soil underneath is exposed, the ten holes are easy enough to dig. Creating the stone cairns that will protect the dead from being dug up again is another matter.

But they definitely need protection. The birds of prey ride the sky in endless circles as the men lever rock out of the sides of the arroyo, haul it to the burial site, pile it into place, then scour the death site once again to make sure there's nothing left for the birds or any other scavenger. In the process, Michel Robidoux stumbles on a cache of beaver traps, most of them mangled beyond repair. He picks through them and grimly collects the twelve that appear to be most mendable.

It's a two-day task that leaves no time for anything else, so it's easy enough for Gregorio to avoid any interaction with Jones. But once the trappers are back on the Salt and have returned with relief to the business of trapping, Jones picks up his program of harassment.

There's a new edge to his attention, now. His eyes follow Gregorio around the camp. And he seems to be spending more time there than the other men. His trap lines are set in remarkably short order and he's back with his morning haul well before any of the other men.

Under the constant surveillance, Gregorio's work appears to slip. The sugar he's left on the rock slab that serves as a table tumbles to the ground for no reason, the beaver skins he's stretched fall from their tree branches in the night, the food he serves the men is sprinkled with grit or is too salty to eat.

Jones points out every error. Gregorio keeps his eyes down and goes about his business without comment, without apologizing for the mistakes he hasn't made. At first, Ignacio tries to intervene, to point out Jones' proximity when the sugar falls or to monitor the cooking pot so Jones can't get near it. The trapper simply begins playing tricks on Ignacio, too.

Gerald watches it all helplessly, well aware that any intervention on his part will only make the situation worse. What he doesn't understand is why Ewing Young doesn't step in. Can't he see what Jones is up to? But Young seems oblivious to what's going on.

But then, Young has other things to worry about. He's pulled the trappers off the Gila River and turned them northeast, up the Black. The narrow river canyon is thick with beaver. The big rodents have created a series of dams and the water seeps for miles between the dry hills at the base of the rugged cliffs on either side of the stream. The men have to wade through knee high marsh and fight through dense

165

thickets of scraping willow, but the take in pelts is worth the discomfort. They trap steadily onward.

The hills on either side are dry rock spotted with patches of dusty juniper. Their bleakness makes the valley, with the long-stemmed grasses, bushy willow, and wild rosebushes that crowd the edges of the beaver ponds, even more inviting. Beyond the smaller stuff, where the ground is more elevated, is a narrow strip of juniper, cedar, and occasional ponderosa, the ground underneath crowded with undergrowth. Even in February, with no leaves showing yet, the brush makes for hard going unless a man stays at the base of the dry hills or is lucky enough to stumble onto a dim animal track.

Eighty miles up, the river forks. Young divides the men into two groups, one to each branch, separating Jones and Gregorio in the process. Jones, Pattie, Smith, and Maurice LeDuc move with Young's party up the fork that heads due north. Gregorio, Ignacio, and Gerald join Robidoux, Sublette, and George Yount in the party that moves up the northeast branch.

Not having Jones around makes life more pleasant, although there's little time for anything but the drudgery of trapping, butchering, and stretching skins day in and day out. The scenery changes as they move upstream, and the air cools as the elevation rises. Gerald is surprised at the relief he feels at the temperature change. Then he realizes it's not really the heat he objects to. It's the fact that it's this hot in February. It just doesn't feel natural.

But as they move upstream, it begins to feel more like the way February had felt in the Sangre de Cristos. The streams are frozen solid and the beaver are deep in sluggish winter sleep. There's little point in breaking through the ice to set traps they aren't likely to investigate.

Gerald's team turns downstream, moving rapidly now. They reach the rendezvous point at the river fork half a day ahead of Young's party. Jones seems quiet enough when he rides into camp behind Young, but his eyes narrow when he sees Gregorio. It's clear the man's attitude hasn't changed.

The group trapping the west fork has gathered about a third more pelts than Gerald's party. Ewing Young shrugs. "You just never can tell," he says.

"Mollie's got other things t' do," Enoch Jones smirks. He crouches beside the fire and pokes at it with a stick. "Ain't figured out yet not to use green firewood, either." He grins maliciously at Gregorio, who's on the other side of the fire, stirring the stew for the evening meal. "'Fraid t' go inta the woods to collect dry fuel, little boy?"

Just then, Ignacio enters the clearing, his arms full of broken aspen branches. He drops them onto the ground beside Jones, then begins cracking the smaller pieces over his knees and tossing them into the flames. Sparks shoot up and Jones jerks back. "Watch what yer doin'!" he growls.

Thomas Smith laughs. "Too bright fer ya, Jones?" he asks. He turns to Gerald. "How far'd that fork go, anyways? Does it really head as far as the San Francisco?"

"Nigger mollie lover!" Jones spits. He glares at Smith, stands, and stalks into the woods. Gerald focuses on Smith. As he begins describing the terrain near the head of the Black's northeast fork, Smith, LeDuc, and Young all lean forward attentively.

~ ~ ~ ~

The trappers move down river the next day, back toward the Gila. Since they're travelling through an area they've already trapped, there

167

are no pelts to process, and little to do once they've made camp. Young has slowed the pace and they make camp before nightfall each day, giving the men time and daylight to mend traps and take a breather.

And to clean up a little. On the third afternoon from the fork, Gerald slips through the brush to bathe in a side stream. He's returning along a narrow deer trail, half-bent to avoid the crowding willow branches, when he hears a guttural man's voice in the small clearing just ahead.

He slips closer and peers through the bushes. It's Jones, growling deep in his throat as he shoves Gregorio Garcia, chest first, his arms twisted behind his back, into the rough bark of a wind-battered ponderosa. As Gerald watches, Jones grabs Gregorio's hair and grinds his face into the thick bark.

Then Jones releases the boy's head. He grips Gregorio's arms with his right hand and fumbles at his crotch with his left. "I'll show you how it's done, Miz Mollie boy!" he growls. His cock springs free of his clothes, and he grabs Gregorio's cotton trousers, and gives them a yank. The back seam gives way with a ripping sound and exposes the boy's bare buttocks. "I'll teach you t' be a man!"

Gerald moves then, and the sound of dry sticks breaking underfoot catches Jones' attention. As the big man's head swivels, Gregorio twists free. His right hand sweeps to his waist. Gerald glances at him in surprise, and Jones' head swings back to the tree.

There's a ten-inch long knife blade in Gregorio's fist. It glitters in the sunlight as his knees bend slightly, balancing his weight. Jones' eyes narrow as Gregorio's arm swings up and out.

The knife slashes into Jones' right shoulder, but he doesn't flinch. "Little bastard!" he grunts. "I'll teach ya a lesson you won't forget!"

168

He grabs Gregorio's wrist with his right hand and twists the knife from Gregorio's grasp as he reaches for his own blade.

Gregorio shrinks against the ponderosa, his eyes wide with fear and Gerald steps free of the bushes at the edge of the clearing. He pulls his maple-handled knife from his belt as he moves across it.

Jones, focused on Gregorio, seems to have forgotten anyone else exists. He chuckles as his bone-handled knife moves to Gregorio's throat, then lifts a small piece of the boy's cotton shirt with the blade's tip. Jones grins maliciously. "I think I'll just start here and work my way down," he says. "Give ya somethin' to think about before I get to where I'm goin'." He glances down at himself, still uncovered and bone-hard. "We got time."

"Time to reconsider," Gerald says to Jones' back.

Jones glances around in surprise. "Oh. Ya wanta share?" he asks with a lascivious grin.

"Let him go."

Jones releases Gregorio's shirt. "You wanta play too?" He snorts as he adjusts his trousers to cover his crotch. "I can take on both of ya and whup ya solid!"

Gerald glances at Gregorio. The boy pulls at his clothes, trying to straighten them. "You all right?" he asks.

As Gregorio nods, Jones lunges. Gerald's head snaps toward him and his hand lifts, his big steel blade steady. They edge around each other, watching for an opening, as Gregorio clutches at his clothes.

For a big man, Jones is surprisingly agile. But Gerald, slimmer and younger, is still quicker on his feet. They dance around each other for an endless ten minutes, sizing each other up. Jones' eyes become mere slits as he realizes the man facing him isn't going to be cowed.

Suddenly, the big man darts in, slashing past Gerald's blade, but Gerald slips sideways and away. As Jones turns to follow, Gerald makes his move, reaching in to slice Jones' left wrist and force him to release the bone-handled knife.

Jones staggers back and drops his weapon. He steps sideways, but the grass has become compressed and slick from the men's maneuvering and his feet slip out from under him. As he drops to the ground, he leans forward and grabs the dropped knife with his right hand.

"Just let it go," Gerald pants, stepping back. "Leave him alone and we'll call it quits."

"You ain't bested me yet, ya molly-lovin' nigger bastard," Jones snarls. He presses his left hand against his side, trying to staunch the blood from his wrist. "I ain't through with you."

"Enough blood's been shed," Gerald says. He glances toward Gregorio, who still stands frozen by the big ponderosa. "Go on," he tells him.

Jones scowls. "He ain't goin' nowhere and neither are you." He staggers to his feet. "I ain't through with either of ya!" He lunges on the last word and his blade slices Gerald's right forearm as Gerald dances away.

Then they close again, but Jones is awkward now, wielding the bone-handled knife right-handed. Even his feet seem to behave differently.

But Gerald is also weakening. He reverses his grip on the maple handle, holding it waist level, the steel blade broadside against Jones' weapon. As Jones moves forward to take advantage of this adjustment, his feet slip again on the crushed grass. His weapon drops to the ground as he lurches chest-first toward Gerald and his upraised knife.

As Jones tilts toward him, Gerald jerks his knife up and away from the man's belly. The steel slices upward and twists sideways. As

Jones sinks onto the mashed-down grass, Gerald's blade sinks sickeningly between the ribs into this big man's right side.

They're both on their knees now. Gerald, still clutching the maple-handled knife, has been carried forward and down by the force of Jones' fall. He catches himself and leans backward, releasing his grip on the knife.

"Nigger bastard!" Jones growls. He wrenches himself up and back on his heels, glares into Gerald's face, then grabs the hilt of the knife with his bloody left hand. He grits his teeth and yanks the blade free. Blood gushes from the wound, but he barely glances at it. He tosses Gerald's knife toward him contemptuously. "That the best you can do?"

Gerald opens his mouth, but Jones clearly isn't looking for an answer. Instead, he scrabbles in the grass for his knife and staggers to his feet. He points the big blade at Gerald, then Gregorio. It wavers slightly and he tightens his grip and presses his right hand against his bleeding chest. His eyes are icy-blue slits of fury.

"I ain't done with you yet," he growls. "You follow me an' yer a dead man, ya mollie bastards." Then he turns wildly away and crashes through the brush toward the riverbank, moving upstream.

Gregorio stares at Gerald. "He is—." He takes a deep breath and puts a hand on the ponderosa's thick bark, steadying himself. "You killed—"

"That may be," Gerald agrees. He pushes himself to his feet. "It's hard to say just how badly he's hurt." He looks toward the trail that Jones has left in the undergrowth and suppresses the sudden bile in his throat.

He feels drained, all the tension gone out of him. He tries to stiffen his resolve. Will Jones return? If he does, his anger toward the boy will be ten-fold. Curiously, Gerald feels no anxiety for himself. He

171

stands, breathing in the knowledge that he's knifed a man, perhaps killed him, feeling again the sensation of the knife sliding almost softly between Jones' ribs. He feels curiously detached. It's quite a different sensation from shooting at fleeing Indians. He looks down. There's blood on his knife and his hands.

"You're hurt," Gregorio says.

Gerald lifts his right arm and looks at the cut in surprise. He'd forgotten it was there. Now that he's remembered it, he can feel the pain stinging along its length. He wipes at it with his left hand. "It's only a scratch," he says. "Smith'll fix me up nicely." He glances down at the boy's torn cotton trousers. "Can you twist those together enough to keep them up until we get back to camp? We need to tell the Captain what's happened."

Gregorio pulls at his trousers, trying to make himself presentable, and looks at Gerald anxiously. "But not everything," he says.

Gerald turns away, toward the path to camp. "I don't think we need to go into particulars," Gerald agrees.

And he's right. In fact, he's a little startled at the lack of surprise when he announces that Jones has fled upriver with a wound in his chest. They all seem to have a pretty good idea of what's occurred in the woods. Smith silently bandages Gerald's arm and Young doles out a small dose of whisky.

Gerald explains three times that Jones may be fatally wounded before Ewing Young details a group to search for him. Smith, LeDuc, and Pattie head reluctantly into the brush while the others wait out the next three days, desultorily repairing traps and other gear, and speaking of anything but the events in the clearing.

When the three men return, they report that they followed Jones up and then across the river, across the dry hills, and through a break in the canyon walls. Then the tracks disappeared. Although there's little cover in the rock-and-sand terrain above the canyon, they didn't spot Jones or see any sign of a body.

"Probably holed up somewhere to die," Thomas Smith says with a shrug. He nods at Gerald. "Serves the bastard right."

Ewing Young frowns. Regardless of the man's character, Young is still responsible for him and it irks him to not know for certain what's happened to him.

"That's some knife arm you got there," James Pattie says to Gerald. He shakes his head and glances at Gregorio. "It must of felt good to finally shut that man's mouth."

"We're gonna hafta give him more opportunities with the Injuns," Smith jokes.

Gerald smiles thinly and looks away. He's cleaned his knife blade a good half-dozen times, but it and his hands still feel unclean. He wonders what his father would think about the use he's put the knife to.

He studies his fellow trappers. Only Young seems concerned that they haven't located Jones or know what's happened to him. Is this the way of these men? Are their trapping partners as expendable as the natives? Their attitude sheds a new light on their lack of interest in his own status. Is it possible that they don't care about the color of his skin simply because they don't care about him? He stirs uneasily.

"Griz'll get him," George Yount suggests.

"Too tough t' eat," Thomas Smith snorts.

Gerald grins in spite of himself. Too poisonous to eat, is more like it. And yet—. He shakes his head. Jones is an insatiable bastard, but he's still a human being. It doesn't seem right to leave him or his dead body alone in the wilderness. And Gerald's hands still shake slightly when he remembers the way the man's chest gave under his knife blade, the gush of hot blood. His stomach twists and he flattens his hands against the piece of cottonwood log he's sitting on, pressing them down on the soft gray wood. He gazes into the fire.

Inexplicably, his thoughts turn to Suzanna Peabody. What would she think about the trappers' indifference to Jones' fate? And how will she feel when she learns Gerald has killed him? Will she think his actions were justified? Not that she'll ever know the worst of what Jones did, the reason for the fight in the first place. Not from Gerald's lips.

And Gregorio won't tell her. Even these hard-boiled trappers are unlikely to speak of such things in the Peabody's parlor. She's safe from the worst of it. She'll only know about the man's attempt to force a kiss from herself. And that certainly won't justify a knife fight. Or a death.

Gerald shrinks away from the thought of those black eyes directed angrily at him and resolutely turns his mind to the hunting of beaver. They'll be back on the Gila soon, and moving down it toward the Sonora's Red River, what the Mexicans calls the Colorado. That's where Ewing Young believes they'll do most of what he calls their 'real business'—trapping the furry banknotes that will recoup the expedition's expenses and make some money besides.

Young seems to have put Jones's almost-certain death behind him. Gerald wishes he could do so that easily. Maybe trapping will help. It's an exhausting business, but he was relieved to get back to work after the Papago fight, and it'll be a relief to get back to work yet again. This time, Jones and his crudities won't be shadowing the campfire. Though the big dirty-blond man shadows Gerald's dreams now in a way he never did before the altercation in the clearing.

Yet, if Jones is truly dead, he won't be in Taos again, shadowing Suzanna Peabody's footsteps. The thought produces a guilty lightness in Gerald's chest. He shakes his head. It's a strange mix of emotions.

A sense of relief beside a deep guilt at feeling relieved. And guilt that he stabbed the man. Surely there was another way to deal with Jones' animosity toward Gregorio and himself. Though Gerald can't think what he could have done differently.

Gregorio himself has grown quiet and avoids Gerald's eyes when he distributes the food at mealtimes. Is he also suffering from guilt? Or shame that he wasn't able to handle Jones on his own? Gerald shakes his head and lifts himself off the old cottonwood log. They'll be moving out tomorrow and he needs to reorganize his possibles sack.

CHAPTER 21

"My cousin Antonia told me a story yesterday that I think you will find of great interest," Encarnación says as she stirs the mixture of milk and sugar in the pot on the wood stove. Spring sunlight pours through the window, whose wooden shutters are thrown back to allow air into the room. The wooden grate in the window opening casts a shadowy grid on the opposite wall.

"What story is that?" Suzanna asks absently. She shakes the container of black tea leaves, then pries off the lid and peers inside. There's less here than she'd thought. Prices are so high right now. Perhaps she should switch to strawberry leaf or rosehip tea.

She looks up at the cook. Encarnación has set the hot pan on the wooden table top to cool, and is separating the yolks and whites of six brown-speckled eggs. "What did Antonia tell you?" Suzanna asks.

Encarnación twists her face in disgust. "That man, that Jones." She moves to the stove. "Here, can you add the yolks to the milk and stir it? Slowly now, and steadily."

Suzanna places the canister on the table and moves to the stove as Encarnación begins beating egg whites as if they were Jones himself. "Ugh. I can hardly speak of it," she says.

"Now you must tell me!" Suzanna says. "What happened?"

Encarnación's hands slow a little. "You know how it is with Antonia's casa, how it's out of sight of all of the others." She shakes her head and peers at the egg whites, which are frothing nicely. "That man came to her house in the spring, while Gregorio was at the market, and he tried to attack her." Her head jerks up. "Do you still have that knife I gave you?"

Involuntarily, Suzanna glances at the door to check for her father, then nods. "He attacked Antonia Garcia?" she asks. "And she said nothing?"

Encarnación sets the bowl of egg whites down, moves to the stove, and takes the spoon from Suzanna. She moves it carefully through the custard, scraping along the edge of the pan. "He tried to attack her," she says grimly. Then she grins and glances slyly at Suzanna. "He was unable to accomplish his task."

Suzanna steps away from the stove. "He was unable?"

"That's what she told me." Encarnación chortles. "It would seem that el amador potente is not all its owner would prefer."

"Oh, my goodness!" Suzanna moves to the table. Her hand drops to the tea canister. "So perhaps he's not as dangerous as we think."

Encarnación frowns. "Perhaps." She leans toward the pan, studying the thickening mixture, then moves to the table for the egg whites. "Or perhaps el amador springs to attention only for others of his kind." She shakes her head and glances at the girl. "Certainly I would continue to carry el cuchilitto. And ask Ramón to accompany you on your errands."

Footsteps scuff the hard-packed clay floor at the other end of the hall and the two women exchange a mute nod.

"That Jones!" Encarnación says, a little more loudly than necessary. "But if I think of him further, I will curdle les natillas."

"Oh, Chonita!" Suzanna laughs and turns to place the tea canister back on its shelf. "That would be a shame!" She grins mischievously. "You should think of Ramón Chavez instead!"

177

The cook gives her a half-amused look as she moves the pan to the side of the stove.

Jeremiah Peabody appears in the doorway and Suzanna abruptly changes her tone. "Where did you store the dried strawberry leaves?" she asks. "I think I'm going to start drinking that for tea, instead of the black. This February cold has begun to make my chest feel a little constricted."

Encarnación begins to spoon the frothy egg whites into the hot pan. She nods toward the wall by the window. "It's in the alacena."

Suzanna moves to the wooden cupboard set into the adobe wall as her father moves across the room toward Encarnación. "Custard?" he asks with a pleased look.

"The hens have begun laying again," Encarnación tells him. "It's a way to use the extra eggs."

"It is also a most excellent way to welcome the spring," he says. He turns to Suzanna. "Are you ready for your Latin lesson, my dear?" He frowns. "Unless you are tired? Did you say your chest is constricted?" He glances at the open shutters. "Is that window too drafty?" He turns to Encarnación. "Perhaps we should install mica in this one as well."

Encarnación scowls and Suzanna chuckles. Her father and the cook have this discussion every few months. She knows Encarnación's opinion. "Oh, it's not truly uncomfortable, papá," the girl says easily. "The strawberry is merely a preventative. It will make a nice change."

He peers into her face, humphs, and leaves the room. The two women smile at each other companionably. Encarnación turns back to her natillas as Suzanna locates the dried strawberry leaf among the other herbs in the wall cupboard.

NOT JUST ANY MAN

CHAPTER 22

Those among Ewing Young's men who've tasted Encarnación's custard think of it longingly as they trap down the Gila. Game is scarce and even the fish are wary of these men who invade the beaver ponds. The trappers' diet has shrunk to beaver carcasses and the little corn they can trade at the occasional Papago village, villages which are warily courteous to the foreigners.

The monotony of beaver and occasional corn stew is wearing. Gerald finds himself thinking wistfully of white flour biscuits and black tea. And narrow brown hands holding out a small china plate— But he stops himself. He has no right. He busies himself mending traps and creating willow frames for the pelts he collects every morning.

Young's party is ten days on the Gila before it reaches the Colorado River. Here their diet expands to include beans traded with the Uma Indians. Then the trappers turn north, up the Colorado. They begin to see cultivated fields again, planted by Indians that Ewing Young says are called 'Mojave' and James Pattie insists are the Maracopper. What matters to Gerald is that, although it's still only late February, the squash plants in the fields are already well up and looking remarkably healthy.

There's no apparent design to the way the squash is planted, except that each hillock lies on the edge of layers of silt still moist from the river's spring flood. It's a very different farming pattern from the irrigation ditches among the Papago fields on the Gila, or the ones at Los Chavez.

The fields expand as the Americans move upstream. In startling contrast to the flat lands along the Gila, brown as far as the eye could see, the Colorado's valley is a swath of green bounded by high stony bluffs that block a man's view of anything but the river and its valley. Dense thickets of cane and arrow weed line the river banks, and beaver lodges bulk from its sides. As the expedition's fur take increases, the trappers' pace slows. There's beaver enough here to last them a good while.

It's a pleasure to work and rest here. Gnarled cottonwoods cluster wherever the ground is slightly raised. Under the trees, the grass is thick and green. The mules and horses bend toward it eagerly.

But then it begins to rain, and the reason for the river's width and the lush growth beside it becomes clear. The rain here isn't like New Mexico's: a half day of moisture, then sun again, sparkling on a newly-cleansed world. On the spring-time Colorado, the rain comes hard and solid, a steady downpour that lasts all day, then into the next, and the next after that.

The trappers sit gloomily under makeshift tents of heavy canvas that they've had no use for until now. They huddle the tents as close as possible over the cooking fires, trying to protect the flames from the rain while also making sure the canvas doesn't catch fire. Gerald hunkers down with Thomas Smith and Maurice LeDuc under a square piece of tenting strung between two young cottonwoods.

On the third afternoon, the rain begins to ease. As the clouds pull back, a band of half-naked Indians appears among the trees, red, white, and black designs painted on their chest.

Thomas Smith mutters "Shit!" and cocks his rifle as Gerald reaches for his pistol.

Then Ewing Young emerges from his own shelter. He waves impatiently at the weapons. "They're friendlies," Young says. He gives Smith a sharp look. "Unless you're fool enough to start shootin'."

Smith lowers his gun, his eyes narrow. "I ain't never seen a friendly Injun that couldn't turn unfriendly in a blink," he says.

But Young's eyes are on the Mojave leader moving toward him, his black-tattooed chin jutting belligerently.

"Pee-Posh," the man says. He touches his black-striped chest, then makes a sweeping gesture toward the men behind him. Then his hand sweeps toward Young and his trappers. "Americano?"

Young nods, then they move into sign language. Smith leans toward Gerald. "They're all named Peeposh," he chuckles. "And they've all got tattoos on their chins like true savages."

Gerald smiles, watching Young at his work. His hands move so swiftly Gerald has trouble understanding what he's saying. But then one of the Indian men moves forward carrying a basket and he understands. This is a trading mission.

When it's over, the trappers have two baskets of beans and more of the everlasting corn, and the Indians have red strips of cloth and eight skinned beaver carcasses.

But the Mojave don't leave. The rain has finally drizzled to a stop and the sun is out. Gerald stands under a cottonwood and watches as, thirty feet away, the Indians dig several large holes in the ground, build fires in them, then add the gutted beaver. They cover the holes with dirt, leaving small apertures for the smoke. It's a kind of pig roast, he realizes. Only with beaver.

By some mysterious process Gerald can't ascertain, the Indians seem to know when the meat is ready. He watches as they claw the dirt aside, scrape the burnt crust off the meat, and proceed to feast.

Ignacio comes to stand beside Gerald. "It is like our matanza," he says. "Although we might cook a sheep or a goat." He chuckles. "I wonder what mi mamá would say to beaver. Or whether mi papá would be willing to eat it." He shakes his head. "He is doubtful of the ways of the trapper. He says los americanos break the law for the joy of it."

Gerald frowns. "What law are we breaking?"

"Not you, señor." Ignacio glances over his shoulder. "It is Señor Young with whom he is concerned. He believes el señor does not deal honestly with our officials."

Gerald looks at Ignacio, who continues to watch the Indians eat, their long black hair kept carefully away from their faces and food. "Does he have reason for his distrust?" Gerald asks.

Ignacio shrugs. "There have been incidents," he says reluctantly. He glances at Gerald, then turns away. "I'm sure it is nothing."

The Indians hang close for the next two days, eagerly accepting more beaver to roast. There's plenty, as the traps yield thirty plews the first night, then another twenty. On the third day, the catch has dropped to ten and Young announces that it's time to move out. The Indians drift away, presumably back to their village, and the trappers head upstream.

As far as Gerald can tell, the village the trappers come across three days later doesn't belong to the men they traded with. The hamlet consists of two rows of brush and thatch huts. The trappers and their mules proceed between them. Tall woven baskets stand on low stilts beside the buildings, their contents protected by woven lids. Naked children and bare-breasted women with tattooed chins peek from behind the baskets and from inside the huts. There's no sign of the men.

The trappers establish camp under a cluster of giant cottonwoods three miles north of the village and within a stone's throw of the river. There's a break in the thickets of cane and arrow weed, so they can get to the water easily, and a grazing meadow that surrounds the other three sides of the cottonwood grove.

Ignacio and the other camp keepers are just starting the evening meal when a group of Mojave men appear. Although their women had been timid, the men hold themselves proudly and look the Americans in the face. They're dressed in breech clouts of woven strands of wood and the same paint as the Mojaves the trappers had traded with downriver.

Their leader is a thick-set man with a broad forehead and a black design tattooed on his chin and red and black stripes painted on his chest. His eyes are narrowed from years of sun glare. A bow and a quiver of arrows hang from his naked back.

He seems unconcerned about the language barrier. Even though Young has a rifle in his hands, the man confronts Young confidently. He points toward the river, then himself, the packs of furs, then himself again. Then he waves his hand at Young's men, ranged around the camp fire, and shakes his head. He makes a dismissive gesture.

Gerald frowns. The man seems to be saying it's his river, not theirs, and what comes from this river is his as well. He has a point. It is his land—his peoples', anyway.

The Chief points at the mules and horses grazing nearby, then makes a scooping motion toward his chest.

Young's eyes darken. "I ain't givin' you a horse," he growls.

There's no need to shake his head in denial. The Mojave understands. He frowns, points toward the river again, then himself. Then he gestures at the horses and makes another scooping gesture.

183

He holds up a forefinger, then repeats the entire set of motions: the river, himself, the horses, the scoop.

"He just wants the one," James Pattie says.

"And then he'll want more," Thomas Smith says. He turns and spits. "And more after that! You gonna give him your daddy's mare?"

"Ain't mine to give!" Pattie protests.

But Ewing Young and the Mojave ignore the side play. They face each other like two men about to duel, eyes steady, jaws set. Suddenly, the Chief's hands move again, this time over his shoulder to the bow and arrows. In one fluid movement, there's an arrow pointing at Young's chest. The Mojave grins, almost playfully.

Thomas Smith's rifle clicks. The Chief gives no notice he's heard. He lifts the bow slightly and releases his arrow up over Young's head, where it lodges solidly in the trunk of a big cottonwood.

Young turns and lifts his gun. A shot rings out and the arrow's shaft breaks apart, the end tumbling to the ground. There's a long silence, then the Chief nods and turns. His men follow him out of the grove.

The trappers watch them go. "That ain't the last of him," Thomas Smith says.

Young studies the arrowhead still stuck in the tree. He nods grimly. "There'll be no trap setting tonight," he announces. He turns and considers the campsite and the area between it and the river. "With the river behind us and the grassland on the other side of the trees, I suppose this is as good a place as any. And there's plenty of deadfall." He turns back to his men. "It's time to fort up."

Trappers and camp keepers work side by side to pull deadwood and branches into position on the three sides of the tree-shaded camp not protected by the river. They herd the unwilling animals inside, then go back to work on the waist-high bulwark, reinforcing it with the packs of beaver pelts.

It's dusk before they finish. They eat a cold meal, then settle down for the night. Young orders a double guard: two men on each side of the enclosure, one along the river, two-hour shifts, no smoking or talking. For once, no one complains.

No one sleeps much either. The horses and mules move restlessly as the guards pace inside their sections of the bulwark. Gerald lies with his eyes open, staring into a moonless sky, trying not to think about why the Indians will attack in the morning. The Chief's request seems such a trivial thing. And such a fair one.

Young's stubborn response, and the other trappers' apparent agreement with him, makes Gerald wonder what really happened between Robidoux's party and the Papago villagers. What triggered that initial attack? What small thing resulted in the death of all those men? He stares up at the sky. Even the stars seem dimmer than usual.

He doses off, then a mule snorts and he's awake again, staring into the night. The waiting seems more painful than an attack could ever be. He knows this thought is nonsense. Yet time drags unnervingly in the unmoving blackness. Only the changes in guard mark its passing.

His own duty comes just as the sky begins to lighten and he's finally drifted into a semi-sleep. Suddenly George Yount is shaking his shoulder and muttering, "Your time!" in his nasal Pennsylvania Dutch accent.

Gerald sits up sharply and his skull connects with Yount's with a dull thud. The big man jerks back and glares at him, then breaks into a grin. "Didn't think you was asleep, did ya?" he asks.

Gerald grins sheepishly and shakes his head.

Yount rubs his forehead. "That is one hard skull you got," he says.

185

Gerald chuckles. "So my daddy says." Smith, lying nearby, raises his head and growls wordlessly, and Gerald lowers his voice. "Which section?"

Yount gestures toward the center, facing the meadow, and Gerald nods, reaches for his rifle, and heads toward the wall of wood and beaver pelts.

It will be a beautiful day. He peers over the bulwark at the silent grass. Dew has collected on its long slender blades. The moisture glitters in the rising light, then evaporates as he watches. To his left, Michel Robidoux leads a small group of hobbled horses through the break between the fort and river and stations them to graze on the south side of the improvised wall.

Gerald glances at the trees overhead. A light breeze moves their leaves, setting up a small, joyful sound. The peacefulness of the morning is at odds with the tension of the night. He takes a deep breath.

As he lets it out, a man on horseback appears at the top of a small rise on the other side of the meadow. Gerald stiffens. It's the Mojave Chief, a spear in his hand, a small collection of men on foot behind him.

Gerald opens his mouth, but Thomas Smith's voice overrides his. "We've got company!"

Smith is beside Gerald before Ewing Young reaches the bulwark. Smith braces his rifle barrel on a convenient notch in the uppermost log and sights on the Chief. Then Young steps forward and pushes the barrel up and away. Smith scowls.

"Don't go giving them any provocation," Young says.

Smith mutters an imprecation Gerald can't hear, but Young ignores him. He glances at Gerald. "Yours, too," he says.

Gerald glances down. His rifle is also angled toward the oncoming men. He lowers the barrel and glances behind him. Trappers are scattered in small knots across the impromptu fort's interior, all of them casually holding a loaded firearm as they appear not to watch the Mojave warriors. Only Young gazes straight at the Chief and his clutch of men as they move toward the American encampment.

When they're close enough for conversation, the Chief reins in and begins making the same gestures he'd made the day before. He waves a hand at the grazing horses, still grazing outside the makeshift fort.

Young glances at the animals and scowls. He lifts his chin at the Chief. "I told you 'no'!" he shouts. Then he raises his rifle barrel toward the sky. It roars defiantly.

The Chief's mount stirs anxiously and the man's eyes narrow until they're mere black slits. His horse wheels, circling toward the grazing animals, and the Chief lifts his spear. As its point bites into the nearest horse's side, the trappers' rifles speak from the bulwark. The Chief tumbles from his mount. Two warriors gallop forward and gather him up. Then the Mojaves move off. Rifle fire follows them as they disappear over the rise.

"Any bets on how long it'll take 'em to try it again?" Milt Sublette asks.

"I'm thinkin' an hour or two," Thomas Smith says. "They'll need to sort out who's gonna lead 'em the second time around."

"I'm betting it'll be longer than that," Sublette says. "They'll wanta dance a little and work their dander up."

George Yount turns toward the opening by the river. "We must bring in the horses and tend to the wounded one."

Ewing Young paces along the front of the bulwark, pushing branches into place, shoving fur packs more tightly into the gaps. "Yes, bring them in," he says. "Then move them as close as you can

187

toward the water, out of the way." He tilts his head and looks up at the tops of the cottonwoods. "Garcia, you and Sandoval climb up into the branches there—" He points to a gnarled tree just inside the fort's right hand wall. "And there—" He points to a slightly smaller tree on the left. "Keep your eyes peeled and let out a holler as soon as you see them red devils comin' back."

The two young men nod and scramble into the trees. Then nothing happens. Young keeps them up there most of the day, spelled by Gerald and James Pattie when there's food to be prepared and distributed.

The meal is stark, but no one besides Thomas Smith thinks fire is a good idea. He wants his coffee. There's been none since the previous morning. No one pays much attention to his grumbling. They're all too busy watching for the warriors who don't come.

Darkness falls and the rain starts up again. Putting up any kind of shelter against the downpour will reduce the trappers' ability to monitor any activity outside the bulwark walls. Even Thomas Smith doesn't suggest it.

Instead, they sit in disconsolate huddles inside the makeshift fort, pieces of blanket, tent, or buckskin draped over their heads and shoulders, and try to catch a little sleep. Even guard duty is better than sitting in the mud. By the time the rain has stopped, the ground's a muck-ridden mess.

They're all stiff and cold in the morning, but the rain has stopped. As the trappers stretch themselves awake and beat warmth into their arms and legs, the Mojaves appear at the top of the rise, just out of rifle fire range. The dull thud of a drum reverberates across the meadow, setting up a steady heart beat, then the warriors begin a shuffling dance, occasionally moving to one side to shoot a challenging arrow toward the fort. The arrows bite the ground well short of the bulwark, but the message is clear. We're coming.

"Just limberin' up," Smith observes laconically. "'Fraid to get closer, I guess."

"Unusual for Mojaves," Ewing Young says. He strokes his chin. "As a general rule, they like surprise attacks. But I'm guessing they'll be massing up shortly." He turns to Gregorio. "Shimmy on up that tree again and see if you can spot anything beyond that bit of hill they're dancin' on."

The camp keeper scrambles up the nearest cottonwood and cranes his neck. "There is nothing, señor," he calls down. He gestures toward the Indians. "There are no more than what you see."

Young nods thoughtfully, studying the rise. He turns to ask another question, but the warriors have spied movement in the tree. As Gregorio begins clambering down, they group together and move forward, their taunts filing the air.

Smith rushes past Young to the bulwark. "Alrighty boys!" Smith yells. "Have at 'em!"

Young scowls but doesn't contradict the order. He moves to one side and checks his primer, then nods at Gerald. "Are you ready?" he asks.

Gerald nods grimly. Personally, he would have given the Chief a horse. Even two. It is his people's river, after all. But it's too late now for second guessing. He double checks his load and braces the rifle barrel in a branch that protrudes from the bulwark.

The trappers' first volley stops the warriors in their tracks. Two Mojaves warriors go down and another staggers and grabs at his right shoulder. The rest dash to their fallen men, grab them up, then turn and flee toward the village.

Thomas Smith scrambles over the bulwark wall and races after the fleeing warriors, LeDuc and Yount close behind him. Ewing Young watches them dispassionately, then turns to the remaining men. "All right, let's pack up and head out," he says. "It's just not profitable to waste time arguin' with a bunch of savages. They've learned their lesson. And there's not enough beaver left along here to make battling them worth our while, anyway."

And with two men dead and another injured, the Mojaves are likely to return, looking for vengeance, Gerald reflects as he helps disentangle the packs of beaver pelts from the fort's improvised walls. Young is wise to move on. But Gerald is careful to keep his expression blank. After all, Young is the man paying the bills. He notices that when Smith and the others return, they don't object to the move either.

CHAPTER 23

The trappers march steadily up the Colorado, covering as much ground as possible, not stopping to trap. Each night, they raise a rough barricade around their fireless camp and post a two man, two hour watch. There's plenty of beaver sign and Thomas Smith complains that they're wasting good territory, but Young pushes everyone forward. Even the animals feel the impact of long days crossing unfamiliar ground. They stamp and nip impatiently as the camp keepers load them each morning.

To top it off, the rain starts up again: a steady drizzle more disheartening than any solid downpour with a defined beginning and end. Gerald feels as if he's moving in an drearily endless nightmare of wet clothes, slippery mud, cranky mules, and anxious men.

On the fourth night, the rain stops and the mood lightens. Young seems to think the worst of the danger is past and allows the camp keepers three small fires for the evening meal. He details Thomas Smith for the first watch, and he and the others wrap themselves in their still-damp blankets and lay down beside the smoldering flames.

It's full dark, and Gerald has been asleep perhaps two hours, rolled into his blankets just beyond Young and the camp fires, when the arrows come pouring in. They thud heavily into the wet ground.

"What the hell?" Ewing Young exclaims. He rolls from his blankets, bumping up against Gerald's legs as Gerald sits up and reaches for his gun. "Get down!" Young barks and Gerald drops, his hands clutching the rifle's smooth stock. "Won't do you any good!" Young says. He half rises, peering into the night. "Use your knife!"

Gerald fumbles at his waist and sits up. Crab-like, he moves toward Young and crouches beside him.

"Douse those fires!" Young barks. Blankets fling up and out, covering what's left of the flames. But it's too late. The damage has been done. As the light dies, the Indians disappear into the night.

The trappers rise cautiously and look around the clearing, trying to assess the damage by the dim light of a clouded moon.

"Get me outta here!" James Pattie gasps. He's still in his blanket. Smith moves closer to examine him. He chuckles and shakes his head. Arrows project from the ground on either side of the younger man, pinning his wool trade blanket in place. Pattie looks back at Smith in terror. "I can't move!" he says. "I'm paralyzed!"

"You ain't hurt." Smith reaches down and yanks on one shaft, then another. The fire-hardened wooden points pull smoothly out of the wool and Smith kicks the blanket aside. "Come on out of there," he says. "You're all right. Those arrows don't even have a real point on 'em." He turns and tosses them to the ground.

"Pointed enough to do damage if they hit you," Maurice LeDuc says, looking down at the man who'd been lying next to Pattie. "This one is gone."

"And this one," George Yount says from the other side of the clearing.

"And I got hit," Milton Sublette says, his voice coming from the darkness on Gerald's right. Gerald turns to see Sublette holding the fleshy part of his upper left arm, blood oozing from his bicep.

"First the right leg, then the left arm," Young says. "Next time, it'll be your head if you're not careful."

Sublette scowls and looks at Smith. "Do you think you can fix this one up better'n you did my leg?"

Smith humphs, leans his rifle against a tree stump, and turns to find his pack. "Only thing wrong with your leg is your head. You should of let that Mexican woman medicine it."

"I ain't lettin' no witch woman doctor me," Sublette says sourly. "You gonna bind this up, or not?"

Maurice LeDuc appears at Smith's elbow and mutters something in his ear. Smith drops his pack and turns on Young. "Dammit, they got my horse!" he shouts.

Young raises his hand. "Quiet now," he says. "They may still be out there."

Smith pays him no heed. "Damned thieving coyotes! Sneaking cowards!" He reaches for his rifle and starts across the clearing. "I'm goin' after 'em." He turns to glare at Young. "I don't care what you say! Those Injuns need a lesson they won't forget!"

Ewing Young looks at the two dead men, then the wounded Sublette. "Wait until morning," he says. "Then we'll cut out after them."

Smith and a dozen of the others ride out at first light, Gerald among them, James Patty on his father's sorrel mare. Gerald can't say why he accompanies the posse. Some atavistic desire to see the thing through, he supposes. Blood's been shed. Or perhaps it's simply that, after four days of fighting and waiting, waiting and fighting, he's tired of living in fear and wants to put an end to at least this particular threat.

He realizes guiltily that he wants the sense of relief that he felt after the fight with Jones. A release of the tension, no matter the cost. He grimaces. He's no better than the men on either side of him, who

193

are urging their mounts forward so eagerly. He's just a man like any other man. In this case, he's not sure that he likes the idea very much.

It's just dusk when they find the Mojave camp. It seems that Thomas Smith has a nose for Indians. Or at least the smell of broiled horseflesh on the early evening breeze. Sweet but with an overlay of charcoaled bitterness. Smith reins in at the top of a small hill and nods grimly to the left and a cluster of cottonwoods beside a small stream that empties into the river beyond.

Smith reaches for his rifle and checks the primer as the other men draw up beside him. Gerald cranes his neck to peer past LeDuc's shoulder. A group of bare-chested Mojave men cluster around a campfire beneath the gnarled cottonwoods. As the trappers watch, there's a hoarse exclamation from the branches of one of the trees. The warriors turn in unison toward the hill, strung bows materializing in their hands.

"Arrows!" Smith says contemptuously. He heels his horse and charges down the slope, his rifle blasting as he goes. The young warrior in the cottonwood tumbles out of its branches and the other Indians break for cover as the rest of the trappers follow.

Gerald pauses long enough to check his powder, then urges his horse forward, weapon at the ready. But by the time he reaches the thicket of streamside willow where the Indians have turned to make their stand, his rifle is only a distraction. There's no room here for arrows or gunfire. Knives and spears are the weapons of choice and both sides use them fiercely, the mounted trappers leaning forward and jabbing downward, the Mojaves sidestepping the blood-wild horses while maneuvering for a spear thrust that will silence them or their riders.

Gerald's horse shies from a thrusting spear and Gerald leaps off, letting him run. Then a warrior rushes him. The Mojave's tattooed face and the red strip of cloth binding his hair are spotted with blood and his eyes are mere slits of fury. He raises an arm, swinging a two-foot-long wooden club. Gerald ducks and swings his rifle.

The rifle butt hits the warrior broadside in the chest and the man falls into the dirt. Gerald straddles him, flips the gun into position, and fires. The bullet explodes into the man's chest, but Gerald doesn't stay to inspect the damage. He leaps away, every sense heightened, braced for the next onslaught.

But there is no onslaught. The fight is over and the other trappers are already celebrating. Pattie and two other men prance in a mock war dance between dead and dying Mojave warriors. The normally phlegmatic LeDuc has his trousers down, his urine spraying triumphantly. "Iiiiiiyee!" he yells.

Gerald winces and looks away only to see Thomas Smith looping a lariat around the neck of a Mojave who's attempted to escape. A section of spear projects from the man's back, apparently wrested from one of his fellow warriors and used against him. The three feathers on the end of the spear wave jauntily as Smith yanks the man toward one of the cottonwoods.

Smith tosses the loose end of his lariat over a thick branch and begins pulling the Mojave inexorably to his doom. The warrior closes his eyes for a brief moment, then his jaws lock stubbornly. Gerald feels a twinge of sympathy and respect.

Milton Sublette moves toward Smith, waving a long black scalp and dragging the body it came from by one leg. "Here's another one!" he says.

Smith grins and nods. "That'll show 'em what happens when they attack white men!" In his distraction, he pauses in his work. The Mojave man's feet are still on the ground and he gives a sudden twist, trying to slip out of the rope. A rifle blasts, and the man crumples.

Smith nods at LeDuc. "Fast thinking!" he says. He kicks at the warrior, assuring that he's truly dead, then turns and looks around for more. "Hey Pattie! Bring that one, too!"

Bile rises in Gerald's throat. He moves away, toward the hill. The animals are clustered behind it, milling anxiously. He finds his horse and starts to lead it away, but finds himself drawn to the hilltop.

Six warriors dangle from the cottonwoods. Except for the man Sublette scalped, the warriors' long lustrous black hair splays awkwardly over their shoulders, canted to one side by their broken necks. Under the trees, Smith slaps Maurice LeDuc on the shoulder, as if congratulating him on a job well done. Gerald's throat fills with bile as he turns away and mounts his horse.

~ ~ ~ ~

While the fight with the Mojaves leaves Gerald feeling sick, the other trappers seem filled with a strange exhilaration. They move up the Colorado in a whirl of hunting, albeit mountain sheep and deer rather than beaver. In fact, they feel so powerful, they become magnanimous, leaving the few Indians they encounter at little risk of the indignities they inflicted on the Mojave.

Still, Gerald braces himself for trouble each time he sees a native hut and feels a surge of relief when the encounter is over. He wonders how long the magnanimity will last. Hardly any pelts have been added to the packs since the trappers' first interactions with the Mojave, and beaver are thin along this part of the Colorado. There isn't much overt grumbling, but there is a sense that things could be better.

Smith, of course, is more free with his opinions than the others. He blames first the Indians and then Ewing Young. From his perspective,

Young wasn't firm enough in the first place and, in the second place, the route Young has chosen is just plain stupid.

His comments are particularly strong on mornings when he's found only one beaver in his six-trap set. He's so disgusted that he's started muttering that he'd just as soon give up trapping altogether and head on back to the settlements by way of the Zuni. They apparently have some good looking gals there that would ease at least some of his frustration.

Maurice LeDuc chuckles at Smith's more colorful grumbling and adds comments of his own, but Young ignores them both. Young's lack of response seems to goad Smith and, as the trappers move up river, he and LeDuc begin spending more time apart from the others, occasionally pulling in Pattie, Solomon Stone, and even Ignacio.

They make no effort to lower their voices. "East," and "Zuni villages," and "more beaver" drift to the others around the fires. Young remains aloof. After all, Smith and LeDuc are free trappers. They can do and say what they like. Only the camp keeper is under contract and Young seems confident that Ignacio will remain with him.

Gerald watches the friction uneasily. The larger the band, the more secure it is and the more likely to produce a favorable beaver harvest. And Ignacio's contract with Young is as binding as his own. Will the boy break it and become known as a man who doesn't keep his word?

But it's none of Gerald's business and he turns to his own work. He oils his traps, considers the kinds of crops that might grow in nuevomexico, and lets himself wonder what Suzanna Peabody might be doing at this particular moment.

In spite of his concern about Ignacio, Gerald feels a sense of relief the night Smith and LeDuc announce that they're pulling out the next morning, along with Solomon Stone and Alexander Branch.

Young looks at Pattie. "You and that horse of your daddy's goin', too?"

Pattie hesitates, then shakes his head and runs his hand through his curly blond hair. "I'll be staying along with you, if that's all right," he says meekly. Young nods brusquely, then turns toward Ignacio.

"I made a contract, señor," Ignacio says stiffly. He looks away. "I will honor it."

"I should hope so," Young says. As the Captain turns back to Smith, Ignacio's face darkens. He moves stiffly toward the food.

Gerald frowns. What is it about Young that the boy dislikes so thoroughly?

CHAPTER 24

Suzanna looks up from her novel and rubs her eyes. Although the mica filters the winter light, there's enough to read by if she sits on the adobe window seat. Yet her eyes are tired. She closes them, then glances at the door. Her father is going to appear any minute now and ask why she's not at the table, where her Latin grammar lies unattended.

If she tells him she can't concentrate, he's going to want to know why. He'll probably decide that she's been drinking the strawberry leaf tea because she's unwell, and then banish her to bed.

She shudders. Inactivity in bed is the last thing she needs. Lack of exercise is probably the real reason she's so restless. It's been an exceptionally cold winter and she hasn't been outside in a week. She leans closer to the window. The dim light may be adequate for reading, but she craves sunshine as if it were a food.

Her mind strays to Young's trappers somewhere far to the west, where she's been told its warm even in winter, where there's no lack of sunshine. She sighs. That would be nice. To walk forever across the landscape, soaking in the light, moving in time with the long strides of her companion— She catches herself and her lips twitch. And who would that companion be? A stride equal to hers, gray eyes in a brown face, smiling at her in bemusement. His sturdy square hands—

Suzanna feels herself flush and she leans her face against the cool milky panes of the window. She wishes winter was over, that there's some way to hear from the men in the field. They've been gone such a long time. The waiting is so difficult. Especially when she has nothing to occupy herself. Nothing except Latin and novels.

Then she hears her father's step in the hallway. She rises abruptly and goes to the fire. The flames will be reason enough for the heat on her cheeks. She takes a deep breath and turns to face the door as it opens.

He glances at the book in her hand. "Miss Rowson?" he says in mild surprise. "Is the Latin not engaging enough for you this morning, my dear?"

She drops her eyes. "I stumbled on the grammar and need your assistance, papá," she says. As she goes to the table and lifts the Latin text, he watches her in bemusement, but his face is studiously blank when she turns back to him with the book in her hand.

CHAPTER 25

The reduction in Ewing Young's forces shifts his group's momentum once again. A smaller party makes better time and there's more beaver to divide between the remaining men. Although there still aren't many beaver overall. Milton Sublette shakes his head bitterly and Michel Robidoux looks anxious, but there's little real grumbling until the canyon of the Colorado becomes so deep that its shadowed sides keep parts of the river in almost perpetual darkness. Granite walls tower above it and allow little space for travel along the river. The water churns around massive rocks in the riverbed and the trappers can hear the sullen roar of rapids upstream.

The men's disquiet comes to a head the morning they wake to fog so thick they can't see their own feet, much less the top of the canyon. They're camped on the south bank, in a spot slightly wider than usual, where there's browse for the animals beside the river. The water runs a little more quietly here, because the channel is wider. The fog has dropped heavily in the night, reaching from one granite wall to the other.

As Gerald opens his eyes and blinks in confusion, Milton Sublette and George Yount rise simultaneously from their blankets on opposite sides of the fog-muted campfire. They loom out of the whiteness like two young giants, hair on end and rifles at the ready. Their heads turn wildly. "I can't see!" Sublette roars.

Overhead, a stone rumbles down an invisible slope. Then there's a crunching sound on the upstream bank. Sublette whirls and aims into the fog.

"Hold your fire!" Ewing Young snaps. A mule's head appears from the mist. Gerald, still in his blankets, suppresses a chuckle.

Sublette glares at Young. "How was I supposed to know?" He jerks his rifle barrel at the white dampness, which seems to be getting thicker by the minute. "Can't see a damn thing."

The figure of a man resolves itself from the fog, leading a mule with one hand and flailing the other as if trying to beat the mist into submission. It's Michel Robidoux.

"Could of been a Mojave," Sublette grumbles.

"That's why you need to hold your fire," Young says.

"And get killed!" Sublette snaps. But he lowers his rifle and turns away.

Robidoux moves to the fire. "Sacrebleu, it is impossible that we stay down here like this," he grumbles.

The normally taciturn Richard Campbell speaks from his blankets. "Ach, there's no beaver to speak of and it's lookin' like this canyon's only goin' to get deeper. We'll be forced to go up top soon enough."

"We need to get out now," Sublette says flatly.

Young's eyes narrow. "Who's leadin' this outfit?"

Sublette's chin lifts. "I'm a free trapper."

"Then go if you want to." Young jerks his head down river. "Go and find Smith and LeDuc and them. Head on out on your own and see how far you get, just you and your mule. At least Smith had some idea of where he was going."

"I ain't that kind of fool," Sublette growls. He turns to Robidoux. "Better watch goin' off on your own in this fog. It ain't likely you could find your way back."

Robidoux shrugs and waves a hand at the canyon walls. "That I could stray far is also unlikely," he says. "The canyon itself embraces us."

"That's for sure," Sublette grumbles.

"I suppose the canyon and the fog provide as much protection as they do danger," James Pattie says. He looks up, toward the invisible top of the mist-enshrouded granite walls. "No one up there can see us down here."

"We can't see them neither," Sublette says. "And there ain't no way out of here that I can see, except up." He glares at Young, inviting a response. "Unless we follow this damn river to its source, wherever that is. Whether there's any damn beaver on it or not." He turns away in disgust. "Some trappin' expedition this is turning out to be."

Young doesn't answer. He's staring up at the cliffs, first one side, then the other. The fog is slowly lifting away from the water and the canyon walls. The rock overhang here is so deep that he can't see more than fifty feet up. "I saw deer tracks last evening," he says thoughtfully.

Gerald is out of his blankets now, rolling them into a compact bundle. Young turns toward him. "Come have a look," he says. He turns and wades into the river, toward a shallow bar of gravel about a third of the way across.

Gerald follows him out of the shadow of the rock, fighting the current. The two men turn and look up, studying the face of the south cliff. The fog is dissipating rapidly now, though a few wisps still cling to the side of the cliff.

Young points at a seam in the rock face. "There, to the left of that crevice. Does that look to you like a path?"

Gerald examines the granite wall. "It does look like some kind of trail," he says. "Although it could drop off at that big boulder there on the right." His eyes swing left. Here and there, evergreens cling in impossible crevices. "What about there, by that cedar?"

Young studies the tree, then shakes his head. "If that's a trail, only a mountain goat could climb it to the top. It breaks down halfway up, by that big outcrop." He grimaces and nods downstream. "We passed what I'm looking for yesterday." He points again. "See there?"

Gerald's eyes track Young's arm. There's a shallow indentation in the almost-vertical rock, worn down by generations of game picking their way to the water below. The trace appears to extend to the top of the cliff. "That looks like it could work," he says doubtfully.

Young chuckles and pats Gerald's shoulder. "Only one way to find out," he says.

It's a hard climb, and dangerous. The horses roll their eyes as the men lead them upward and the pack mules balk and snort irritably when their loads scrape the granite cliff face. Gerald wants to balk himself, but the only other option is to remain beside the river. So he and the others coax the reluctant animals upward, into an unknown land.

When they finally negotiate the last twist in the narrow trail and scramble up and over the rim, they all stare in amazement. The land lies flat and wasted before them, the sun beating fiercely on scattered and dusty piñon and juniper scrub. Here and there, a single ponderosa breaks the monotony.

"Flatter'n hell and almost as hot," Sublette mutters. "What is this, March? I ain't never seen anything as bleak as this. Even that stretch of the Rio del Norte there north of Taos has more green to it." Then he turns and looks back at the canyon. "Now ain't that somethin'," he says.

204

The others turn to follow his gaze into the ever-widening yawn of the canyon of the Colorado. From this vantage, the river appears to wind through a whole set of canyons, great gashes in the earth, some with entire mountains rising from their base. They're mountains of sheer stone, jagged pyramids of rock, striped a muted red and dirty yellow, the only plant life an occasional tree that juts precariously from a stony cleft. The Colorado is lost in the depths of the maze and from here it's impossible to tell which north-running gash it might descend from. The tremendous chasms that slice the earth at their feet seem to go on forever. Gerald's mule snorts anxiously.

"Sacrebleu!" Robidoux swears.

"It is a grand sight," George Yount says reverently.

"Indeed," Richard Campbell says, a little grimly.

"This land up here may be wasted, but it's better than being down there," Sublette says.

Gerald feels himself shiver, in spite of the sun burning his shoulders. Who knows what might have laid in wait for them there?

But when he turns to face the landscape above the rim, another shiver runs through him.

The land here is not only flat and dry, with little cover, it holds no sign of recent rain. And, after the dim canyon, the bright March sun beats down mercilessly. He narrows his eyes against it and wishes for some of Old Bill's charcoal.

But the lack of water is the worst of it. Gerald touches his tongue to his already-parched lips, sets his jaw grimly, and follows Ewing Young east along the edge of the immensity, with only the creak of mule harness and his own bleak thoughts to occupy him. No one speaks.

The trappers follow the canyon rim for five days, husbanding the water in their canteens, moving north and east in a country scorchingly inhospitable by day, bleakly beautiful in the late afternoon light, when a small breeze makes itself felt, and well below freezing at night. The juniper and piñon are too widely spaced and hug the ground too low to provide any real shade or night shelter. Even the ponderosas seem inhospitable, too dusty for their long needles to sparkle in the sharp sun.

There's little to eat besides what the mules carry. The game that made the trail the trappers followed up the cliff side have made themselves scarce. But then, there's no browse here, to speak of. And no morning dew to freshen it, if there had been.

To their left, the canyon grows deeper, wider, then deeper still. Great crevices seem to appear out of nowhere at the trappers' feet, blocking their way forward, forcing them into circuitous routes that move the exhausted men farther south before they can proceed east again.

Gerald begins to feel as if the canyon is alive, is opening new cracks each freezing night in order to force them south into even hotter, dryer country and back to the Gila itself. At least there's water on the Gila, he thinks deliriously. Perhaps Jones is there. Perhaps this is his punishment for the man's death. They will meet here somewhere in this bleak land and their bones will mingle, killed and killer bleaching together in the sun.

Is there water in the afterlife? What he would give for just a touch of moisture on his lips. He looks enviously at the dusty trees. How do they survive in this dry land, this rocky soil? But then, they are evergreen. Nothing with a leaf could last long in this desert. And certainly nothing with blood in its veins. No wonder there was a game trail leading down the precipitous cliffs to the canyon. His carefully-husbanded canteen has been empty since yesterday morning and his tongue is swollen with thirst.

He tries to stop himself from biting it. The wet blood moistens his throat, but the biting only makes his tongue swell even more. But it's difficult to force himself to do anything more than move blindly forward in the dryness, the haze of dust kicked up by his fellow trappers and the animals they lead. Even the thought of Suzanna Peabody has dried up, a mere wisp of a concept burnt out by the beating sun, the heat that rises from the crusted soil under his feet, the dust coating his tongue. Only Jones remains, chuckling grimly.

He can see Jones' face in his mind, but not his companions. Only Jones' face and his own feet, moving numbly forward. The other trappers are also silently delirious, throats too dry to waste on mere words, their focus limited to the ground directly before them. Only Milton Sublette's eyes move, and then only toward Ewing Young, whom he glares at bitterly.

But Young has other things on his mind. Somehow he keeps them all heading in the same direction until, on the sixth day from their climb over the rim, they reach water again. Somehow, they've turned northeast and found their way down a gradual, rock-strewn slope into a canyon that's almost as spectacular as the one they've escaped from, but much wider and not nearly as deep. The tops of its red and yellow-striped walls are visible from the stream at its base.

The trappers hardly notice the canyon's side. They surge gleefully toward the water, then remember their animals. They approach cautiously, letting the gaunt horses and mules drink sparingly. They'll make themselves sick if they drink as much as they'd like.

They camp one day and two nights, letting the animals adjust enough to drink their fill. They don't dare stay longer. Now that they've all revived a little, the trappers see that the food supplies are astonishingly low. They bathe their dust-ridden heads, drink their own cautious fill, and reload their canteens, then head upriver. The canyon shallows steadily, but there's little browse and still no game to speak of. An occasional snare-caught rabbit is the only supplement to the remnants of flour the camp keepers scrape from the sides of the remaining barrel.

Gerald loses all sense of the number of passing days. Time is a blur of pain as he hobbles painfully forward. Each morning, he forces himself from a stone-cold bed, moves to bring in the bony animals from their attempts to locate a little grass, then helps the camp keepers lift the cumbersome packs of beaver pelts onto the mules.

Then they set out again. The landscape is still stony and bleak and there's less cover here than at the top of the Colorado's canyon. Although the trappers are grateful for the water, the paucity of plant life means there's no beaver. But it isn't the pelts that Gerald longs for. It's the meat underneath them. It's hard to believe he once yearned for something besides beaver tail.

Finally, they reach the foothills of the Rockies. Mountains have never looked so beautiful, so inviting. The vegetation on the lower slopes is sparse, but more than what was available between the striated walls of the canyon behind them.

And there are meadows. Thin with grass, because it's still spring, but still meadows. They not only provide grazing for the animals but the open spaces attract other browsers. James Pattie kills a mule deer and the trappers feast royally, not saving any for the coming days, confident that there'll be more meat as they move farther into the hills. Ewing Young breaks out two bottles of whisky from a hidden stash and the jollity increases.

"If I was less footsore, I'd show you all a proper Scottish reel!" Richard Campbell laughs. He takes a healthy swig of liquor and passes the bottle to Gerald, who hands it on to Michel Robidoux.

"It is a day most marvelous," Robidoux agrees. "My throat, it is content." He pats his shrunken waistline. "And the gut, it is also content."

"That was one hell of a long haul," Milton Sublette says. He twists around to look at the fur packs on the ground under the scrub oak at the edge of the clearing. "Not much to show for it, neither."

"It'll pick up now," Ewing Young says. "We'll have so many furs we'll need to build us a press."

CHAPTER 26

And they do. Within a week, they're taking beaver pelts still thick with winter fur, and plenty of them. Three weeks later, there are too many for the mules to comfortably carry and Young sets Ignacio and Gregorio to constructing a fur press. They drag half a dozen ten-inch-thick aspen poles into camp, set them into post holes dug in a rough three-by-four-foot rectangle, then lash shorter lengths to the top of the frame and down its sides, with more-or-less twelve-inch spaces between them.

In the meantime, the trappers open the packs of pelts, shake out the furs, and refold them to fit the dimensions of the press. When the press form is ready, they lay long strips of rawhide on the ground crosswise inside the frame and flip the ends beyond the side pieces. Young brings out a tanned deerskin and James Pattie positions it inside the press and up its sides.

Gerald, Gregorio, Pattie, and Ignacio station themselves around the outside of the press and hold the ends of the deerskin in place while Michel Robidoux carefully stacks beaver plews inside the frame. When it's full, he nods in satisfaction and lays a stiff piece of rawhide on top of the plews.

Young paces around the press, checks the alignment and positioning of the furs, then produces a length of chain that his mule has packed all the way from Taos. Under his direction, Gregorio and Ignacio lay one end of the chain on the ground about five feet away and pile large rocks on it to hold it down.

While they're doing this, Gerald chips a notch in the end of a six-foot long pole about six inches thick. Ignacio carries the free end of the chain to the press, jingling the links straight as he goes.

Gerald glances at Young, who gestures to the end of the press opposite the chain and says, "Just maneuver that stick up into the press and toward Sandoval."

Gerald nods, feeds the pole between the top of the pelts and the nearest sidepiece, and pushes it toward the other end of the press. It's tilted at an angle across space, and he raises an eyebrow at Young questioningly.

"Just leave it there," the Captain says. "Garcia, you and Sandoval go ahead and take out the side pieces there on the other end.

The two camp keepers move forward as if they understand exactly what Young has in mind, and work the two end pieces directly above the furs on the other end of the press free of the side posts. Ignacio grabs the end of the angled pole and pulls it toward himself.

Gregorio hands him the end of the chain and Ignacio wedges the chain firmly into the notch. Then they move around the press to where Gerald is standing. They grasp opposite sides of the pole and press steadily downward, forcing it against the rawhide and the pelts under it until the plews are compressed to a third of their original thickness and well below the edge of the tanned deerskin.

"That'll do it," Young says. The camp keepers hold the pole in place as Robidoux and Yount grab the rawhide strips, pull them up and over the pack, and knot them tight before the pelts can spring back into shape. Young steps forward with a small branding iron heated over the fire, and sears his mark into the top and sides of the pack. Then he motions to Gerald to remove enough poles from the press so the pack can be lifted out, and the process begins all over again: furs laid carefully in, buckskin on top, pole inserted and used to wedge the plews into a compressed block.

By the end of the day, the original twelve mule loads of pelts are seven tightly-bound bundles, each about 90 pounds and half as bulky as the original loads. Four of them are Ewing Young's, while James Pattie, Michel Robidoux, and Milton Sublette each put their marks on one of the other three.

"Room for more!" Young tells Milton Sublette with a rare smile.

"Not enough," Sublette grunts as he turns away.

But Young leads the band further into the mountains and within a month even Sublette is satisfied with the catch. The Rockies have been kind to them. So kind that Sublette begins to mutter about the difficulty of traveling with thirteen packs of compressed furs. There's little room on the mules for anything but beaver plews, and the trappers are forced to carry their supplies on their backs instead of looping their possibles sacks and traps onto the pack saddles each morning.

With the mules at carrying capacity, Young decides it's time to head south. In late April, the trappers begin winding out of the mountains, moving slowly back toward the Mexican settlements. Young swings clear of the occasional band of Utes, even though the Indians would gladly trade their own plews for any small thing about the camp.

Young's attitude seems odd, since the Utes are generally friendly toward American trappers and Mexicans. But now that the trapping's done and they have a good take, all the men are eager to get back. No one questions the Captain's actions until they top a sparsely-junipered hill and look unexpectedly down on a tree-shaded adobe village that straggles alongside a burbling creek.

Young moves back and clucks his mount to the back side of the hill, out of sight from the houses. Gerald turns his head, puzzled. "Come on!" Young says from the bottom of the hill. "Get on down here!"

"What the devil?" Milton Sublette mutters, staying where he is. "I've got me a powerful thirst that's in dire need of a quenching!"

"Ach, there's most likely a señorita or two in that village just pining for the likes of us," Richard Campbell says mournfully. He maneuvers his mule down the hill as Gerald steers his own animal around a fat juniper and begins the descent.

"He's got his reasons, I guess," James Pattie says as he and his father's sorrel lag behind Campbell. "But I'd sure like to know what they are."

"Just be quiet and get on down here," Young growls. Sublette turns, gives him a long look, then grudgingly moves down the slope.

Young insists on a single fire that night. "What the hell are we doin', anyhow?" Sublette demands. "You tryin' to avoid taxes or somethin'?"

Young allows himself the flash of a smile. "Somethin'," he says.

Robidoux clicks his tongue disapprovingly and Sublette says, "Those Mexicans are gonna find out sooner or later. It ain't like we just snuck out of here last spring. You got a permit and all."

"I'll pay what I need to," Young says.

"Just not on all of it," Sublette says.

Young shrugs as Ignacio slips past him with an armful of firewood.

"Don't go putting all that on there at once," Young tells him.

"We can pretty much cache our plews anywhere," James Pattie observes.

"We won't need to cache them," Young says. "I've got storage lined up."

At the fire, Ignacio looks up sharply, his face dark with anger. The fire flares and Young scowls. "I said to keep that down."

Ignacio nods and picks up a small branch to poke at the logs, but Gerald, on the opposite side of the fire from Young, can see that his jaw is clenched.

"And does it happen that we know where this storage place is?" Richard Campbell asks.

"You'll know in another few days," Young says.

"The way we're headin', we're gonna be in Taos in another few days," Sublette observes.

Young shakes his head. "We swing south tomorrow. Have you ever seen the white tent rocks?"

"Those ones by Cochiti Pueblo?" Sublette grimaces. "You hiding furs at Cochiti?"

"Or south of there at Santo Domingo?" Michel Robidoux suggests.

Young shakes his head. "Wait and see," he says. "We'll get them stored and then we'll head to Taos and you all can get back to your women."

Sublette chuckles. "I'm pinning my hopes on Peabody's cook. I don't care if I get a kiss. I just want some real food."

Michel Robidoux laughs. "Is it your plan to steal her from Jeremiah, or simply to visit?"

"I hear she carries a stiletto," Young says. He grins. "That gal's got a bit of a temper."

"Don't blame her, what with Jones prowling around last spring," Sublette says.

"And a good riddance to him," Campbell says.

Gerald braces himself, expecting a glance in his direction, but the talk passes on to other households, other women, and other entertainments, past and future, especially those involving alcohol and cards.

Gerald looks into the fire, his thoughts on Suzanna Peabody. How will she greet him when he returns? He has no right to expect anything but politeness. Yet a man can't help but wonder. But that's foolishness. Especially since she knows nothing about who he really is. What will she say when she discovers that he's killed a man?

Gerald's hands twitch, feeling again the way Jones' chest gave under his blade. He forces himself not to shudder and his mind to move on to other topics. Will his earnings from Young be enough for land and an outfit? Can he dare hope that Suzanna Peabody— But he moves his thoughts away from that, too.

The white tent rocks come into sight two days later, after a long trek through a narrow canyon studded with piñon pine. When the trappers emerge from it, they're directly above the drooping conical tips of a veritable city of vaguely tent-shaped white rock formations three times the height of the average man.

Gerald shakes his head, not sure why these are worth seeing. They just look like clumps of rock. But as the trail descends and winds through the towering cone-shaped mounds, their complex colors become apparent. The rock is swirled with pink, gray, and white streaks that twist this way and that in the sunlight.

There's something eerie about the way stacks loom overhead, their tops twisting down as if to peer at the men below. Gerald tells himself he's simply reacting to the path's narrowness and the rocks' proximity. This would an excellent place for an ambush. The mule he's leading tosses its head anxiously and Gerald grins. She thinks so too. He pats the animal's neck. "I don't think it'll be long now," he says.

Ahead of him, LeCompte bends to pick up a small rock. Gerald glances at his own feet. Shiny pieces of black obsidian reflect the light. Arrowheads? But they aren't all shaped in the same way. A source of arrowheads, perhaps.

The path widens as the trappers reach the far edge of the final cluster of rocks and Gerald's breath comes more easily. Ignacio Sandoval eases up beside him on the trail and Gerald turns to welcome him.

"The mule, she is restless?" Ignacio asks.

Gerald nods. "She doesn't think much of Ewing Young's rock tents," he says wryly. "Nor do I."

"They leave a bad feeling." Ignacio gestures toward the men and animals ahead of them. "As does this."

"Going home?"

"This is what my father believes all Americans do," he says. "This hiding of the furs. What El Joven is intending."

"To find a way not to pay all the duties he owes?"

"My father is an upright man and he hates men who cheat. He also worries that he and his family will be caught up in the cheating of others."

Gerald looks at him. So this is what Ignacio had been trying to say that day in the Gila. "And you?" Gerald asks.

"When I went to Taos for my studies, he warned me of men like Young." The younger man's face is bleak. "He bade me report to the authorities any fraudulent activities I might see."

This is the young man who pretended to be in Taos at his studies and went trapping instead. But Gerald only says, "And will you do so?"

Ignacio makes a helpless gesture. "It is a commandment to obey one's father." His jaw tightens. "And what Young is doing is wrong."

So it's not obedience to his father so much as Ignacio's own convictions that propel him. Gerald feels a surge of admiration mixed with pity for the younger man.

They walk on, the mules' creaking packsaddles filling the silence.

"I was wrong to lie to mi papá in that way," Ignacio says somberly. "About the trapping." He glances at Gerald. "Though I did not directly tell him an untruth, it was still a lie. I will not do so again." He shakes his head. "I have learned much on this adventure," he says. "Both good and bad."

Gerald nods. "As have I."

Ignacio glances at him, then keeps his eyes carefully forward. "That Jones. Gregorio told me what happened."

Gerald's stomach clenches, but he only says, "That was certainly bad."

"I must thank you. On Gregorio's behalf."

Gerald turns his head, checking on his mule. "I would have preferred a different ending," he says. "But I couldn't stand by and watch him do that to Gregorio."

"I hope that man is truly dead," Ignacio says bitterly.

Gerald pauses, not quite knowing what to say, not wanting to prolong the discussion. Although flashes of memory still occur to him, Jones has finally stopped appearing in Gerald's dreams, burnt out by the blinding sun and heat of the long trek beside the great canyon, and Gerald has no wish to relive the incident. He forces himself to smile. "Isn't there also a commandment about that?" he asks lightly.

"It says thou shall not kill. It does not say anything of wishing or gladness."

Gerald inclines his head, acknowledging the distinction. "That would be an interesting point to discuss with Señor Peabody," he says. His heart sinks at the thought of telling the tall black-coated man what he's done. But it's bound to come out. And he owes Peabody a debt of honesty, if only for the man's kindness. Better to tell him before someone else does.

And if Suzanna's father knows, she will almost certainly learn of it. His stomach clenches. How will she feel about what he's done? Will she look at him differently? In disgust, repelled by his violent solution to the problem of Jones? Or will she be delighted, happy that the man is no longer a threat to her or to the cook?

Gerald finds it hard to believe that Suzanna Peabody would react in that way to any man's death, but he has to admit that he doesn't really know her thinking on such matters. And he isn't sure just what he hopes she will say or feel when she learns of the events by the Salt. He only knows that his mind shrinks from both the idea of telling her and of her hearing the tale from somebody else. Even her father.

Ignacio seems to have read his thoughts. "And then there is la señorita," he says. "I understand that she is likely to have an opinion on the matter."

Gerald chuckles. "From what I've seen, she generally has an opinion about most things."

Ignacio grins. "Gregorio says she is more opinionated than my mother or my mother's cousin, Encarnación."

"You're related to the Peabody's cook?" Gerald shakes his head. The relationships here are endless. But it's a safer subject than Enoch Jones, Suzanna Peabody, or the hiding of beaver furs. "Are strong opinions a characteristic of all Spanish women?" he asks lightly.

But the hiding of beaver furs can't be so easily dismissed, since Ewing Young is leading them to the place where the plews are to be stored. The trappers skirt Cochiti pueblo, its two story adobe walls bulking in the distance, and move south along the Rio del Norte.

The spring runoff has swollen the water levels to three times their normal size. Young studies the currents carefully before he decides on a location where the previous-years' sand bars have divided the channel into four apparently-shallow strands. The trappers gingerly make their way across, Richard Campbell in front with a long cottonwood pole to monitor the silt-laden bottom for sinkholes.

It's getting on toward evening before the last of the pack mules stands safely on the eastern bank and noses at the greening grass under the big gray cottonwoods. Gerald looks back across the river. The setting sun silhouettes the Jemez mountains, black against a salmon sky. To the north, its' rays brighten the outcropping of red rock that is La Bajada, the bench of land between Cochiti and Santa Fe.

But there's little time for appreciating the sunset. Young moves downstream, the trappers strung behind him.

"We stoppin' tonight?" Milton Sublette calls.

"Soon enough," Young's muffled voice answers.

CHAPTER 27

It's almost too dark to see when they arrive at the long, white-washed adobe. Lantern light gleams from its deep windows. Even the milky white mica in the window panes can't block the yellow comfort of the lamps. Gerald feels a sudden jolt of joy, a sense of homecoming. Which is ridiculous. This house is not his home, nor does he have another to go to.

A short man, almost as wide as he is tall, steps from the shadowed portal. "El Joven!" he says jovially.

"De Baca," Young answers. Gerald glances at him in surprise. Even Young isn't usually this succinct.

"Luis Maria Cabeza de Baca at your service," the portly man says with a formal little bow. Then he straightens and gives the Captain and his trappers a wide smile. "Come in! Come in! We've been expecting you!" The door behind him swings open and a woman appears. She's almost as broad as he is. "My wife has prepared a meal," he says.

She moves onto the porch. "It is not much," she says apologetically. "Only tortillas and goat stew."

"To not eat the beaver or the venison will be a great thing indeed," Michel Robidoux says.

Ewing Young gestures toward the mules. "These first," he says. "They need to be under cover."

Cabeza de Baca nods. "Yes, of course," he says happily. "Los mulos, they must be disburdened." He turns toward the door. "Eduardo!"

A boy of perhaps ten appears. The man says something in Spanish, too low to hear, and the boy moves into the yard and toward the far end of the house.

"There are sheds there behind," de Baca says. "Will that be sufficient for now?"

Ewing Young nods curtly and reins his horse to follow the boy. De Baca steps off the porch. "I will take el caballo, if you like," he says. "You must be weary from your journey."

"I'll do it," Young says, not looking at him.

"As you wish." De Baca falls into step beside Young's mount as the trappers cluck their animals into action. "Did you have a good hunt?"

"Good enough."

"And now you are returned. There is much news of interest." As they round the house, a low adobe building bulks out of the shadows. "But here is the shed. Is it sufficient?"

"For tonight. We'll shift tomorrow if we need to." Young dismounts and moves to the nearest pack mule. He begins unfastening its straps, something he normally leaves to the camp keepers. His men follow suit, working quickly to unload their goods into the dark shed. Then they turn the animals into the adjoining corral and move to the house.

Only when they've all eaten does Young begin to unwind. De Baca has talked solidly through the meal, complaining about the authorities in Santa Fe, bragging about the quality and quantity of his goat herd, grumbling about the pretensions of the Cochiti people on the north and the Santo Domingans on the south, Indians who think they can push good Spaniards off their own land. Apparently the government authorities are more apt to side with the Pueblans in the ongoing boundary dispute.

"The bastards won't even stand up for their own!" he exclaims, slapping the table.

"They're too busy trying to take advantage of us Americans," Young agrees as he wipes his bowl with the last of his tortilla.

"More wine?" de Baca asks. He signals to his wife, who moves forward.

Young nods at her and looks across the table at de Baca. "You said there was news that will be of interest to me."

The other man nods. "You know of Ira Emmons, the one who trades in Santa Fe?"

"Irish Emmons? What about him?"

"That Vicente Baca who calls himself the alcalde of Santa Fe confiscated the Irishman's furs. He had one hundred eighteen pelts. Good ones from the Gila. Even though Emmons trapped under a license, Baca has taken the furs for himself."

"Emmons had a license?"

"Well, it wasn't his, precisely. He bought it from Manuel Sena. Pobre Sena, he says he didn't know foreigners were now disallowed from the trapping. And that Baca, he believed him and let Sena go without a fine. But then he sold the Irishman's furs. That Emmons is a fool. He told Baca there were other furs of his that he had cached, and now soldiers have been sent to the copper mines to collect them."

"The copper mines? The ones south, there at Santa Rita?"

"Si, all the way south to Santa Rita." The fat man shakes his head. "This administration will go to great lengths to steal another man's property."

Young's face has suddenly become impassive. The fat man studies him with hooded eyes, then pushes his bowl toward the center of the table.

Young looks down the table at Michel Robidoux. "Didn't your brother have a scrap with Governor Narbona last spring about that? Didn't Narbona return Antoine's furs and apologize?"

Robidoux shakes his head. "It was my brother François. He had over 600 pounds of fur. I tell you, he was most anxious!" He shrugs and rubs his right thumb and index finger together meaningfully. "But it was all settled peaceably. That Narbona is a sensible one."

"He has become quite unsensible since news arrived that he is to be replaced," de Baca says. "He is in fear of what Armijo will report that he has done."

Young raises an eyebrow.

"While you were out, everything changed." The fat man spreads his hands, palm upward. "Narbona, that more or less sensible man, is to be removed as el jefe politico—what you call el governor—and replaced with Manuel Armijo of Plaza de San Antonio de Belen. The Armijo who thinks he is next to el diós himself because his mother is of los Chavez."

Gerald's head swivels. Chavez? So the new Governor's mother is related somehow to the Señor Chavez who hosted them beside the Rio del Norte while they waited for reinforcements from Taos? He shakes his head. Yet another example of the interrelationships of the people here.

"The Manuel Armijo without children," de Baca's wife sniffs from the corner. She moves forward, lifting a long-necked pottery jar. "More wine, señors?"

Young nods at her and turns back to her husband. "So now Narbona is confiscating furs regardless of license arrangements?" he asks. "Even the licenses that he approved?"

De Baca leans back with a satisfied air. The trapper captain has finally understood. "It is very bad, señor," he says solemnly. "Very bad indeed."

Now Young's eyes are hooded. He doesn't respond.

"The risk, it is much greater now," de Baca continues. "Not only is Narbona of a different mind, but it is unclear what Armijo will do when he takes over. I may not be able to provide the protection to your furs that we originally discussed."

A flash of amused irritation quirks Young's lips. "I wouldn't want to put you at risk," he says calmly. He reaches for his cup of wine. "I'll have to find someplace else to stash them."

"Oh no, señor!" de Baca says. "It will be safer for them to remain here until you can transport them to Taos, where the politicos are more sensible." He spreads his hands again. "It is just that the protection must be enhanced to ensure the packs are safe until you return." He reaches out to poke at his empty bowl. "It will require more men and more money to ensure the silence of everyone involved."

"More money," Young says drily.

"Si, Don Joven," de Baca says, giving the trapper the honor of Spanish status. "More money will be quite necessary if you are to protect the results of your labor from el arunscel, the tariff."

Young turns his head, slowly looking around the table at his men, then at de Baca. "I will decide in the morning," he says.

Anger flashes across the other man's face, then is replaced with a smile that does not touch his eyes. "I agree," he says. "Consider it well my friend, and I believe you will understand all that I have said.

This new governor who is about to take control does not appreciate you americanos as I do."

Young chuckles. He pushes back from the table, and Gerald and the others follow suit. "I bid you good night."

Gerald wakes to the sound of red-winged blackbirds singing in the fields that lie beyond the house and the river. He smiles contentedly. He's been dreaming of Suzanna Peabody, beside him on a path that lies along brimming Taos acequia ditches and greening fields.

Then he remembers last night's dinner conversation. His mouth twists in distaste. People and their greed, their presuppositions, and their problems. How does Young know Cabeza de Baca is telling the truth about the confiscations? What makes both of them so determined to cheat the government of its rightful share? After all, the gathered furs are all from Spanish waters, as far as Gerald can tell. He remembers Young's argument with the Mojave Chief and grins. Well, Indian waters.

But that's a whole different issue. The Spanish control the country clear to the California coast, so they're responsible for the Mojaves and the Apaches, too. Gerald chuckles. He suspects that the Indians would find that idea merely amusing.

He turns his thoughts back to the present situation. What will Young decide to do about de Baca's demands?

Whatever the Captain has decided in the night, it seems to satisfy Cabeza de Baca. He and his wife are quite jovial at the morning meal, plying the trappers with food and liquor, and assuring Young that the furs will be guarded as if they were their own.

"Some o' those are mine, ya know," Milton Sublette puts in, but Ewing Young swings his head and asks, "You want to help with the payment?" and Sublette subsides.

Young orders the supplies and the few furs he's taking in for tariff purposes to be redistributed among the mules, so they're all carrying something. As the camp keepers are finishing this task, De Baca approaches Ignacio Sandoval, who's tightening a cinch.

"I believe we are related through my wife," de Baca says jovially.

Ignacio turns to the older man and lowers his eyes respectfully but does not speak.

"Your father is Felipe Sandoval of Socorro?" de Baca asks.

"Si, señor."

"I saw your father in Santa Fe last week. He said he was searching for you, that you were to be in Taos but were not there."

The younger man grimaces unhappily and the fat man laughs. "Ah, I see. You accompanied Don Joven without permission, did you not?" He grins and wags a finger in Ignacio's face. "That was very bad of you! Very bad!" He claps the younger man's shoulder. "But we will not tell tu papá, will we now?" He rubs his right thumb and index finger together. "You will owe me for this secret, will you not?" The fat man laughs again and moves away. "I will seek payment another time!" he laughs.

Ignacio's face twists in disgust. He turns back to the mule and yanks the cinch tighter.

De Baca laughs again and continues toward the house, nodding to Gerald as he passes.

CHAPTER 28

Young leads his men north through the sage and juniper-spotted hills west of Santa Fe, well beyond the plaza and the Mexican customs officer. His plan is to report his arrival and pay his fees in Taos, where he has friends among the local officials.

Halfway through the morning, Ignacio leaves the group to head into the city to make amends with his father. "Better sooner than later," Young says. "Come on up to Taos when you're ready for your pay."

Ignacio nods respectfully, but there's a determined look in his face when he pauses beside Gerald to say goodbye.

"Vaya con diós," Gerald tells him. "Is that how you say it? Go with God?"

The younger man smiles somberly. "That is most correct," he says. "And you also." He glances toward Young, at the head of the line of men and pack mules. "And with great carefulness."

Gerald frowns. "Are you expecting that we'll have an problem?"

Ignacio shrugs. "Are there not always problems?" Then he turns and moves on, only pausing for a moment to speak to Gregorio before he heads across the dusty hills toward Santa Fe.

Gerald shakes his head. Great carefulness? Always problems? Ignacio is merely anxious about meeting his father and confessing where he's been, Gerald tells himself. That's what's making him so pessimistic. But the look on the younger man's face lingers in his mind as he moves north along with the rest of Young's trappers and mules.

The rocky soil on the road is still dusty underfoot, but Gerald catches glimpses of the cultivated fields below. The ones nearest the river are an emerald green. In spite of Ignacio's elliptical warning and his own anxiety about meeting the Peabody's again, Gerald's spirits lift as the trappers move north toward Taos and its broad plains.

When they top the hill that overlooks the valley, his breath catches. The fields are dotted with men and women bending over the tilled soil. Children drive cattle out of pastures destined for another round of barley or oats. It seems as if every valley inhabitant, except for the trappers and the taberna people who serve them, is in the fields. The acequia ditches brim with water and the bushes along the paths beside them shimmer with fresh green leaves.

Gerald buys a wash tub on credit from Ceran St. Vrain's shop and carries it back to the trappers' camp site, once again in a field controlled by Ewing Young. First a bath, then clean clothes. He can't stand the smell of himself another moment.

He places the tub in the middle of a small cottonwood grove, requisitions a pot to haul water from the acequia, then uses it to heat water over the fire. There's a sense of release in the preparations for being clean. A kind of promise. As if the process will also wash away the smell of other men's dirt and attitudes. Even Enoch Jones.

He turns his thoughts firmly away from Jones and kneels in the spring grass beside the metal tub. Dry leaves from the previous fall crinkle under his knees. He pulls off his shirt and drops it on the grass beside him, then leans over the tub, dips the pot into the water, and douses his head. The tub erupts in dirty brown swirls. Gerald grimaces. How many times will he need to do this before he's truly clean? And that's just his hair. What about his clothes?

He glances at the shirt on the grass. It was once the pale tan of unbleached muslin, now it's a sort of grayish brown. Is it even possible to get it back to its original state? He wonders how much credit St. Vrain would give him for new clothes and when Young will be back in Taos and able to pay him off.

Behind him, feet crunch on broken leaves. Gerald turns.

Gregorio Garcia is standing at the edge of the trees, looking sheepish, a pile of clothing in his arms. "Hola," he says. "You are well?"

"Well enough." Gerald gestures to the wash tub. "I'm just trying to get clean again." He shakes his head ruefully. "It may take a while. And you? You are well?"

The boy grins. "I was not allowed into the house until I bathed and replaced my clothes." He shakes his head. "My mother refused to touch me, so much did I stink." He chuckles. "I did my best in the wilderness to stay clean. I thought I had done well. But a man does not know how he smells until a woman tells him."

Gerald chuckles and nods toward the brown water in the tub. "I tried to wash my hair."

Gregorio holds out the clothing in his arms. "Mi mamá sent these to you," he says. "I am to bring the old ones to her to be laundered."

Gerald frowns. "I have no money just yet," he says. "As you know, we haven't been paid yet." He begins running his hands through his hair, trying to squeeze out the dirt along with the remaining water.

"It is a loan." The boy moves forward to put the clothes on a section of clean grass. "It is to say gracias for your friendship to me."

Gerald's hands freeze. "You told her what happened?"

"No. Only that you were a friend to me."

"Anyone would have done the same."

The boy gives him a pitying look. "I wish that is true, but I am only a mexicano."

Gerald shakes his head, but Gregorio continues. "In any case, she sent the clothes." He turns back toward the campsite. "I will be by the fire heating more water." He looks back at Gerald and grins. "I think you will be needing more!"

Gerald laughs and looks down at the wash tub. He might as well dump this and start again. It won't do any good to continue with sandy water. He shakes his head. This is going to take a while. He grabs the nearest handle and begins pulling the tub toward the stream.

As much as he wants to see Suzanna Peabody, Gerald waits until Gregorio returns to the campsite with his newly-cleaned clothes before he ventures into the village. He wants to present himself in his own things, not something borrowed.

The laundered clothes and a barber visit for a haircut and shave help to restore him to something like his former self, but he still feels uneasy. His breath tightens as he moves through the streets toward the Peabody casa. He shakes his head at his own anxiety. He's crossed a mountain range with men he barely knows, battled Papagos and Mojaves, killed a man— His thoughts veer off.

Battled Mojaves, survived the great canyon, and the lands on its precarious brim, he tells himself firmly. He's faced all of that and earned the respect of his fellow trappers in the process. Survived hunger and thirst beyond most men's experience.

Yet his stomach clenches with anxiety at the thought of seeing Suzanna Peabody again. Will she greet him with gladness or indifference? There's been time enough while he's cleaned himself up for Young or one of the other men to visit the Peabody casa and tell the story of Enoch Jones and his flight into the wilderness.

Gerald's jaw clenches. He's a damn fool for waiting so long to go to her. Will she be repelled by what he's done? Will she even want to speak to him again? And if she does, will she talk of some other man who arrived while he was away, who's wormed himself into her heart? Or someone who's been here all along, who she neglected to mention during their conversations last fall? After all, Gerald isn't necessarily important enough to her to need to be warned off.

He has no right to hope. Of all men, he has the least right to hope. After all, there's much about him that he hasn't told her and he has little to offer. Yet he has to admit that he does hope and that very hope makes him reluctant to face her. Afraid he'll discover he truly doesn't have a right or reason for his dreams.

When he turns the final corner to the house, his feet slow even further. The big wooden gate in the adobe wall is shut tight.

Who does he think he is, after all? And then there's the issue of his race. He clenches his fist at himself. He thinks he's so brave. Yet he didn't have the courage last fall to tell her the truth and he still cringes at what she will say if—no, when—he does. What if she's learned while he was gone that he's not as white as she thinks?

Gerald stares at the wooden gate. It's not the color of his skin. After all, she seems to hold the brown-skinned Encarnación in high regard. Certainly, Suzanna treats the Peabody cook more as a friend than a servant. The problem is that he's entered the Peabody casa under false premises and now he doesn't know how to correct those false impressions. Bringing the subject up now would imply that he has a right to her heart, that he believes she would be interested to know about his ancestry.

Perhaps he should just slip away. Disappear into the mountains as his father did. After all, other men come and go in Taos without making a point of visiting the Peabody parlor. And his funds are safe

231

with Jeremiah Peabody until he calls for them. For that matter, he could send someone else for them. Gerald half-turns, back toward the corner and safety.

"Why, Mr. Locke!" a glad voice says behind him. He wheels to see Suzanna's face beaming at him from the half-open gate. She comes toward him with her hands out, then glances down self-consciously and lets them fall to her sides. She stops, leaning imperceptibly toward him, then her back straightens. "You've returned safely," she says, her head slightly turned. It's almost as if she's afraid to look him in the eyes.

"Yes." He stands looking at her, her straight black brows above dark eyes that still don't meet his, the black hair coiled neatly on top of her head, her slim frame brimming with suppressed energy under the old-fashioned dress. He fights the urge to touch her, to turn her face toward his own. His throat feels unaccountably dry. He swallows and forces his lips to move. "And you?" he asks.

She shrugs and moves slightly back. "I am the same." She turns toward the gate and glances back at him. "Will you come in? My father will be glad to see you."

"And you?" he asks impulsively. His breath catches at his audacity, but he forces his eyes to stay on her face.

She turns back to him, tilting her head, smiling into his face now, a hint of mischief in her eyes. Gladness sweeps over him.

She glances away, then meets his gaze. "Yes," she says honestly. "I am very glad to see you."

His hand lifts toward her, but she turns again toward the gate. "Come inside," she says abruptly.

Gerald's forehead wrinkles at the change in tone, but he follows obediently.

By the time they reach the parlor and her father, Suzanna has returned to her open-faced self. "Here's Mr. Gerald Locke Jr. returned from the mountains," she says gaily as they enter.

Jeremiah Peabody is alone in the parlor. He puts his book aside, rises, and comes across the room to take Gerald's hat and shake his hand. "It's good to see you again, my boy!" he says. "Was your venture successful? We've seen no one from your party yet, although we knew you had returned. Come! Tell us where you went and all that occurred!"

Encarnación enters the room, a tray of tea things and sliced white bread in her hands, and beams at him. "He knew you were back because Antonia told Ramón that Gregorio had returned, and Ramón brought us the news," she says. She glances down at the tray. "I thought you might like some civilized food."

Gerald smiles at her, a wordless gladness washing over him. He isn't sure who this Ramón is, but the cook's assumption that Gerald knows him fills Gerald with a sense of belonging. For a welcome like this, he'd almost be willing to go out to the mountains again.

"Come! Sit down!" Jeremiah Peabody urges him. "Suzanna, are you going to make tea, or just stand there and look at the man?"

233

CHAPTER 29

But the glow of Gerald's welcome doesn't last more than an hour. Ewing Young and James Pattie also show up at the Peabody casa that afternoon. Pattie has brought his father's sorrel mare to show off and they all troop into the courtyard to admire the beast. It shows little sign of its ordeal among the Apache and then the canyon wilderness, and nickers politely at the strangers it's introduced to, especially after Suzanna produces a small handful of carrots from her winter cache.

The mare delicately takes a single carrot and Suzanna gives Pattie a delighted smile. "She's remarkably polite!" the girl says.

Pattie runs a hand through his blond curls and smiles into Suzanna's face. Gerald's stomach clenches. She smiles that way at everyone. There's no special welcome here for him. He's just one of many. Just any man.

Still, he finds himself returning with the others to the parlor and taking tea and sandwiches from her hands. Ewing Young ensconces himself in the window seat. Then Richard Campbell and George Yount show up. The Pattie mare is still in the courtyard, and there's general talk of the sorrel, horses in general, and Pattie's father at the Santa Rita mines in particular, and how glad he'll be to see his Kentucky riding horse again.

Suzanna's eyes meet Gerald's more than once as the talk flows around the room and he begins to relax a little. Perhaps there's something here for him, after all. Something just for him.

But there's still the matter of Jones. Gerald's stomach tightens as he waits for the talk to turn to the trapper who was part of the party that found the horse, the man who didn't return with them.

But the conversation hasn't arrived anywhere near that subject when Milton Sublette bursts into the parlor. "That damn Armijo!" he says as he enters abruptly, his hat still on his head.

Jeremiah Peabody's eyes move from Sublette to Suzanna.

"Beggin' your pardon, ma'am," Sublette says. He snatches his hat from his head and nods to her father. "Jeremiah." Then he turns to Ewing Young. "I just got in from Santa Fe. Your man in Peña Blanca's been shot!"

Young lifts his chin. "I don't have a man in Peña Blanca."

Sublette makes an impatient gesture. "De Baca, the one who was storin' our furs. I guess he was serious about protectin' those plews as if they was his own, because he put up a fuss when the Santa Fe alcalde showed up with his soldiers, and they killed him."

"Damnation!" James Pattie says. He turns toward Suzanna. "Beggin' your pardon, ma'am."

Suzanna nods at him abstractedly, her eyes on Milton Sublette.

Sublette thumps his hat against his leg and shakes his head. "I shouldn't have left my pack there. I should of just taken them in and paid the full duty on 'em. It would've been easier all round."

"What's done is done," Ewing Young says. He glances at James Pattie. "We'll get them back."

Jeremiah Peabody leans forward. "Who is it that's been killed?"

Ewing Young turns his head. "Luis Maria Cabeza de Baca," he says evenly. "Of Peña Blanca. He was storing some furs for Sublette, Pattie, and me until we could take them into the customs house." He nods toward Sublette, who's moved toward the table and is taking a teacup from Suzanna's hands. "Apparently, the Santa Fe alcalde decided to bring them in sooner."

Sublette jerks around, his teacup rattling in its saucer. "It's Governor Narbona that ordered it. Alcalde Duran was just doin' his job. But who did it don't matter to de Baca or his family. He's dead!"

"I heard you. And the furs?"

Sublette grips the teacup so hard Gerald thinks it might snap in two. Sublette stares at Young, his jaw clenched. "All thirteen packs were taken into custody and moved to Santa Fe." He sits down at the table, opposite Suzanna and as far away from Young as he can get. He carefully places the cup and saucer on the table, then turns in his chair to face the room.

He puts a hand on each knee. "De Baca was tryin' to protect the furs. He started waving a gun around and one of Duran's soldiers got excited and shot him." Sublette shakes his head in disgust and looks at Jeremiah Peabody. "Narbona seems to have forgotten all about the fact that he issued us licenses last spring."

Young stands in one fluid motion. He looks around the room at the men who've been with him all winter. "I haven't paid you all yet," he says. "If you want to see your money, you'd best come with me to Santa Fe." He nods to Sublette. "We don't need everyone, but see if you can at least round up Michel and LeCompte. Tell 'em to catch us up on the road." Sublette nods abruptly and disappears into the hallway. Young turns to Jeremiah Peabody, then Suzanna. "Ma'am," he says as he puts on his hat.

The trappers gather themselves together, nod politely, and move out of the room door. Gerald is the last to stand. "I'd best go with him," he says apologetically. "Or I'm likely to not see any of the wages I'm due."

Suzanna nods reluctantly. Her father's thin face darkens. "I'll be glad when you're out of it," he says.

And what will Peabody say when he learns that these same men left Jones in the wilderness to die? Gerald wonders uneasily. But he only says, "I look forward to being done with it," and lifts his hat from the peg by the door. He looks for a long moment into Suzanna Peabody's anxious eyes, then turns silently to let himself out.

It's a hard and silent ride to Santa Fe, dust thick in the air as the cantering horses throw a haze over the road across the Taos plain and along the ridges above the Rio del Norte. Young stops fifteen miles south to grab a cold meal and let the horses blow.

There's no time even for brewing coffee, but no one grumbles. Young's grim face stops complaints before they can become thoughts. The trappers move out again, at a steady trot, conserving their mounts.

They canter into the Santa Fe Plaza early the afternoon of the third day with dusty clothes and sleep-deprived faces, and rein in at the door of the long low adobe building that houses the Governor's offices and living quarters and forms the north side of the plaza.

Ewing Young stalks through the palace's massive wooden doors and the trappers sit their horses and gaze at the goods for sale under the building's portal. Early squash, peas, and last summer's corn compete for attention with Pueblo pottery and Navajo blankets. But none of Young's men have money to spend. Not until the confiscated furs are released.

The winter's catch is still confiscated when Young strides angrily out of the building and mounts his horse. The trappers follow him to a campsite beside the Santa Fe River, just outside of town in a spot that's easily located. By noon the next day, a small group of American merchants has found them and they've all hunkered down

237

to consider what's to be done. If the furs aren't returned, if trapping isn't going to be allowed, there'll be little reason for any of them to continue on in New Mexico. They all might as well head back to the States.

But a new Governor's about to be sworn in and nothing's likely to happen until he's in office. They can only hope that the rumors about Manuel Armijo's attitude toward the Americans aren't true. Especially his reported attitude about American trappers.

"There's no real law sayin' foreigners can't trap," one of the merchants observes as they sit around the campfire. "This so-called proclamation is just hearsay."

"Well, somebody's seen something written down or Narbona wouldn't be carrying on like this." Milton Sublette shifts his position on a large sandstone rock and adjusts his wounded leg. "His attitude is quite a change from how friendly he was just last fall."

"Has anybody seen this so-called proclamation?" Ewing Young asks.

The merchants shake their heads. "Cristobel Torres told me he was shown something, but then the man who showed it to him whisked it away," one of them says. "Chris says it looked more like a letter than a formal proclamation. But he didn't get a good look at it."

James Pattie runs his hand through his hair. "They must have somethin' to go on," he says.

"This Armijo sure don't like Americans much," the merchant says.

"Like we're all the same," Milton Sublette says bitterly.

"I'm thinkin' we should ask to see this here proclamation they keep talkin' about and get someone to translate it for us," the merchant says. "Someone like Torres, who we can trust to say it straight."

238

"Isn't Torres the one with the house opposite the Governor's so-called palace?" Young asks.

"The one with the big wooden gates? That's Cristobel's cousin, I think. Agustín Torres."

Young nods. "Do you think he'd be willing to give us room and board on credit until this thing is settled?"

The merchant shrugs. "He's generally friendly toward Americanos," he says. "He might take you all in, depending on how long it takes to get this mess dealt with and how much you'll pay him once it's over with."

Milton Sublette scowls. "Some of us have families to feed and plans to make. We can't be waitin' around all summer for governors to change in the hope that Armijo'll be more sensible than Narbona."

Young turns his head. "You'll get what's yours."

Sublette hoists himself awkwardly to his feet. "Everything I've got is bound up in those furs." He scowls at Young. "I don't know why I didn't just take what was mine and go on by myself."

"But you didn't," Young says coolly. "You decided throwin' in with me made more sense."

"Shouldn't have." Sublette kicks at a piece of firewood with his injured leg, sending up a shower of sparks. "And it's the last time I do." He turns away. "I'm goin' to town. Anyone coming with me?"

George Yount stands and looks at Gerald questioningly, but Gerald gestures at the fire, indicating that he's staying where he is.

"Oh, I forget. Your gal is in Taos, is she not?" Yount grins at Gerald companionably and turns to follow Sublette.

Gerald shakes his head and notices Jim Pattie watching him. He turns his attention to Ewing Young.

239

"I need to lay low, or whoever is governor will try to arrest me," Young is telling the merchant. "If that happens, someone else is likely to die."

The other man nods. "I'm goin' to ask the alcalde about that there piece of paper and see if he can produce somethin'."

"How'd he find out about the furs, anyway?"

The other man shifts uneasily. "One of your men reported you to Governor Narbona," he says reluctantly. "That Mexican Sandoval."

Young nods grimly. "His Daddy told him to."

"It's likely he did. They say Felipe Sandoval is worse than Armijo when it comes to his feelings about Americans."

Young looks across the fire at Gerald. "This is what happens when you take them in, try to teach them a trade," he says bitterly. "They'd just as soon turn on you as thank you for your help."

Gerald looks back at him, recalling Ignacio's frustrated desire to trap and his anger when he realized that Young planned to circumvent the law. There are two sides to this question, but now doesn't seem a good time for that discussion. Gerald shrugs noncommittally and looks into the fire.

CHAPTER 30

Gerald has plenty of time to fire-gaze over the next few weeks, although the flames are now on a hearth in Agustín Torres' wooden-gated adobe on the south side of the Santa Fe plaza. Manuel Armijo has taken over as governor and, though the Santa Fe alcalde immediately asked for a copy of the proclamation, it takes two weeks and a second request before the bureaucracy produces the document.

Young's jaw tightens when he hears Cristobel Torres' careful translation. Mexico City has indeed forbidden foreigners to trap. The licenses Narbona issued the previous year are technically invalid. Manuel Armijo is free to dispose of the confiscated furs in any way he sees fit.

"Not that they're going to be fit to be disposed of," Sublette grumbles. He rubs his leg and moves his foot a little, easing the discomfort. "No American merchant is likely to touch 'em. These Mexicans don't know anything about storing furs and those packs have been in that old cracked-roof adobe behind the Governor's so-called palace all this time, gettin' rained on. Even if they aren't wet, they've been packed up longer than they should've been. They're likely to be in a hell of a shape by now."

Ewing Young studies him for a long moment, then lifts himself from the adobe wall bench where he's been sitting in the Torres sala. "Well, I guess that's something the Governor ought to consider," he says. "His furs aren't going to have much value unless someone who knows what they're doing dries them out." He brushes past Gerald in the doorway, crosses the Torres courtyard, and lets himself out the big wood-plank gate and into the plaza.

The mid-June sunlight glares down at the dusty plaza and the people meandering across it. The sellers under the palace portal look up as Young strides across the square, then down at their wares as he barges through the building's heavy wooden doors.

Gerald, watching with James Pattie and George Yount from the Torres gate, senses a general pulling together of goods and blankets. Business doesn't stop, but the vendors are definitely aware that violence could erupt and flight might be necessary. The set of the sellers' shoulders reminds him of the turkeys he and Old Bill observed in the canyon of the Cimarron: not taking flight just yet, but positioning themselves for it, if flight should be necessary.

When Young returns, he's shaking his head in disgust. It takes another three weeks and a deputation of Santa Fe's American merchants before Governor Armijo is convinced that the confiscated plews are truly in danger of moldering into worthlessness. He reluctantly orders them hauled out to the plaza in two wooden carretas, there to be shaken out, inspected, and repacked. But only under Alcalde Duran's supervision, he says sternly. The trappers are not to be left alone with the furs, and the plews are to remain at all times on the portal in front of the gubernatorial palace.

The July sunshine is hot and clear when Young, Gerald, and George Yount go to work on the water-stained packs in the shade of the portal. The trappers have displaced the vendors, who've shuffled their goods to the few shady spots on the three other sides of the square, including under the adobe walls of the Torres casa.

At either end of the portal, a Mexican soldier leans against the massive cottonwood columns that support its portal roof. The Alcalde is closer, hovering nearby.

The trappers lay the packs in a line under the portal, then start at the western end. When Young cuts the rawhide straps around the first pack, the compressed plews expand, bulging against their deerskin cover as if trying to escape. When Gerald and Yount peel back the wrapping, the furs expand further. The stack of plews leans dangerously, threatening to topple.

They steady the stack as Ewing Young carefully pulls off the top plew. He shakes it flat, then carries it to the edge of the portal and holds it up to the sunlight. He and the Alcalde examine it for damage, then Duran gently places the fur on a blanket spread in the plaza sunshine, a few yards beyond the portal. The next plew is damaged and the Alcalde sets it aside on a separate blanket that he's laid beside the first one.

As the men work through the stack, other trappers wander by, some of them Young's men, some from other groups. They pause to watch Young at work, then move to the furs on the blankets and shake their heads at the damage. About half the plews have lost their luster or are missing clumps of the thick bottom layer that makes winter beaver so valuable.

Alcalde Duran is intent on his work and doesn't see the dark looks or notice Milton Sublette's scowl when he limps by, then steps onto the other end of the portal, and moves back down the porch to examine the still-unopened packs.

Sublette speaks a word of acknowledgement to Yount and Gerald as he reaches them, nods curtly to Young, then disappears around the corner of the building. Yount watches him go. "He don't look too happy," he says.

243

"Aren't his furs at the other end?" Gerald asks.

"One of his packs is there at the end and another is toward the middle," Yount says. "His marks are plain enough, if that's what he's lookin' for."

Young and Duran finish the first pack and move to the second. Young bends over it, then grimaces. "Look at the stain on that cover," he says to the alcalde. "This one is going to be nasty." Gerald and Yount cut the straps and peel back the water-marked buckskin. As the first plews bulge out, the stink of mildew fills the air.

"They must have been just sitting in water," Young says. He puts a palm on the top plew, then reaches down and jams his other hand into the middle of the pile. "The farther down they are, the wetter they get." As he tries to lift the top pelt, the fragile skin rips under his fingers. He grips it with both hands, pulls the pelt off the stack, gives it a shake, and turns to Duran, the "V" of the tear between his hands. "Look at this!"

Duran nods, his eyes anxious. "It is bad," he agrees. "We must begin a new stack of these more ruined—"

"Cuidado!" The soldier nearest them exclaims. They turn toward him, then again, following his pointing finger. At the other end of the portal, the soldier on guard has dozed off in the sunlight. As Young and the others turn, he straightens with a jerk, but it's too late. Milton Sublette has hoisted a pack of furs over his left shoulder and is off the portal and limping rapidly across the plaza toward the Torres gate.

The soldier lifts his weapon. The vendors along the Torres wall scatter, their goods still on the blankets in the ground below the wall.

But then Duran roars "No!" at the top of his voice. The soldier glances toward the alcalde and lowers his gun as Sublette disappears through the big wooden gates.

Duran turns to scowl at Ewing Young. Young's lips twitch.

"It is not a thing to amuse," the alcalde says stiffly. He nods grimly toward the palacio's heavy wooden doors. "His Excellency el jefe politico must be informed and he will not find it a thing of amusement."

Young spreads his hands, palm upwards. "His Excellency ordered the furs to be aired and cleaned. There's always a risk in any activity."

Duran's scowl deepens.

"Sublette acted on his own," Young says. "He's a free trapper." He glances down the row of packs. "I believe you'll find that he's only taken what is his. And not all of those, for that matter."

Duran turns and barks a command at the soldier at the far end of the portal. The man moves toward him with his head down. Duran snaps something in Spanish and the man spreads his hands in a helpless gesture. Duran swings around, squinting across the plaza. "Torres!" he says bitterly. Then he turns to Young, who's gone back to pulling furs from the pack.

"Here, Locke," Young says, lifting a plew toward Gerald. "Let's keep moving."

As Gerald reaches for the fur, the alcalde spits, "His Excellency will hear of this!"

Young looks up. "They weren't my plews," he says. "They belong to Sublette, not to me. And you still have his other pack. Jim Pattie's too, for that matter."

The American's apparent lack of concern seems to infuriate the alcalde, whose eyes narrow. He turns sharply and waves his two soldiers closer. He barks an order, then turns on his heel and marches into the adobe palacio.

Young pulls another plew from the stack. "We'd better get a move on," he says dryly. "I doubt we've got a whole lot of time before His Excellency sends out more troops to guard his vast wealth."

245

Gerald is reaching to cut the straps on the third pack when a dozen soldiers march into the square. The few vendors still in the plaza melt into the side streets.

Young straightens to watch the soldiers, a contemptuous smile on his lips. "They're quite a sight, aren't they?" he asks no one in particular. He glances at Yount and Gerald. "You might want to move off a little. There's no use in you being arrested, too."

Gerald returns his knife to its sheath and he and Yount move to the end of the portal and step onto the dusty street beyond.

Young waits for the soldiers to cross the plaza to him, his head contemptuously erect. They move into place, an armed man on either side and two more behind him, and he steps into the plaza and then down the nearest side street.

The remaining soldiers begin collecting the beaver plews and reloading them onto the carretas. Gerald and Yount look at each other grimly and try not to watch as the carefully sorted furs are tumbled into a single heap.

There's a sudden shout across the square. They all turn to see James Pattie in the Torres gateway. "You'll ruin 'em, doin' that!" Pattie yells, his voice high with strain. He spreads his hands in front of him, palms down. "Flatten 'em out, for God's sake!" He takes a step into the plaza, but then a soldier appears from the corner of the casa, a musket in his hands. Pattie's head swivels toward the weapon, and he takes two steps back, into the safety of the Torres compound.

Then Agustín Torres appears at the gate. He says something to the soldier, who shakes his head disapprovingly, but lowers his musket. But he doesn't leave. He turns and moves to one side of the gate, facing the square.

Gerald glances around the plaza. It's empty of vendors.

"It is time, I think, to return," George Yount says. He moves toward the Torres house. The soldier eyes him warily, but Yount ignores him and walks firmly into the courtyard.

As the tall wooden doors start to swing shut behind Yount, Sublette's head and shoulders appear in the gap. His head turns, studying the plaza. He sees Gerald and lifts an arm to make a sweeping gesture, pulling him toward the house. Gerald hesitates. But he has nowhere else to go. And he still hasn't been paid. He moves reluctantly across the square.

Inside, he finds a dozen trappers scattered around the walled courtyard, sitting on bedrolls or leaning against the adobe walls. Milton Sublette is bent over his pack of furs, checking the straps. He looks up and grins at Gerald. "Looks like we're in for it now!" he says.

Agustín Torres comes out into the sunlit courtyard. He's a short stocky man with a wide, usually cheerful face, but now he looks anxious. "I have just received word that the soldiers are coming for you," he tells Sublette. He tilts his head toward the gate. "It would be well if you and your furs are not here when they arrive."

Sublette's eyes narrow. "You don't want a fight, huh?"

Torres spreads his hands, palms upward. "I offer you my home, señor. But not the lives of my wife and my children."

"And this just isn't the time and place for battle," Richard Campbell says mildly.

Sublette nods impatiently. "I know it. I don't like it, though." He shrugs, then crouches down next to his pack of furs. He flips it onto his shoulder, then straightens carefully, favoring his injured leg. He turns to Torres. "You got another way out of here that's not through that gate?"

"Gracias, señor," Torres says. He turns and gestures toward a small door at the opposite end of the courtyard. "This way, if you please."

Sublette follows him across the enclosure. He turns at the door. "Hold 'em off as long as you can, boys!" he says with a grin.

There's a general chuckle as Sublette ducks through the door, then the remaining men look at each other warily. "I hope this doesn't turn itself into a fight," Richard Campbell says. "It'd be a bad thing indeed to wreak damage on this fine house."

"They've got my furs," James Pattie says bitterly. He runs his hand through his curly blond hair. "Every single one of them. And all of them mixed in with Young's now, like as not."

"The adobe walls, they are easy to fix," Michel Robidoux says. "And the repair of them is women's work, not Torres'."

"Well now, that thought seems most, how do you say, unchivalrous," George Yount says. He lifts an eyebrow at Robidoux. "Is that the right word?" Then he shrugs and lifts his muzzle loader to check his powder. "It is my hope the shooting will not happen."

"But 'tis better to be prepared than not," Richard Campbell says as he lifts his own firearm.

The pounding at the gates comes a full hour later. The men inside are ready for it. They're scattered casually around the courtyard, Gerald leaning against the far wall, Robidoux and LeCompte crouched near the gate with playing cards in their hands, George Yount and Richard Campbell sprawled casually on benches placed along opposite walls. Only James Pattie moves, restlessly stalking the space between Yount and Campbell. Every man has a weapon either in hand or laying across buckskin-covered knees.

The gate shakes again and Pattie stops in his tracks. No one moves.

Agustín Torres hurries out of the house and across the courtyard without looking at the trappers. He swings the gate open just far enough to allow the soldiers to enter. He bows slightly, his head erect, eyes arrogantly sharp. Watching him, Gerald marvels at the man's transformation from placating host, when he asked Milton Sublette to leave, to Spanish aristocrat.

The man in charge of the soldiers explains apologetically that they have orders to search the house for Sublette and his furs, and Torres regally nods permission. The soldiers ignore the trappers as they move across the courtyard. Torres, his arms crossed over his chest, stands at the gate and waits impassively for their return. A small boy appears at his side and Torres puts his hand on the child's shoulder and speaks a few quiet words. The boy nods, his eyes large in his small face, but stays close to Torres.

When the soldiers reemerge, their leader apologizes once again. Torres and he speak together in Spanish, their words rapid and liquid in the sun, then Torres gestures to the boy, who runs to the gate and swings it fully open.

Only after the gate has closed behind the governor's men do the trappers finally stir. "We didn't expect to bring such trouble on your head," Richard Campbell says apologetically.

Torres shrugs. "Ah, there is always some trouble in this life. And it is possible that we have now finished with this thing."

But the thing isn't finished. Two hours later, Young appears. "After all that time waiting, His Excellency wasn't available for an interview," he says drily. "I guess he was too busy countin' the furs he's worked so hard for. I hear there's a market in Mexico City for beaver plew."

But the Governor is apparently available the next day, because two soldiers show up at the Torres casa with a notice that bids "Señor

Joven" to an audience. Young's jaw tightens, then he moves so quickly past the soldiers and across the plaza that they're forced to half-run to keep up.

He returns almost as quickly, looking pleased with himself. "Almost got myself thrown in the calaboose," he tells Agustín Torres with a grin as the massive gate swings shut behind him. The small boy who'd opened it for the soldiers heaves the wooden bar that latches it into place.

"El calabozo?" Torres says in alarm.

Young shrugs. "Your governor sure does like to bluster and threaten," he says. "He's claiming me and Sublette had some kind of arrangement, that I talked his Excellency into having those furs hauled out to the plaza just so Milt could steal what was his." Young shakes his head. "Armijo sure don't let go of an idea once he gets it in his head." He laughs. "I finally just walked out on him."

Torres' eyes widen. "You walked away from His Excellency? El jefe?" He looks apprehensively toward the wooden gate, then at Young. "You left his presence without his permission?" Someone raps firmly on the other side of the gate, and Torres sighs and gestures wearily for the boy to open it.

A cluster of men in uniform stand outside. "The house, it is surrounded, Don Torres," their leader says apologetically. He looks over Torres's shoulder to Ewing Young. "You must come with us now, Señor Joven," he says. "It is on the order of el jefe politico."

"There are other ways of settlin' this," James Pattie says from his seat on the other end of the courtyard. They all look toward him as he lifts his gun from his knees.

Torres sucks in his breath. Young puts his hand on Torres' forearm and shakes his head at Pattie. "There's no call for bloodshed," he says. "I'll go with them."

"Gracias, señor," Torres says.

The soldier makes a polite gesture. "This way, please."

Young is gone two weeks, held in the Santa Fe prison while his men sit in the Torres courtyard or wander the town, looking for something to do while they wait for their wages. Those who have the resources and inclination spend their time gambling at monte or visiting prostitutes. James Pattie spends a good deal of time grooming and exercising his father's sorrel mare.

Gerald and George Yount wander into the hills and do a little hunting. From the higher slopes, Gerald notes that every bit of land here suitable for farming is irrigated and in use. Chile and corn seem to flourish in the well-tended soil.

And the hunting in the hills is productive. He and Yount are in the courtyard late one afternoon, presenting a brace of rabbit and grouse to Torres, when there's a dull thud on the big wooden gate. As the small gatekeeper opens it, Ewing Young appears, Michel Robidoux supporting him on one side, Richard Campbell on the other. Young's face is thin and pale. His big frame shrinks into itself and his shoulders sag with exhaustion.

Torres springs forward. "My friend!" he says. He looks at the men supporting Young. "What happened?"

"He is with fever," Michel Robidoux says. "His Excellency the Governor has ordered him released on condition of bond."

A smile flashes across Young's face, then his head droops again.

"We didn't know where else to carry him," Campbell says apologetically. "You must be weary of us all by this time."

"No, no," Torres says. "It is well." He motions them toward the house door. "Please, bring him within." He turns to Gerald. "Will you assist?"

251

They maneuver Young across the courtyard and into the house, Torres and the others following close behind. In the sala, Gerald rearranges a bench so one end is against the adobe wall, and Robidoux and Campbell settle Young onto it, back against the wall, legs stretched out on the bench.

Torres hovers anxiously. "Is it well with you, mi amigo?" he asks.

"A little water and I'll be just fine." Ewing Young grins and nods toward George Yount, still holding the rabbits. "And a piece of that hare you'll be stewin' up pretty soon." Young grimaces at Torres. "That's one nasty calabozo your Governor has there. No light and no blankets to speak of. And the food is an abomination."

Torres' back straightens. He crosses his arms. "Your recovery has commenced con rapidez," he says drily.

Young winks at him as Robidoux and Campbell chuckle. "Armijo seemed to think it might be so," Robidoux says. "He demanded our guarantee that the Captain would not disappear."

"Well, I'm disappearing as far as Taos anyway," Young says. "And my furs are going with me." He rubs two fingers together. "It's amazing what a protestation of innocence accompanied by a small gift can accomplish."

"And what about my furs?" James Pattie asks.

Young looks at him sympathetically. "I'm sorry, son," he says. "The governor won't release them unless you put yourself in his hands."

Pattie runs his hands through his hair. "In his jail?"

Young grimaces and nods. "It's your choice," he said. "You might be able to talk him out of them at the right price."

Pattie takes a step back. "I don't want to go anywhere near that bastard!"

252

Young shakes his head regretfully. "I'm afraid they're lost to you, then."

Pattie stares at him, then says flatly, "There's no reason to stay here, then."

"Come on to Taos with us, give Armijo a little time, and he might change his tune."

Pattie frowns and turns to Torres. "Do you think that's possible?"

The Mexican man shrugs. "I suppose anything is possible."

Pattie runs his hand through his hair again. "Maybe I'll go see him," he says.

"I'd wait until tomorrow, if I was you," Ewing Young says. "He may be a little testy today, after dealin' with me. I don't know that he thinks he got the best of our arrangement. And his price is bound to be higher if we all look too eager."

But by the next afternoon, it's too late. Pattie returns to the Torres casa in a pale rage. "That bastard took everything!" he says as he storms into the courtyard. "Sold it all off! Mine and Sublette's too!"

Ewing Young looks up from the bench where he sits against the sunny adobe wall. "He sure didn't waste any time."

"I don't know what to do," Pattie says. He half-turns and looks at the other trappers questioningly. They all look uneasily away.

"There's not much you can do now," Young says.

"All I've got left is my daddy's horse." Pattie rubs a hand through his curls. "I guess I can take it to him, see what he's got to say about it all."

Young nods. "That might be best. And there's no need to reimburse me for your food and all."

Pattie stares at him, then looks down. "I'd forgot about that," he admits. "What I owe you."

Young raises a hand, waving the younger man's concerns away. "You brought in meat enough to cover it," he says. "We'll call it even."

Pattie hesitates, then nods. "I'm gonna go get that horse," he says, and goes out.

Ewing Young's eyes follow him and a satisfied look flashes across his face. Gerald's eyes narrow. Was this part of Young's deal with the governor? A few coins and the other men's furs in exchange for his own?

Gerald turns away, disgust in his throat. Is nothing straightforward in this country? Suzanna Peabody's direct gaze rises in his mind. Not everyone is like Young. He knows that. But, the fur trade seems to bring out the mischief in people. It isn't just the trappers. First the government allows trapping, then trapping's allowed only under certain conditions. Then it isn't permitted for Americans at all. Although that hasn't seemed to slow anyone down much. The trade in pelts is still brisk. Beaver plews aren't called 'furry bank notes' for nothing.

Jeremiah Peabody had said "It's a bad business." He'd been referring to Young's response to de Baca's death, but Gerald's beginning to think anything connected with the fur trade is a bad business. It's too uncertain, too ephemeral. Too filled with tension and suspense and, finally, downright chicanery.

CHAPTER 31

When Gerald repeats this observation a week later in the cozy Taos parlor, Jeremiah Peabody chuckles and Suzanna laughs out loud. "I've never thought of the fur business as ephemeral," she says as she pours Gerald's tea. "Those plews certainly seem solid enough, although lightweight."

"The trade certainly has become complicated." Her father turns to Gerald. "While you were in Santa Fe, Thomas Smith and Maurice LeDuc hid their furs in a cave somewhere near La Cienega and then came into Taos to make sure the coast was clear before they brought them in. They'd apparently had a run-in with someone in authority northwest of Santa Fe." He nods at Gerald. "I hear they also exchanged money and goods before a resolution was found. Deception and half-truths seem to be very popular these days."

"The truth certainly doesn't seem to be very popular," Suzanna says. "Ignacio Sandoval's father was assaulted by an American trapper because Ignacio reported Ewing Young to the authorities. Fortunately, the alcalde was nearby and intervened." She shakes her head. "I hate to think what might have happened to Señor Sandoval simply because he believes people should obey the law."

"There aren't many like him, either Spanish or American," Gerald says glumly. "Too many people either change the rules or don't want to live by them. Personally, I'd prefer to make a living doing something less subject to interpretation."

Jeremiah Peabody hefts the Latin tome he's been holding. "This is why I prefer books and teaching," he says. "Ultimately, my interpretation is mine alone." He places the book on the small table beside him and grins at Suzanna. "Is there tea in that pot for me, my dear, or is Mr. Locke the only recipient of your largesse this afternoon?"

"You were busy with your book," Suzanna teases. She fills a cup and hands it to him, then turns to Gerald. "Would you like more bread and butter?"

"No, thank you," he says. He hesitates. "Did James Pattie send word that he had gone to Santa Rita?"

Suzanna shakes her head. "I don't think so." She turns to her father. "Did he have reason to inform you of his whereabouts, papá?"

Her father shakes his head and lifts his cup to his lips. Suzanna turns back to Gerald. "The plot that you found for my potatoes has produced beautifully!" she says eagerly. "Ramón helped me plant seed potatoes from last year's crop and they seem to be doing nicely!" She glances at her father. "There were differences of opinion about how best to store them, so I tried three different methods, and both the straw and sand seemed to work equally well—"

Ramón? The name is familiar, but Suzanna's eyes are on his. Gerald pushes the question aside and leans toward her, absorbed by both her words and her enthusiasm. Jeremiah Peabody returns to his book, a small smile on his lips.

CHAPTER 32

Ewing Young disposes of his furs, damaged as they are, and Gerald receives his pay—a little over $300. It's now mid-August and the fur brigades for the coming season are starting to form, but Gerald's aversion to the entire process hasn't receded. Or maybe it's just Ewing Young who no longer feels honest to him.

Not that Young has asked Gerald to participate in another hunt. The older man is staying in Taos this winter. He claims to be recuperating from his Santa Fe imprisonment, but Jeremiah Peabody seems to think Young is simply lying low.

Gerald has to admit that there are some things he does like about trapping. The wilderness has a definite appeal, and he enjoyed his time with Old Bill Williams, even if the man did have an opinion about just about everything. There are men like Ewing Young in any walk of life. Certainly, there are bound to be men like Enoch Jones in any given group of Americans. Staying away from trapping is no guarantee that he won't meet someone else with Jones' attitudes. But Gerald's mind veers away from that topic, which still hasn't come up in the Peabody parlor.

His discomfort with trapping really began with the ugliness that erupted on the Gila and again outside the Mojave villages. The killing there, and then the unremitting butchering when beaver was plentiful. There was just so much blood. He grimaces. And then the blood from

Enoch Jones' chest. His hands twitch, remembering the feel of the blade, the way is sank so easily—

He pushes the thought away and focuses on the recent events in Santa Fe. That whole episode was also slippery and uncomfortable. The kind of transaction that seem to be central to the life Ewing Young and the other trappers seem to glory in.

Is he being too squeamish? He doesn't think so. But he needs to do something. As he walks the dusty Taos streets, Gerald ponders his options. There are other trapping groups forming, in spite of the government prohibition against American trappers. Word has filtered north from the copper mines that James Pattie and his father are recruiting men for another trip into the Gila. Rumor has it that they plan to push west from there, into California.

Here in Taos, Sylvester Pratte is putting together a group of thirty men for a venture north into the Rockies. Old Bill has signed up with them. Gerald chuckles. Williams working with a large group of trappers. Given the man's strong opinions and his antipathy toward trapping with others, that should be interesting for all involved.

Gerald stops in mid-stride. Pratte's group is heading to North Park and the Platte River. Which means Old Bill will be far north of the mountains east of Taos, the long valley and the streams that flow from it and the peaks around it—Red River, the Cimarron, Coyote Creek. Is there enough beaver there to justify a trapping excursion of his own? Would such a venture net enough that he could return to Taos with enough funds for land and a cabin?

Suzanna Peabody's dark eyes flash into his mind. Gerald forces the thought to one side. Land and a cabin are enough to hope for. He shouldn't set his sights too high. She may very well prefer to set up housekeeping with someone else.

And she doesn't know what he's done. What he's capable of doing. Who he really is, on several levels. His courage shrinks when he thinks about telling her. Yet how can he not? He who disdains the dishonesty, the slipperiness of others, still hasn't been forthcoming about his own failures. Regardless of how she might feel about his ancestry, there's always the death of Enoch Jones.

He wants to forget it all, to push Jones and the events in the Gila wilderness into a dark hole in his memory. But the man haunts him even when he doesn't haunt him. The dreams are mostly gone now, but still there's the constant dread that someone will tell the Peabody's about what happened. Suzanna will be puzzled and hurt that he hasn't told her, and yet he somehow can't find the right time or the words.

But the story of Jones' death is a small thing compared to the issue of his own heritage, of who his father is. He's going to have to tell her. But here too, Gerald finds himself putting it off. She has a right to know. At least, he hopes that she has a right to know. Yet his stomach twists when he considers how she may react. Will she despise him for something he can't help but be? Or will she feel only contempt for a man who hasn't been truthful with her from the beginning? Or will she not care, because she doesn't really care about him, one way or another? He can't bear to think about how she might react, yet he knows delay is only going to make the discussion more difficult when—if—it comes.

He turns his thoughts to the streams that surround the long valley to the east. It's dangerous to venture into the mountains alone, yet the beaver would be all his, the rewards higher. Gerald grimaces. And then there's the moral dilemma. Americans are forbidden to trap in nuevomexico. All of Mexico, for that matter. But there's little else he

259

can do to earn money, unless he hires on with one of the outgoing Santa Fe trains and returns to Missouri.

But there's nothing for him in Missouri but repression and insults. Besides, Suzanna Peabody—although so far out of reach to him—is here in nuevomexico. He can't bring himself to truly consider leaving.

He sets himself to considering his options, instead. If the beaver have returned to the Red River, the Cimarron, and Coyote Creek, the trapping is simple enough. Smuggling the plews into Taos that will be the problem.

Not that it would be very difficult. It's just that it's against the law. Is he really willing to take part in the subterfuge men like Young engage in? Yet it might be necessary to accomplish his goal. He's mentioned the idea to Suzanna, the idea of going east into the Sangres to trap. She seemed less than enthusiastic. The illegality of it seemed to concern her.

There's another option. A citizen can trap legally, no matter where he's originally from. Some of the American and French-Canadian trappers are turning Catholic and becoming Mexican citizens in order to have free access to Mexico's hunting grounds.

But even if he was willing to become Mexican, there isn't time to complete the naturalization process before the season begins. It takes a good year or more. And, given Governor Armijo's attitude toward Americans, he's unlikely to support an application for citizenship that isn't accompanied by considerable financial incentives. Gerald suspects that even all he has wouldn't be enough.

He's still frowning over his lack of options when he turns into the Peabody gate. Suzanna is bending over her pepper plants, which are planted along the courtyard's south wall. She's pouring water from a small wooden bucket into the ground at their roots. A short wiry

Mexican man who looks vaguely familiar is at the well on the other end of the courtyard, transferring water into a larger bucket.

Suzanna looks up as Gerald comes through the gateway. "Hola!" she says cheerfully. She turns to the Mexican man with a smile. "Ramón, this is the gentleman we were speaking of earlier." She nods to Gerald. "This is Ramón Chavez, a cousin—" She looks at Ramón, who grins at her. Suzanna chuckles. "A relation," she corrects herself. "A relation of both our Chonita and her cousin Antonia."

Gerald and the shorter man nod politely at each other. Ramón hefts the bucket toward Suzanna and gives her a questioning look. "Oh, yes!" she says. She puts her container on the ground and the Mexican man crosses the courtyard and begins filling it from the larger one.

Suzanna looks at Gerald. "Ramón has been helping me water the plants and giving me advice on the best way to keep everything from wilting in this heat." She glances at the sky. "The monsoon rains should have started by now, but they haven't been cooperating."

Ramón chuckles. "They are testing your faith, señorita," he says.

"My faith in the monsoons, at any rate!" she laughs. She turns, empties the small bucket around the pepper plants, sets it down, and turns to Gerald. "Will you come in? My father will be pleased to see you."

It's her standard formula, which usually fills him with pleasure, but there's something about the way she says it today, a kind of tentativeness to her look, that sends a unexpected chill down his spine. Will only her father be pleased to see him? What about herself? Has someone told her about Jones? His race?

But he can't bring himself to ask any of these questions, especially in front of a stranger. Especially one who looks at Suzanna as this Ramón Chavez does. There's no deference in the man. The affection in his glance says he's confident of the girl's good opinion. Almost as if there's an understanding between them. Gerald follows Suzanna numbly into the house.

"Ah, just the man I wanted to see!" Jeremiah Peabody says as they enter the parlor. He stands and crosses the room, reaching for Gerald's hand. "I have a proposition for you that might benefit us both."

"Papa, you're beginning to sound as hasty as you claim that I am," Suzanna says with amusement. "At the very least, let Mr. Locke take off his hat and sit down."

Peabody laughs and gestures to a chair. "That was rather precipitous of me!" he says ruefully. "Please forgive me. How are you today, Mr. Locke? Have you decided what you will do with your time, this coming season?"

Gerald shakes his head, his fear lifting as he takes his seat. "I'm still undecided," he says. "Somehow another expedition like last fall's doesn't appeal to me."

"I'm going to see about the tea things," Suzanna says. She crosses the room and goes out.

The men watch her go, Gerald trying not to let his eyes linger.

"Was Ramón Chavez still here when you arrived?" her father asks.

Gerald's chest tightens. He forces himself to nod calmly.

"I've known Ramón many years," Peabody says. "He and I trapped together my first season here." He smiles ruefully. "He trapped, at any rate. I discovered that such a life is not truly my calling." He smiles a little. "As I think you have also." He pauses, and Gerald gives him a rueful smile. Peabody nods. "Ramón's a good man, and a valuable one," he says. "He seems to know or be related to everyone in nuevomexico, which is a valuable thing in an associate here."

Suzanna returns, carrying the tea tray, and Gerald leaps to take it from her and place it on the table. As she begins to pour the tea, she glances at her father. "Have you told him about Ramón?"

Gerald's chest tightens again at the tone in her voice. He looks at her father.

"I was just about to explain his relationship to us," Peabody answers. "It might be easier if you did so."

Suzanna chuckles and hands Gerald his cup. She tilts her head. "Let's see. Ramón Chavez is the brother-in-law of Chonita's sister's husband and the son of Antonia Garcia's uncle by his second wife."

She frowns. "I think that's correct." She frowns, considering. "I'm not sure what that makes Ramón and Chonita to each other." She shrugs. "At any rate, he's also a dear friend of my father's and is my godfather, although I wasn't technically baptized, since we aren't Catholic." She glances at her father. "Although Ramón was hardly more than a child himself when I was born, he agreed to provide for me if something should happen to papá before I was of age, God forbid."

Gerald feels the clutch of discomfort in his stomach easing. "He seems a nice man," he concedes.

"Ramón has been in and out of Taos the past eighteen months, and his presence never seems to have coincided with your own," Jeremiah says. "That's why you haven't met him." He shifts in his chair. "But now he's decided that he'd like to find a way to make a substantial sum and is searching for a way to do that." He gives Gerald a small nod. "He feels as you do about the trapping business, especially about how the American trappers manipulate the government officials to achieve their ends."

Gerald looks at him, wondering where this is going. Jeremiah turns to Suzanna. "Could I trouble you for another cup of tea, my dear?"

Suzanna nods and crosses the room to take his empty cup. Gerald feels his eyes following her, then wrenches them back to her father.

"It seems to me that you might do worse," he is saying.

"Worse?" Gerald asks.

"I think that Ramón might be of assistance to you," Jeremiah Peabody says, apparently repeating something he's already said. "It's never wise for a man to go alone into the mountains, but he has a particular desire to trap this next season. Regardless of the business's less savory aspects, it still has the potential to bring a high return. If the two of you partner as free trappers, there would be a mutual benefit. Also, since he is Mexican, the legality of your activity would not be questioned."

"And Ramón is an excellent and enthusiastic cook," Suzanna says. "I suspect he'd be more than happy to take on that responsibility."

Jeremiah Peabody flashes a smile. "That would certainly be a consideration if you were going with them," he teases. "Given your lack of enthusiasm for cookery."

She chuckles. "And lack of skill," she says ruefully. She turns to Gerald. "I hope you'll consider partnering with him," she says. "You mentioned going back into the Sangres. It would be a comfort—" She stops, her face flushing. She looks down and smoothes the fabric of her dress across her lap. "That is, I would be glad to know he had someone with him in the wilderness. The mountains are not safe for a man alone."

So it's Chavez's safety she's concerned about. Gerald turns to Jeremiah Peabody. "I would need to speak with him," he says stiffly.

Peabody's eyes drift from his daughter's face to Gerald's. A smile twitches his lips. "Let me see if he is still in the house," he says as he rises. "I suspect he will be in the kitchen with Encarnación."

264

As he leaves the room, Suzanna lifts her gaze from her skirts. She gives Gerald a conspiratorial smile. "When he's in Taos, Ramón spends as much time as he can in Chonita's kitchen," she says. "Since he can cook and bake as well as she can, we believe that the attraction is not truly the food."

Gerald raises an eyebrow, trying to keep the hope from his face.

"He doesn't quite have the financial resources he believes he needs in order to offer her a home." Suzanna turns her dark eyes on him, the pleading plain. "He is very dear to us and it would be a gift to my father and to me if you would agree to partner with him." She smiles mischievously. "And to Chonita, as well."

The knot in Gerald's chest smoothes itself out. "It seems a good plan," he says. "But of course I'll need to talk with him myself. He may not be agreeable to the idea."

She gives him a glowing smile as her father ushers Ramón Chavez into the room.

CHAPTER 33

Gerald finds to his surprise that, in the company of Ramón Chavez, some of the pleasure of trapping returns. The man is quiet, but certainly not taciturn or sullen. He is simply who he is, with no axe to grind, nothing to prove. Unlike the querulous and opinionated Old Bill Williams, Chavez rarely speaks. But when he does, what he says is sensible and without rancor, even when he talks of the Indians.

After William's loquacity and the casual violence and deceptiveness of the men in Ewing Young's trapping party, Ramón's temperament and attitudes are a welcome change. His deep affection for the Peabody's, which is apparent in any reference to them, also goes a long way toward fueling Gerald's respect for the older man.

They take the same route into the mountains that Gerald and Williams had used. Ramón has trapped the Red River before and can give advice on side streams that might be of value, especially in the upper forks. While Gerald's instinct that there will once again be beaver where he and Old Bill trapped proves valid, Ramón's knowledge adds even further to their take. They work their way steadily to the river's headwaters.

Two days after they reach the mountain lakes, the first snow hits. There isn't much, perhaps two inches. But Ramón looks at their icy blankets and the lead-gray sky and shakes his head. "There will be more today and then tomorrow," he predicts. "It is time to head downward." He turns to Gerald. "We can move back down the river,

266

or we can work south through the mountains toward Mora, or move east to the dark valley."

"The dark valley?"

"The one they call the Moreno." Ramón shrugs. "The pines, they are very dark on the mountainsides there."

"I have seen that valley twice now," Gerald says noncommittally. "There are streams from it that hold beaver. But there are no beaver in the valley itself."

"But the valley itself is a thing to be seen," Ramón says. "I have not been there in many years and would view it again."

Gerald gives him a surprised look. Is this man drawn to those slopes the way he is?

"I have been told there is gold in the streams that flow through the valley," Ramón continues. "Not much, but a little." He looks up at the gloomy clouds overhead. "Though this is not the season for searching for such things."

"Perhaps in the summer," Gerald agrees. "The valley grass is long and green in the summer. The water there seems to run year round."

"It is very cold in the winter though," Ramón says.

Gerald looks up at the snow-heavy clouds moving steadily down the mountain toward them. "It's still a thing worth seeing."

Ramón grins. "Then let us see it," he says.

Moving directly east requires them to flounder up a rocky bank that seems almost vertical in places. The mules snort disapprovingly as the men lead them over the slippery rocks. Finally, the slope levels out and they stand at one end of a rock-covered saddle between two boulder-strewn slopes. The mountain peaks behind them are shrouded in clouds.

The storm has begun in earnest now and the ground is slick underfoot. A cold wetness swirls into their faces and seeps into their clothing. They move forward slowly, glad for the saddle's relatively flat terrain but wary of its broken slabs of sandstone and shale. The mules twitch their ears and snort irritably but keep moving, picking their way across the field of rock.

Ramón and Gerald pause at the point where the saddle widens and begins to slope downward. They exchange grim looks through the haze of white flakes. The spaces between the rocks underfoot are filling rapidly with snow, making the surface look deceptively smooth. One false step will twist a man's ankle for him. With this downward slant, the resulting fall would be nasty and long.

"I think perhaps the mules should lead us," Ramón says. "They will feel a footing where we cannot see."

Gerald nods, too cold to argue. Ramón pats his mule's shoulder, speaks a few words into its ear, then moves backward, playing out the lead rope as he goes. When he reaches the animal's rump, he snaps it with the rope. The mule turns its head and gives him a reproachful look. Ramón snaps the rope again. The animal snorts in annoyance and starts down the slope, the man well behind, letting the mule take the lead, careful to hang onto the rope but not to put any pressure on it. Gerald follows numbly beside his own animal, keeping to the track Ramón and his mule are creating, fighting for traction on the slick snow.

It's two frozen hours before they drop into a narrow ravine, out of the worst of the storm. Because the walls of the gulch block the wind, the snow is thinner here. Gerald's very knees are numb with cold. He hears Ramón speaking to his mule and realizes the other man is once again level with his animal's head. Gerald moves forward stiffly.

Ramón grins. "He did well, did he not?"

"He did." Gerald looks around. "Do you think we're far enough down to safely shelter for the night?"

Ramón shakes his head. "It is hard to say." He looks around. Two massive sandstone slabs twice a man's height jut from the slope to their right. The big rocks are perhaps eight feet apart, but lean into each other and form a sheltered space between them. Ramón moves toward it and peers in, then turns, his eyes amused. "There is strong evidence this will provide the shelter we seek," he says. "Someone has been here before us."

Gerald moves up beside him and peers into the space. There's a circle of stones on one side and a small collection of broken deadfall tucked under a cleft in the far rock. With a little crowding, there's enough space for two men and their mules. The surface of the boulders are marked with figures and symbols scratched deep into the sandstone surface, some of them partly obscured with lichen. "Indians?" he asks.

"So it would seem."

He frowns. "Is it wise for us to use it?"

"No one else is here," Ramón points out. "And we need shelter."

Gerald nods and clucks at his mule.

There's something about an enclosed space and a warm fire that brings out reminiscences and confidences in the most reserved of men. Ramón speaks of his childhood, the simple poverty that seemed a kind of wealth, and an uncle who killed a man but didn't suffer any consequences, because his vecinos considered the death justified.

Gerald stares into the fire. "I also have killed," he says. He grimaces. "Or I believe that I have." He glances up. Ramón watches him impassively. Gerald turns his head away. "Last season. With Ewing Young's expedition."

"Enoch Jones did not return," Ramón says.

Gerald looks up in surprise, but now the other man's head is turned away. It's somehow easier to say the words to the back of his head. "I

269

stabbed him," Gerald says. "He was threatening harm and I stabbed him." His hand twitches, feeling the blade sinking inexorably between Jones' ribs. His breath catches, but he forces himself to finally say it. "I stabbed him in the chest. Hard. Not enough to simply stop him, but also to cut open the flesh between his ribs." He swallows. "He ran into the woods and there was no sign of him after that." He shakes his head. "But no man could live with that kind of wound and no doctoring."

"Jones is the man who followed la señorita," Ramón says. "And also Chonita."

Gerald looks up. "He was bothering her also? Even after that time in the plaza? What a bastard!"

"A good man to be killed."

There's a long silence as both men stare into the darkness. Then Gerald says, "I haven't told the Peabody's."

"And will you?"

"I should. I must, if I am to—"

"Ask for her hand?" Ramón sounds a little amused.

Gerald studies the fire. "I have no right," he says. "And certainly no resources. And she's given me no encouragement."

"Hmm."

"And there's the matter of Jones' death."

"Por que?"

"Because a man should tell a woman everything about himself."

There's a long silence. "Por que?" Ramón asks again.

Gerald glances at him in surprise. "Because— Well, because it's right, I suppose. It's a matter of conscience, of being honest and truthful."

Ramón stirs and stands, stretching his legs. "I have learned much since you americanos have come to my country," he says. "One of the things I have learned is that truth is not always what it seems and to be honest is sometimes to lose more than the honesty is worth."

Gerald raises an eyebrow.

Ramón shrugs and lifts his hands, palms up. "But to each of us a different thing is important," he says. "To Suzanna Peabody the death of Jones may come as a welcome piece of news. She may find what you have done a cause for rejoicing." He frowns and tilts his head. "That is perhaps too strong a word. I cannot imagine that she would rejoice at the death of any man. But surely it is for her to decide what secrets must be told and which truths are necessary." He shrugs and moves away to lay out his blankets and prepare for bed.

Gerald stares into the flames for a long while before he follows the other man's example and composes himself to sleep as the mules send their breath into the space over his head.

CHAPTER 34

In the morning, the men and mules move down the ravine, following the half-frozen water that trickles through it. The gulch runs straight south for a long while, then swings north until Gerald begins to wonder if they're wise to follow it. After all, the valley lies to the south.

But they're still headed downhill and the snow is still falling on the slopes behind them, so he doesn't voice his concern. Though he does breath more easily when the stream turns again, twisting northeast and then south.

They camp that night at what appears to be the fullest part of a deep curve that bends north and east. The ravine has widened a little and its slopes are more broadly angled and lower than they've been.

Snow still threatens and there's no sign of huntable wildlife. Even the birds are stilled by the heavy clouds. The two men are reduced to eating flour and water mashed into a paste, then spiraled around green sticks and cooked over the smoky fire.

At least there's water. In the morning, Gerald breaks ice from the edge of the tiny stream and gingerly fills his canteen. With luck, the liquid will warm a little before his thirst compels him to try it. At the moment, it's bound to be toothbreakingly cold.

When he returns to the fire, Ramón has his rifle in his lap, checking the load. "It may be that the elk have all moved into the valley," he says. "Perhaps there will be meat to eat with our bread tonight."

Gerald grins. "Oh, is that what you call what we've been eating?"

Ramón's smile flashes. "It is not the bread of Encarnación," he says. "But for that we must return to Don Fernando de Taos."

Gerald looks at the pack on his mule's back, ready for the day. "There aren't enough furs in that pack to warrant a return just yet," he says. "More's the pity."

Ramón grins. "But how delicioso that bread will be when we taste it again," he says. "After my poor attempts."

"I wasn't criticizing your bread," Gerald says apologetically. "I'd just like some meat to go with it."

Ramón chuckles. "I also am weary of my so-called bread," he says. "And I too wish for meat." He turns his head and tilts it to look at the just-visible mountain peaks to the west. "Let us hope those clouds stay behind us and do not descend with us down the ravine."

They kill the fire and head out, still following the stream, which is starting to actually look like it means to become a creek at some point. Gerald shakes his head ruefully. Back in Missouri, this trickle of moisture wouldn't be given the honor of a name. But he's willing to bet there's a map somewhere where it's drawn clearly and given a label. He chuckles. If its water runs all year, it'll even be designated a river.

The sun is doing its best to make itself seen through the bank of clouds in the east. It isn't producing much light or much warmth, but it seems to promise an end to the grayness and snow.

There's a break in the trees ahead and Gerald's heart lifts. The valley, at last. But when they reach the open space, he sees that the stream is merely curving south through a frozen meadow toward yet another mountain. Snow-bound grassy slopes block the view on either side.

Gerald suppresses a groan of frustration. The grass is a hopeful sign, but the mountain ahead is discouraging. Yet, the mules' heads are up and Ramón is nodding in satisfaction. As they swing south alongside the rivulet of water, frozen grass crunching beneath their feet, Gerald sees why.

The narrow stretch of grass between them and the mountain ahead curves around its base and stretches beyond to form a peninsula of grass that reaches into the larger valley below. As Gerald pauses to take it in, the sun breaks through the clouds. The white snow gleams joyfully back at him.

He jiggles his mule's lead rope and follows Ramón along the stream. The ground is slightly mushy underfoot now and the snow is already melting from the grass. The mules snatch mouthfuls as they pass, and the men slow a little to allow them to forage and to adjust their own eyes to the brightness.

Ahead of him, Ramón suddenly raises his arm and waves it toward the base of the mountain that had seemed so ominous. Gerald turns, narrowing his eyes against the glare. Elk scatter the lower slopes, browsing contentedly, apparently oblivious to the men and their mules. Ramón's arm moves again, to the south, and Gerald sees another hillside with yet another herd. Ramón turns toward Gerald and grins. "Meat for our bread," he calls.

Gerald chuckles and nods. What a valley it is. A snowy Garden of Eden. Water, browse, meat. What more could a man want? Suzanna Peabody's bemused eyes rise before him. Well, that also. If that's possible. But, for now, the meat and the beauty seems almost enough. He lifts his voice toward Ramón. "Shall we find a place to camp and then go hunting, or shoot first and camp later?"

~ ~ ~ ~

But of course, no section of real estate is truly a Garden of Eden unmarked by human activity. The report of Ramón and Gerald's rifles and the subsequent elk stampede down the valley is bound to be noticed by other meat seekers.

Gerald and Ramón are hunkered over an afternoon fire at the base of one of the half-dozen long low rises that bisect the valley when the mules nicker anxiously. Immediately, the men are on their feet, rifles in hand, the fire between them as they stand back to back, eyes scanning the snow-spotted slopes.

An Indian man, in the long braids and beaded buckskins of the Utes, rises from the grass twenty yards out, palms up to show he comes without weapons. Ramón says "Heh!" and Gerald turns his head slightly.

"How many?" Gerald asks.

"Just one, I think. No, there's another."

Gerald nods, his eyes sweeping the grasses within his gaze. "I think— No, there's another." He frowns. "A youngsters," he says in a relieved tone.

"Ute youngsters can also shoot."

Gerald chuckles. "Very true." He swings his head. "Just the three, then. All with hands open. Shall we call them in?"

Ramón shrugs. "If we don't, they may shoot. If we do, they may shoot."

Gerald laughs and raises his arm to beckon the Utes forward. As they come closer, he squints. "I think I may know the tall one."

Ramón nods. "As do I. It is Stands Alone." He looks carefully at the boy. "And his son Little Squirrel. They come to Taos sometimes,

275

to trade. It is three years since I have seen them." He lifts a hand in greeting as the tallest of the men reaches the campfire.

"My friend," Stands Alone responds. He nods to Gerald. "You I have met before. With the Lone Elk of the red hair. Did you find the beaver you sought?"

Gerald nods. "You directed us well. We made a good catch."

"And now you have returned." It isn't a question, but somehow it requires an answer.

"Yes." Gerald turns. His eyes sweep the valley, then move to the Ute. "It is a good place."

"It is." Stands Alone turns and nods toward his companions. "This is my friend Many Eagles and my son Little Squirrel." The men and boy nod to each other. "I see you have found meat," Stands Alone says.

"But not beaver just yet, so we were forced to shoot elk," Gerald says, remembering their previous conversation.

A smile glimmers across the Ute's face. "So you have no fat." He turns to his son and says something in Ute. The boy pulls a section of beaver tail from the pouch at his waist. "It is now we who have fat."

"Perhaps we should combine them," Ramón says. He turns to the boy. "Yours and mine together will make a fine meal. And we have flour for bread."

~ ~ ~ ~

They eat until they are satiated, then Ramón places thin strips of the remaining meat on the rocks that fringe the fire. "The jerked meat will be good for your travels," he tells Stands Alone.

"It is good," the Ute says. "No waste."

"It would be a shame to waste anything of this valley," Gerald says. He looks out over the broad sweep of it. The snow is melting in earnest now. Elk and deer graze the hillsides, although well out of gunshot range. A business-like coyote trots across a boggy area below, nose straight before him. "The grasses indicate that the soil here is rich."

Stands Alone looks at him. "The grass is good feed for the elk and deer. And sometimes the antelope and buffalo."

Gerald adds a small piece of wood to the fire. "And would also do well for beef cattle."

Stands Alone grimaces. "Sharp hoofed and stupid. Bad for the stream banks." Then he grins mischievously. "But good for the wolves and the catamount."

"If a man lived here and watched over them, cattle might do well."

On the other side of the fire, Many Eagles moves impatiently.

"If a man lives here, the eagles might leave," Stands Alone says.

"If a man who respects the eagles lives here, he will not encroach on their nests and they will not wish to leave."

"The big eagles, the ones you call the golden, will eat small calves."

Gerald shrugs. "If most of the calves survive, the ones that are taken will not be missed."

"Rich man," Stands Alone observes.

Gerald shakes his head. "No, not a rich man. Just a realistic one. We must all pay for what we use. A calf now and then to the eagles or the wolves is a fair trade for use of the land."

Ramón glances at Stands Alone. "And to those who have used it before you?" he asks.

Gerald spreads his hands. "Surely there is room for all."

277

"One American comes and others follow," Many Eagles says grimly.

Ramón grins. "But not to last through a winter."

Stands Alone chuckles. His eyes slide to Gerald, then back to Ramón. "The winter winds here will push them away," he says. He and Ramón chuckle companionably.

Gerald raises an eyebrow. "I have encountered these winds," he says mildly. "I was here last winter with Old Bill."

"You would be without a woman." Stands Alone grins at Many Eagles and says something in Ute. Many Eagles chuckles and shakes his head. "Women do not like the winters here," Stands Alone says to Gerald. He gestures toward the Cimarron. "They stay below in the warm valley, the one of the Utes."

"I don't have a woman," Gerald says.

"You never know what might transpire," Ramón says.

Gerald glances at him, then returns his focus to Stands Alone. "A man who lives here will be rich enough to share with his friends," he says. He glances at Many Eagles. "And their friends."

Stands Alone nods, then shrugs. "It is not for me to say. Many bands of differing tribes travel these mountains to hunt and trade."

Gerald nods. He looks up and his eyes touch the grassy swales, the marshy area where the Cimarron River heads, and the green-black mountain slopes on the valley's eastern edge. "It's only an idea," he says. "Something to think on." He glances at the other men. "There's also the matter of money and cattle, which I don't possess." He shakes his head. "I may never have the means to do what I wish."

"You never know what might transpire," Ramón says again.

"The meat, it jerks?" Little Squirrel asks his father, and the men turn to teasing the boy about his two hollow legs.

CHAPTER 35

After the meat is jerked and divided between them, the Utes and trappers go their separate ways. Gerald and Ramón move east into the small valley Old Bill and Gerald had trapped two years before, then south toward Coyote Creek, gathering beaver pelts as they go. Gerald revels in the shadows of sun and cloud chasing each other across the green-black peaks, the exhilaration of the clear mountain air. In spite of Stands Alone's cautions, he finds himself continuing to ponder the possibility of a spread at this altitude. He can't seem to let go of the idea.

They make a good catch. Two ninety-pound compressed packs of furs weigh down the mules. More streams beckon in the mountains and valleys between them and Taos, but as the weather lightens in early February, the two men begin to contemplate a return to Taos.

"We'll get there before most of the big parties return and we'll be able to set our own price," Gerald says hopefully as he warms his hands at the campfire one night.

"The arrival we can control, I think," Ramón answers. "The price is up to el dios."

"The price for quality pelts was good last spring," Gerald points out.

"That was last spring," Ramón says. "Who knows what will happen this year? But I agree it is time to return. I am hungry for Encarnación's raised biscuits." He smiles at the trees beyond their camp site, then at Gerald. "She has said perhaps I may ask for her hand, if we return well."

Gerald smiles at the hopefulness in his friend's voice, though a pang of jealousy touches him at the same time. What he would give for such a 'perhaps'.

"And you will be glad to see Señorita Peabody, I think," Ramón says.

Gerald nods and looks away. Will she be glad to see him? He shakes his head at himself. Each time he goes away, he hopes she'll greet him especially joyfully at his return, give him some sign that he means more to her than the other men who visit her father's parlor.

He reminds himself that she did seem especially pleased to see him when he arrived in the spring. Then he remembers the admiring looks she gave James Pattie's horse. He grimaces. Maybe that's not a good comparison. The problem is, the longer he's away, the more his doubts creep in, the more he realizes the audacity of daring to tell her how he feels. And then there's the matter of Jones.

And his own race. Jones' death is a small issue compared to this thing about himself that he hasn't confessed. Despite Ramón's opinion that Suzanna has the right to decide which truths she wants to hear, telling her this fact seems fraught with danger. And there's also the fact that it seems audacious to simply blurt it out as if he has the right to think she ought to know everything about him. If she doesn't love him, then why should she or her father care about his race? He has about as much right to tell Suzanna Peabody the truth about himself as he does to ask for her hand.

Which is no right at all. He crosses to his mule and checks the straps around its pack of furs for the third time. This, at least, is something he can control. "Shall we plan to head out tomorrow then?" he asks over his shoulder. "To get you back to Encarnación in good time?"

~ ~ ~ ~

Neither man's predictions about the price of beaver furs is quite met: they are neither as high as Gerald hoped or as low as Ramón feared.

Because his expectations were lower, Ramón has an extra bounce to his step as he and Gerald leave Beaubien's mercantile. "Shall we go now to the Peabody casa?" he suggests.

Gerald grins at him. "I think you should wait at least a week before you press your suit," he teases. "After all, it isn't good for a woman to know you're too eager."

Ramón flashes him a smile. "I have waited long for this day," he says. "And I owe it to you, my friend."

Gerald shakes his head. "It's I who owe you," he says. "Your mountain skill and your trapping." He grins. "And your cooking."

Ramón chuckles. "My cooking is as nothing compared—" He stops, embarrassment shading his face. "But perhaps I speak of her too often."

"Is it possible to speak too often of a woman you admire?" Gerald asks.

"But you do not speak of la señorita."

Gerald tilts his head in acknowledgement. "I should have said, 'of a woman you admire and of whom you have reason to hope,'" he says.

Ramón shoots him a glance and turns his eyes back to the dusty street in front of them. "You do not believe you have reason to hope?"

"I don't have her father's status and resources," Gerald says simply. "I have no right to such hopes. And there are things I haven't told him. Things he has a right to know."

Ramón smiles. "I do not think it is her father's ideas or opinions that should concern you," he says. "La señorita's mind and opinions are her own."

Gerald chuckles. "That is true." Then he sobers. "But I don't know her mind on this matter."

Ramón shrugs. "There will be time to discover that, now that we have returned."

They reach the Peabody casa's wooden gate, which stands slightly ajar. Ramón puts his hand on the heavy wooden bar which serves as a handle. "Are you ready?" he asks as he swings the gate open and steps forward.

They stand just inside the courtyard. It's bright in the early February sun. Bits of green poke through the soil in the neatly dug garden beds. Yet there's an unusual silence and no sign of activity. The heavy wooden kitchen shutters are closed. Gerald and Ramón exchange an apprehensive glance.

Then the house door opens and Encarnación appears and turns to the kitchen shutters without glancing toward the gate.

As she lifts the wooden bar that holds them shut, Ramón moves forward. "With your permission," he says.

Encarnación whirls, her hand reaching for her skirt pocket. Then she realizes it's Ramón and her face relaxes. "Oh, Ramón!" she says. "Such a time we have had."

"Is there sickness?" Gerald asks from the gate, trying to keep the anxiety from his voice.

She looks toward him. "La señorita is well," she says, answering his unasked question. She shakes her head. "The señor has been taken by an ague and has fever." She looks toward the gate disapprovingly. "Suzanna seems to have gone in search of herbs."

Ramón raises his eyebrows. "En febrero?"

Encarnación shrugs. "There are places where the grasses have begun to green, where herbs can be found." She gestures toward the courtyard's southern wall, where the tendrils of plants are taller than anywhere else in the bright space. "As you see." She shakes her head. "We have dried forms of what she needs and a few leaves here are already producing. But la señorita believes the wild plants are stronger in value."

"El señor, he is quite ill?"

Encarnación nods, her face troubled. Then there's a movement at the gate and her lips tighten. "You left no word!" she says.

The men turn to see Suzanna, her skirts damp and carrying a small basket half full of reddish-brown twigs and sprigs of green.

Suzanna gives Gerald a glad look, then turns to shut the gate. He hurries forward to help her. She turns toward Encarnación as he lifts the bar that latches it into place. "I left you a note," she says mildly.

The other woman humphs and turns back to the kitchen shutters. "With these shutters closed, who can see?"

Ramón leaps to her side and swings the wooden squares away from the window. As he latches them out of the way, Encarnación turns and goes into the house. Ramón looks at Suzanna and raises his eyebrows. Suzanna chuckles and gestures for him to enter the house. He shakes his head and waves her ahead of him.

Suzanna and Gerald grin at each other and move across the courtyard toward the door. "I hope your father is not as unwell as Encarnación indicated," he says gravely.

She turns her head, her dark eyes anxious. "She's right to be concerned," she says. "He's suffered a great deal from the cold this winter and nothing I gave him truly eased his discomfort." She nods at the plants in her basket. "I did find some willow that was already producing new growth. Its spring bark will be more efficacious than what I dried last fall." She sighs. "I hope it will help."

Then she brightens. "And I also found poleo, which is very rare this early in the year. I don't know that it's of any value for what ails him, but he loves the taste of it, especially with a little black tea added." She chuckles. "It will also help to stretch the black tea, which is his only beverage of choice at the moment."

"It's good to know that he has the energy to make choices," Gerald says.

She laughs. "Yes. As long as he's asking for black tea and Encarnación's natillas, I think we have a reasonable hope of recovery."

CHAPTER 36

Jeremiah Peabody is well enough the following week to sit in his parlor chair and receive visitors. Gerald takes the opportunity to repeat all he's told Suzanna about the winter's hunt. The older man listens quietly, his illness making him less likely to interrupt with questions, more likely to watch the younger man's eyes stray to Suzanna. She sits in the window, demurely stitching a new shirt for her father when she isn't glancing at Gerald.

Peabody's eyes close, then open again when Gerald stops speaking. "Go on," he says. "About the valley?"

"I'm tiring you," Gerald says apologetically.

"No, no." Jeremiah's hand waves toward the window. "The light is a little bright today."

Suzanna's eyes lift from her work. "Shall I adjust your chair?"

"No, no." He smiles. "I like to watch you sitting there. It reminds me of my mother."

She smiles and looks down at the cotton fabric ruefully. "I don't sew as well as she did."

He chuckles. "No, but your knowledge of plants and herbs is far superior to hers." He turns to Gerald. "The early willow she found saved my life."

"Oh papá, you exaggerate," Suzanna says. "You weren't in any real danger."

"It felt as if I was." He takes a deep breath. "It is good to feel my chest expand fully again."

She looks at him affectionately and turns back to her work. "This thread has knotted yet again," she grumbles. "How I wish clothes could make themselves as plants do!"

The men look at each other and chuckle. "So, tell me more of this valley," her father says.

Gerald could sit in the Peabody parlor forever, feeling the calm of its adobe walls and mica-paned windows, talking quietly with Jeremiah Peabody, watching Suzanna stitch her father's shirts. But she grows restless in the half-light of the parlor and the temporary February thaw.

"I know it isn't time yet to plant," she tells the men one afternoon. "But I'd like to at least check on my potato plot. I left some plants in the ground, to test if they would overwinter in place." She turns to Gerald. "Would you accompany me? I'm hoping to return with enough for a few meals, and the basket will be heavy."

Jeremiah Peabody raises his eyebrows at the sight of his daughter playing the weak female, but Gerald feels only the sweetness of being asked to help. He's instantly on his feet.

"You may need an additional wrap," her father tells her. "I suspect it is cooler out there than it appears."

As she goes to retrieve her cloak, Gerald turns to him. "I suspect it's the exercise that she's truly after. But I'll make sure she stays warm, sir."

Peabody smiles at him. "I know you will. I believe you care for her welfare almost as much as I do."

Gerald's chest tightens and looks away, his face red. "I do care for her very much, sir." He forces his eyes up. "I know I am not worthy of her, sir."

Now Peabody looks away. "No one is worthy of her," he murmurs. He glances at Gerald, then turns his gaze to the window. He chuckles. "Not until she decides they are, at any rate."

Gerald waits, his breath suspended, anxiety threading through him. Should he speak now? Should he tell the man the truth about himself? But then Suzanna appears in the doorway, wrapped in a knee-length gray-and-red-striped woolen cloak, a large wicker basket on her arm.

Her father's head swings toward her. "Do you think that basket will be large enough for a only few meals worth of potatoes?" he teases.

She chuckles. "I'd rather take too large a basket than one that's too small!" She turns to Gerald. "Are you ready?" She lifts a short spade from the bottom of the basket and waves it at him. "I hope you're prepared to dig!"

Gerald moves toward her, his heart light.

But as they walk through the village's adobe-walled streets, Suzanna becomes uncharacteristically silent. Gerald's heart sinks. Has she heard about Jones? Does she suspect the truth about his race? He slides a look sideways. There's no longer a smile in her eyes. In fact, she seems to be looking everywhere but in his direction. As if he's a stranger she's trying to avoid, not a friend walking beside her.

He tries to think of something to say, but everything that comes to him seems either too innocuous or too intimate. He studies his feet as they move out of the village and onto the network of paths that lead to the acequia and the potato patch.

The only sound is the tramp of their feet on the path and the chatter of an occasional bird in the narrow leaf cottonwoods overhead. Suddenly Suzanna stops and clutches Gerald's arm.

287

"Look!" she gasps. She nods at the path ahead, where it curves around the corner of a field. She turns to him, her eyes shining. "Did you see it?"

He shakes his head and tears his eyes away from hers. The path bends to the right, following the line of the irrigation ditch.

Suzanna frowns. "I'm sure I saw a wild turkey. A hen, I think. It went into the field."

"If we're quiet, it may still be there," he whispers.

She nods and they move cautiously ahead. Just before the bend, they step off the path and toward the field, holding their breaths. On the far side of the rows of corn stubble, a lone turkey hen pecks at the debris. Her dark brown feathers gleam in the sunlight.

Suzanna looks at Gerald in delight and he smiles into her eyes, all discomfort gone. She turns back to the field. The turkey, apparently unaware of their presence, moves slowly but steadily toward the row of bushes that divides the field from its neighbor beyond. Gerald and Suzanna look at each other, then the path. If they follow it around the corner of the field, they'll be closer to the bird.

They move cautiously back to the path and then slowly along it, eyes glued to the bird. As they round the corner, the turkey hen begins to move along the bushes at the edge of the field, and away from the path. Head down, pecking at the grass, it seems to be unaware of the humans. But it still moves steadily away as they approach.

Gerald chuckles. "They're intelligent creatures," he murmurs.

Suzanna grins. "You'd think it knows that we're here," she says. As she speaks, the turkey slips through the bushes and disappears into the opposite field. Suzanna shakes her head. "They're so beautiful," she says. "And so shy."

"Old Bill and I saw whole flocks of them in the canyon of the Cimarron," Gerald says. "I suspect they also spend time in the valley above during the summer months."

"You certainly seem enamored of that valley," Suzanna teases. Then her face flushes and she looks away, up at the sky and the sun. "It's getting late." She turns and strides away from him down the path. "We need to get those potatoes and get home— Get back before dark falls." She looks up again and laughs awkwardly. "The days are still short, even if it does feel like spring."

Gerald hurries after her. She seemed so sweet, so normal, just a moment ago and now the curtain has come down again on her face. Despair overcomes him.

Suddenly, Suzanna's foot twists against a rock in the path and she lurches to one side. Gerald reaches for her elbow, but she pulls away with a little jerk and hurries on.

He feels a sudden surge of anger. He should just turn back, let her gather her potatoes herself. Clearly, she doesn't want him here. Her attitude toward him has definitely changed over the winter. But he hasn't done anything to precipitate such a change. Has he? He tries to think back, to what was said in the parlor, to her father's expression of good will.

Or does she know something her father doesn't? Has she heard about Enoch Jones or, worse still, learned who Gerald's father is? His jaw tightens. He should just leave her to her opinions, whatever they are. Yet he finds himself following her down the dusty acequia path. The cheerful early-spring green that dots the bushes and trees seems to mock his discomfort. Yet he follows her.

By the time they reach the potato patch, Suzanna seems to have walked off her irritation, if that's what it was. She wades eagerly into the middle of her plants and bends over the half dozen hills she's left to overwinter.

Gerald follows her through the fence and watches her use her hand spade to push aside the slimy, freeze-blackened potato leaves. She shoves the blade into the ground and looks up at Gerald in surprise. "The soil is still quite soft!"

He kneels beside the hill, oblivious to the plant matter under his knees, and begins sifting dirt through his fingers, feeling for knobs of potato. When he finds one, he presses his thumb against its resisting skin. "They're very firm," he says. "They seem to have survived nicely."

Suzanna crouches beside him. "They're beautiful!" She leans closer, her face inches from his.

He smiles into her eyes. "Beautiful as a turkey?" he teases.

She laughs. "In their own way!" As she reaches for the tuber, her fingers brush his palms.

"Beautiful as you," he says softly.

She glances up, startled, and he holds her gaze. Then he turns his head and sifts his fingers through the cold and damp earth. "I have no right to speak," he mutters.

But she's still looking at him, the potato in her hand. "You have every right," she says softly. She tilts forward, as if drawn to him by an invisible string.

He lifts a hand, whether to keep her from falling or pull her closer, he doesn't know. Then he sees the dirt on his fingers and grimaces. "My hands are soiled," he says.

"We are all soiled, one way or another," she murmurs. Then her head is on his shoulder and they're crouched in the middle of the potato patch, his arms around her, kissing her gently.

She moves closer in response and he loses his balance and falls backward into the dirt. Suzanna laughs helplessly. She stands up, drops the potato in her basket, and gives him her hand. "I didn't mean to topple you!"

He pulls himself up and faces her. His stomach clenches. If he doesn't say it now, he never will.

Her smile fades. "I—"

"I need to tell you—" He breaks off and looks away. Then he gathers his courage and faces her, his hands clenched. "I killed a man," he blurts.

She tilts her head enquiringly.

"I stabbed him. In the wilderness." He turns his head and studies the cottonwoods on the other side of the acequia, not daring to watch her expression change.

"There was cause," she says gently.

He turns back to her. "You know?"

She nods, watching his face. "Gregorio told his mother." She smiles slightly. "I don't believe he told her everything, but enough that she understood that Jones was attacking him when you came upon them. He says you saved his life."

Gerald shakes his head. "It wasn't his life Jones was after."

"I know," she says simply. "Although I don't believe Antonia does. There are some things a boy can't tell even his mother." Her lips twist. "If Jones had achieved his goal, Gregorio would have been deeply ashamed. There's no telling what he might have done." She shudders. "Jones was a beast and much bigger than Gregorio. He—" She turns away, looks at the trees, and takes a deep breath. "I know it's wrong to be glad for a man's death, but I can't help it." She faces him, her eyes anxious. "I'm glad you did what you did. Does that make you think ill of me?"

Gerald shakes his head. "Given the threat he was to you, I can understand how you feel."

"But he was no threat to you," she says. "You acted to protect others, not yourself."

He absently brushes his hand against his leg, bracing himself to tell her that Jones was indeed a threat to him, that he'd guessed Gerald's most important secret, but before he can speak she begins to laugh. She points at the the dirt his hands have streaked across his trousers.

"You're just making it worse!" she says.

He stops brushing and reaches for her, dirty hands and all. "If it makes you laugh, then it doesn't matter."

She leans into him again, hiding her face in the curve of his shoulder as his arms slip around her waist. "If you will only do this, nothing else matters," she murmurs.

He pulls back, holding her at arm's length, looking into her face. "There is something else I need to tell you. Something about me—"

She shakes her head and puts her fingers to his lips. "I know everything about you that I need to know," she says firmly. She leans forward, into his chest. "Nothing else matters. Only this is important."

A wild, unbelieving joy fills his heart as he pulls her still closer against him.

~ ~ ~ ~

They're a long time returning to the Peabody casa, neither wanting to break the spell that holds them beside Suzanna's patch of potatoes. Finally, the late afternoon chill drives them back to the village.

When the gate comes in sight, their steps slow.

"I will speak to your father now," Gerald says. "Though I'm not sure just what to say." He looks sideways at her and smiles. "You haven't actually said that you'll marry me."

She laughs. "You haven't actually asked me."

He chuckles and releases her hand. Then he takes off his hat with a flourish and kneels before her in the dirt street. Out of the corner of his eye, he sees Encarnación at the gate, her hand to her mouth, her eyes gleeful.

Gerald focuses on Suzanna's face, which is suddenly still. "Señorita Suzanna Peabody, will you do me the immense honor of being my bride?" he asks solemnly.

Suzanna nods wordlessly and Gerald raises an eyebrow. "You have no words?" he teases.

"You have left me speechless," she says, smiling at him. Then she reaches for his hand. "Yes," she says simply. "Most certainly, yes."

He rises and they lean into each other, his lips on her cheek.

At the gate, Encarnación wipes a tear from her face and slips back into the courtyard. Ramón is sitting on a stool near the kitchen door, cleaning out a gourd as a first step to making her a new dipper. She crosses the yard and smiles down at him. "It is as you said." She gestures toward the gate. "They are just there. He has spoken to her."

He looks up. "And she has answered?"

Encarnación smiles. "She has answered."

"And you, sweet Chonita?" Ramón asks. He places the gourd and his knife on the ground and stands, reaching for her hand. "Will you give me the same answer?"

She smiles affectionately. "Ah, Jesús Ramón Chavez. My dearest amigo."

His face darkens. "Only amigo?"

She closes her eyes. "I swore to myself that you would be merely my friend." She bites her lip and nods toward the house door. "He needs me. Now more than ever, with Suzanna to marry." She gives Ramón an anguished look. "When he took me in, I made a vow to stay as long as he needs me. You know that."

Her suitor nods, remembering the troubled teen who refused ten years before to marry the man her parents had chosen for her, the shelter Jeremiah Peabody gave her in exchange for help with his small daughter and the household work. Peabody never attempted to expand on that exchange and this fact only deepened the girl's loyalty to him, especially after her parents died.

"Surely your debt to him has been paid," Ramón says. Then he pauses and reaches gently to turn her chin toward him. "Surely he would not begrudge you this thing." His eyes look into hers. "You have my heart. Are you ready now to swear another vow? To give me yours?"

She moves, half turning toward the door, but he reaches for her arm and the slight pressure is enough to stop her. "Por favor," he says gently. "I think you will not deny me."

Her eyes fill with tears and she gives him a little nod. "Si," she whispers.

His hands move to her shoulders and she bends her head. He kisses her hair, inhaling the warm fragrance of her skin, mixed slightly with the dust of corn flour and the faint sweet scent of caramelized onion. "But I cannot leave him," she says into his shoulder. "Not just yet."

He nods. "There will be time," he says soothingly. "I must prepare a home for us. And speak to Señor Peabody and the Padre. There will be time."

She nods and turns her head to smile up at him. "You are a good man, Jesús Ramón Chavez."

He shakes his head and smiles at her. "I am only a man. And I have waited this long. A little longer will be of no importance."

As his arms tighten around her again and she lifts his face to his lips, there's a slight rustle at the gate. They turn, his arm around her waist, to see Gerald and Suzanna, linked in the same way. The two women look at each other and laugh in delight.

Suzanna slips from Gerald's grasp and crosses the courtyard. She reaches for Encarnación's hand. "Shall we tell him together?" she asks. She turns to the men and makes a shooing motion. "Go on!" she says, smiling. "We'll let you know when he's ready to speak with you."

Gerald and Ramón look at each other and shrug ruefully. Ramón gives the two women a small bow. "As you wish," he says.

"We await your summons," Gerald says from the gateway, and Suzanna flashes him a dazzling smile as she and Encarnación turn to disappear into the house.

CHAPTER 37

"He sees me, papá," Suzanna says. As she settles onto the stool beside his chair, the firelight casts a glow on her creamy-brown face and dark eyes. "He sees me in a way that no other man has ever done. In a way that not even you can."

"You are my daughter."

She smiles. "Yes. And I'll always be a part of you, as you will be a part of me. But you can't help but see me as your daughter, as part of yourself." She shakes her head wonderingly at the fire. "He sees me as me."

"Not as an extension of himself?"

"No." She twists around to look up at him. "That's what's so unusual about him." She turns back to the fire. "I've never met anyone like him."

"There are many men you have not yet met," Jeremiah observes mildly.

Suzanna snorts. "I've met enough. Including some I wish I never had."

Jeremiah grimaces, then glances at the book in his hands. "I thought Carlos Beaubien might be interested in you, and you him."

Suzanna makes a face. "Monsieur Beaubien is only interested in short young Spanish señoritas with a flirtatious air. Also, he wants a Catholic girl. His religion is important to him." She grins. "I hear Paulita Lovato is interested in him, even if she isn't quite fourteen.

She wants a wealthy man. He comes from aristocracy and money, and I suspect will be wealthy in his own right. She's young, but she knows what she wants."

"And you, at not quite sixteen, are so much older than she," Suzanna's father says dryly.

She moves to the window and leans toward it to peer through the milky-white panes.

"And Ceran St. Vrain?" he asks.

She sighs in exasperation and turns back to him. "Now, why would I be interested in a man who chases every skirt he encounters? He's already had a child by at least one of the local women."

Her father chuckles. "St. Vrain does seem to have a roving eye," he admits. He turns and puts his book on the small table beside his chair. "Though he would undoubtedly settle down if the right girl encouraged him to do so."

"I doubt that very much," Suzanna says tartly. She shrugs. "Besides, he's also a devout Catholic. If he ever does marry, he'll want a Catholic girl."

"And what is Mr. Locke's view on religion?"

She shakes her head. "We haven't even spoken of it. It seems to have no weight with him." She grins at her father. "I've noticed that, in all the time he's spent in this parlor, he's never expressed an opinion on the matter."

Her father chuckles. "You mean that he has never contradicted my somewhat Protestant bias." Then he sobers. "But it is something to consider."

"Yes." She gazes out the window again. "I will ask him," she says absently.

"And what of this young man who came last Sunday with Matthew Kinkaid? This Christopher Carson?"

"He seems nice enough," Suzanna says carelessly. "Though he's very young."

"He is just about your age."

"Men take much longer to mature." She gives him a stern look. "You've said so yourself."

He raises his hands in a helpless gesture. "You have an answer for my every argument."

She chuckles. "I am my father's daughter." Then she sobers. "I love him, papá. And we share a love for plants and the land that I've never seen in another man."

"What of his people?"

"What of them?"

"Has he spoken of them? What are they like? After all—"

"I'm a half-breed," she says. She sighs. "Well, a quarter breed. Although I'm sure there are some men who would consider the French part of my ancestry to also be a cause for concern." She shakes her head. "No, we haven't spoken of it. But he isn't interested in going back to the States. As long as we stay here in nuevomexico, my ancestry won't be a problem."

There's a long pause, then Jeremiah says, "I was thinking of his ancestry, not yours. He has told us of his Irish mother, who is no longer living. What of his father?"

"He hasn't spoken of him, except in a general sense." She leans forward. "But I don't think his father will object to my background. A man of Gerald Locke's caliber and kindness can only come from parents of the same quality." Then she straightens and grins at him. "Besides, in this matter, it's my father who has the final say, not his."

He grimaces at the fire and her unwillingness to catch his meaning, but then she crosses the room to him, and resettles herself on the stool at his feet. She looks up at him, then into the fire. "I hope you will be glad for me."

"I will be glad if you are glad." He says it so stiffly that she turns her head in surprise.

His face is averted, staring at the door to the hallway, his hands clasped tightly in his lap. His lips are pressed together, as if he's afraid to open them. She looks into his face, then leans her head against his black-trousered leg. "I will always be your daughter," she says gently. "But I believe that Gerald Locke will make me happy. And if he's willing to take me as I am then I am willing to take him as he is, with no questions about ancestry or anything else."

Jeremiah Peabody sighs. His hand caresses her hair. "I agree that Mr. Locke seems to love you very much and that you have much in common," he says. There's a long silence, then he says, "And you will do as you see fit." He leans forward to peer into her face, his blue eyes sharp. "But your happiness must come from within you, not from anyone else. He cannot give you everything. He is only a man."

She smiles slightly. "He's not just any man. He's Gerald Locke Jr., the kindest man I know, besides my father. And he's the man that I love." She shakes her head slightly. "I feel a connection to him that I can't quite express." Then she tilts her head and looks into her father's face. "But I take all this to mean that you approve."

"'Approve' may be too strong a word." His smile is bittersweet. "I cannot happily approve a thing that will deprive me of you. But I acknowledge your right to live your life and Gerald Locke does seem a good man, that we know so little about his background." He looks again into the fire. "And so yes, I suppose I approve."

She stands then, and kisses his averted face. "Thank you, papá," she whispers, and slips toward the door.

"And what of Encarnación?" he asks from behind her.

She turns and looks at him sympathetically. "You must ask her that yourself," she says.

CHAPTER 38

It's a long two days. Gerald and Ramón try to busy themselves with organizing the campsite, cleaning their equipment, and caring for the mules. Ramón snares a couple rabbits and cooks them, then scrapes the skins and begins the initial tanning process while Gerald chops enough firewood to last them a month.

Late in the afternoon of the second day, a small boy with black hair hanging in his eyes shows up. He carries three small white envelopes, one for Gerald and two for Ramón. When Gerald opens his, he reads:

> *Mr. Locke,*
>
> *It would be my pleasure to speak with you tomorrow morning on a matter which I believe to be of some interest to you and my daughter. It is my understanding that what I have to say will be to your mutual benefit.*
>
> *Yours,*
>
> *Jeremiah Peabody, Esquire*

Gerald's forehead wrinkles, then he grins. What a formal man. What a generous man. What a good man. If all goes well, this man will be his father-in-law.

Gerald takes a deep breath and swings toward his gear, pushing away the anxiety in his chest. Peabody has the right now to know about his ancestry. Suzanna may say she doesn't care, but surely her father will.

But first things first. He needs to brush his coat and clean his boots. And perhaps a haircut—

But his planning stops instantly when he sees Ramón's face. The other man stares blankly at the mountains beyond, shaking his head.

"What is it?" Gerald asks.

Ramón lifts a white square of paper. "She has decided that we must wait two years." He looks at Gerald, his lips twisting. "I told her I was willing to wait for her. I thought perhaps six months."

"Perhaps she will change her mind."

Ramón gives a little snort. "Once that woman decides a thing, that is an end to it." He lifts the letter helplessly. "That fact was once a comfort to me."

"Why so long?"

"She will not leave el señor. Not just yet." He glances at the note. "She says that with la señorita marrying, it is important that she stay. She must find a suitable replacement for herself and train that person to care for him properly."

"Yet Suzanna will go."

"She says it is her wedding gift to la señorita, that she may go freely, without worry for her papá."

"She is a good woman."

Ramón nods glumly. "She is."

"So you have time to prepare a home for her."

The other man nods. "That is true." He nods to the other envelope. "This is from el señor, asking me to come and speak to him on the day after tomorrow." He grins ruefully. "It is doubtless to ask about my plans."

"And what are your plans?" Gerald stops. "I'm sorry. I don't mean to pry. It's just —"

Ramón lifts a hand, waving Gerald's apology aside. "I will provide for her as would any other man. By the sweat of my brow. A little trapping, a little labor in the fields."

"I know I have no right to ask," Gerald says. "But would you consider throwing in with me? Going with me to make homes for our wives in the black valley?"

Ramón raises an eyebrow. "Will la señorita go with you?"

It's not the only question about his future that remains unanswered. He doesn't yet have Jeremiah Peabody's approval of his suit. But Gerald steels himself against his anxiety about his appointment with Suzanna's father, and nods. "I think so. But it's not a thing for one man to do alone. It would be good to have your assistance. Your partnership."

"I can bring little silver."

"But much experience and knowledge of the land. I'd want us to be true partners. You can give Encarnación a home with your portion. And one near Suzanna, which I think they would both like."

"After two years," Ramón says glumly.

"Who knows? She might decide to make it shorter. A woman is always free to change her mind."

Ramón chuckles. "If el diós grants me a miracle." He holds out his hand. "Partners," he says. "Gracias, amigo. And I can provide the cooking until Chonita joins us. When she does come, I'm sure she will be delighted to have more than one person for whom to cook."

"Thank you," Gerald says, taking his hand. "Thank you, my friend."

They grin at each other, delight in their eyes.

"They said 'yes,'" Gerald says wonderingly. For a moment, the anxiety lifts and he breaks away, swinging his hat in the air. "They said 'yes'!"

CHAPTER 39

"I have not asked you many personal questions," the tall thin man in the black coat says. His eyes sharpen on the younger man's face. "My daughter says they aren't important. I disagree, but she insists."

Gerald steadies himself and looks into Jeremiah Peabody's face. "If you ask it of me, I will tell you everything," he says.

Peabody's face darkens. "I have determined not to pry," he says stiffly. Then his lips twitch and he waves his hand in the air. "It is between you and Suzanna," he says. "You will answer to her, anyway."

A great wave of relief unbinds Gerald's chest. He tries not to smile too giddily. "Suzanna has spirit as well as brains," he acknowledges.

"And that is what I wish to speak to you about," her father says. "Your history is a matter between you and my daughter. But your treatment of her is a matter between you and myself."

Surely it can't be this easy. Gerald opens his mouth, but Peabody raises a hand to silence him. "As you know, I have not raised Suzanna to be a common household drudge," he says. "She has been carefully educated. If she wished, she could make her way in the world alone. She does not wish it and she will be a fine helpmate to any man she chooses. She has chosen you. She was raised to choose, not to be chosen."

Jeremiah Peabody smiles ruefully, his eyes a little sad. "She has a will, and where her will and her heart are engaged, she will be a strong support. She was not trained to cookery and such. I think you know that she has no aptitude in that direction. She will need assistance. I trust you will be able to provide her that aid."

All the obstacles are gone now. Gerald tries to keep the gladness from brimming over too far. He works to keep his voice steady. "Suzanna has been clear with me on that point," he says. "Ramón Chavez has been kind enough to agree to assist with the kitchen work for the time being."

Jeremiah Peabody raises an eyebrow. "You will employ him?"

"We are to be partners. He will provide me with much needed expertise and I will contribute what cash I have." Gerald sobers as he looks into Peabody's face. "He hopes to make a home for Encarnación and himself alongside us. In the meantime, he will be of great assistance to both Suzanna and me."

"And this home? It will be in your black valley?"

Gerald smiles. "A portion of the valley I have spoken of, yes. With Suzanna's agreement."

Jeremiah Peabody permits himself a small smile as Gerald continues. "It's a fine country," the younger man says eagerly. "I believe we can prosper there. And with Ramón accompanying us, I'll feel more secure in taking her to such a remote location." He pauses and looks firmly into Jeremiah Peabody's eyes. "I treasure and respect your daughter, sir. I know I am only a man, but I will do all I can do to make her content."

The older man's lips twitches. "She tells me you are not just any man and I'm not sure contentment is something she wishes to find," he says drily. Then he moves forward and takes Gerald's hands in his. "But I am relieved to hear that you have considered her safety and her happiness," he says. "I believe you are sincere, sir, and Suzanna loves you dearly. I give you my blessing."

They smile into each other's eyes. "I aim to make you glad that you gave it, sir," Gerald says.

CHAPTER 40

Suzanna scowls sleepily at the lopped-off branches that brace the hillside lean-to. She burrows deeper into the bedding. At least there's a bear skin to add some warmth. It's early May in Taos. Everything's blooming there. Here, it's icy cold. If that man thinks she's going to actually live permanently in this God-forsaken place, he isn't thinking clearly.

"Wife?" Gerald asks from the open side of the lean-to.

She burrows deeper, covering her head.

Gerald chuckles and comes to kneel beside her. "I have a fire going," he says. "I've toasted some of the bread Encarnación sent with us and am heating water for tea."

Suzanna sighs and reluctantly uncovers her head. "All right," she says.

"There's a herd of elk on the other side of the valley," he says. "I thought I'd try for one after breakfast. We could use the meat. Do you want to come with me?"

"I'm not staying here by myself." She sits up. "Not until you've built me a cabin."

He leans in to kiss her forehead. "I love you," he says.

"And I you." She shakes her head. "Though I still think you're soft in the head. This valley is so isolated and cold. How does anything grow up here?"

He grins, stands, and goes out. "The water's hot!" he calls from the fireside.

Suzanna grimaces and pulls the bear skin around her shoulders as she leaves the blanket. The shaggy skin drags the ground around her feet as she steps outside. The fire is crackling with warmth and the sky overhead is a luminous blue. She takes a deep breath of the clear mountain air.

The marsh where the Cimarron heads is at the base of the hill she's standing on. On the other side of the marsh is yet another hill. Ramón moves among a half-dozen downed and debranched trees. Two mules browse on the grassy slope below, waiting to pull the logs to the cabin site.

Suzanna shakes her head and looks at Gerald, who is carefully pouring steaming water into a tin mug. "You do know that you're both crazy, don't you?"

He hands her the mug of steeping tea, then turns and waves his arm toward the valley below. "Just look at it," he says.

She follows his gaze. The morning sun touches the long grasses on the valley floor and the tiny silver streams that weave through the spring green. A coyote trots purposefully along the base of the hill, where a cluster of elk browses peacefully. Nearer at hand, a red-wing blackbird trills in the marsh.

"There's plenty of water," Suzanna acknowledges. "And that vega grass should make excellent hay. I wonder what other plants lurk in it. Wild onions, I would imagine. And garlic." She purses her lips. "There's likely to be mint along the stream banks."

Gerald chuckles. She narrows her eyes at him, then grins.

He moves to stand beside her. His arm slips around her waist. "Hmmm," Suzanna says. She tilts her head and lets it rest in the hollow of his shoulder. "I still think moving here is a crazy idea." She shivers a little. "It's much cooler here than in Taos. I suppose that'll be nice in June and July, but right now it seems a bit chilly."

Gerald nods noncommittally but doesn't answer. They gaze at the long valley before them, the black-green of the pines on the slopes of the snow-topped mountains opposite, the brighter green of the grassland below.

Suddenly, Suzanna twists out of Gerald's arms and leans forward to peer at the flat piece of land between the hill they're on and the marsh. "I wonder if I can get corn to grow up here," she says. "Certainly potatoes."

Gerald grins triumphantly, then wipes his face smooth as she turns back to him.

Her eyes narrow. "If you think I'll be satisfied that easily, you'd better think again, Mr. Locke," she says severely. Then she laughs. "That cabin had better have glass windows!"

"Yes, ma'am, Mrs. Locke," he says, his eyes dancing as she leans in to be kissed.

EPILOGUE

"Well, that young Gerald Locke has gone and got himself set himself up in conjugal bliss." Old Bill turns the bent beaver trap in the firelight. He can't righteously plan on it holding together until they get back to Taos. He sure hopes Jerry Smith has showed up by then. This needs the touch of an expert.

"Yeah?" Milton Sublette asks. "Who to?"

"Señorita Suzanna Peabody, no less."

"Well, I'll be." Sublette frowns. "Does her daddy know about Locke? What he is?"

"Oh yeah. He knows Locke's Daddy. Trapped with him back when they both first come out here. Him and Locke and that Ramón Chavez. They were quite a team."

"And?"

"The girl says she don't righteously care what Locke is or where he comes from. He's the man for her."

"Does she actually know? Did they tell her?"

Old Bill shrugs. "Now that I don't truly know, but I wouldn't think so. Not unless she wanted to know. And if she doesn't, I'm sure not going to be the one to inform her. Our Suzanna's a strong-willed piece, but she's ours and I don't aim to spoil her pleasure for her, if knowing who her man's Daddy is would spoil it. Besides, Locke's a good man and that's all that righteously matters."

"Yeah, it don't matter. And the only man stupid enough to care and bastard enough to tell her is dead and gone."

"And by the hand of her man."

"Fair fight and a man who deserved to die, if ever there was one." Sublette stirs, easing his leg and grunting a little at its stiffness. "Well, I wish young Locke luck," he says. "With that gal's opinions, they could be in for quite a ride."

Old Bill chuckles. "That they righteously could be."

THE END

NOTE TO READER

Although the main characters in *Not Just Any Man* are fictional, their story is framed by historical events and the men and women who participated in them. One of these men was Tennessee-born Ewing Young. By Summer 1825, Young had been based in New Mexico about two and a half years. He and his business partner William Wolfskill had two primary sources of income: trapping during the fall/winter fur season and freighting merchandise to and from Missouri the rest of the year. When Gerald Locke Jr. meets Young's wagon train on the Santa Fe Trail, Young is returning to New Mexico for the second time that summer.

We don't know for certain that Young sent most of the merchandise from that second 1825 train directly to Taos in order to avoid paying customs duty in Santa Fe. However, traders on the Trail routinely loaded their goods onto pack mules at Point of Rocks and took them west across the Sangre de Cristo mountains instead of south to the Capitol. The route to Taos crossed Gerald's long mountain valley near what is today the Angel Fire Ski Resort.

We do know that Major George C. Sibley's Santa Fe Trail Survey Expedition used the Point-of-Rocks-to-Taos route that fall, reaching Taos in late September. William Sherley Williams (aka 'Old Bill' Williams) was Sibley's expedition guide. A red-headed self-confident man with strong opinions and a gift for languages,

Williams left the Expedition shortly after Sibley reached Taos and spent the winter of 1825/26 trapping in the mountains.

Where Williams trapped that season is anyone's guess, but he had a reputation for going out alone or with only one companion. This enabled him to trap areas that other trappers didn't know about and weren't likely to venture into even if they did, because there wasn't enough beaver there to support large groups of men. The Red River, Cimarron River, and Coyote Creek region of the Sangre de Cristos, where I place Williams and Gerald in Winter 1825/26, may well have been such a location. Although old beaver sign and current lodges still exist along these and nearby streams, all the waterways are relatively small and are spread some distance apart. It's doubtful that a large group of trappers would have been able to gather enough plews there to make it worth their while. However, one or two men might have done well.

Old Bill's habit of solitary or near-solitary trapping was the exception. Large parties of trappers like the one Ewing Young and William Wolfskill led into what is now southwest New Mexico and southeast Arizona in Fall 1826 were more typical. The Young/Wolfskill group trapped the Gila River's tributaries, then followed the river across Arizona. At the Colorado River, they moved north and then finally east into what is now western Colorado. This is the party into which I've inserted my fictional characters Gerald Locke Jr., Enoch Jones, and Gregorio Garcia. Its real-life participants included 'Thunderbolt of the Rocky Mountains' Milton Sublette; Thomas L. Smith, who would lose a foot and become 'Peg-Leg Smith' the following season; Smith's trapping partner, Maurice LeDuc; George Yount, the Pennsylvania-born mountain man with roots in Alsace who his fellow trappers called 'Dutch George'; a

Mexican camp keeper named Ignacio Sandoval; and James Ohio Pattie, who joined the group during their expedition.

Much of what we know about this trip is chronicled in the 1831 book *The Personal Narrative of James O. Pattie*. The scenes in *Not Just Any Man* that occur after Pattie joins Young's party, including the trapper interactions with the Papago and Mohave tribes, are based on Pattie's account. However, Pattie's story becomes geographically garbled shortly after Thomas Smith's tiny party takes off on its own. Young and his remaining men seem to have moved off the Colorado River near the southwest end of the Grand Canyon, made their way along the Canyon's rim and into what is now Colorado, then worked southeast to New Mexico's Jemez Mountains and the Spanish settlements.

My fictional take on the events before Pattie joined Young's group and then after the trappers returned to New Mexico is based primarily on the account David J. Weber provides in *The Taos Trappers* (1968). This includes the interactions with the Apache on the Gila River and then, after the expedition returned to the settlements, the storage of the group's furs in Peña Blanca, Cabeza de Baca's death, and the subsequent events in Santa Fe, including Ignacio Sandoval's role in reporting Young's attempt to dodge custom duties, Milton Sublette's theft of his own pack, and Young's incarceration and release.

Of course, the conversations, motivations, and personality traits of the historical characters in this novel are as much products of my imagination as are those of the fictional ones. What is not a product of my imagination is the likelihood that 1820s New Mexico would have been more welcoming to persons of African descent such as Gerald Locke Jr. and his father than was Missouri at the time.

When Missouri became part of the United States in 1803, the new Territory was characterized by small farms with relatively few slaves and a fairly liberal policy toward free persons of African descent. Although free Blacks didn't have the social or economic mobility of Whites and most of them subsisted as menial laborers, they could legally hold property and enter into apprenticeship agreements. Work in the countryside was readily available, especially during harvest and other high-activity seasons, and there was also ready employment on the river.

These legal rights and economic opportunities, such as they were, held throughout the 1810s, even as Missouri Territory's slave population steadily increased. This growth—the number of slaves had more than tripled by 1820—ensured that Missouri entered the Union that year as a slave-holding State. But even then, the new State's free Black population may not have felt particularly anxious. After all, their civil rights still held.

However, as the number of slaves in Missouri continued to grow after statehood, the State's laws began to change. These changes are best illustrated by the 1825 legislative decision to reduce the punishment for enslaving a free Black. Under Territorial law, this crime had carried a mandatory sentence of death without benefit of clergy. Now, the penalty was a maximum of thirty lashes and ten years in prison. Unless the person enslaved was returned. Then the punishment was only a $1000 fine and costs.

With changes like this taking place, free Blacks in 1820s Missouri may very well have wanted to leave the state as quickly as possible. For a single man, the Mountain West was a logical place to go. The Lockes wouldn't have been the first men of African descent who headed for the Rocky Mountains in search of a freer way of life. They would have been joining men like Jim Beckworth, who hired on with William Ashley's expedition to the Rockies in 1824 and went on to become, like many of his fellow mountain men, famous both for his exploits and his capacity to stretch those adventures into memorable stories.

Prior to 1821, Beckworth and his fellow Americans hadn't been particularly welcome in New Mexico. They were technically illegal aliens and subject to arrest at any time unless, like my fictional character Jeremiah Peabody, they'd been given special permission to remain. But when Mexico moved from Spanish to self-rule, this situation changed. Foreigners were not only allowed to remain in the country, they were invited to become full citizens, as long as they met certain basic requirements.

The invitation to citizenship was open to anyone, regardless of skin color. This absence of a racial qualification reflects a difference in attitude about ethnic backgrounds that distinguished Mexico from the United States at the time, a difference that began early in Mexico's history as a Spanish province, when the first influx of Spaniards included persons of African descent.

As the conquistadores moved into the far north, including what would become New Mexico, they were accompanied by First Nation (aka 'Native') auxiliary soldiers and black slaves, some of whom stayed behind when Coronado's expedition returned south in 1542. Subsequent settlement and relief caravans into nuevomexico included both free Black soldiers and Black slaves, a number of whom married into the peoples already settled in the region. In fact, some historians believe that the 1680 Pueblo revolt against the Spanish was actually led by a man born from one of these unions.

In addition, Diego de Vargas' resettlement caravan twelve years after the 1680 conflict included free families of African descent. As citizens, these households had the right to participate in government land grant programs, a privilege exercised by African descendent Melchor Rodriguez and his children, who participated in the 1751 Las

Trampas settlement south of Don Fernando de Taos. With persons of this type of heritage living in the Taos area, it's unlikely that Gerald's skin tone would have attracted much notice. After all, he would have looked remarkably similar to others in the community.

I am not saying that nuevomexico has always been a shining example of racial tolerance. Its record is far from perfect. Certainly, the upper classes in the 1800s could be quite proud of and concerned to maintain their Spanish heritage and limpieza de sangre, or 'pure blood,' and, after the 1846 American conquest, these attitudes were reinforced by American racial prejudices.

However, during the Mexican period (1820-1846), nuevomexico reflected the federal government's relaxed attitude toward racial difference. This was in sharp contrast to the United States' official stance at the time. In fact, while America continued to add more slave-holding Territories and States to its Union, Mexico passed laws that forbade legal documents and census data to reflect racial distinctions. Also unlike the U.S., marriage between members of nuevomexico's various ethnic groups was relatively common in the 1800s, as it still is today.

Given nuevomexico's comparatively relaxed attitudes about race during the 1820s, it seems feasible that an African-American man could live there either as Black or White, depending on how he chose to present himself. Or chose to allow others to see him, as Gerald Locke Jr. does in *Not Just Any Man*.

Whether Gerald's choice is the best or wisest of his options is another question entirely. While his decision not to tell the woman he loves about his heritage is not the first issue they will face in their married life (see *Not My Father's House,* 2019), eventually Suzanna will learn the truth. I hope you'll be as interested as I am to discover (in *No Secret Too Small,* 2020*)* what she says and does when she realizes her husband has tacitly lied to her. Given Suzanna's strong opinions and her ability to articulate them, I suspect it won't be a muted reaction.

HISTORICAL CHARACTERS IN *NOT JUST ANY MAN*

Apache Chief (?-?) Headman of the small band of Apache that confronted the William Wolfskill/Ewing Young trapping party on the Gila River in Winter 1826/27. The little information available about the Chief is from James Ohio Pattie's *Narrative*. The red shirt Pattie says the Chief wore was atypical. In the first half of the 1800s, Apache men were more likely to wear long white cotton shirts.

Armijo, Manuel (1790-1853) Governor of nuevomexico 1827-1829, during which he had a complex relationship with the expatriate American trappers and traders. Armijo was appointed Governor again in 1837, following the 1837 Tax Revolt, and served until 1844. His attitude toward Americans seems to have changed during this second term in office, because he signed off on a number of government land grants to naturalized citizens like Charles Beaubien and Ceran St. Vrain. Armijo served as governor again from Fall 1845 until mid1846, when he ordered his militia not to fight the invading American army, then fled south across the receding U.S./Mexico border.

Baca, Vicente (?-?) A Santa Fe alcalde in 1827. The alcalde, or local magistrate, was an elected position. The man chosen was head of the municipal council and also justice of the peace. Two alcaldes, the alcalde de primer voto (senior alcalde) and the alcalde ordinario de segundo voto (junior alcalde), served together. It's not clear which position Baca held in 1827, when he was ordered by Governor

319

Narbona to confiscate and sell the furs American trapper Ira A. Emmons had hidden at the Santa Rita copper mines in southern nuevomexico.

Baillio, Paul (?-?) Business associate at one point or another in the 1820s of George Champlin Sibley, future Missouri Governor Lilburn Boggs, Ceran St. Vrain, and William Sherley Williams. When Missouri's Fort Osage closed in 1822, Baillio and Sibley bought up the post's remaining government supplies and traded directly with the Osage tribal members. Baillio then moved on to New Mexico, where he arrived around 1824. He seems to have owned mercantile businesses in both Taos and Santa Fe. He and Ceran St. Vrain were business partners from 1825 to 1828.

Baird, James (1767-1826) Mountain man who arrived in nuevomexico in 1811 as part of the Robert McKnight party. The entire group was arrested by officials in Santa Fe and sent to Chihuahua, where they were held until 1820. After Baird's release he returned to the States, then made his way back to New Mexico, where he trapped, co-owned a still that specialized in the distilled grain and wheat based liquor called Taos Lightning, and became a Mexican citizen. He died at El Paso in 1826 en route to a trapping expedition in the Gila Mountains. At least some of his party, including Luciano Grijalva and the Chalifoux brothers, Jean Baptiste and Pierre, went on without him.

Beaubien, Charles 'Carlos' (1800-1864) Quebec-born trapper of aristocratic French-Canadian descent who arrived in New Mexico in early 1824 and settled as a merchant in Taos. Beaubien married María Paulita Lobato of Taos in 1827 and applied for Mexican citizenship in 1829. In 1841 he was co-grantee, along with Provincial Secretary Guadalupe Miranda, of what would become the Maxwell Land Grant in Colfax County, New Mexico. Following the 1846 American invasion, Beaubien was named one of New Mexico's three Superior Court judges. His 14-year-old son Narciso was killed during the 1847 Taos Revolt.

Branch, Alexander (1798-1841) Virginia-born trapper who settled in New Mexico in 1825. He converted to Catholicism in 1828 and in 1829 married Paula de Luna, the daughter of Taos alcalde Rafael de Luna, and became a Mexican citizen.

Cabeza de Baca, Luis María (?-1827) Resident of the hamlet of Peña Blanca on the Rio Grande south of Santa Fe, between the Native American communities of Cochiti and Santo Domingo Pueblos. Cabeza de Baca was killed in Summer 1827 while trying to keep the furs Ewing Young's trapping party had cached on his property from being confiscated by government officials.

Campbell, Richard (?-1860) American trapper who arrived in nuevomexico around 1824. Campbell was a member of the 1826/27 Wolfskill/Young trapping expedition described in this novel. He married María Rosa Grijalva of Taos in 1828 and remained in New Mexico for the next thirty-two years.

Carson, Christopher 'Kit' (1809-1868) Mountain man and trapper famous for guiding Colonel John Fremont to California in the 1840s and infamous for his part in forcing the Navajo from their lands and onto the Bosque Redondo reservation in the 1860s. Carson was a teenager when he arrived in nuevomexico in late 1826, toward the end of this novel.

Chalifoux, Jean Baptiste (?-?) One of two brothers with the James Baird trapping party when Baird died in El Paso. After Baird's death, the Chalifoux brothers and other members of the group continued into the Gila Mountains and may have crossed paths there with the Wolfskill/Young trapping party. Jean Baptiste led a horse-raiding expedition into California in the late 1830s, operated a trading post beside the Rio Grande at Embudo, New Mexico in the 1840s, and moved to Colorado in the 1850s. He is said to have built the first house (in 1860) at Trinidad, Colorado.

Chalifoux, Pierre (?-?) One of two brothers who were members of the 1826 trapping party being led by James Baird when Baird died in El Paso that fall. After Baird's death, the Chalifoux brothers continued on into the mountains and may have encountered the Wolfskill/Young party in the Gila Mountains. Pierre married a Taos woman in 1829.

Chavez, Francisco Javier (?-?) Wealthy patriarch of the Los Chavez Land Grant on the west bank of the Rio Grande between Belen and what is today the village of Los Lunas. Chavez was the first Governor of nuevomexico following Mexican independence from Spain. A descendant of a member of the original Oñate colony of 1598, Chavez had four sons and five daughters. His sons Mariano and José both served as Governor during the Mexican period. Chavez hosted the Wolfskill/Young trapping party in late 1826 while William Wolfskill travelled to Taos to recruit more men to assist in dealing with the Apaches on the Gila headwaters.

Duran, Agustín (?-?) Santa Fe alcalde, or local magistrate, in 1827 when Governor Narbona ordered him to confiscate the Young party's furs from the Cabeza de Baca property in Peña Blanca. The raid resulted in de Baca's death. Later that summer, Duran supervised the airing of these same furs in the Santa Fe Plaza and was present when Milton Sublette stole an unopened pack of plews. Duran would continue to serve in positions of authority in Santa Fe where, as alcalde de primer voto, or senior magistrate, he supported Governor Perez during the 1837 Tax Revolt.

Emmons, Ira A. 'Irish' (?-?) American fur trapper of Irish heritage who arrived in nuevomexico around 1825. In 1827, Emmons trapped on a license borrowed or rented from Santa Fe military garrison armorer Manuel Sena. Emmons cached the resulting plews at the Santa Rita copper mines in the southern Gila mountains. Government officials confiscated and sold the furs as part of a larger crackdown on illegal trapping by American expatriates.

Grijalva, Luciano (?-?) Trapper in nuevomexico in the 1820s. Grijalva was a member of the group of men with James Baird when Baird died in El Paso. He and some of the other trappers went on to 'hunt' in the Gila Mountains after Baird's death. Grijalva may have been the father of María Rosa Grijalva, the Taos woman who trapper Richard Campbell married in 1828.

LeDuc, Maurice (1808-?) Thomas Long Smith's French-Canadian trapping partner at the time of this novel. LeDuc was in New Mexico as early as 1824 and was a member of the 1826/27 Wolfskill/Young trapping expedition on the Gila and Colorado Rivers until he joined Smith in splitting from the Young party on the Colorado. In the 1830s, LeDuc built a trading post on the Hardscrabble Trail in Colorado. He was still in the Rocky Mountains as late as 1866.

Martinez, Padre Antonio José (1793-1867) Member of a prominent Taos family and the Catholic priest at Taos from 1826 to 1857. Padre Martinez also operated a printing press, a school, and a seminary in Taos and played a leading role in nuevomexico politics under both the Mexican and American administrations.

Mojave Chief (?-?) War leader of the Mojave band that confronted the Wolfskill/Young trapping party on the Colorado River in early 1827. The little information known about the Chief is from James Ohio Pattie's *Narrative*. For more about the Colorado Mojave, including traditional body ornamentation and war tactics, see

Dreamers of the Colorado by Frances L. O'Neil and Paul W. Wittmer.

Narbona, Antonio (1773-1830) Jefe politico, or civilian governor, of nuevomexico from September 1825 to Summer 1827, when he was succeeded by Manuel Armijo. During Narbona's tenure, he sought to enforce Mexico's ever-changing laws regarding the activities of expatriates, including trappers.

Pattie, James Ohio (1804-1833?) Kentucky-born trapper who accompanied his father, Sylvester, to the Rocky Mountains in 1824. He was a member of Michel Robidoux's failed 1826/27 trapping expedition on the Gila River. After a subsequent ill-fated expedition with his father to California, Pattie returned to the States in 1830 and wrote *The Personal Narrative of James Ohio Pattie*. The *Narrative* was edited and published by newspaperman Timothy Flint, who freely added what he called "geographical details."

Pattie, Sylvester (1782-1828) Kentucky farmer and War of 1812 veteran who took his son, James, with him to New Mexico in 1824. During the winter of 1826/27 Sylvester worked as a supervisor in the Santa Rita copper mines while James accompanied Michel Robidoux's ill-fated trapping expedition to the Gila. In 1827, Sylvester and James led a small party of men to California, although none of them had government permission to travel there. Sylvester died in a California prison in 1828.

Pratte, Sylvester (1799-1827) Trapper and investor who arrived in nuevomexico in 1825. He funded trapping endeavors like Michel Robidoux's 1826/27 expedition and also led efforts of his own. Pratte died in late 1827 in what is now Colorado on a trapping party that also saw the self-amputation of Thomas L. Smith's left foot. This expedition is said to have been the last of the large fur parties that originated in nuevomexico.

Robidoux, Michel (1798-?) One of six Robidoux brothers of French-Canadian heritage who arrived in nuevomexico in the 1820s. Robidoux led a Sylvester Pratte-sponsored trapping group to the Gila River area in 1826/27. The Americans were attacked by Indians, believed to be Papago, and only three of the original twenty-three trappers survived: Robidoux, James Pattie, and another man. These men subsequently joined Ewing Young's trapping group. The story of the initial Papago attack and the trappers' subsequent revenge is detailed in *The Personal Narrative of James Ohio Pattie,* which forms the basis for that section of this novel.

Sandoval, Felipe (?-?) Father of Ignacio Sandoval, the camp keeper who in 1827 informed Santa Fe officials that Ewing Young had hidden his party's furs at the Cabeza de Baca home in Peña Blanca. Felipe was believed to have ordered his son to report on Young.

Sandoval, Ignacio (?-?) Camp keeper with the 1826/27 Wolfskill/Young trapping expedition on the Gila and Colorado Rivers. After the group returned to nuevomexico, Sandoval informed Santa Fe officials that Young had cached the party's furs at Luis María Cabeza de Baca's home in Peña Blanca. The resulting raid to confiscate the furs led to Cabeza de Baca's death.

Sena, Manuel (?-?) Armorer for the Santa Fe military garrison in 1826. Sena acquired a fur trapping license from Mexican officials that year and then lent or sold it to Ira A. Emmons. The transaction seems to have taken place before the law forbidding foreigners to trap in Mexico was passed or, at least, before news of it reached Santa Fe. Emmons used the license as the legal basis for trapping beaver in the Gila Mountains.

Sibley, Major George Champlin (1782-1863) One of three United States Commissioners appointed by Congress to complete an official survey of the Santa Fe Trail. Sibley was the only Commissioner to cross the international boundary into Mexico. He seems to have had a rocky relationship with William S. 'Old Bill' Williams, whom he hired as a guide for the expedition. After his Survey work was completed, Sibley returned to Missouri, where he and his wife established what is today Lindenwood University.

Smith, Thomas Long 'Peg Leg' (1801-1866) Trapper who would become famous as the mountain man with the missing foot. Smith was in Santa Fe by 1824. He tended to work as a free trapper connected with, but not under orders to, other trappers. He was probably working in this capacity as a member of the 1826/27 Wolfskill/Young party. For a description of Smith's adventures after his small band of men left the Young party somewhere on the Colorado, see Daniel J. Weber's *The Taos Trappers* and *Fur Trappers and Traders of the Far Southwest,* Leroy R. Hafen, editor. The following year, Smith joined Sylvester Pratte's trapping expedition to Colorado. During that hunt, Smith received a leg wound that required amputation of his left foot. He would be known as 'Peg Leg' Smith the rest of his life.

St. Vrain, Ceran (1802-1870) Taos-based trapper and trader who was a descendant of French nobility. St. Vrain grew up in St. Louis and arrived in Santa Fe in March 1825 with a William Becknell wagon train. He remained in nuevomexico the rest of his life, working as a trapper, trader, and owner of a Mora grist mill. He had four children, each by a different woman, and is buried in Mora.

Stone, Solomon (?-?) Fur trapper who may have been part of the 1823/24 Thomas Fitzpatrick party that discovered the South Pass in what is now Colorado. He was a member of the 1826/27 Wolfskill/Young trapping expedition.

Sublette, Milton (1801?-1837) Kentucky-born descendent of French Huguenot refugees and one of five brothers engaged in the Rocky Mountain fur trade. Milton and his oldest brother William went West in 1823 as trappers for the William Ashley expedition. Over six feet tall, Sublette had a reputation for audacity and recklessness that earned him the nickname 'Thunderbolt of the Rocky Mountains.'

Torres, Agustín (?-?) Resident of Santa Fe who provided Ewing Young and the American merchants in Santa Fe with the 1827 translation of a government proclamation that banned noncitizens from trapping on Mexican waterways.

Torres, Cristobal (?-?) Santa Fe resident who owned a home on the south side of the Santa Fe Plaza in the late 1820s. Torres provided shelter to Ewing Young and his trappers in the summer of 1827 while Young negotiated with Governor Armijo for the return of the group's furs. The following year, Torres also stored Missouri merchant Phillip Thompson's furs, although the plews were eventually seized by Santa Fe's presidio commandant, presumably on orders from the Governor.

Williams, William Sherley 'Old Bill' (1787-1849) North Carolina-born mountain man who spent his formative years in Missouri. At sixteen, Williams left home to live among the Osage Indians. After the death of his Osage wife twenty-one years later, he headed west. Based in Taos, the lean, red-headed Williams had a taste for gambling and Taos Lightning, and a propensity for trapping on his own or with only a camp keeper as companion. A self-confident man with strong opinions, he eventually ran afoul of John C. Fremont, who hired Williams to guide his 1848 expedition across the Rockies. The party became trapped by harsh winter conditions and Fremont refused to follow Williams' advice, then blamed him for the subsequent death of twenty-one of the group's thirty-two men. Williams himself died during an attempt to retrieve the equipment and records left behind in the expedition's scramble to safety.

Wolfskill, William (1798-1866) Kentucky-born merchant and trapper who arrived in nuevomexico as part of William Becknell's 1822 train over the Santa Fe Trail. Two years after the trapping expedition described in this novel, Wolfskill led a party of about twenty men across the Great Basin into southern California. He decided to settle in California and, when fur trapping proved an impractical way to make a living, took up farming. He and his brother and sons created an agricultural venture that introduced the Australian eucalyptus, the soft-shelled almond, the chestnut, and the persimmon to California.

Young 'Joven', Ewing (1793?-1841) Farmer with carpenter's training who became a mountain man. In early 1822, Young sold his newly-acquired Missouri farm to join William Becknell's second train to nuevomexico. There, Young and his business partner William Wolfskill traded goods from Missouri and also led trapping expeditions, including the Gila/Colorado River trip that forms the basis for part of this novel. In 1832, Young led a party of trappers to California and stayed on the West Coast, eventually moving to and dying in Oregon.

Yount, George (1794-1865) Carolina-born mountain man with grandparents from Alsace. Yount may have retained some traces of his family's original speech patterns, because his fellow trappers nicknamed him 'Dutch George.' He arrived in Santa Fe in Fall 1826 as a Santa Fe Trail teamster and almost immediately signed on with the Wolfskill/Young party to trap the Gila and Colorado Rivers. In 1830, Yount joined William Wolfskill's California expedition and did not return to Santa Fe. He died in the Napa Valley on ranch land granted to him by the Mexican government.

SOURCE LIST

Batman, Richard. *James Pattie's West, the dream and the reality.* Norman: U of Oklahoma Press, 1986.

Brooks, James F. *Captives and Cousins, slavery, kinship, and community in the Southwest borderlands.* Chapel Hill: U of North Carolina Press, 2002.

Donnelly, Thomas. *The Government of New Mexico.* Albuquerque: U of New Mexico Press, 1953.

Favour, Alpheus H. *Old Bill Williams, Mountain Man.* Norman: U of Oklahoma Press, 1936.

Glasrud, Bruce, ed. *African American History in New Mexico, portraits from five hundred years.* Albuquerque: U of New Mexico Press, 2013.

Hafen, Leroy R., ed. *Fur Trappers and Traders of the Far Southwest.* Logan: Utah State U Press, 1972.

―――. *The Mountain Men and the Fur Trade of the Far West,* Vols. I and IV. Spokane: Arthur H. Clark, 2000 & 2001.

Johnson, Michael G. *Encyclopedia of Native Tribes of North America.* Buffalo: Firefly Books, 2014.

Márquez, Rubén Sálaz. *New Mexico, a brief multi-history.* Albuquerque: Cosmic House, 1999.

O'Neil, Francis L., and Paul W. Wittmer, eds. *Dreamers of the Colorado, the Mohave Indians, their land and religion.* Farmington: Tunxis CC, 2013.

Paterek, Josephine. *Encyclopedia of American Indian Costume.* New York: W.W. Norton, 1994.

Pattie, James Ohio. *The Personal Narrative of James Ohio Pattie.* Cincinnati: John H. Wood, 1831.

Rockwell, Wilson. *The Utes, a forgotten people.* Montrose: Western Reflections, 2006.

Russell, Carl P. *Firearms, Traps, and Tools of the Mountain Men.* New York: Skyhorse Publishing, 2010.

Simmons, Marc. *Coronado's Land, essays on daily life in Colonial New Mexico.* Albuquerque: U of New Mexico Press, 1991.

Trexler, Harrison. *Slavery in Missouri, 1804-1865.* Baltimore: Johns Hopkins U, 1914.

Weber, David J. *The Taos Trappers, the fur trade in the far southwest, 1540-1846.* Norman: U of Oklahoma Press, 1970.

Loretta Miles Tollefson

Made in the USA
Middletown, DE
29 December 2018